THE HELLS OF NOTRE DAME

[signature]

Printed in the United States of America
First Printing, 2023

ISBN 978-1-960411-00-6 (eBook)
ISBN 978-1-960411-01-3 (paperback)
ISBN 978-1-960411-02-0 (hardback)

Published by Night Muse Press
Cover art by JV Arts
Edited by Nastasia Bishop in collaboration with Stardust Book Services
Illustrated by Nathan Hansen Illustration
Stepback art by Haflacky

NIGHT MUSE PRESS
EST. 2020

ACKNOWLEDGEMENTS

To Jena – without you, I'd have surrendered to my demons long ago. Most days I feel like I don't deserve you in my life, but thank you for sticking with me regardless.

To KR, my inspiration, and for reminding me that if you can do it, I can, too. I want to be you when I grow up.

To Victoria, Ted, and Zoltan, my dear patrons whose unwavering support makes all I do possible.

To everyone who tried to tell me I couldn't do this – thank you very much. Spite is a powerful motivator.

And to Claude and Esmeralda, for insisting that your story was one worth telling. I couldn't agree more.

ALSO BY R. L. DAVENNOR:

The Curses of Never Series:

A Dance with the Devil

A Land of Never After

A Sea of Eternal Woe

A Forest of Blackened Trees

The Phantom of Notre Dame Series:

The Hells of Notre Dame

The Masque of Crimson Shadow

Others:

Dragon Lake: A Swan Lake Retelling

To anyone who was ever told their existence was a sin.

It's not.

BEFORE YOU BEGIN:

Content warnings for this novel include adult language, graphic violence, explicit sexual content, homophobia, transphobia (misgendering) and mentions of gender dysphoria, body dysmorphia, and past childhood sexual assault (implied).

This novel is not intended to be historically, geographically, or socio-politically accurate to the period in which it is set. It is a work of fantasy fiction set in an alternate universe similar but by no means identical to our own, and as such, many liberties have been taken.

A note regarding Claude's identity: while today their label would be a nonbinary lesbian, their arc is an exploration of gender identity and how it shifts given one's surroundings. Instances in which Claude refers to themselves with gendered terms, both masculine and feminine, help illustrate that as understanding evolves, so does confidence. The correct pronouns for Claude are either she or they—though given her masculine presentation, note that there are also instances in which Claude allows themselves to be referred to with he/him pronouns both for safety and comfort.

Please also note that while Claude and Esmeralda are only involved with one another for the entirety of this book, they enter a consensually polyamorous relationship in which they are both permitted to seek out other partners, and will do so in subsequent books in the series.

Thank you, dear reader, for giving this story a chance.

I. THE SCARF

Claude

"Ave, María, grátia plena, Dóminus tecum."

Hail Mary, indeed. I had survived another week, gotten through another Friday, and at last, my mask could begin to slip without consequence. It was the moment I looked forward to the most: the blessed quiet following Vespers and the evening Mass where it was only me and Saint Mary. I had recited her prayer every dusk since I was old enough to speak, and as always, I went slowly, placing weight on every sacred word.

"Benedicta tu in muliéribus, et benedíctus fructus ventris tui, Iesus."

I didn't dare lift my head from where it rested atop my clasped hands and instead marveled at the gorgeous array of colors painting the otherwise drab stone floor. Notre Dame was breathtaking at sunset, when the stained glass sang for a final time before going dormant for the night.

A smile crept to my lips at the thought, because tonight, I'd be long gone by the time darkness fell.

But I couldn't so much as stand until I finished my prayer, and that would never happen unless I stilled my mind and focused. Inhaling deeply, I recited the final line, willing Saint Mary to sense my devotion.

"Sancta María, Mater Dei, ora pro nobis peccatoribus nunc et in hora mortis nostrae."

On any other night, here was the part I would say *amen*. I would rise, lock up my office, and meet Quasimodo upstairs, where we would have dinner, talk, and read before retiring to our rooms for the evening.

But today was Friday, the night we visited a place where I needed Saint Mary's strength more than any other. I couldn't end my prayer before asking for her blessing, not if I had any hope of keeping my wits about me. Here, I may be Archdeacon of Notre Dame, but there, I became a woman stripped down to my most primal urges. And those urges wanted nothing but *her*.

Closing my eyes, I squeezed my hands together so hard they hurt. My voice came out raspy and hoarse, and the words garbled due to the excess saliva pooling in my mouth. "Blessed Virgin, you know of the sin that tempts me." It had far more than tempted me—I had shattered my vow of celibacy all to Hell, acting upon my impure urges more times than I could count—but I shoved the ugly truth aside. "Forgive me. Break these chains that bind me. Cleanse my heart and soul, and free me from this ceaseless torment."

Said torment's beautiful face flashed in my mind. With luscious raven curls, rich umber skin, and eyes like emeralds, it was little wonder The Embermage had haunted my dreams these past months, but acknowledging her beauty didn't make the burden any easier to bear. I couldn't close my eyes without picturing the near-constant sheen of sweat clinging to flesh whose gleaming silver undertones were revealed only in moonlight, couldn't place my hand anywhere on my body without it wanting to migrate between my legs. The punishing hold she had over me was as maddening as it was intoxicating… but one way or another, it ended tonight.

One final visit to the street faire in which The Embermage regularly performed. Yes, that was what I needed to get her out of my system—to watch her dance among the flames one last time, to meet her gaze in a sea of hundreds, to look and marvel, but never touch. Never, *ever* touch, not even if she begged me to.

But God, envisioning The Embermage on her knees, pleading for—

"Protect me, Mother Mary, as you protected your son, and I will do the same for mine," I blurted out, horrified at where my thoughts had strayed. That was what I needed to remember, why I needed to keep myself pure. If for no one or nothing else, I needed to think of Quasimodo, my son and my responsibility. No more sneaking around with Mercedes, no more lusting after The Embermage, and after tonight, no more visits to the faire. Ever. I'd accepted my place at Notre Dame for a reason, and it was high time I began living what I preached. It was one thing to damn myself to the pits of Hell, and entirely another to drag my innocent son along with me.

Tonight it was, then. But no more.

"In the name of the Father, and of the Son, and of the Holy Spirit," I whispered solemnly, unclasping my hands to make the sign of the cross, "Amen."

When I stood, I immediately felt lighter. Freer. The ever-present ache in my chest lifted as I turned toward Saint Mary's likeness depicted in stained glass, and a familiar calm washed over me the moment our gazes locked. There was a reason I prayed to Saint Mary rather than God in the evenings. I loved Him dearly, but as a fellow mother, Saint Mary understood me in a way He simply never could. Sunlight filtered through the dazzling display, bathing me in a rainbow of color and informing me of a single truth: even after all these years, despite all my sins and flaws, a higher power still watched over and protected me. No matter what vitriol my peers in the clergy spouted about people like me, to some higher power, I was accepted. I was enough. Grateful tears welled in my eyes, because whether it was Saint Mary's or God's doing hardly mattered. I'd accept whomever's blessing I could get.

After regaining my composure and collecting my prayer cushion from the floor, I made the short walk back to my office. The door was closed, which surprised me only because the maids were usually here cleaning by now, but it didn't upset me—not when it meant I'd have even more quiet time to myself. I loved Quasimodo dearly, but given that we were about to spend an entire evening together, I fully intended to wait until the designated time to meet him, and not a moment sooner. He wouldn't expect me for another fifteen minutes. *Perfect.*

I closed and locked the door before placing the cushion on my desk. Leaning my palms against the cool wood, I scrutinized its surface. Everything was exactly as I'd left it: neat, orderly, and organized, all yet another indication no one had been in here, and that I was alone. Truly alone, especially now that I'd begged forgiveness for my immortal soul. The afterglow of my prayer, and presumably God's watchful eye, had faded.

What I chose to do next would be for me and me alone to know.

Heart pounding, I reached within the neck of my robe and pulled out my prize, carefully and gently so as not to tear the sheer fabric. A scarf, but not just any scarf. It had once belonged to *her*.

I recalled the night I'd acquired it in exquisite detail. I'm still not sure what possessed me to stand so near the stage, but it was an inexplicable pull I didn't bother to fight, and Quasimodo was thrilled to be in the front row. Our proximity hadn't escaped The Embermage's attention. About halfway through her performance, she'd leaned down, yanked the scarf from her neck, and wrapped it around mine, pulling our faces so close I could have pulled back my hood and kissed her. For the rest of my life, I'd regret that I hadn't.

But as quickly as it happened, the moment shattered, leaving me breathless and with the scarf still draped over my shoulders. It was a beautiful, delicate thing, and its violet fabric smelled of smoke and the faintest hint of lilac. As my most treasured possession, the scarf hadn't left my person since the moment I'd acquired it, but not only because I couldn't let anyone else find it.

I may be a holy woman, but I sure as hell wasn't a saint.

My free hand had already drifted below my waist to gather up my vestments. There were quite a few layers to get through, but my practiced fingers made short work of them, fueled by the need pulsing between my thighs. Just my undergarments stood in the way now, and then—

"Did you two finally fuck?"

I nearly screamed. With trembling, careless hands, I shoved the scarf back into its prison and yanked down my robe before whirling around, both surprised and somehow not at all to see a red-haired woman leaning against the far wall. Though half-bathed in shadow, it was easy to make out the sea of freckles dotting her porcelain skin, though her maid's uniform concealed that they extended down her shoulders all the way to her hands, as well as other places I'd seen more times than I could count. Arms crossed, she raised an eyebrow, clearly not planning on saying anything else until I did.

"Mercedes." Her name came out more breathless than I intended. I wish I could have attributed that to her use of profanity, but if I allowed her crassness to bother me, we'd never be able to have anything resembling a civilized conversation. "The door was locked."

"Since when has that ever stopped me?"

Like the other maids, Mercedes had keys to just about everywhere, but last I was aware, that wasn't meant to include my office—for good reason. "What the hell are you doing here?"

She held my gaze, her expression impassive. "Watch your tongue. Father Laurent wouldn't like it. Me, on the other hand…"

"Stop that."

"Stop what?"

"Don't be coy," I snapped, having regained my composure. "You know precisely what you're doing."

"Do I?" Mercedes cocked her head. "I'm not sure I'd say that, as it's not yet had the desired effect."

I bit back a groan and instead bit my tongue. *Lord, give me strength.* This woman knew precisely how to push my buttons, and I hadn't yet decided if it was infuriating or thrilling, especially given what she'd interrupted. It took every ounce of energy I possessed to rein in my impulses, but despite my efforts, my defenses were rapidly crumbling. "You're not supposed to be here."

"You're not supposed to have that scarf."

That smart little mouth of hers was going to be the death of me. "Why *are* you here?"

"What are you doing with that scarf?"

"Answer the question."

"Make me."

My body reacted before my mind caught up. One moment I was at my desk, and the next, I undid weeks of good behavior, and my hand was around Mercedes's throat. She gasped the moment I touched her, but not in pain—I knew the difference intimately well. The corners of her mouth twitched up, hinting at a smile, and her hips bucked against mine, seeking friction rather than escape. I gathered both her wrists in my free hand before raising them above her head, shifting my weight forward, and tilting her chin up at a near-harsh angle, effectively immobilizing her against the wall. She moaned then, soft and restrained, but given that my own constraint had already snapped, I wasn't sure what to feel. Shame? Regret? Disgust?

Any of them would have been appropriate, because everything about what I had just done was wrong. A *sin*. My silver hair may be cropped as short as the rest of the clergy, my breasts bound for most of my waking hours, and my garb identical to my male counterparts, but beneath the modifications I found necessary to better serve my church and my God, I was every bit as womanly as Mercedes. Both nature and my religion dictated that I should find men appealing… or ideally, no one at all, given my vows.

But I couldn't deny my attraction to other women any more than I could deny my God, and my sexual preferences were a festering wound I'd wrestled with my entire life. By day, I was a devout, pious Catholic, performing my duties as Archdeacon and far more whenever necessary, but by night, I sinned, recklessly pursuing pleasures of the flesh. My lust was overpowering and often insatiable. I'd even been known to have multiple women in the same night and still be left wanting more… though when Mercedes was willing and available, other partners were rarely necessary. She had a sexual appetite to rival mine, one of the many things I found appealing about her.

And though I'd never admit it aloud, *God*, I'd missed her. Avoiding her had been pure torture, and now that she was here and my hands were on her, I couldn't resist indulging. "Is this what you wanted?" I breathed against her cheek, lightly nipping at her earlobe. It may have been weeks since I'd touched her—or anyone—but I hadn't forgotten how to handle a woman, nor the games Mercedes liked to play. "To be at my mercy? I bet you'll do anything I ask so long as it ends with my hand up your skirt."

"I will." Her response was more a whine than anything else, and she bucked her hips against mine before meeting my gaze. "Please, Claude. It's been so long."

She was right about that, and I couldn't remember the last time we'd slept together or even come close. Just four months ago, Mercedes and I couldn't go more than twenty-four hours without undressing one another, but circumstances had changed, especially after we'd nearly been caught one too many times. With Mercedes already on thin ice given her past and me unwilling to risk endangering my son, we'd agreed to end the relationship that had never truly been one to begin with, and return to being friends without benefits.

But there was more to it than that, a truth we had yet to acknowledge aloud. Around that same time was when I began visiting the street faire and participating in its festivities every Friday night. It had started innocently enough with my sole intention being to bring a smile to Quasimodo's face, but one look at *her* and it became anything but. The Embermage and her dazzling performances had enchanted me mind and soul, but I wanted and needed far more. She had become an addiction, a compulsion overshadowing my desire for anyone and anything else. Mercedes knew me well enough to notice all of it—my change in demeanor, and certainly where I'd been going—she'd just kept her mouth shut.

Until now, apparently, because she was still giving me an

identical look to when she'd first questioned the scarf. A flash of anger had me gripping her throat slightly tighter. She knew damn well why I'd been avoiding her, but if she wanted me to say it, she would leave here disappointed.

And what had she said? Right—that it had been a while. "It has, and you know why."

"No, I don't," Mercedes shot back, voice slightly hoarse. "If we need to be careful, then let's be more careful. If you no longer want me, just say so. But it's neither of those things. You're rejecting me for someone else. For *her*."

I almost flinched at both the pain in Mercedes's voice and her mention of The Embermage. "I'm not rejecting you, and there *is* no one else."

"Then fuck me."

I swallowed the sudden lump that had formed in my throat. "I... I can't."

"See?" Mercedes's eyes glistened in a way that suggested she was about to claw my eyes out or cry; perhaps both. "Rejection."

"That's not rejection. I said I can't, not that I won't."

"Then why won't you? Are you two exclusive?"

"I'm never exclusive."

"Then, does her cunt truly taste that much better than mine?"

Christ, she was getting loud. "Keep your voice down—"

"Is she prettier than me?"

"Of course not."

"Do you love her?"

Oh, God—the 'L' word, the one I loathed above all others, and the one Mercedes knew better than to utter. My control snapped yet again, and for the second time, my body took over without conscious or rational thought. Stepping aside, I released Mercedes's throat to snatch the nape of her neck, walk her forward, and bend her over my desk. I ignored her startled yelp as I tangled one hand in her auburn curls, forcing her head up, and only barely resisted the urge to smack her rounded bottom. She more than deserved it for what she'd insinuated.

"I love no one but my God and my son, in that order. Is that clear?"
"Yes."
"Yes, who?" I tightened my already punishing grip on her hair.
"Yes, Mis— I mean, Archdeacon Frollo."

"Good." Before I could give in to any more of my sinful urges, I stepped away, leaving Mercedes a breathless, trembling mess as I slumped against the far wall, sinking to my knees. My heart was racing, and my hands shook when I lifted them to where I could examine them. Making the sign of the cross didn't help ease the panic, nor did trying to picture Saint Mary's likeness just down the hall. An icy chill crept over my skin as the reality of what I'd just done set in. I had touched a woman in a sexual manner *again*, and very well may have bedded her if I wasn't already lusting after another. I remained captive to these urges, these cravings, this torment that refused to leave me alone, and had no end in sight.

What if God had been watching us just now and I'd failed Him? What if my very existence was a sin, an abomination, a mistake, and that everything my colleagues whispered about me was true? What if no amount of penance would ever be enough? What if my immortal soul was already damned straight to Hell?

"Are you all right?" Mercedes asked quietly, and only then did I realize I'd been raking my nails over my arms with such violence that there was a bit of blood. I yanked down my sleeves and lifted my head, only for another wave of shame to wash over me when I took in the sight of Mercedes, her disheveled hair and flushed cheeks. I should be asking if *she* was all right, but I didn't move or speak at first, focusing instead on regulating my breathing and keeping my pulse steady. I was no stranger to panic attacks, but it had been over a year since I'd had one in the presence of anyone else. The fact that I'd had one here and now, less than an hour before—

"Claude?" Though she remained where I left her, Mercedes spoke my name again, her tone firm enough to tear me from my rapidly spiraling thoughts. "Tell me what's going on."

"No." I pressed my lips together as I shot her a glare. She knew better than to order me around. "I'm fine."

Mercedes snorted. "Like hell you are."

My breath still came in heavy pants as she closed the distance between us, leaning down to sit beside me. I didn't protest as her fingers entwined with mine. Both reassuring and grounding, the gentleness of it felt far better than I wanted to admit.

"I'm sorry." She paused, her gaze slipping to the floor. "I shouldn't have pushed you like that."

"You shouldn't have asked me if I loved her," I said, low and almost more to myself than her. Love was… a complicated thing. I didn't want it anywhere near the women in my life, because ultimately, it was a weakness. And of all the things I couldn't afford to be, weak was at the very top of that list. Let it show, and Notre Dame would eat me alive even more than it already had.

"I shouldn't have," Mercedes agreed, "but I'm your friend, I miss you, and I worry about you. It's not just me you've been avoiding, and people are starting to notice. You haven't been yourself for months, Claude. Not since—"

"Don't."

She bit her lip and shook her head, causing her red curls to tumble over her shoulders. Despite how irritated I was with her, I reached out and tucked the runaway strands back behind her ear. Mercedes leaned into my touch, covering my hand with one of hers to keep it in place on her cheek. "I know I can't stop you from going to see her, and I won't try. But can you blame me for worrying? It's dangerous out there, and if you were caught, especially with what she…" Her voice trailed off when I shot her another glare. "Just… be careful, all right? And remember that you have people within these very walls who love you."

I chuckled darkly. "At Notre Dame? Besides Quasimodo, the only person with any love for me is you."

Only when I felt Mercedes's breaths on my neck did it register how close we were. She had shifted so she was nearly in my lap, and at some point, I must have turned so that I was fully facing her. My hand remained on her cheek when she lifted her gaze to mine, and I

13

didn't miss the way it had been previously fixated on my lips.

"Mercedes..."

"Please," she whispered, so softly I barely heard her. "I know your rule. But I don't want to leave this room without having kissed you at least once."

The pain in her voice twisted my stomach into knots. Mercedes was far from the only sexual partner I'd confused and hurt over the strange fact that of all the things I was willing to do in bed, I drew the line at kissing. They all followed the same train of thought: how could I possibly have an issue with another woman's lips on mine when I was perfectly comfortable with lips touching any other part of my body? That was precisely it, though—the intimacy of such an act. And much like love, intimacy was something I avoided at all costs.

But Mercedes... oh, my Mercedes. I'd wanted to kiss her since I'd first laid eyes on her gorgeous auburn locks all those years ago. Like me, she'd lived and worked in Notre Dame for most of her life, and for that reason alone there had been an instant connection between us; completely platonic at first but one that rapidly grew into something more. She had been everything I'd ever needed her to be: my friend, my confidant, my colleague, and eventually the closest thing I'd ever had to a lover. Much as I wanted to keep up my stony façade, I couldn't deny the depth of our unique bond.

I certainly couldn't deny her now.

Mercedes leaned forward slowly, giving me ample opportunity to pull away or tell her no. When I did neither, she moaned before closing the remaining distance between us, tentatively pressing her lips to mine. Soft yet desperate, her kiss was far more innocent than I had expected, and it sent a shiver down my spine that kept me rooted in place. It had been so long since I'd been kissed, let alone kissed like this, that neither my body nor mind knew what to make of it.

But to my surprise, it was over as quickly as it started, and Mercedes all but ripped herself from me. Without another word or glance, she rose, pausing briefly to fix her hair and skirt, departing my office before I could so much as blurt out whether I'd done something wrong. I tried to ignore the way my heart ached, or at least not flinch when the door clicked shut, but Mercedes's unspoken message was loud and clear. Her kiss wasn't intended to be a comfort, hopeful, or even sad.

It was simply goodbye.

II. THE PLOT

Esmeralda

"Well, that's certainly a look."

The voice, familiar as it was, succeeded in shattering my concentration and nearly caused me to smear my rouge. *Fuck me, tonight of all nights?* Frowning, I turned from the mirror and twisted in my chair, tossing my carefully styled curls over my shoulder to face the intruder with as much nonchalance as I could muster. Much as I wanted to snap, any reaction at all would only add fuel to the fire, and not in the fun way. "What's that supposed to mean?"

Jules tilted their head and shrugged before leaning against the doorframe. The cocky grin plastered across my sibling's features was more than enough to inform me how pleased they were at having donned their costume quicker than I had, and I fought the urge to roll my eyes. It may have been a game we'd played since we were children, but given that was one I'd stopped trying to win a decade ago, beating me was hardly the accomplishment they seemed to think it was. "I've just never seen you wear that much paint before," Jules said innocently. "What's the occasion?"

"What, would you rather I not take the stage tonight?" I scoffed. "Fine by me. It's all yours. Set your lightning upon some unsuspecting fruit stand. That should go about as well as last time."

"Says the one who's never, ever set anything on fire by accident." Their tone was thick with sarcasm.

I barely bit back the fact that I'd very much like to set *them* on fire right about now. "What do you want? Surely you didn't come here to insult me."

"Of course I did. You make it far too easy."

"Don't you have somewhere to be?"

"Don't you have a reason for getting this prettied up? You still haven't answered my question."

"In case you've forgotten—and judging from the way *you're* dressed, it looks like you have—looking nice is part of our job." I gestured to my hair and face, though the latter wasn't nearly finished thanks to the interruption. Jules, on the other hand, hadn't even buttoned their shirt up all the way, but knowing them, it was probably on purpose. "My attention to detail is hardly the revelation you seem to think it is."

"See, that's just it. Looking nice is one thing, but you're acting weird on top of it. Well, weirder than usual."

"Am I?"

That was clearly the wrong thing to say, because Jules immediately narrowed their gaze. "Out of snippy retorts already? Antoine was right. You *are* hiding something."

Oh, shit. "That's ridiculous," I said, though I could barely hear myself speak over the blood roaring in my ears. "What could I possibly have to hide?"

Everything. I had everything to hide, and the less who knew, the better. If my plans were to go awry, anyone with any knowledge of my plot could be in danger—especially a fellow mage like Jules. My sibling made me want to tear my hair out on a daily basis, but I certainly couldn't bear the thought of anything happening to them.

"Given the innumerable layers in that skirt of yours, practically anything."

"It's a petticoat. And you're welcome to go through it if you'd like," I said coolly, but apparently not coolly enough, because the next thing I knew, Jules rubbed their hands together. Blue sparks danced across their fingertips before floating to the floor, with several settling on the rug.

"Watch it!" I bolted upright, prepared to stamp them out if need be, but thankfully, the sparks dissipated quickly. Shooting Jules a glare, I swore under my breath before hissing, "You ass. You know I can't put out the fires you start!"

"Nothing in your skirt, then." Jules clicked their tongue disapprovingly. "But you're still going to tell me everything."

I glowered. "There's nothing to tell."

They raised an eyebrow. "Don't lie to me, Es."

Scowling, I waved them away before settling back into my chair—which took effort, given the elaborate petticoat and the specific way it forced me to sit. "Believe what you want. But if you're not out of this room in ten seconds, I swear to God, I'll start a fire that *you* can't put out."

"Now wait just a minute." Ignoring my yelp that was equal parts protest and pain, Jules closed the distance between us and snatched one of my hands. The blue sparks rippling across my skin were the least of their concern. "Immaculate hair. All this effort on your face, with particular attention paid to your lips. Manicured nails, with those two fingers specifically looking very—"

"*Jules.*"

They smirked. "Who's the lucky lady?"

"There isn't one." I wrestled myself from their grip, resisting the urge to make good on my threat from a minute ago. "And it's not what you think."

"Ha! So there is a secret." Jules laughed triumphantly, jingling the dozens of tiny bells sewn onto their elaborate costume. "Does the secret's name happen to be Isabelle?"

"What? No! Jesus, I could do far better than Isabelle."

"Agreed. So who is it, then? Jacqueline, Agnès, Emile—"

"You're just listing every woman we know."

"Rossella, Bonnie, Mabile—"

"Enough!" At my outburst, several of the room's candles

extinguished, forcing me to light them again with a flick of my wrist. "It's… not a woman," I admitted through gritted teeth. "It's a man."

Jules's expression immediately switched from one of teasing to understanding, informing me I should have gone with this from the start. "*Oh*. A special showing, of course! Why didn't you just say so? I can still help, you know. He may not know what he's missing, but I can still show him a good time—one he'll readily empty his pockets for."

"That won't be necessary."

"Oh, I didn't mean like *that*. I won't touch him… unless he wants me to, of course." They winked, and I fought the urge to roll my eyes. "So, who's the lucky lad, then?"

I groaned. "Will you just drop it?"

"Can't be any of the men I know if he prefers a woman's company. A hint, please?"

I found myself unable to do more than stare at Jules, still processing their clear and unspoken *No, I won't drop it*. I knew my sibling well enough to know when I was fighting a losing battle, and much as I was loath to admit it, it was time to bow out. The evening had hardly begun, and already I was exhausted from playing this game. For it to be a success, I needed both my wits and my magic at their full strength, and at this rate, I'd have neither. Maybe there was a way to compromise; I could tell Jules just enough to get them off my back without endangering them, and perhaps I could get something out of this in return. After all, there was still a variable for which I had no solution.

"All right. Your hint is that you do know him. Not personally, but you've seen him around."

"Ah ha!" Jules clapped their hands so close to my face I flinched. "Men I've seen around, men I've seen around... oh, there's so many, aren't there? The streets are always so crowded, especially on Friday nights. There are the obvious choices: that man who treats his cigar like a third arm, that silver-haired man in the hood, that man with the ragged hat I've never heard speak a single—wait. It's the silver-haired man. Of *course* it's him. You haven't stopped staring at him for weeks now!"

"Noticed, have you?" I did my best to keep my expression and voice impassive. This had to be handled carefully and specifically.

"Everyone has. Every week he's here, seemingly for no other reason than to watch you perform. So much for him to see, so much for him to indulge in, yet all he ever wants is you. Isn't that enough to stroke your massive ego? Or would you prefer him enchanted, devoted to you and only you? Is that the reason for the private showing?"

My lips twisted into a smirk; finally, something I could work with. "That's precisely it. I don't intend to enchant him. I intend to seduce him."

Jules nearly choked. "You? Seduce a man? Since when have men appealed to you?"

"Since always. It's hardly my fault most can't perform in bed."

"Or perhaps I've already fucked the talented ones," they fired back, crossing the room to sit in the stool opposite me. "But I'd prefer not to compete with my own sister."

I raised a brow. My sibling definitely had a type, and it would shock me beyond measure if the silver-haired man appealed to Jules's tastes. "What, do *you* want him?"

They scrunched up their nose. "Not in the slightest."

"Then there is no competition. Besides"—I paused, turning back to the mirror to finish applying my rouge—"I could use your help."

"Help with seduction?" Jules cackled again. "I know it's been a while since you've bedded one, Es, but rest assured, men are far easier to coax into bed than the women you fuck. And from the way that one's been staring, I can't imagine it will take much more than a single crook of your finger."

"But he doesn't come alone. There's that boy he always brings. His son, perhaps?" I faced Jules again, hoping their perceptive ass wouldn't pick up on the fact that this was the variable. "If anyone needs enchanting, it's the boy. We need to reassure his father he's safe and looked after before I can make my move."

They blanched. "You want me to babysit?"

"Call it what you like, but he's not a baby. He'll be a man in a few years by the looks of it."

"You can't be serious. Antoine and I—"

"Were going to fuck in the alley again, yet still within earshot of half the neighbors?" I shook my head. "No. Tonight, it's my turn."

Jules immediately brightened. "You and him, in the alley? How filthy."

"No!" I snapped, too quickly once again, so I had to blurt

out a way to cover my ass. "I only meant that he looks rather conservative, don't you think? I'm sure he won't want to risk being out in the open like that. It's likely we'll come back here, so see to it we're not disturbed."

Jules glanced at my bed and mimed a gag. "I see why you asked me to watch the child if this was the alternative."

I sighed. "Jules..."

"Fine. Fine!" They threw up their hands in defeat. "I'll tell Antoine to spread the word that you're not to be disturbed tonight."

My heart skipped a beat; had I truly done it? Had my sibling given in? "Thank you."

"Thank me when it's over and you're safe." Jules ran a hand through their braided hair before eyeing me up and down. "I know you can take care of yourself... but you know I worry. You don't even know his name."

I snorted. "And you know the name of every man you've fucked?"

The corners of their mouth twitched. "Point taken. It's just... You could have anyone you wanted, Es, and there are plenty of people you've known far longer perfectly willing to bed you. Why him? And why the insistence on him?"

Because he's one of Notre Dame's clergy. Because he may one day help or even save us. And because he's clearly infatuated with me; why not use that to our advantage?

But I didn't say any of that—I couldn't, so I shrugged. "I want something different, that's all. You've heard the whispers about silver-haired people—a Starchild, some might call him, blessed and chosen by gods worshiped across the sea. And that hood adds an air of mystery, don't you think? I've been dying to see what's underneath for weeks." That much was true. Though the robe concealed most everything, it couldn't hide his tall, broad frame, and I'd caught glimpses of other tantalizing secrets, too: his forearms, his jaw, his lips, his eyes…

"Or perhaps he wears it because he's horrifically ugly." Jules scoffed, tearing me from my thoughts just in time. "And Starchild, my ass. How do you know he's not old and wrinkled?"

"Beauty is in the eye of the beholder, and he's young. Just a few years older than me, perhaps." I squeezed my sibling's upper arm. "I'll be fine. And if I begin to suspect otherwise, my magic is more than enough to protect me."

"The same way it protected Mère?"

The air around us went icy as Jules sucked in a breath. I could tell by that reaction alone they hadn't meant to bring up our mother, much less compare her to me, but it was far too late to take it back. Stiffening, I pulled my arm away, my own retort hovering on the tip of my tongue. *Don't you understand? I'm doing this for her. So that her fate is one you nor I may never suffer.*

"I'm sorry, I only meant—"

"I know what you meant," I cut across them. "But my mind is made up."

Jules didn't argue further, but I could tell they wanted to. I didn't need them to voice aloud what the look on their face was screaming: this was a risk. Maman took risks, and it got her killed. I knew that, even more than they thought I did. *Much* more than they thought I did. But this was hardly the first time I'd put myself in danger to keep them safe, and it wouldn't be the last.

Because if there was one thing Maman had taught me, it was this: if the Church was so determined to see mages burn, we'd just have to burn them first.

Finally, Jules met my gaze. "Good luck, then."

"You as well." I turned back to the mirror and finished touching up a few spots on my face before standing up and giving myself one last look over. Taking a few calming breaths, I weaved a few stray hairs back into place, concentrating simply upon breathing in and out as I stared at my reflection. I looked lovely, truly. The red of this dress complimented the brown of my skin, and I was even wearing Maman's necklace: a teardrop-shaped ruby pendant on a thin gold chain. I'd convinced Jules to help me without sending them into a panic or revealing too many details. The hard part was over, and there was no need to still be anxious... right? So why was my heart beating out of my chest and my magic swirling in a way that made every nerve ending feel as though it was on fire?

Fire. I hadn't donned the final piece of my costume, and surely that was what the prickles dancing across my skin were picking up on. Jules, too, for they stood holding the cloak ready for me to slip into it.

"Thank you." I pulled my hair aside so they could fasten the tie loosely around my throat, but we both knew it wouldn't remain there long. Not long into my act, I'd lose the garment discreetly, replacing its shape with a plume of actual fire, but the unsuspecting crowd thought the cloak and the plume were one and the same. Did the silver-haired man, too? Or had he caught on to all my tricks by now?

I turned to the mirror a final time, styling my hair back into place and making sure everything was just so. All the while, Jules's outline remained visible in the dimming candlelight, and when they made no move to leave, I frowned. "Go on, then. I know the way."

Jules nodded, pulling me into a quick hug before heading out the door. I almost regretted shooing them out, because the moment it clicked shut, I became hyper-aware of the crowd that had gathered outside—the one waiting for me. Their chant was as insistent as it was deafening, shouted like an incantation... or a prayer. "*Embermage. Embermage. Embermage.*"

Was the silver-haired man shouting, too?

Inhaling deeply, I closed my eyes and pictured the little I'd seen of his face. He had high cheekbones, narrowed eyebrows, and sharp, almost harsh features, but his lips were plump and soft, as if begging to be kissed. We nearly had, once, the night I'd given him my scarf. It had been the start of my seduction... and also the night I'd first dreamed about him. I'd had too many to count since, but the first remained the best as well as my favorite. Tonight wasn't about pleasure, but if the opportunity presented itself?

I wouldn't hesitate to recreate that dream in painstaking, toe-curling detail.

With those images at the forefront of my mind, my magic calmed nearly instantly, as did my heartbeat. Before the anxiety could creep back, I marched toward the hidden door that would lead me straight to the stage, yanked it open, and slipped into darkness. My cloak and skirt trailed behind me as I walked the short distance to the curtain, but I knew better than to pick them up; if I left it on the ground, it was far easier to make it appear as though they were on fire, and the crowd always went wild for that.

Judging from their cries alone, they numbered in the hundreds, easily the largest crowd we'd managed to gather in weeks. The thought briefly thrilled me—more spectators equaled higher pay— but the moment I pulled open the other end of the trapdoor and my gaze swept over the handful of city guards placed in strategic positions among the sea of Parisian citizens, my exhilaration turned once again to paralyzing fear. The guards took their orders from the Church, who claimed their presence was simply to ensure everyone's safety at such events, but those of us blessed with magic knew far better. They weren't here to keep the peace.

They were here for *us*.

Mages, they'd deemed us, but the term was hardly fair. Though it fit people like me and Jules who regularly utilized magic to perform and entertain, there were plenty of mages content with simply using their abilities to enhance their daily lives. Magic was a gift anyone could possess; man, woman, or neither, brown, Black, or white, and its uses were as varied as the people who wielded it. I'd even met a few who never used their magic at all. Every mage's choice was their own, and I would never dare pry, but I strongly suspected what these guards represented to be the root of that so-called 'choice.' Magic wasn't, and had never been illegal, so long as it wasn't used to harm another person… but the Church had never been content with that. Why would they be when the very existence of magic threatened their God? All they needed was an excuse—one spark out of place— and they would be justified in beginning the crusade that had hung over the mages' heads for generations.

Which was why I had resolved to be two steps ahead. Acting only as a reaction was never a strategy that had sat right with me, so from the very first night the silver-haired man stood in my crowd, of course I'd taken notice. At first it was simply the hair that intrigued me, but it didn't take me long to recall the rumors of a Starchild serving among the current members of Notre Dame's clergy. If the rumors were to be believed, he'd risen up quickly through the ranks and now served as Archdeacon. I smiled as his handsome face flashed in my mind's eye; to think that just a few months ago, I'd have settled for any random guard who would have me.

This was my way in. This was the opportunity I'd been waiting for: someone powerful I could sway to our side, or at the very least sympathize enough with our plight to delay the inevitable. The Church would come for us—of that I had no doubt—but with their Archdeacon in my back pocket, perhaps not nearly as soon. And all of it hinged on tonight.

No pressure.

Sarcasm was apparently not what my anxiety needed. My confidence vanished, my heart skipped a beat, and my breath froze in my lungs as I stepped onto the stage and bowed, managing to sweep my arms in their usual grand flourish despite wanting to leap out of my own skin. It was as if I were a spectator to my own actions rather than in command of them. My body moved, but my mind couldn't recall giving the orders. The roar of the crowd swelled and surrounded me, like a thunderous wave that threatened to swallow me up whole. The stage was a precipice, and I stood barefoot on its edge, with no way down and no way back.

I may have fallen prey to the fear completely if not for the flames there to ground me. A small fire had been lit center stage, crackling and hissing like a feral beast waiting to be fed… and reminding me that I was one, too. Raising my chin and setting my shoulders, I walked the full length of the stage once, then twice before coming to a halt before the fire. All mages were immune to the element they wielded, so I was in no true danger, but I'd never quite gotten over my curiosity over what such pain might feel like. I stretched out my arm, ignoring the cries of the crowd as the fire engulfed me up to my shoulder. Though there was a vague bite to it, the heat was comforting, welcoming even. I leaned closer, wanting to feel the sting of an almost-burn on my face—but someone cried out in a voice that I recognized.

Him.

Immediately I scanned the crowd, searching for the silver-haired man I was convinced had spoken. But there were too many faces, all blurred together in their eagerness for what might come next, and not a single trace of that distinct silver. A dull ache erupted in my chest as a paralyzing fear took hold.

He wasn't here.

Of course he wasn't. Why would he be? I had been a fool to wait so long to make my move, especially given his position at Notre Dame. It would have only taken one person to recognize him, one person to inform his superior, and he'd never be able to show his face anywhere near this district again. Ripping myself from the flames, I opened my mouth to call the entire performance off, to scatter the crowd or send them into a riot for all I—

But then, I saw him. He wasn't near his usual spot, which explained why I'd missed him before, but it was unmistakably him, a fact that made my heart skip a beat. He met my gaze without flinching, his eyes bright and unblinking beneath that shock of silver hair. It felt as though he was looking straight into my soul, searching for truths hidden and long buried but that he alone wished to know.

When he smiled, something inside me lit up in recognition or perhaps relief; whatever it was, it was precisely the motivation I needed to begin my dance. It was no different than any other, save for one simple thing.

This dance was solely for him.

III. THE FAIRE

Claude

*M**aman,* Quasimodo signed into my open palm. *You're smiling again.*

Hell, that wouldn't do. Tearing my gaze away from the maze of tents pitched in the middle of the street and their dazzling display of lights, I reset my expression to a neutral one before meeting my son's gaze and signing back, *Better?*

Only if smiling is a crime. He squeezed my hand once his fingers finished forming the shapes, not quite hard enough to hurt but certainly enough to make his point. *I like your smile. Why do you hide it?*

A dull ache blossomed in my chest, as did the urge to pull him into a fierce hug. I settled for guiding us out of the crowd we'd been navigating, coming to a halt near one of the closed-down shops with my hand still in his. A year ago I'd have needed to kneel if I wanted to face Quasimodo at eye level, but now a boy of fifteen, it wasn't necessary. *You know why*, I signed. *We cannot draw attention to ourselves. If we smile too much, strangers might talk to us.*

"You mean *you*," he said aloud, his tone thick with frustration. "No one ever wants to talk to me."

That's not true. I want to talk to you.

"You always talk to me," he snapped, but softened his tone at my no-doubt-wounded expression. "I want to make a friend and meet someone new. I know my way around. I'll be safe."

It wasn't an unreasonable request. Whether I was ready to admit it or not, in a few short years, Quasimodo would be a man—a decent one at that. He had a good head on his shoulders, a kind heart, and could speak and lip read well enough to communicate with most anyone.

It wasn't his deafness that worried me, though. Despite the disguises we both wore in the form of heavy cloaks with hoods, there was no concealing the disfigurement that had plagued Quasimodo since infancy. His spine hadn't formed correctly, and it left him with a large, humped back. At best, his appearance drew questioning glances; at worst, scathing whispers. And I wanted to shield him from all of it.

But I couldn't protect him forever, especially outside the confines of Notre Dame, and tonight was our final visit to the street faire... a fact I hadn't yet been brave enough to confess. These trips were the highlight of his week, and to cease coming here would crush him. We'd need to find another excuse to venture outside the cathedral every now and again, I'd already decided, but it couldn't be this—not as long as The Embermage remained a regular performer.

"All right," I found myself saying, and having read my lips, Quasimodo's face immediately lit up. *You may go. But you're not permitted to leave this block. Don't take off your cloak, don't go into anyone's house or shop, even if you're invited, and meet me at our usual spot in an hour.* The Embermage's performance would be over by then, and I knew better than to linger.

Quasimodo frowned. *An hour and a half?* he signed hopefully.

An hour, I insisted, my movements sharp and firm. *Have fun. And please, be safe.*

"I will," he said, beaming as he turned to walk away, straight toward the rapidly gathering crowds. "Thank you, Maman!"

I immediately clenched my teeth and yanked my hood farther down, but it was far too late to scold him for breaking another of my rules. While in public, I insisted upon masquerading as a man, and when in earshot of said public, Quasimodo wasn't permitted to refer to me as 'maman' or anything else that might give away the fact that I was a woman. Given my height and the broadness of my shoulders, it was both for safety and my own personal comfort, as well as to lessen any chance I might be recognized. The silver hair I'd possessed all my life was already a dead giveaway to my identity to anyone paying any attention. I didn't need to make it any easier for them.

But other than a few curious glances, Quasimodo's outburst had been swiftly swallowed over the roar of the crowd and forgotten. It was as relieving as it was unsurprising. In all of Paris, if there was anywhere

I could truly be myself, it was on these streets, for I was far from the only one unwilling to conform to society's rigid gender standards. Just a few paces away, a person with a generous amount of facial hair skipped and twirled, showing off the bright yellow dress that more than suited them. Two others were helping to braid the impressively long locks of someone dressed in a waistcoat. And a quick scan of the crowds wandering the busy streets revealed they weren't made up solely of women and men; there was more diversity in my current field of vision than I'd ever seen step foot inside Notre Dame. People of every race, class, and gender mingled openly. It wasn't simply that everyone who presented a little differently blended in with the performers gathered on every corner, whose bright and elaborate costumes were as eye-catching as the yellow dress, it was that their differences were accepted, welcomed even. I supposed it made sense, considering who put on these faires...

The mages.

No sooner had the thought entered my mind than a plume of water shot up and over my head before colliding with a plume of fire of an identical size and shape. Canceling one another out, they vanished with a crackling sizzle, the noise quickly followed by *oohs*, *ahhs*, and applause. The pair of mages responsible for the display, a white woman and a brown-skinned man, each sank into a quick bow, taking only a moment to acknowledge the recognition before gesturing toward the main stage. Unlike the tents and stands pitched specifically for the faire, the stage's presence was permanent.

"That was just a warm up for the main event," the man called out. "Hurry, now—The Embermage begins in a few short minutes!"

It was more than enough to get the crowd moving. The existence of magic was nothing new, but the way these mages wielded it in the form of entertainment certainly was. Masters of various elements, every mage was born with an affinity to one in particular. Despite my conservative upbringing and the Church's attempt to shield me from such things, I'd witnessed affinities ranging from earth to air to lightning. Less common ones were things like flora and weather manipulation, and I knew without a doubt there were far more. Many mages gravitated toward the profession which might utilize their affinity the best, while others chose not to tap into their magic at all.

Only one mage had ever caught my eye enough to want to know more, though: *her*. The raven-haired dancer, The Embermage, and the one I hadn't been able to get out of my head since the very first time I'd witnessed her captivating performance. Her power should worry me at best, and terrify me at worst—she commanded flames, after all—yet all I cared to know was what her heat might feel like on my skin... among other things.

Swallowing, I kept my head down as the crowd grew ever thicker, hoping desperately no one had noticed my flushed cheeks. I was quite literally flirting with fire and needed to be more careful, even tonight. I was better than this. I *had* to be better than this. It didn't matter how The Embermage's dark skin lit up in the glow of the firelight, or that I longed to touch her the way her fire did. It didn't matter that we'd locked eyes more than once, and it certainly didn't matter that her scarf remained tucked against my chest.

She was sin, and it could never be.

With that thought front and center, I lifted my gaze just enough to make out my immediate surroundings. Jugglers and acrobats had taken the stage, there to pass the time before the main event, but hardly anyone spared them a glance. Buzzing with excitement, the sizable crowd talked among themselves, with most of the conversations I could make out predicting what The Embermage might perform for us tonight. I felt a twinge of sympathy for those already on stage whose talents were all but going to waste. They were skilled, undeniably so, but we'd come for her and her alone.

In just a few short minutes, she'd come bursting through that curtain with a plume of fire trailing after her. With glittering emerald eyes, the way her dress barely clung to her shoulders, and that flirtatious smirk, it was little wonder that half a dozen men were already quite literally fighting over the positions near the front. I rolled my eyes and steered well clear of the careless brawl. I'd seen her act dozens of times and didn't need the best view, but if I was being honest, I could hardly blame those vying for such a coveted spot. The Embermage was mesmerizing and had developed her abilities well beyond any of the other fire mages in attendance.

One of the many things she alone could do was mold her fire into animals. She'd mimicked wolves, bears, and even a legendary phoenix, but the grandest of them all was the dragon. I'd only seen her do it once, but it hadn't stopped me from hoping for it every time since, but not for the display. While everyone else was fixated on the dragon, I was fixated on her—specifically, her smile. That look of pure joy was one I'd craved ever since, and I'd do unspeakable, sinful things to witness it again.

I may have indulged in picturing said things in my mind's eye had a body not slammed into my front, nearly causing my hood to fall back. Oblivious to my cry of indignation, the drunken man stumbled off, but it was equally likely he simply hadn't heard me. Either the restless energy from the brawl had spread, the masses had grown impatient, or both, for a deafening chant had risen:

"*Embermage. Embermage. Embermage.*"

It was only then that I realized just how many people were here. The Embermage never failed to draw a large crowd, but this was the largest she'd attracted in weeks, if not months, and people continued to file in by the dozens. Bodies soon pressed against me from all sides, rooting me firmly in place, and for once, I was thankful for my height; if I were any shorter, I wouldn't have been able to make out the stage from where I stood.

The only ones who didn't have trouble carving out their own space were the city guards, mostly because they were given as wide a berth as possible. I counted no less than five in a quick scan, but none I recognized. *Good.* The last thing I needed was for one of them to report me to Father Laurent. I had what I would consider a friendly relationship with several members of the guard, but even then, I wouldn't trust them to carry a secret as heavy as this one. To come here was to mingle with mages, and mingling with mages could get me confined to the cathedral at best and stripped of my position as Archdeacon at worst.

But that was why tonight was the last time, my final visit. Though I'd never admit it aloud, Mercedes had been right: this was as risky as it was dangerous, and I'd been damn lucky to have gotten away with it for as long as I had. An idle part of me had wondered if I *hadn't* gotten away with it and permitted me to keep coming here regardless, but I shoved the ridiculous notion aside. I could already hear the scathing disapproval in Father Laurent's tone should he ever discover my disobedience, and I could probably recite the lecture I'd receive here and now.

Thankfully, I didn't have to. The noise crescendoed to a peak, and I snapped my head up just in time.

There she was.

Though the other spectators cheered and clapped as she glided to center stage, my breath caught in my throat. Holding her head high, The Embermage bowed low, sweeping her arms in a dramatic arc. Draped over her shoulders was a cloak of pure fire, invoking cries of alarm from the first-timers in the audience, but those who knew better only cheered louder. Unbothered by the flames, her dark hair bounced as she walked, spilling over her back to mix with the fire. She was too perfect to be real, yet I couldn't deny that she was, for the scent on the breeze confirmed it. *Her* scent. Smoky and with the faintest traces of lilac, the same that I inhaled from her scarf every single night. Despite the crowd's demands, she didn't begin right away. She walked the length of the stage once, then twice, seemingly allowing a better look at her gorgeous dress. The red suited both the flames and her dark skin, accentuating her breasts and curves all in the same fell swoop.

Though I wanted nothing more than to simply get lost in this moment, in her, questions that had relentlessly plagued me drifted to the forefront of my mind, each one boiling down to a single, mystifying word: why? Why had she given me her scarf, and why did she keep staring at me, singling me out? Why was there this inexplicable pull between us, an attraction more powerful than gravity? The looks she gave me were as intense as they were invasive, and if I didn't know any better… seductive.

No. Surely that was my imagination and the attraction I felt toward her playing tricks on me. I came here in disguise, for God's sake—any attention she'd paid to me, a stranger wearing a hood, had to be a coincidence. If I were smart, I would consider myself lucky, leave it at that, and leave this faire for real, never again to return.

But I wasn't smart. Week after week and month after month I'd come here, risking more each time I dared to make the trip. I'd made excuses. I'd angered my peers in the clergy. I'd altered my steadfast routine to fit around seeing her, which was more effort than I'd ever made with any woman I'd bedded, but The Embermage was different. She felt… worth it. She'd enchanted me in mind, body, and soul, and there was only one truth of which I was undeniably certain: I never wanted it to stop.

Startled gasps jolted me from the uncomfortable revelation. I raised my gaze to the stage, only to cry out in horror at the sight of The Embermage half-engulfed in fire. Some faraway voice at the back of my mind reminded me that mages couldn't be harmed by their own element, but far too concerned for her safety, I barely heard it.

Her head snapped up. Only once she backed away from the flames did I allow myself to breathe—but just for a moment. Because then she began scanning the crowd, her brow furrowed in what was a familiar and rather endearing look of concentration. She was searching for someone.

And if I wasn't totally delusional, she was searching for *me*.

It didn't take her long. The Embermage's entire demeanor shifted when she landed upon me, her body relaxing, expression darkening. When our gazes locked, the rest of the world melted away. I became lost in the sea of her eyes, and even if it meant that I'd drown, I never wanted to surface. More truths reared their terrifying heads, truths that paled in comparison to simply wanting her. If she was wrong, I didn't want to be right. If she'd have me, I'd worship her as my new God.

And if she was Hell, I'd go willingly.

Though I practically knew The Embermage's steps by heart, my lips still parted in awe the moment she started dancing. Her bare feet drummed the stage at a frantic, yet perfectly controlled pulse, but if there was music, I couldn't hear it. My ears picked up only the sizzling of her cloak, the noise quickly drowned out by the roaring of the crowd as she pulled the garment from her shoulders. Those at the front stepped back to get away from the heat, but she didn't flinch. She grinned as if fueled by their fear.

The moment it left her hands, rather than turn to ash in the wind, the cloak transformed. Following the shape of The Embermage's hands, the plume grew longer and longer until it could wrap her entire body in its embrace several times over, the very same way that I wanted to, *needed* to. God, I craved her laugh. I lived for her smile. I yearned to feel her touch and desperately wanted her to feel mine. I envisioned her writhing beneath me, yanking my hair and clawing at my back until she was screaming my name.

Yet I didn't know hers. I'd asked around, to no avail, but it seemed her people were as keen to protect her as she was herself. Following each show, she quickly disappeared into the hidden door from which she emerged, as though she was as legendary—as temporary—as her fire. Part of me hoped she was. It'd make my plight a whole lot easier.

But as The Embermage was about to prove, nothing was ever easy with her. Most nights, she started off slow. She'd get the crowd clapping but refuse to up the tempo of her dance until she was good and ready, teasing us each time her leg slipped through the slit in her dress. She'd toss her head, sending her curls cascading down her back, and strut around while her fire trailed behind like the obedient servant it was.

Tonight was not one of those nights.

I couldn't tell what gripped her, but something had. With a single flick of her wrist, she signaled the drums to start before launching into a frenzy. She was anywhere and everywhere, crooking her finger and daring the fire to catch her. A time or two, it appeared that she was beckoning *me*, but at the speed she was moving, it was impossible to be sure. Each time they failed to engulf her, the flames grew, upping the intensity with a vengeance.

Finally, she was cornered. Back pressed against one of the pillars holding the stage's roof upright, the fire surrounded her, blocking all routes of escape. I could barely make out her silhouette through the curtain of orange and red, and from the shocked murmurs surrounding me, several couldn't see her at all.

The logical part of me knew this was likely another one of The Embermage's tricks, but she had me holding my breath. Several more moments passed as the fire closed in, and despite my best efforts, after glancing up, I lost sight of her. Anyone else would have been screaming for mercy by now, their flesh sloughing off in pieces... but she was silent.

A single clap thundered through the campsite then, followed by a rush of hot air almost strong enough to blow the hood from my face. Ash caught in my throat, and the sting of it brought tears to my eyes, but it only lasted a few moments before passing. Incredulous cheering and applause erupted before I'd fully registered what happened. "She's alive!" someone next to me declared. She was more than alive.

She was magnificent.

From where The Embermage stood center stage, regarding the crowd with icy, calculated calm, she looked like royalty. Not a single bead of sweat dripped down her face, and her dress and curls remained intact. Even if she hadn't been elevated by the stage, the regal angle at which she held her chin informed all of us we were beneath her, which still wasn't enough for me.

I got on my knees for only my God... yet I wanted to worship her.

As she bowed low to acknowledge the well-deserved praise, I forced myself to look away. Though she'd somehow managed to hold herself together after a literal trial by fire, after simply witnessing the marvel of her, I was in pieces. My hands quivered, my heart fluttered, and most embarrassingly, there was a need pulsing between my thighs. With each passing moment, that need—and the wetness—grew.

I swore under my breath then muttered, "Father, forgive me." It was an ongoing battle not to make profanity a habit, and I certainly didn't need two to break. But as I smoothed my cloak and adjusted the covering concealing my face, I knew that The Embermage was far more than just a bad habit. She was an addiction.

"Merci, merci!"

My head snapped up. Had The Embermage just spoken?

"You're too kind." She spoke again as though my jaw wasn't on the ground, and as if addressing the crowd was a normal part of her performance. I'd been coming here for damn near four months, and not once in that time had I heard her speak, much less to her spectators. "A show is only as good as its audience, and you've been an excellent one. I've been saving this next trick for a special occasion and the perfect crowd since I'll need a bit of help." She gestured to a fellow mage occupying what little space existed between the stage and the crowd: a mage who bore a rather striking resemblance to her. "Jules, would you be so kind as to select someone for me?"

My mind screamed *me*, but my body took a step back. Nothing good could come from me and The Embermage being that close. Either I'd go up in flames or only torture myself further, and I wasn't certain which was worse. As most of the crowd threw their hands in the air and begged to be chosen, The Embermage scanned the sea of faces, and I knew from that look in her eyes she was searching for me. I glanced down, forcing myself to stare at the patterns in the dirt. *Not me. Not me.*

After an eternity, the crowd burst into applause, cheering and whistling as the person Jules had chosen for her ascended the stairs to stand on the stage beside The Embermage.

I didn't expect that person to be my son.

Biting my lip to keep from screaming Quasimodo's name, I rubbed my eyes to be certain they weren't deceiving me. They weren't.

He truly *was* with her.

I could have sworn a shadow crossed The Embermage's face as she regarded my son, but it was gone when I blinked. She sank into an even deeper bow than she had at the beginning of her performance, all the while holding Quasimodo's hand. Wordlessly, she gestured for him to stand to the side, taking his arms and bending them into various shapes. Though my heart fluttered wildly, I could hardly complain at the gentle way she treated him.

She left him where she'd placed him before skipping back to center stage, addressing the crowd with a twinkle in her eye. "I give you: Dancing with the Dragon."

This time, more than just drums joined in. A low drone rattled my bones while a slow melody began on the pipes. I wanted desperately to watch The Embermage but couldn't take my eyes off Quasimodo, whose face betrayed none of the worries I felt in my core. Neither she nor Jules had given him any instructions, nonverbal or otherwise. How would he know what to do?

I couldn't let this stand. Ignoring the grunts of protest and the way my bindings shifted when I moved, I tried to shove my way through the tightly packed crowd. I made a bit of progress, but the closer I drew to the stage, the more futile my mission became. People began shoving me back, spewing vile curses, and one man even took a swing at my face, a blow I barely dodged. I wouldn't be nearly as lucky a second time, because I wasn't lithe and nimble; I was a woman tall and broad to a fault.

Defeated, I glanced up. The music was much louder now, and the drums beat at a heart-stopping, frantic rhythm. A plume of newly conjured fire trailed behind The Embermage, who strode to the beat.

When she stilled, so did the music—as well as my very soul. She nodded to Quasimodo before summoning the dragon.

In an instant, the harmless plume transformed into a monster of behemoth proportions, complete with muscular, bat-like wings and a gaping maw. Its eyes glittered with a vengeance, its tail lashing in anticipation. Covered in fiery scales and armed with alarmingly realistic horns meant for goring, I had no doubt the dragon could burn as well as act as a deadly battering ram.

It was all I could do not to scream Quasimodo's name; I bit my lip until I tasted blood. Out of all of us, out of hundreds of perfectly willing adults, why had she and Jules chosen *him*?

The Embermage ducked her head as the dragon dove from the sky, its maw aimed for her face. Leaping forward, she took her weight on her hands, doing several acrobatic flips before coming to land on her feet. The dragon continued its pursuit, forcing her to duck and weave as deadly a dance as she'd promised. My mouth hung agape, but not for the reason I'd expected.

The beast took its direction not from The Embermage, but from Quasimodo.

I'd never seen such delight on his face. He remained where she'd placed him, far out of harm's way, and whatever way he waved his arms, the dragon followed. He alone controlled the beast, and he alone decided whether or not The Embermage burned. I could tell from the look on his face the power intoxicated him… but it wasn't long before it grew to worry him. The drums began beating faster, vibrations he would be able to feel through the stage floor.

His gaze darted to the crowd, no doubt searching for me. Waving my arms, I mouthed over and over for him to end this. Even from where I stood, I could clearly make out the sheen of sweat that clung to The Embermage's dark skin, as well as the way her breast heaved each time she attempted to catch her breath. This wasn't sustainable, and the dragon seemed to agree.

As the music built to a climax, for the first time, the dragon disobeyed Quasimodo's command. Though he repeatedly pointed toward stage left, the beast had The Embermage cornered in stage right. As before, her back pressed against one of the pillars while the beast stared her down. She held its gaze, returning its glare of defiance. I realized what she intended to do before she did it, but I didn't have time to scream.

Throwing her arms out at her sides, The Embermage allowed the dragon to swallow her whole.

"No!" My son's piercing cry tore through the stillness following her collapse. Before the flames had fully dissipated, Quasimodo was by her side, cautiously poking the heap of red fabric. It was impossibly hard to tell from where I stood, but I swore that The Embermage wasn't moving, not even to breathe. All of us, mages and citizens alike, waited in stunned stillness. Even Jules's lips were parted in shock.

Tears streamed down my son's face, and the sight summoned my own. Whatever sorrow I felt over The Embermage's tragedy had been momentarily replaced by rage: how dare she let my son feel responsible for her own careless accident? My fists clenched at my sides, angry that I couldn't even comfort him given that I remained trapped by the crowd.

"Your hope is too easily extinguished."

A chorus of astonished gasps, and The Embermage rose unburnt and unscathed.

The crowd burst into a deafening celebration before I'd had a chance to take it all in. A sea of arms waved in my face, obstructing my view of her, Jules, and my son. But I could swear they were moving, turning toward the trapdoors—and *not* the stairs.

"Move!" I hissed, shoving my way through the bodies yet again and meeting much less resistance than before. It helped that the crowd had begun to disperse, but what made the most difference was my own inner resolve. Quasimodo had been parted from my side for too long and had participated in one too many near-death experiences for my liking. Weaving through the maze of oblivious spectators, I looked up just in time to see The Embermage take a final bow before disappearing back into her trapdoor. She was the final performer to remain on the stage; Jules and Quasimodo were already gone.

"Wait!" I shrieked, but there was no way my voice wasn't lost among the cacophony. Fueled by reckless abandon and sheer desperation, I barrelled through the crowd with the intention of striking down any who dared to stand in my path. It wasn't necessary, though; now that the show had ended, the barrier ahead of me grew thinner, and it wasn't long before I reached the stage.

Chest heaving, it was a moment before I could form a coherent thought. *The trapdoor.* Yes, that was what I needed to find, where Quasimodo had most likely disappeared to. Barely contained rage coursed through me as I stomped up the stairs, and even if there wasn't a fire still burning in the center of the stage, I'd be seeing nothing but red. How dare those two put my son through such an ordeal—but more importantly, how dare Quasimodo disobey me? I'd explicitly told him not to follow anyone inside, to stay in the streets, but at the first opportunity, he'd done the opposite. What in God's name was he thinking? What in God's name had *I* been thinking, letting him wander around alone?

"You cannot be here, Monsieur."

I whirled around with murder in my eyes, glaring daggers at the pair of mages who had followed me onstage: the man and woman from earlier. "I assure you, no part of me wants to be here," I snapped. "But that boy was my son, and it's high time we headed back home."

"Boy?" the man echoed, taking a step toward me. "He looked more like a capable young man, one who can find his way home on his own."

Heat prickled beneath my skin, threatening to boil over at any moment, mostly because he was right. Still, it was far too late to rein in my overprotective tendencies. "You presume to know my son better than me?"

"We know only that you shouldn't be here," the woman said, flicking her wrist and producing a plume of fire. The glow of it accentuated the shadows on her face, and if I wasn't so angry, the warning display may have scared me. "Please, just go. No one needs to get hurt."

I couldn't help it. I laughed, shaking my head in disbelief. The movement dislodged my hood, causing it to fall past my forehead and expose more of my face than I'd ever shown in public before, but I didn't bother to fix it. Let them see. Perhaps they wouldn't recognize me for who I was, but my rage at least would be on full display. "For all any of us know, my son could already be hurt."

The man's gaze flicked to my hair and back again before he clenched his jaw. "He's not."

"Then, take me to him."

"Go home, Monsieur." His voice was low as he stated what was clearly my final warning.

I should heed it. It's what anyone with half a brain would do, especially when faced with two fully fledged mages, one of whom appeared to be as pissed off as I was. What the woman had said about Quasimodo wasn't wrong: he was no longer a boy, and it wasn't more than half an hour's walk back to Notre Dame. But we'd arrived here together, and damn it, I wasn't leaving without him. Besides... part of me wanted to test these two. Magic only landed mages in trouble when it was used to harm another person, so either they were bluffing, or they were hiding far more than Quasimodo behind that trapdoor.

Raising my chin, I looked him in the eye and said, "No."

He moved so fast I didn't have time to flinch. A jet of water shot out from his outstretched arm, forming into a whip-like shape before darting toward my shoulder.

But it never touched me. The moment a third voice snapped, "Antoine," from behind where I stood, the water lost its shape, splattering into the stage rather pathetically. "Stop this. He's with me."

My heart skipped a beat. Not simply because of the 'he's with me,' but because I knew that voice. I turned around slowly, both terrified and exhilarated at what I knew I'd find.

The Embermage stood so close I could reach out and touch her.

IV. THE SEDUCTION

Esmeralda

He was even more handsome up close—and tall. He was very, very tall.

His eyes were blue, just as they'd been in my dreams. The faintest of freckles dotted his cheeks, still visible despite his white skin currently flushed with color. One rather prominent beauty mark sat on the left side of his face, near the bridge of his nose. And his hair wasn't silver, I realized—it was white. Pale, ghostly white, which was somehow fitting given how he'd haunted me as of late.

But as fascinating as all of it was, one thing stood out above all others: the vague air of femininity that grew stronger the more I stared. It didn't lessen the attraction I felt toward him—if anything, it enhanced it—but the smoothness of his skin, particularly around his chin and jaw, felt telling.

An intriguing thought surfaced. What if this man wasn't a man at all?

No matter the answer, it changed absolutely nothing. Even if I hadn't come this far and sacrificed as much as I had, something as irrelevant as gender was hardly enough to keep me from moving forward with my plan. Tonight wasn't about pleasure, but the fact that I was attracted to people of all kinds certainly was a bonus in this scenario.

Still, given that he hadn't corrected Antoine after being called 'Monsieur,' I decided I'd refer to him as a man and with the applicable pronouns until told otherwise. If growing up around my sibling had taught me anything, it was never to assume such things, but this felt like a rather delicate exception. This man had secrets, it seemed, and I'd allow them to remain his own.

Because after all… so did I.

I'm not certain how long we stared at one another, but it was long enough to make Antoine uncomfortable. Clearing his throat, he said, "I was just following Jules's instructions."

Jules. My absolute idiot of a sibling who had somehow interpreted 'distract the child' to mean 'invite him on stage,' leaving me with no choice but to play along. His poor father had been worried sick judging from the wide-eyed look on his face, and I could hardly blame him. "Then I shouldn't be surprised you're as incompetent as they are," I snapped, sidestepping the man but placing my hand on his shoulder; I wanted desperately to talk to him, to apologize for Jules's poor judgment, but needed to diffuse what could have been an absolute nightmare of a scenario first. "You were to make certain I wasn't disturbed—but tell me, where did that include using your magic on a guest?"

Water began creeping up Antoine's arm. A mage's element mirrored their inner emotion, so this was a clear indication his temper hadn't gone anywhere. "We asked him to leave. He wouldn't."

"I was looking for my son!" the man snapped over his shoulder, but he silenced when I gave him a squeeze.

Lowering my voice for his ears alone, I met his gaze. "Your son is unharmed, and I'll take you to him in a moment."

"With all due respect, I'll believe that when I see him. And please, hurry."

Though he hadn't spoken impolitely, I didn't miss the desperation only barely concealed in his strained tone. Even if I had, the worry etched on his face would have been impossible to deny, and guilt knotted in my chest. *Thanks a lot, Jules.* "I completely understand. Let me deal with these two, then we'll go right away. He's not far."

When he nodded, I turned my attention back to Antoine, speaking through gritted teeth but keeping my voice low. "And what if you had been spotted?" I jerked my head toward the handful of guards prowling the rapidly emptying streets. One stood with his arms crossed and eyes narrowed, making no effort to hide what I knew beyond a shadow of a doubt. "Give them a reason—any reason—and that's it. You know that."

Antoine scoffed. "If you expect me to apologize—"

"Not to him, or even me. To Jules. They'd be inconsolable if anything were to happen to you. God knows why, but that's a mess I'd rather not deal with." Sighing, I glanced at Isabelle, a fire mage like me. She'd retreated into the shadows while Antoine and I argued. "Now go, both of you. I'm still not to be disturbed, but should anyone threaten that peace, you're not to use your magic to deal with it. Is that understood?"

Isabelle nodded immediately, but Antoine hesitated, because of course he did. Finally he, too, uttered a guttural *hmph*, which was the closest to a 'yes' I was going to get. The pair departed the stage, each headed in separate directions to cover as much ground as possible.

It was only when the man drew a ragged inhale that it dawned on me that we were alone.

And that I was touching him.

Heat that had nothing to do with my fire crept to my cheeks as I pulled my hand away. He held my gaze, silent and unmoving as ever, and not knowing what else to say, I blurted out, "Sorry."

He cocked his head. "For what?"

"For, ah, touching you. I should have asked first." Shit, this wasn't at all how this was supposed to go. It was all Jules's fault for taking matters into their own hands, for forcing our introduction under these awkward circumstances, and I could strangle them. I'd planned this—every moment of it. I'd rehearsed what to say. Hell, I'd even rehearsed what to think, what to feel… or rather, what *not* to feel. This wasn't about attraction, and it certainly wasn't about feelings.

So why was my heart beating out of my chest, and why did those flutters feel suspiciously like butterflies?

"It's all right." His voice, soft, smooth, and intriguingly formal, pulled me from my thoughts. "I apologize as well. I didn't mean to antagonize your friend."

I scoffed. "Antoine is hardly a friend. Just someone my sibling likes to fuck that I'm forced to put up with as a result."

His jaw clenched at my use of the word 'fuck.' I very nearly said it again but caught myself just in time, lifting a hand to my mouth to prevent myself from blurting out anything else. "I'm sorry—"

"Stop apologizing." He ducked his head suddenly, repositioning his hood so that it masked most of his face once again. I almost stopped him—his face was beautiful, and he ought not to hide it— but given that I just pointed out that I should have asked permission before touching him, I didn't. "You have nothing to be sorry for. If anything, I should thank you for defending me, especially after I invaded your space."

It was my turn to be affected by his choice of words; a shiver ran through me at the phrase 'invaded your space.' Oh, yes. I'd like him to do that very much, and with any luck, he would, too. "There was no intrusion," I somehow managed to utter without my voice cracking. "We may be strangers in the true sense of the word, but I certainly feel as though I know you... and you me, yes?"

Despite Jules's interference, I'd managed to turn it around. *Yes, perfect; make it intimate, get a little personal.* I studied his reaction carefully, equal parts nervous and exhilarated. Lifting his gaze to mine, he swallowed, nodding after a moment. I didn't miss the way his hands clenched at his sides, nor how his cheeks flushed an even deeper red. It was a few seconds more before he spoke. "Only from your p-performances," he stammered, tripping over his words. "You're quite gor— I mean, g-good."

It seemed I had him flustered—not bad—but flustered wasn't good enough. I needed him so aroused he wouldn't be able to think of anything but taking me to bed. "Thank you," I said, smiling. "You're quite impressive yourself. If I remember correctly, you haven't missed a single one of my shows in damn near twenty weeks."

"Eighteen," he admitted sheepishly, "but who's counting?"

You, apparently, I bit back. "You must be one of my most devoted fans. Such loyalty deserves a reward, don't you think?"

His eyes nearly bulged out of his head. "I—I h-hardly think—"

"I'm going to tell you a secret," I cut across him, stepping forward to close the already narrow space between us. "One that only a select few know. May I?"

Chest heaving, he nodded, so I leaned in. Our height difference meant that I needed to stand on my tiptoes to reach him. It took effort not to brush the hair from his face, but I did adjust the hood slightly, allowing easier access to his ear. He'd gone as still as stone, so I rested a hand on his arm—ever so lightly—before beginning my whispered confession. I went by a stage name for a reason, and only family and trusted friends knew my real one. Entrusting him was a risk, but if we were going to sleep together, it didn't sit right with me to withhold this from him… not when I was already withholding so much else.

"My name is Esmeralda."

I pulled away too quickly to be certain, but I could have sworn a visible shiver ran through him. He looked at me, lips parted in wonder—almost as if seeing me for the first time. "Esmeralda," he echoed softly, and my gaze darted to his lips, fascinated at the way they formed every shape.

I nodded, hoping the darkness concealed the blush creeping to my cheeks. "And my pronouns are she and her."

This, I hadn't planned or even premeditated. It just slipped out, but it felt more than right; perhaps now he might feel safe enough to correct me if wrong assumptions had been made. But he said nothing. If anything, he looked even more terrified, so I asked, "And whom do I have the pleasure of meeting?"

More silence lingered and swiftly grew awkward, but just as I was about to blurt out that he didn't need to tell me anything, he said, "You may call me Claude."

No pronouns, but at least I had a name. Simple yet elegant, and it fit him well. I extended my hand, bowing my head before saying, "It's very nice to formally meet you, Claude."

Another pause, but this one was much shorter. After cupping his fingers beneath my own, he dipped his head, mirroring my greeting... then lifted my hand to—oh, fuck—

Claude's lips grazed my knuckles.

It was the briefest of kisses, but what lingered was his stare. Never once did he break eye contact, and if I didn't know any better, what quite resembled a wicked grin played at the corners of his mouth. But it was gone when I blinked, the moment broken save for the electricity still dancing between us. Or the way my skin already longed for more of his touch.

Understanding dawned on me then. It took two to conjure the types of things I was feeling, the depth to which my body was reacting to his physical cues, however subtle. He knew precisely what he was doing, didn't he? It prompted a rather terrifying question. What exactly *was* his goal—and did it include beating me at my own game?

I may have launched into a mental tirade had Claude not interrupted. "It's very nice to meet you, too, Esmeralda. But as lovely as this has been, my son—"

"Shit. That's right, I'm sorry. Come." Gesturing for him to follow, I turned on my heel and marched toward the trapdoor, immensely grateful for the opportunity to hide my face and for something to do with my hands. After pulling it open and conjuring a small ball of fire for visibility, I descended the stairs into darkness.

I had some time alone with my thoughts while waiting for Claude to make his way down. This was going well—a little too well—and honestly, I didn't know what to make of it. On one hand, he was undoubtedly receptive to my advances. On the other... perhaps a little too receptive. This wasn't intended to be or become anything more than a transaction, but the way he was looking at me, the way he'd touched me... it felt like something else entirely.

And as his footfalls descended the stairs, I wondered if such a conservative-looking man was far less so than I had first presumed.

Claude appeared at my side a moment later. The dimly lit hall's narrowness forced him both to duck and to stand so close we were nearly touching, but I certainly didn't mind. Taking advantage of the fact his sight wouldn't have adjusted to the darkness quite yet, I eyed him up and down, drinking in any bit of him that wasn't concealed by that cloak. My fire's light flickered around his silhouette, bathing him in a mysterious orange glow and accentuating every line on his face, almost as if to say *Look, isn't he beautiful?*

I know, I thought back, averting my gaze before Claude could catch me staring. *Trust me, I know.*

"So… this is what's down here," he said kindly, but I just scoffed.

"No need to pretend it's impressive. It's just an empty hall."

"True," he conceded, "but how many others can say they possess a secret hall concealed by a secret trapdoor, leading to even further secrets?"

Claude's tone was teasing, but a lump formed in my throat regardless; he had no idea how right he was. "Not many," was all I answered but didn't offer anything more. It was far too difficult to concentrate given the way his arm rubbed against mine with every step, and my palms began to sweat as I became hyper-aware of his proximity. I increased my pace in hopes we might reach our destination faster, but not only did he match it—we touched yet again.

The backs of our hands brushed. Though not nearly as intimate as the knuckle kiss, the skin-to-skin contact was still more than enough to send a jolt through me, one that ignited every nerve in my body. My inner flame turned to molten metal, heating and spreading until nothing but desire coursed through me, pooling and gathering in the space between my thighs. It was all I could do not to throw myself into Claude's chest and beg for more, but I forced myself to be patient, if only for a little while longer.

I'd first let him see that his son was safe… but then he was all mine.

I managed to keep my hands to myself, and we reached the end of the hall not a moment too soon. After extinguishing my fire, I opened the door, gesturing for Claude to enter first. I lingered in the hall, needing a moment to gather myself, to steady my breathing, to—

"Maman!"

Maman?

My head snapped up, and gripping the doorframe, I dared a peek into my bedroom. Jules sat in the chair at my vanity, but they weren't facing the mirror; they were facing Claude's son, a hunchbacked red-haired teenager who stood in the center of the room, cradling a glowing orange ball of... *no.* Surely that wasn't fire?

I was unable to get a better look given that Claude darted into my field of vision, headed straight for their son. Lowering their hood, they knelt before him, forming their hands and fingers into various, frantic shapes. Though the language wasn't verbal, it wasn't difficult to guess the kinds of things Claude might be asking.

But I wasn't fixated on that or even the fire; I was still hung up over 'mère.' Was that just how Claude's son referred to them as a parent, or...?

"I knew it. I *knew* you wouldn't take a man to bed."

My sibling's joking whisper nearly made me leap out of my skin. When and how had they gotten over here? "Keep your voice down!"

"Looks like you were right though—she's all right, for a woman. What's her name?"

"Claude, and don't assume. They didn't tell me their pronouns, even when I asked."

Jules clicked their tongue. "Ah. I remember those days."

I narrowed my gaze in confusion. "What do you…"

My voice trailed off when Claude turned to us with an arm draped over their son's shoulders. The fire was gone; had I truly imagined it, after all? An awkward smile played on their lips, and their voice came out strained and formal. "Thank you for keeping Quasimodo safe. He had a wonderful time—as I did with you, Esmeralda." Claude nodded in my direction. "It's late, however, and we really must be going. We cannot miss morning Mass."

Claude turned to depart, but Quasimodo stayed put, glancing at Jules and back again. "Wait, we're leaving? Why? Jules was showing me how to—"

"Play with fire? Don't you think you've had enough for one evening?" Claude spoke both aloud and in sign, though I suspected they told Quasimodo something entirely different given the firmness of their movements. "Again, thank you. But it's time we went home."

Before Claude could take another step, Jules shook their head, a smirk creeping onto their cockier-than-usual features. "You think he was just playing? Oh no—those flames were all his." They glanced at Quasimodo. "He's a fire mage."

I blinked in disbelief. *A fire mage?* But Claude had seemed so terrified when Quasimodo acted as my assistant on stage, surrounded by all those flames. Were they not aware that mages couldn't be harmed by their element? Had they not wanted me to know? Or did they truly not know of Quasimodo's abilities, and this was the first time anyone had voiced it aloud?

The past few hours had gone by incredibly fast, but I forced myself to recall the performance, how Quasimodo had fared when entrusted with my power. I'd been too distracted to realize it at the time, but come to think of it, he had picked up on what to do unnaturally fast... as if such things were instinctual. Because they were.

Whether Claude liked it or not, their son was one of us.

I exchanged a glance with Jules. Quasimodo would need a teacher, and he'd need one soon, because if there was anything more dangerous than an untrained fire mage, it was an untrained fire mage who also happened to be a teenage boy.

Jules met my gaze and shrugged, still grinning like a fool. They didn't say anything, but I knew my sibling well enough to know when they were gloating. God damn them—had they sensed Quasimodo's power all along? Had that been why they'd chosen him? Why the hell hadn't they told me sooner?

Claude remained wide-eyed, shaking their head. "No," they said simply, though their voice wavered. "That's not true. If it were, wouldn't I have known?"

My sibling just nodded to Quasimodo. "Show them."

Panic constricted my chest, and I tensed to dart across the room; was Jules out of their mind? To command a newly awakened mage to conjure fire in my *bedroom* of all places—

But I halted when it became clear we weren't in any danger. The flame Quasimodo produced was small, unassuming, and didn't have much life behind it. The plume burned out as quickly as it had been summoned, leaving the boy looking nervous and unsure as to what our reaction might be.

For a few moments, all was silent. Then came Claude's shaky whisper: "He... he can do that? How? And when—"

"Not all mages manifest their powers in early childhood. Some show no signs until adolescence," I cut across them, more desperate to soothe Claude's panic than I wanted to admit. "This doesn't mean that you, nor he, did anything wrong."

"But now that he has manifested," Jules said, taking a few steps in Claude's direction, "he will need a tutor. Whether or not Quasimodo chooses to utilize his magic, he must learn to control it. Fire in particular can be... unpredictable."

Claude's jaw clenched as they stared at Jules. "And I suppose you wish to be that tutor?"

Jules scoffed. "Hardly. As a lightning mage, I am unsuitable long term. However, I'm more than qualified to teach him the basics. And we can begin right now if you'd like."

A beat passed before Claude's gaze flicked to me. "But Esmeralda—"

I opened my mouth to speak, but Jules interrupted, even going so far as to dart between us. "My sister is a fire mage, yes. But she wishes to speak to you in private. Isn't that right, Es?"

Taken aback at what Jules was insinuating, I stumbled over my words. "Y-yes, but that was before this particular revelation came to light." I met Jules's gaze, speaking with more confidence as I glared at them. "It's quite a lot for Claude to trust you alone with Quasimodo, and more than we have any right to ask. We are strangers, after all. I think that if they wish to go home, we shouldn't interfere."

My sibling's brow furrowed in confusion, but they didn't protest as

I sidestepped them to address Claude. "If you've had enough for one night, by all means, go. But perhaps next time, we can plan a lesson?"

A shadow crossed Claude's face when I brought up a next time, but it was gone when they nodded. "He'd love that, I'm sure. But you're right—it's getting late, and I really should be getting him home."

"Of course." I forced a smile even as disappointment knotted in my chest. "Jules can see you out."

They did a double take, their mouth dropping open. "Es, are you—"

"Jules can see you out," I repeated firmly.

The weight in my chest only grew heavier and more painful as I watched Claude sign to an obviously disappointed Quasimodo, and they didn't offer me more than a curt nod before following Jules out the door. I blurted out the words festering inside me just in time, halting Claude in their tracks right before they disappeared from my view entirely.

"I know it's late, but once you do what you need to, and if you'd still like to have that talk... I'll be here waiting."

Claude hesitated, then departed without a word.

"You're such an idiot."

I fought to keep flames from erupting along my arms. "Haven't we established that already?"

"Apparently not, given what you just did."

"And what was I supposed to do?" I whirled around to face Jules, who had made themselves quite at home on my bed. "Did you think for one second that Claude would have let Quasimodo out of their sight after the stunt you pulled on stage? They were worried *sick*, and you know damn well that was never part of the plan. So don't act like this is my fault. It's yours."

Jules held up their hands in surrender. "Easy, Es. I was only trying to help."

"Well, you didn't," I snapped.

"There's no need to get yourself this worked up about it. They'll be back—"

"Will they?" I laughed darkly. "After what happened tonight, I'm honestly not so sure."

Silence descended upon us then, broken only by Jules's heavy sigh. "If there's nothing I can say to make you feel any better, at least let me help you out of that dress."

"No," I said quickly; perhaps too quickly. Crossing my arms over my chest, I shook my head. "I want to be alone." A lie, but I certainly didn't want to be in my sibling's company for a moment longer.

They frowned. "Can you even undo those laces yourself?"

"Get *out*, Jules!"

Finally taking the hint, they scrambled from my bed and made their way toward the door. Jules hesitated then, looking very much like they wanted to say something else, but thought better of it at the last second, and slipped from my room, closing the door soundlessly behind them.

Only once completely certain I was alone did I collapse on my bed, my hair and dress pooling around my quivering body. I felt like crying, but the tears wouldn't come, which only intensified my paralyzing emotions. A mixture of shame, guilt, and regret were swirling within me, and if their sheer force wasn't confusing enough, even more so was the sadness that threatened to overwhelm me at the mere thought of never seeing Claude again.

But why? We were strangers. We hadn't spent more than an hour together, hadn't engaged in more than a single conversation. And as for my plan, I'd have wasted time and effort, certainly, but it wasn't as if I couldn't begin my search anew. My plot didn't *have* to involve Claude specifically, just a member of the Church—any member who would have me. Jules was right. Getting worked up over this served no purpose. There was no need to panic.

I wasn't panicking, though. I was sad… almost to the point of grief.

"What the hell is there to grieve?" I muttered into my pillow, no doubt smearing makeup all over it. "And don't say 'what could have been.' If Claude wanted there to *be* anything, they would have stayed, or at least come back. The fact that they haven't means it never would have worked, anyway."

In truth, there was still plenty of time for Claude to return, and I had promised I'd be here waiting. But I'd lied to Jules about more than just wanting to be alone; I did want to be out of this dress, and desperately.

I just wanted Claude to be the one to take it off.

"Stop it." I shook my head, only partially succeeding in clearing the filthy thoughts that sprang to the forefront of my mind. "This is torture. *Stop it.*"

Unfortunately for me, nothing stopped it, at least not until the night finally caught up with me and I began to doze off. I fought the exhaustion as best I could, forcing my eyes open before I fell too deep... until a sharp knock sounded at my door.

Bolting upright, my heart fluttered in my chest as I stumbled over to my vanity. *What time is it?* There wasn't a chance to figure that out, not when one glance in the mirror confirmed what a mess I was. I only had moments to scrub furiously at the smeared makeup still on my face and come up with an excuse for Jules, who had no doubt come to check on me. "Come in," I called, clearing my throat when my voice cracked.

But it wasn't Jules who walked in.

Surely this was a dream. Surely my eyes were playing tricks on me, because there was no way that was Claude in my doorway. But no matter how many times I blinked, they were still there, dressed precisely the same way they'd been at the faire—cloak and all.

"You... you came back."

It was all I could think to say, and I stifled a wince at having stated the obvious. But Claude simply held my gaze, nodding. "I came back. But likely not for whatever reason you wished to speak to me."

I swallowed, not uncomfortable with the words themselves, but the formality with which they were uttered. "Oh?"

They didn't answer right away, and the uncomfortable, icy silence threatened to swallow me whole. I remained still as they shut the door, but when I gestured to the chair at my vanity, Claude shook their head. "This won't take long. I just wanted to speak to you regarding Quasimodo's, ah... powers."

"I'm sure you have questions. I'm more than happy to answer them."

The energy shifted yet again when Claude took a step toward

me, their tone taking on an edge of desperation. "Of course I have questions, but far more fears. My son is a mage. A *mage*. Do you know what they'll do to him if they find out?"

It took effort not to snap at such an uneducated question. "By 'they,' I can only assume you mean the Church," I replied icily. "And while being a mage alone isn't a crime, yes. I certainly *do* know what it's like to live in fear that could change at any moment."

Claude's expression softened as understanding dawned. "You're right. I'm sorry. Please forgive my ignorance. This is just so much to take in."

They reached for the wall for support, visibly quivering, and a pang of sympathy replaced my irritation. "You're forgiven," I said quietly. Part of me wanted to go and comfort them, but the other part kept me rooted in place, at least until the tension between us dissipated a little. "I meant what I said earlier, though. I will teach Quasimodo, and that includes teaching him what he needs to know to remain safe."

"Why, though?" Claude's voice shook. "Why would you do that?"

You know why, I wanted to say, but blurted out the other question currently eating me alive. "Why did you come back?" I hadn't meant to ask it, but now that it was out in the open, neither of us could ignore it any longer. "We both know it wasn't just for his sake."

They swallowed. "It wasn't. But in my meager defense, it's all connected."

"How do you mean?"

Claude was silent for a while, but when they did finally speak, their story poured from them like a river. "I have a deep and profound respect for the Church, but particularly my God. It's all I've known all my life. When I had nothing and no one else, He was always there, accepting and willing to forgive me no matter my sins and flaws—of which there were, and still are, many." They paused, inhaling shakily before continuing, "But God isn't the problem; that much I know. When it's only me and Him, I feel more understood than I ever have with another human being. That's not the case with many of His other followers, though… and especially not those who claim to be the holiest of them all. It's the one thing I'll never understand: how those closest to his love are the ones who judge the harshest.

"So in a way, I understand the plight that faces you, and now Quasimodo. I am no mage, but I am…" Claude's voice trailed off. "Well, let's just say the Church hates me, too."

I dared a step closer. "What have you done to deserve such ridicule?"

A bitter laugh. "I exist."

"I don't—"

"I'm a woman, all right?" they blurted out, releasing the wall to fully face me. It was difficult to tell given the current lighting, but it almost looked as if they'd been crying. "I'm a woman who lays with other women. An abomination. It's why I've been coming here all this time. I think you're the most beautiful woman I've ever seen, and I haven't been able to get you out of my head. That's why I came back… but I suspect you already knew that, and just wanted me to say it."

At least a hundred separate thoughts ran through my head in that moment—*They want you, too. They think you're beautiful. They sympathize with the mages, with you*—but I settled on vocalizing the only one that was appropriate. "Claude," I said quietly. "What would you like me to call you, and which pronouns make you the most comfortable?"

They sniffed, confirming they had indeed been crying. "You know, you're the first person to ever ask me that. Both here and in the hall."

"Please don't avoid the question like you did out there. I swear you're safe with me: all I want is for you to be comfortable. To be who you are."

They laughed again, but it felt far more genuine this time. "My name really is Claude. Well, Claudette, but I hate that. Everyone just calls me Claude."

I nodded. "And the other part?"

"And… she and her are fine for now. Truly. Quasimodo isn't my son by birth, but I still resonate quite a lot with motherhood, and Mother Mary."

I smiled, swallowing back my own tears as I took her in. There was an energy radiating from her that most hadn't been there before, and she looked happy, truly happy, for the very first time. "It's lovely to meet you properly, Claude. Thank you for trusting me."

"No, thank *you*."

We stood in silence after that, openly staring at one another. Heart hammering against my ribcage, every ounce of the arousal I'd felt from earlier returned with a vengeance. Her lips on my knuckles, our hands brushing in the hall, the overpowering urge to throw myself into her arms… Fuck. I wanted Claude, and I'd be a fool to let her leave without at least confessing as much. We'd been dancing around this for weeks, months even; it was high time we voiced it aloud, if nothing else.

I first said her name, all but caressing it in a breathy whisper. "You aren't alone in your desire. I want this. I want you."

It was almost impossible to read Claude's expression in the ever-growing darkness. "I doubt you want me, but I certainly want you.

Perhaps more than I've ever wanted anything or anyone."

Too fixated on the second, I didn't address the first half of what she said. "Then, what are you waiting for?"

Her voice was strained. "We… We shouldn't."

"This isn't about should or shouldn't. This is about want, about desire."

"It's not that simple."

I closed the distance between us but didn't touch her. Instead, I leaned in close enough for Claude to feel each of my exhales against her skin. It had the desired effect; a visible shudder ran down her spine. "It *is* that simple. There's the door. Leave now if that is what you wish. But know this," I whispered, pausing to enhance the weight of my words. "If you come here again, you won't find me waiting, at least not for this. I don't play games."

"That's fair," Claude whispered back—but no more. No definite yes or no, and certainly not any action. The frustration festering within me threatened to boil over, as did my flames. For fuck's sake, what was she waiting for? What more could she need to make a decision? At this point, *any* decision would do so long as it broke this vicious cycle of should we, or should we not.

I may have said as much aloud had she not touched me. Her hand curled around my upper arm, the grip both punishing and thrilling, and hopefully an indication she had no intention of letting go. Stilling, I waited, but Claude didn't make a move. If she didn't, I certainly was about to. "Your body tells me one thing—your words another," I breathed against her, my voice hoarse with need. "For God's sake, at least make them match—"

73

"Don't bring God into this." Claude traced circles against the thin fabric of my dress, and I bit my lip to keep a moan from slipping out. "I want you screaming *my* name, not his."

"I'll worship the Devil himself if it gets you to take my fucking clothes off."

An invitation—one *she'd* be a damned fool to ignore. My chest rose and fell in a haggard rhythm, hot and needy, though I'd barely been touched. Didn't she see what she was doing to me, that I was perfectly willing? Didn't she feel this connection between us, one we'd made and solidified long before we'd stood in a room together?

Apparently not, because abruptly, borderline violently, Claude released me. Taking a few steps back, she looked at me as if I were a ghost before glancing away, hands quivering and breaths coming in ragged gasps. "I can't. I took a vow."

"So did all those so-called 'holy' men—the ones who ridicule you. The ones who'd kill me or any other mage given half an excuse." The words tumbled out before I could stop them and kept on coming. "The ones who'd kill your *son*. You'd hold yourself to their standards, above them even, when they don't possess a shred of decency themselves?"

Claude blinked, and for a moment I thought I'd gone too far. But then she shook her head, still refusing to look me in the eye as she said, "But there's still the matter of want. You think you want me, Esmeralda, but you don't. Trust me."

Irritation that bordered on fury ignited within me. I marched toward her with such ferocity that for a moment, her eyes went wide. Halting only when we stood chest to chest, I curled my fingers around her chin, yanking her gaze to mine. It was yet another opportunity to drink her in, to memorize her every feature. I took my damn time, because it very well might be my final chance.

"Leave, or let me pleasure you. Either way, you're going to stop telling me what I do and don't want. *I* decide that. No one else."

Chests heaving, we stood in stalemate. Claude's expression had gone unreadable, leaving me without a clue as to what might happen next. I truly wasn't certain if she would kiss me or storm out into the night.

What I didn't expect was for her to grip my shoulders so hard an involuntary gasp escaped my lips. It was her turn to march forward, forcing me back until my calves hit the bed, at which point she shoved me. I went careening backwards and fell into my sheets with another yelp of surprise—but that was far from the final one Claude had in store.

She was on me in an instant, straddling me before bending over and effectively covering my body with hers. Too distracted by her tantalizing weight, particularly the pressure on my groin, I barely noticed when she gripped my wrists, pinning them on either side of my head before leaning down even farther, her lips hovering against my throat. I writhed and moaned, arching my back in an effort to find the friction I sought, but to my immense frustration, my efforts were ignored.

"Pleasure *me*?" She'd barely gotten started, but Claude's incredulous whisper against my bare skin had my toes curling. "Oh no, Esmeralda. Allow me to pleasure you."

V. THE MIRROR

Claude

Was it me who had spoken those filthy words?

Was this happening?

Or was this all a dream—a lovely dream, but a dream nonetheless—one where I could operate outside the confines and rules that usually kept me their helpless captive? One with no consequences, no expectations, no broken vows, nothing but *us*—

"Claude?" Esmeralda's breathy whisper pulled me from my own head, and she pushed back against my grip on her wrists. "Are you all right?"

I was more than all right. In fact, I felt better than I ever had in my life, like I might burst into laughter or tears of joy at any moment. A breathtakingly gorgeous woman lay beneath me, one who'd listened when I'd opened up to her, one with a deep respect for my identity and gender, and one who claimed to want me. I wanted badly to believe her, because I wanted her, too. I'd deeply regretted not kissing her the night she'd given me her scarf even though that would have violated my rule; how could I live with myself if I denied her tonight, even if it further broke my vow? It wasn't as if it hadn't already been shattered all to Hell anyway. What was once more? What was one night?

But beneath my raw, unfiltered ecstasy, a festering truth remained: this was wrong. Not only that, it was forbidden for reasons that could get us jailed... or worse. I was more than accustomed to living in fear, to keeping my sexual relationships my most carefully guarded secret, but was Esmeralda? Could I forgive myself if I became the reason she always had to look over her shoulder? And more importantly, could she?

I opened my mouth, but nothing came out. Probably for the best. I doubted I could form coherent sentences with the way she was staring at me. She didn't push, but her gaze narrowed, her eyes flicking back and forth as if she wanted to know and memorize my every feature. My sinful thoughts returned with both a vengeance and a need at the idea. *Lord, help me.* I stared right back and couldn't stop marveling at her hair, her shape, her lips... all of it too perfect. All of it off-limits.

Then again, that only made her more enticing. To be human was to crave the unknown, the dangerous and deadly. It was the reason she was able to draw such a crowd on Friday nights, but she and I were a different type of fire entirely. Destructive yet addictive, maddening yet thrilling, taboo but beautiful. Irresistible. More heat radiated between us now than had enveloped the stage during her performance. Too much, if anything. Sweat pooled at my brow, and it wouldn't be long before it started dripping onto Esmeralda. I cringed inwardly; I may not know what I did want, but I certainly didn't want *that*, especially when I had a promise upon which to deliver. Even if I got none of my own out of the encounter—as unlikely as that was—I did intend to pleasure her like it was the last time I'd ever see her.

Because it was.

But damn it, this wasn't going nearly as perfectly as it should. I sat up, breaking our spell, and ran my hands through my hair before wiping the sweat from my forehead. Surely I looked the furthest thing from attractive right now, but Esmeralda simply watched me with interest, propping herself up on her elbows. An amused smirk played on her lips. "You know," she said, her voice low and teasing, "you're probably hot because you're still wearing that heavy cloak. May I?"

I hesitated; I said I'd take the lead, after all, and for good reason. As much as I craved it, another part of me feared her touch. The things it might do, what it might make me want… and worst of all, that I might become addicted to something I could never feel again. But there was something in her eyes that melted me—something that made me feel safe. It was the reason I'd opened up to Esmeralda, told her things I hadn't even confessed to Mercedes, and the reason it felt like tonight might actually be possible.

"Yes," I heard myself whisper, and I let out a deep breath when Esmeralda pushed herself fully upright and began undoing the clasps of the cloak. Though I remained fully clothed underneath, wearing a man's long-sleeved tunic and trousers, the cool night air washed over me as she pulled the garment away from my shoulders and let it fall to the floor.

Only then did I become aware that I was the one sitting in *her* lap, and that she was still touching me. Her hands slid up my chest and neck, settling on my cheeks and pulling our faces closer until our noses were almost touching. The fire between us flared once more as we sat suspended in time, both for what felt like forever and mere seconds. Esmeralda was silent and still, clearly waiting for me to dictate where this went next, and her gentle patience was almost enough to summon more tears.

"I want to kiss you," I confessed against her lips. "But I don't kiss, not mouth to mouth. That's my only rule."

Surprise flickered across her features, but she didn't challenge me on it. "Your 'only' rule? So everything else…?"

She didn't need to finish her question for me to know what she was asking. "Everything else is allowed, provided that my partner—"

"I want it." Esmeralda tightened her grip on me, frustration sneaking into her voice. "All of it. Now take off my clothes before I do it myself."

As much as I wanted to oblige her, she wasn't wearing ordinary clothes—she was in perhaps my favorite dress I'd seen her wear to date. "Do I have to?" I asked quietly, running my fingers from her shoulder to hip and relishing the softness of the fabric. "Don't misunderstand—of course I'd like to see you, but I wonder if it might enhance things if you keep it on."

Esmeralda grimaced. "Actually, that's precisely why it needs to come off. I like it, too, and I'd rather not have to worry about accidentally setting it on fire in case I get too... excited."

"That can happen?"

She grinned. "Oh, yes. But it's not all accidental fires. Others are very, very deliberate."

With that alluring thought left to linger in the air, she slipped out from under me and turned to sit on the edge of the bed, pulling her hair to one side to reveal the intricate lacing up her back. Loosening and undoing it took me a while, but it was both time I had to touch her and to ponder what Esmeralda meant by the comment about her fire. Intriguing imagery flashed through my mind; did she mean we might be able to use it during...?

"That's enough. One moment."

Her voice snapped me out of my trance, and she stood up, taking a few steps toward her vanity. Esmeralda's arms were wrapped around her middle, which was the only thing keeping the fabric clinging to her body. Still facing away from me, she loosened her grip agonizingly slowly, letting the top of the dress pool around her waist. She wasn't bare yet—she still wore a brassiere—but she removed that too, flinging it aside with reckless abandon.

Turn around. The command nearly escaped my lips, but the words died on my tongue as she wiggled out of what remained of her dress, her petticoat, and finally her undergarments. Watching her silhouette move like that had my heart fluttering faster at the start and left far more than my chest throbbing by the end. Only once fully naked did she face me, and I simply forgot how to breathe.

Esmeralda was the most beautiful woman I'd ever seen.

Though her dress hadn't hidden her shape, it had concealed the perfect curvature of her breasts and the healthy thickness of her thighs. She tossed her head, accentuating the warm glow of her cheeks and sending most of her curls tumbling down her back, and only then did I notice the teardrop-shaped pendant sitting in the hollow of her neck: a ruby, by the looks of it. A plume of fire danced in one of her palms, the heat creating both a sheen of sweat and gorgeous flickers of orange light dancing over her skin. Her hips swayed as she approached the bed. Completely and thoroughly entranced, I remained immobile as she leaned forward, placing a hand on my shoulder as she whispered into my ear.

"Do you trust me?"

Still unable to utter so much as a 'yes,' I nodded, and Esmeralda settled beside me on the bed. Rolling up my left sleeve with her free hand, she slowly lowered her palm wielding the fire to my bare skin. My first instinct was to shy away, but when I twitched, she clicked her tongue in disapproval before saying it again—a command this time.

"Trust me."

I tensed, preparing for unbearable heat or perhaps even pain, but none ever came. She grazed her flame-touched fingers up and down my forearm, but it didn't burn or hurt. If anything, it was soothing—comforting, even—and I relaxed into her touch. Esmeralda held her flame steady as I closed my eyes in surrender. But even when she began tracing shapes along my skin, I found myself unable to focus on the warmth gathered there... because even a literal flame paled in comparison to the one burning with a vengeance between my thighs. God, I wanted her. I wanted her so badly I'd do far more than sin to have her.

"Claude," Esmeralda breathed against my neck, prompting my eyes to flash open. "Look."

I glanced down and gasped. A pattern of orange swirls had been branded into my arm: elegant lettering that began at my wrist and ended at my elbow, spelling out the words *I want you.*

"Don't worry—it's not permanent and won't leave any sort of mark or scar. It will fade by mor—"

"This is dangerous." My voice wavered as I cut across her, but I forced myself to keep going. As much as I didn't want to say it, Esmeralda had to hear it. "*I'm* dangerous. It's why I told you not to want me. You have no idea who I am, what I—"

She brought a finger to my lips, shaking her head as something flared in her eyes. "Telling me not to want something doesn't suddenly make it so. And once again, you're underestimating me. Do it a third time and I won't be nearly this forgiving. But Claude—I have to ask." Pulling her hand back, she tucked a few stray hairs behind her ear and gave me a questioning look. "Is it you or me you're trying to talk out of doing this?"

I opened my mouth then shut it again; she was right, and I was a fool. I wanted her, plain and simple, and all my reservations weren't just excuses—they were proof of the fear I'd let rule my life for far too long, proof that I wouldn't allow myself happiness even when it was so close that I could quite literally touch it… touch *her.* I reached out slowly, snaking my arm around Esmeralda's back until my hand rested on her opposite hip. A quick yank in my direction was the only invitation she needed to climb into my lap, draping her legs over my left side before wrapping her arms around my neck, steadying herself while she bared her chest to me. I took the hint, cupping one of her breasts in my hand and fondling the nipple with my thumb.

"Finally," she uttered between breathy moans; she clearly liked what I was doing to her nipple. "I didn't know what the hell you were waiting for."

"And what are *you* waiting for?" The words tumbled out before I could stop them, but in my heart of hearts, I didn't want to. If we were going to do this, we may as well do it properly.

She met my gaze, practically panting now. "*You.*"

We were already joined, but from that point onward, we collided in every way but the one that would break my rule. Esmeralda and I became a tangle of limbs and teeth, utilizing the latter when lips alone weren't enough. I couldn't get enough, even after touching and kissing seemingly every inch of her upper half, so I trailed my hands lower, moaning when I squeezed her rear. I'd never been drunk, but surely this was what it felt like; her mouth on my neck, her hand between my thighs, and her naked form molded against mine. As promised, it wasn't long before fire began igniting in random places on her body, but I wasn't afraid. Though hot and sometimes searing, it never burned, and the slight twinges of tantalizing pain only spurred me on. Taking careful note of my reactions, Esmeralda quickly learned what I liked and how and soon had me bending to her will as easily as her fire.

At some point, we tumbled over, but our exploration far from ceased. Rolling into various positions in a playful battle for control, we somehow landed upon precisely the same position we'd been in before: me straddling a bright-eyed and breathless Esmeralda. Her left arm was completely coated in flame, illuminating her breasts in a way I found irresistible.

I took the closest nipple between my teeth. Her sharp inhale soon turned to a sigh of pleasure. Just as she had for me, I used her reactions as a guide to know how hard I could bite and suck. I moved to her opposite breast just as she began grinding against me, and it quickly became too hard to focus with her moving like that.

I arched my back and closed my eyes, leaning into her groin and gasping her name. "I need you."

Esmeralda's flame-free hand shot out to grip my forearm— the one still glowing due to the letters she'd etched upon my flesh. "Please," was all she managed before intelligible thought escaped me, because when I opened my eyes, a realization struck.

I could see myself—could see us—in the mirror at her vanity. Our writhing bodies, the marks we'd left on one another's skin, all of it in glorious, filthy detail. And if I shifted us into a certain position... we'd both be able to see.

With reawakened fervor, I leaned down, pinning her wrists to the bed before breaking away to trail my lips down her throat. The smallest of whines escaped her, but I ignored Esmeralda until she was practically vibrating beneath me. "Do you trust me?" I whispered into her ear, relishing the way an immediate, visible shiver ran down the length of her body.

Her barely audible "yes" was the only encouragement I needed. Slipping my arms beneath her, I pulled her tightly against my chest before turning, aligning her until she lay backwards on the bed. Only then did I release her upper half to prop up each of her legs, guiding them onto and over my shoulders while I remained in a kneeling upright position. A few pillows to help ease the strain on her back, and a glance in the mirror confirmed it was done.

Esmeralda's gaze widened. Her attempt to say my name turned into a moan, and seeing her like this—flushed, panting, and at my mercy—nearly made me come apart on the spot.

"Tilt your head back," I whispered against her inner thighs, and when she did, the vision I'd seen in my head became a glorious reality. In this position, with me facing the vanity and her head hanging slightly off the bed, we both had a clear view of what I was about to do: make her come until she was begging me to stop.

In the mirror's reflection, Esmeralda's lust-filled gaze met mine. Her hair spilled over the side of the bed, tumbling onto the floor given its length, and her chest heaved with every breath as her flame grew even brighter. A shiver shot down my spine when she asked, "What the devil are you waiting for?"

I didn't hesitate. "You."

Bringing my lips to her felt like the most natural thing in the world. There was a bite to the way she tasted that was unlike any other woman I'd ever been with; she was sweet, but there was also the faintest hint of something earthy, something wild. She tensed and arched her back, gasping and swearing as I flicked my tongue back and forth along her folds, easing her into it, into me. My strokes were long and slow at first, as deliberate as they were teasing, but didn't remain that way for long. Esmeralda gripped the sheets, fighting to steady her breaths while I mostly concentrated on what I was doing. But every time I lifted my gaze and it met hers in the mirror, it only spurred me on, as did the way she kept moaning my name like a prayer.

Her hips bucked against my mouth, informing me she needed more. Without thinking, I slipped a finger inside her, moving my tongue to focus on her clit. One finger soon became two, and by then, my movements were damn near frantic, my lips and hand working in tandem to bring her to climax.

It was shortly after I'd worked her up to three fingers that Esmeralda had her first. She covered her mouth as she screamed, chasing wave after wave as it rippled through her. Each built to a powerful crescendo until the dam within her shattered. She came apart in my arms, her thighs clamping around my head at the height of her pleasure and only releasing once the strongest of the tremors died down. The aftershocks still rippled through her, each one causing her flame to brighten for a split second, and she sighed, blinking up at me with a lazy smile playing on her lips.

She'd never looked more beautiful.

After extracting Esmeralda's legs from my shoulders, I gathered her in my arms and pulled her back into my lap, trailing more kisses down her jaw before pulling her as tightly to me as I could. Was this real? Holding the woman I'd desired for so long, bringing her down from an orgasm I'd given her... it was better than anything I'd ever dared to dream. Our hearts fluttered to an identical rhythm it seemed only they could hear, and if this was how we spent the rest of the night,

I'd have been more than content to remain exactly as we were.

But we were hardly done. Moving my mouth to her earlobe, I whispered into it while squeezing her upper arm. "Are you ready for another?"

Esmeralda gasped; I'd cupped her breast with my free hand while I spoke. My other loosened its hold only to trace fingernails across her bare skin, causing goosebumps to erupt there. "I... I—"

"Say yes," I urged. Though I kept tracing circles, my free hand trailed lower.

"Y-yes, I'm r—"

I didn't wait for her to finish before entering her once again, my fingers sliding in easily given how wet she still was. Esmeralda clenched around me before moaning against my lips, the noise sending a tantalizing jolt down my spine. One hand raked down my back while the other tangled in my hair, and each of her responses only encouraged me to go deeper and faster.

When she began bucking her hips against me, I knew what she needed. Stretching out my thumb, I rested it against her clit, circling gently to start. She pushed into me, so I upped the pressure, but not the speed. Not yet.

Esmeralda panted against my neck, planting half-distracted kisses between breaths. "Claude, please—"

"What do you want?" I spoke casually, doing my best to hide how much this was affecting me, too. "Tell me."

"I want... that, yes, *that!*"

I'd curved the fingers still inside her into a beckoning motion at her guidance. The act hadn't worked with all my partners, but it sure as hell seemed to be working with Esmeralda. She grinded against me, throwing back her head and exposing her beautiful breasts. I kept up everything I was doing, steadying my other arm along her back while I kissed and sucked on her neck.

"Just like that, and don't stop."

To do so would be a bigger sin than the one I was already committing. I continued everything—the motion with my fingers, circling her clit, nibbling at her neck—until she could no longer stand it. Esmeralda tensed around me before another cry tore from her lips. I managed to cover her mouth before anyone had a chance to hear us, but not before making out what she'd said: my name, just as she'd promised. Esmeralda spasmed and twitched, reeling from pleasure, but I held her even after the quivers subsided.

"You're… you're good at that," she finally said, and I stopped playing with her hair to laugh.

"I've had some practice."

She blinked, fighting through obvious exhaustion as she tried to sit up on her own. "You should let me—"

"I'm not letting you do anything but sleep. You gave the performance of your life not long ago, and now this." I brushed my lips against her forehead. "Rest. That's an order."

Esmeralda didn't argue further, and we eventually settled into the sheets, a mess of limbs and caresses. Though no more words were spoken, plenty more was communicated through glances and touch. As both the candles and her fire faded into nothing, the last thing I remember looking at was the way my arm so perfectly draped over her hips.

The last thing I remember thinking was that it should never leave.

I shot awake with smoke flooding my nostrils and ash caked in my mouth.

Sputtering and choking, I doubled over, pounding on my chest in a desperate attempt to clear my airway. Nothing was coming up, but that awful taste remained, as did the panic. My breath came in ragged gasps, and my heart thudded wildly.

I blinked, expecting to see flames, but there was nothing surrounding me now but cool air and tangled sheets. The devastating fire that had consumed everything in its path was long gone, only a figment of my nightmare, but I couldn't escape the awful sensation of burning, searing flesh. As I'd been held in place and forced to watch it come for me, never in my life had I felt such terror.

Until I glanced over to see Esmeralda sleeping peacefully beside me.

Memories came flooding back: her dance, the trapdoor, the mirror, the sex. Even if she hadn't been naked, looking at Esmeralda, there could be no denying what we'd done. Her hair was ruffled, her skin flushed, and worst of all, I'd left faint marks on her neck from the kisses I'd planted there. A quick glance at myself in the mirror revealed that I looked no better; in fact, I looked a hell of a lot worse.

God, damn me to Hell.

But as I sprang from the bed and began searching for my cloak, a more immediate problem presented itself given the shadows stretching across the floor.

It was morning.

And I was *late*.

There wasn't even time to fix or smooth my hair before I fled the room, yanking my cowl over my face and praying that would be enough to disguise me in broad daylight. There was a reason I only ventured from Notre Dame at night; plunging a knife into my own heart would be less painful than getting caught here. Not only that, but it simply wasn't an option.

Bursting from the room, I rounded a corner before stepping into a larger living space where Jules lay draped in a chair, snoring loudly with their mouth wide open. Though I briefly wondered when they'd gotten in last night, given that they hadn't been here when I'd arrived, I was at least grateful that their snores covered my escape from the house. Once outside, I set as quick a pace as my exhausted limbs could tolerate, lost deep in thought the entire way back to Notre Dame.

I couldn't be certain if the butterflies in my chest were from anxiety, adrenaline, or both. If I somehow made it back to the cathedral without being recognized, I'd not only have to slip back in unseen, I'd also need to think of a good excuse for why I'd missed Mass.

This was a disaster. A nightmare, really, but that wasn't the terrifying part. What scared me most was that every moment of the previous night—of Esmeralda—had been more than worth it. And if given half a chance?

I'd happily do it again.

VI. THE GUARD

Esmeralda

She'd fled my presence like a rat caught in daylight, skittering from my bed long before I'd woken. That much I'd expected.

I didn't expect it to hurt this much.

It had been a week since I'd last seen Claude. In that time, I'd become nothing but a bundle of jumpy nerves and a whirlwind of mixed emotions. On one hand, the night and my plot had been a resounding success: I'd ensured her sympathies were in the right place, held and bedded her, and had even gotten a bit of my own pleasure out of the encounter... All right, a *lot* of pleasure.

But on the other hand, I both fucking missed and missed fucking her.

Irritation boiled beneath my skin at the reminder, because not only were my feelings illogical, seeing Claude again—especially in the filthy, borderline depraved way that I so desperately craved—would be a mistake to rival my mère's. The goal had been to rile Claude up, to make her desire me so badly she'd give me what I needed with no questions asked should I ever require a favor, and that much had been accomplished. To waste such a favor prematurely simply wasn't an option. I should hate her, or at the very least fear her. I was a mage. She belonged to Notre Dame's clergy. We weren't simply fire and water: we were fire and kerosene, and to continue this beyond what I'd already risked would trigger an explosion neither of us would be able to contain, mage or not. I knew that.

So why couldn't I get her out of my head?

Everywhere I went, I saw her. White-haired people—Starchildren, as I'd told Jules—weren't especially common, but I began to notice them everywhere, and no matter how much I tried to douse my foolish hopes, even fleeting glimpses got them up every time. I saw her in the mères keeping close, watchful eyes on their children. I saw her any time anyone walked around wearing a hood or cowl. My dreams were what worsened and prolonged my torment most of all. Now that I'd experienced the real thing, they'd only grown more intense and frequent, leaving me in a damn near-constant state of arousal—except nothing helped. Not my own hand, and certainly not any of the partners I'd have happily sought out before. In a single night, Claude had doused my desire for anyone else, leaving nothing but a festering truth behind:

I wanted no one but her.

"…Es? *Esmeralda!*"

The acrid stench of burning fabric yanked me back to reality, and I was greeted by the sight of my own flames eating away at the last of the tapestries Jules and I had been using to decorate my stage for the better part of the last hour. Given that both my hands were occupied, I flicked my fingers, the intent being to extinguish the fire… except all that did was make it double in size.

Jules swore, letting go of their end of the tapestry and shooting me a venomous glare. "Have you lost your mind?"

"I've got it!" Antoine's voice sounded from my left, quickly followed by a conjured stream of water. Landing directly on the flames, it put them out within seconds, but not without soaking the front of my dress in the process.

It was my turn to swear. "Watch it!" I hissed, dropping the soaked and ruined tapestry to wipe the liquid from my eyes, but Jules's response was less than sympathetic.

"You watch it! We were so close to being done, and now we can't finish at all!"

I met Jules's gaze, defeated, because they were right: the poor tapestry was yet another unfortunate victim of the fact that I'd gotten hopelessly lost in my own head. I had yet to find anything resembling a solution. How could I when every idle thought brought me straight back to Claude and the night we spent together? It could never happen again, that much I'd accepted. But God, it felt so good, *she* felt so good…

Jules sighed deeply before turning to Antoine. "Give us a moment?"

He nodded, turning to walk away, but not without casting an irritated glance in my direction. My flames immediately flared back to life—that self-righteous water mage had the nerve to insinuate *I* was the reckless one?—and I'd have raised my arm had Jules not caught me by the wrist.

"What the hell's gotten into you?" they hissed for my ears alone. There were still a few hours to go until the faire officially started, but the streets were already beginning to fill up. The merchants were nearly done setting up their stands, and the tents pitched specifically for faire nights had all been erected. My stage should be fully decorated by now, too, but thanks to my little mishap, a rather conspicuous bare patch of wood remained—directly in the front and on full display, because of course.

"Nothing," I muttered, yanking myself from Jules's grip. "I'm just tired, that's all."

"Tired, my ass. You've been like this all week, ever since…" Their voice trailed off, and when I didn't bother to deny it, they threw up their hands. "Again with her? I swear, Es, she must have some sort of magical vagina if you're this obsessed with her after one night."

I bristled. "That isn't funny."

"It wasn't meant to be," they shot back, though their expression softened into a more understanding one. "Look, I get it. Claude left her mark on you. But we have far bigger problems right now." They gestured to the bare patch. "Got any ideas for how we might cover this up?"

I glanced around at the merchants. Most were selling typical faire wares: trinkets, jewelry, and the like. But when my gaze caught a long-forgotten stand tucked away in a corner, it sparked an idea. Instead of baubles and cheap jewelry, the elderly couple who owned it sold hand-dyed fabrics intended for things like headscarves and layered skirts. Several of those stitched or tied together could certainly work for our purposes.

"What about something like that?" I suggested, pointing toward the stand. "It won't look as uniform, but it's better than leaving it bare."

Jules hesitated before nodding slowly. "It might work," they conceded, and I fell into step beside them as we headed for the merchants. Though I tried to hang back while Jules made their selection, I was quickly recognized as The Embermage by the couple, who were more than delighted to sell to us. They tried to give us a discount, but we insisted upon paying full price plus a tip.

Our goods secured, we headed back to the stage where we made short work of covering up the spot—no fires this time, accidental or otherwise. It ended up looking far better than I expected, which I attributed to both the quality of the fabric and the vibrancy of the dye. Making a mental note to recommend the couple's work to anyone who would listen, I turned back to Jules, gesturing to my still-wet clothes. "I should go get ready."

They nodded. "Go on. I'll make sure Antoine is aware the plan hasn't changed."

"What?" I furrowed my brow, having done a double take at their words. "What do you mean, 'plan?' There isn't one."

Jules's mouth dropped open. "What do you mean? Aren't you seeing Claude again tonight?"

I bit my lip, because the truth was, I didn't know. Part of me doubted she planned to ever come back, but the other part would do just about anything to catch even a glimpse of her. But 'seeing' was far different from 'fucking,' and if anything wasn't happening tonight, it was that. It couldn't—not now, and not ever. "No," I heard myself say. Despite my voice being breathy and hoarse, I pressed on. "I doubt she's coming. But if she is, unless and *only* if it's to give Quasimodo a fire lesson, keep her away from me. Tell Antoine the same."

Before Jules could utter anything resembling an attempt to change my mind, I spun on my heel and fled inside, my thoughts a hopelessly tangled mess as I made my way into my bedroom. Whatever happened later could be agonized over later; for now, all I could do was get ready for my performance.

My first without Claude present in what—nineteen weeks?

Focus, I chastised myself, stripping off my wet clothes and tossing them carelessly to the side. My skirt didn't fully make it to the ground, catching on my bedpost instead. Not wanting to touch any part of the place where Claude had fucked me, I forced myself to ignore it. *Don't think about it—any of it. Not her hands, not her mouth…*

God, her mouth. My heart began beating wildly against my ribcage as I stared at myself in the mirror, clothed only in my undergarments. Flashes of what I'd seen reflected in it that night bombarded my mind's eye: her head between my legs, that triumphant yet oh-so-wicked gleam in her eyes any time I uttered so much as a whimper. Absently, I trailed my fingers over every place Claude's lips had touched, over the marks lingering on my neck, breasts, and thighs. I recalled the marks I'd left on her, too: particularly the 'I want you' I'd etched into her skin.

"I want you still," I whispered aloud.

Did Claude know? Did she have the faintest idea what she'd done to me, what she'd reduced me to? Had she thought of me at all since that night?

Did she want me again, too?

My knees threatened to give out beneath me, but gripping the edges of my vanity, I stood upright and took a deep breath. I could torment myself all I wanted, but none of it mattered anyway, and there was no time left to agonize—not if I wanted to put on a half-decent show. Steeling my resolve, I crossed the room and reached for my chosen outfit for the evening: a midnight-black corset with red and gold accents, a matching skirt, and an extravagantly flowing cape lined with soft feathers to complete the look. It vaguely reminded me of a phoenix—an image I could adopt if only for tonight—because if there was any night I needed to rise from the ashes and be reborn, it was this one.

I entered the hidden hall and took to the stage with a singular goal in mind: forget Claude. Forget *us*. Scanning the crowd as I did prior to every performance, I wasn't sure if it was relief, disappointment, or irritation that I felt upon realizing she wasn't there. No hood, no telltale white hair, and no sign of Quasimodo. Claude hadn't come, which meant only one of two things: I'd scared her off or, since she'd gotten what she came for, a taste of the legendary Embermage,… she never intended to come back. Icy prickles ran down my spine as an uncomfortable realization struck.

I'd been so focused on using her that I'd never once considered if it might be the other way around.

The cloak at my back immediately burst into wild, violent flames. Channeling every ounce of my frustration and grief into my fire, I gave the performance of a lifetime, every move, plume, and gesture an ode to the woman who'd broken me without even realizing it. To my audience, I was The Embermage; what they didn't know was that she was burning away her sadness, one ember at a time. Most of the show went as normal, but by the time I reached the climax, I could no longer contain the rage burning me from the inside out. Spinning and twirling, I summoned the flames and didn't stop until every inch of my body was set ablaze. I became a phoenix in a literal sense, reducing my clothing to piles of ash and embodying my stage persona in the most terrifying way I knew how.

The audience roared as one, and with a final flourish, I fled back into the trapdoor, running the length of the hall with my flames still burning. Only once back within the safety of my bedroom did I fully extinguish them, snatching a blanket to drape over my bare shoulders before settling into the chair at my vanity.

It was there that Jules and Antoine found me. My sibling immediately launched into what sounded suspiciously like a lecture but silenced the moment they met my gaze in the mirror's reflection.

"I need a drink," I said.

An hour later, the three of us sat in a crowded, noisy bar. I'd thrown on an oversized shirt and pants in an effort to conceal my figure, tied my hair back, and paired with a headscarf fashioned from one of the elderly couple's fabrics, I was nearly unrecognizable as The Embermage. Thank Christ for that, because the last thing I needed was drunken fans stumbling up to me. Though Jules had done their best to get me to tell them what was wrong, I knew myself. The moment I opened up about anything remotely emotional— or Claude, for fuck's sake—I wouldn't be able to stop, and the last thing I needed was for Antoine of all people to know my deepest, darkest secrets. I managed the occasional nod in response to Jules's quips, but inwardly, my mind remained a tangled web of conflict. Frustrated and overwhelmed, it was all I could do to keep my flame under control. Though my performance had helped release some of my pent-up aggravation, it had by no means soothed it completely, and the beer I forced myself to keep sipping wasn't helping, either.

Jules and Antoine carried on a lively conversation as if nothing was wrong, flirting, teasing, and clearly enjoying one another's company… yet here I was feeling more alone than ever before. They discussed anything and everything, laughter erupting from their lips every few minutes or so, while I sat brooding in silence.

The sole benefit of being here was that it was so loud and distracting it was difficult to remain in my own head for too long. I swept my gaze over the bar and its patrons, locating a handful of fellow mages, but no one of real interest, save for the trio of city guards, gathered in the far corner. They wore minimal armor and carried only a handful of visible weapons, but their presence alone was enough to make my skin crawl. The one in the middle, a clean-shaven white man with long blond hair spilling down his back, was someone I'd undoubtedly seen before... and as if he could read my thoughts, an arrogant smirk spread across his features. My lips curled into a snarl; why did it feel as if I could never escape these fucking guards? Was I being watched, or worse: followed?

"Stop staring, Es," Jules warned under their breath, kicking my shin under the table when I ignored them.

Reluctantly tearing my eyes from the guards, I shot my sibling a pointed glare. "Don't you think it's odd they keep showing up everywhere we are?"

"Once your performances began drawing larger crowds, they met with Père and the rest of the council, and everyone was in agreement that a larger security force was necessary. What's the big deal?"

"The deal is that it seems far too convenient of an excuse," I muttered, biting back what else I wanted to add: *And Papa can be far too trusting.*

"For once, I agree with her," Antoine said, tightening his grip on his own drink. "I've loathed feeling like they're breathing down my neck, and we aren't the only ones. Many disagreed with Clopin's decision."

Jules shook their head. "You're too paranoid, both of you."

"Perhaps you're not paranoid enough," I snapped before I could stop myself, reaching absently for Maman's necklace. I should have left it at home, especially for somewhere as crowded as this place, but if there was anything I felt naked without, it was her pendant.

My sibling didn't reply right away. I refused to look at them, but it didn't keep their stare from burning a hole into the side of my head. "Are you quite certain there's nothing you'd like to—"

"Excusez-moi," an unfamiliar voice said, but as soft as it was, I nearly leapt from my skin at the interruption. Glancing up, my gaze fell upon a hooded figure, and my breath may have caught in my throat had I not immediately taken note of the red hair spilling from within. Not only that, but the stranger wasn't nearly as tall as Claude, and the hands tightly clasped in front of them were absolutely covered in freckles.

Antoine was first to recover. Waving his hand, he said, "We aren't in need of any service. Leave us."

"I don't work here." What little I could see of the stranger's heavily freckled face reddened even more, and they dropped their voice to a whisper. "I... I'm looking for Es..." Voice trailing off, they hesitated before fixating on me. "Esmeralda?"

Only then did I get my first real look at them. A white woman with thick auburn hair, the corners of her mouth twitched up as I regarded her, but any traces of a smile vanished the moment I hissed my reply.

"Who's asking?" First my rather public loss of control, then the guards, and now this. *Fuck me, could tonight get any worse?*

"M-My name is Mercedes," she said quickly, casting wary glances at Jules and Antoine before turning back to me. "I'm here on behalf of—"

"Are you a mage?" Antoine cut across her, standing up in the process. Mercedes swallowed. "No."

"Were you sent by a mage?"

"No, but—"

"And you," Antoine said, turning back to me. "Do you know what this is about?"

"No. And I don't particularly care."

Mercedes seemed to shrink in on herself, her cheeks paling and her gaze darting around the room. "S'il vous plaît, Mademoiselle. Finding you wasn't easy, and this will only take—"

"You tracked her down?" Jules immediately shot up, their voice low yet still filled with indignation. "For what purpose? Who sent you?"

"That's precisely what I've been trying to tell her," Mercedes said through gritted teeth, and whatever leash holding her back began to snap. "But the information is for Esmeralda's ears alone."

"Anything you have to say to me, you can say in front of these two," I said coolly, folding my hands in front of me. It was both an attempt to look nonchalant as well as to keep my flames at bay; they flared hot beneath my skin, begging desperately to be set free. "Otherwise, leave."

She released an audible exhale. "I really must insist—"

"Upon what, exactly? You heard her." Antoine placed an arm on the table, partially shielding me from Mercedes. A decent amount of water already coated his palm, slowly but surely beginning to creep up his wrist. "Say your piece, or get out of here."

She started to speak, but her words morphed into a yelp of surprise as she was shoved aside. I stood, fully prepared to reprimand Antoine for manhandling her, only to come face to face with the blond city guardsman.

He cocked his head. "Is there a problem here?"

I froze. When had the guards gotten here, and how? Had they overheard us talking? Had they heard my *name*? Questions continued racing through my mind while across the table, Jules reached for and took my hand, regaining their composure long before I did. "No problem at all, Monsieur. We were just leaving." My sibling made an attempt to pull me toward the exit, but with the guardsman blocking both my and Antoine's path, we couldn't move.

"Were you?" the guardsman asked, eyeing us all up and down. "Forgive me—I couldn't help but overhear—but it sounded as though you were requesting that this young lady be the one to leave rather than yourselves." He gestured to a wide-eyed Mercedes, her hood pulled down, held immobile by the other two guards.

"You 'overheard?'" I blurted out before I could help myself, holding the blond's gaze. "How curious. None of us were speaking particularly loud, and last I saw, you three were sitting all the way over there." I managed to look far braver than I felt; inwardly, my heart threatened to leap out of my chest. *Do you know my name? Do you know who I am?*

The guardsman smiled, somehow managing to look even more sinister than before. "Perspective, my dear. You miss quite a lot when you're distracted."

He did *not* just call me a pet name. "I am no one's 'dear,'" I all but growled and would have kept going had Jules not dug their fingernails into my palm.

"Forgive her, Monsieur. She's had a long night. May I take her to rest?"

In any other circumstance, I'd have called my sibling out for daring to apologize for me, but they were right: clearly, I would do far better to keep my mouth shut. The guardsman considered us for a moment, which only enraged me further given that we'd done absolutely nothing wrong. None of us, not even Antoine, had made a scene, but the guards certainly had. The entire bar had gone quiet to gawk at the spectacle that had been made of us.

At last, the blond one conceded, stepping aside to give us room to pass. "See to it you get home safely."

Jules immediately began dragging me toward the exit, nodding profusely. "Je vous remercie, Monsieur. We will."

"Wait," I said, planting my feet and nearly causing Antoine to slam into me. Glancing around him, I met the blond guardsman's gaze and gestured to Mercedes. "What about her?"

"What *about* her?" he echoed, narrowing his gaze. "You asked her to leave."

"Yes, but she's done nothing wrong. Is she not free to go as well?"

"Are you out of your fucking mind?" Jules hissed into my ear, but I ignored them.

"I'm afraid not," the guard answered icily. "We have a few questions for her."

"On what grounds?" Tearing myself from Jules's grip, I sidestepped Antoine until I was once more facing the guard. My flames flared to life beneath my skin and would have come bursting out had I not reined them in at the last moment. "What reason do you have for detaining her?"

"Suspicious behavior," the blond said immediately.

I scoffed. "What, because she came in wearing a hood? Since when is that a crime?"

"When it masks one involved in illegal activities." He stepped forward, his voice dropping dangerously low. "And unless you want the same treatment, I suggest you leave while you still can."

Fury boiled in my veins as I met his gaze, unwilling to back down. Behind me, Jules tugged at my sleeve. We needed to get out of here before anything worse happened, yes, but it simply didn't sit right with me to leave Mercedes behind, not when it was our fault we'd drawn attention to her in the first place. If only I'd just done what she'd asked or at least not antagonized her as much as we did, she wouldn't be about to be carted off to jail—or worse.

"Let her go," I said through gritted teeth, steeling myself against the waves of heat emanating from my body.

The guard pursed his lips. "That's not possible. Now move… unless you want to come with her." His hand moved slightly toward the hilt of his sword.

A threat, one my flames didn't take kindly to. They ignited briefly, bursting from my fingertips, but closing my fist, I extinguished them. As much as I was loath to admit it, there was only one real choice here: Mercedes was a stranger, I owed her nothing, and to start an altercation would not only endanger me but my sibling and their partner as well. So reluctantly, stiffly, I began to move aside… only for Mercedes to collapse on the floor in front of me.

It happened within a matter of seconds. The blond reached for her, but so did I, and our arms brushed. With a grunt, he shoved me aside, causing me to lose my balance. Instinct took over; to keep from falling, I snatched his bare forearm.

That's when I lost control.

Flames leapt from my hand like wildfire, charring the flesh beneath my grasp before either of us could react. I released him immediately, but the damage had been done. Screaming, he cradled his badly burned arm against his chest as he stepped back. The stench of melted skin already hung thick in the air, but though the guardsman had to be in agony, he didn't simply look pained.

He looked murderous.

A gasp of shock ran through the bar, and my heart dropped into my stomach as the realization of what I'd done all but slapped me in the face: I'd burned someone, and badly. I should apologize, speak, anything, but any words I'd been about to utter turned to ash in my mouth as I attempted to wrap my brain around what just happened. My fire had always been volatile—such was the nature of my element—but never once had I lost control this horrifically, this publicly. Was this a result of Claude, of what she'd given me a taste of before vanishing into thin air? Was this who I was without her?

I didn't have time to linger on it. The blond guardsman's face remained contorted in a mixture of pain and rage, and his eyes radiated fury as he pointed a shaking finger at me.

"She burned me!" he shouted, as if that much wasn't obvious. "Arrest her!"

The other two guards surged forward, with one making a grab

for Mercedes while the other stalked toward me with their weapon drawn. Still frozen in shock, I may have been seized had Jules not hauled me back toward the exit. Antoine backed us up, allowing his water to spring to life, but all of it became a blur as panic surged through me. I had just used magic against someone, and not just anyone: an authority figure, in *public*.

Around us, the bar burst into chaos. Shouts of shock and outrage mixed with the frightened cries echoing off the walls. Tables and chairs were swiftly overturned, and fists and elements alike began to fly as both mages and regular citizens sprang into action. Whether the riot was on my behalf or I'd simply been the catalyst, I'd never know. It was mere seconds before a body crashed into Jules, flinging them off to the side, and a moment later, I lost sight of them completely.

"Jules!" I screamed, though I could barely hear my own voice. "Antoine!" I spun around frantically, searching for water, a flash of lightning, anything—

But then, a flash of red, only it wasn't fire. It was hair spilled across the wooden floor. Directly in front of me, Mercedes lay on the ground, kicking and striking at the guard who somehow still had a hold of her. Without thinking, I snatched the nearest chair and bashed him over the head with it, shoving his limp body aside before holding out my hand to Mercedes. She hesitated for a split second before taking it, allowing me to haul her to her feet.

"Have you seen either of the people I was with?" I asked her, breathless. "We need to find—"

"There's no time. Do you have any idea who you just burned?" Without waiting for me to answer, she hissed, "That was Captain Phoebus."

My mouth went dry. "Captain of the Guard, Phoebus?"

"Escape first, questions later." She threaded both her arms around my shoulder, keeping a far better grip on me than Jules had, but I planted my feet when she began navigating us through the frenzy.

"No. I can't just leave my sibling here."

"And what use will you be to them if you're jailed or dead?" Mercedes flinched as a spear of ice flew over our heads, swiftly followed by a chair from the opposite direction. More shattered glass coated the floor with each passing second, and given that I was only wearing dancing slippers, there was a very real chance my feet would get sliced all to hell. I gritted my teeth; whether I wanted to admit it or not, in more ways than one, we truly were running out of time. "Your companions are mages, and those guards are looking for us," Mercedes said, her voice low and deadly serious. "The best way we can protect them is by getting out of here—now."

I hated that she was right. I hated myself even more for nodding. But by holding on to one another as if our lives depended on it, we managed to slip out a shattered window. Mercedes had her cloak to shield her from the exposed shards of glass, but I wasn't so lucky. Blood trailed from the fresh wounds on my face and arms as we sprinted a short distance, the cool night air making me hyper-aware of the location of each shallow cut.

We stopped once we could no longer hear any of the commotion. Uncaring that I stood in the middle of the street, I doubled over to catch my breath, but Mercedes shoved against my chest, pushing me into the nearest alley before rendering me immobile against the stone wall. I opened my mouth to protest, but she covered it with her hand, leaning in until I could feel her breath on my face.

"Now that I have you alone, I may as well do what I came here for." An irritated exhale. "Claude sent me. Told me to look for your necklace as a way to recognize you. No, she didn't want to send a note—too much risk of it being intercepted, she claimed. Didn't consider that the very same might happen to me, apparently."

I stiffened as an icy chill ran down my spine. *Claude* had sent her?

"You know her, then?" Mercedes continued, her hand still over my mouth. "Good. She wants you to know she's sorry she couldn't attend tonight, but that last Friday meant a great deal to her. She hopes you'll be able to forgive her but understands if you can't."

Only then did Mercedes release me, but by then I couldn't breathe let alone form an intelligible response. Claude was not only sorry but missed me by the sounds of it. I'd been on her mind enough for her to realize her absence would be a significant blow, enough to warrant an explanation and apology, enough to consider my feelings. My flames flared to life once again, but the spark that ignited them wasn't hurt or rage… it was hope.

"Why didn't you tell me it was her who sent you?" I asked once I could form words again. "I'd have heard you out immediately if I knew."

"Claude was incredibly clear that her message was for your ears alone. Besides," Mercedes added, "how was I supposed to know that the people you were with were trustworthy?"

I nodded absently. I supposed it made sense.

"You have somewhere to go, right?" Still out of breath herself, Mercedes leaned back against the opposite wall as her chest rose and fell at a frantic rhythm. "Somewhere you can lay low until you're able to escape the city?"

"Yes, my père will protect—*what*? What do you mean, 'escape the city?'"

She looked at me as though I'd just sprouted two heads. "Exactly what I said. Surely you don't intend to stay in Paris, not with Phoebus on your trail. He isn't going to stop hunting you, not until he finds you."

"I'm not going anywhere. Paris is my home."

"That ceased being the case the moment you melted the Captain of the Guard's arm."

"It was an accident," I snapped. "And I mean it. I'm not going anywhere."

Mercedes shrugged before throwing her hood back over her head. "Just know you're a fugitive now. If your plan is to endanger anyone who harbors you, living in the shadows until you're inevitably arrested anyway, be my guest, and good luck." She turned to go but halted when I bit out a reluctant response.

"Wait."

I couldn't ignore what she'd pointed out, because she was right. I'd already done more than enough to place those I loved in danger. With my père, Clopin, and among the Mages' Council would be the first place Phoebus would search for me. Questioning Jules and Antoine would be next. None of them could know where I'd gone—

they couldn't even suspect—but neither could I leave the city. Paris was my home, my family's home, and I wasn't willing to abandon either without a fight.

But I wasn't prepared for one... not yet, anyway. What I needed was a place to disappear. A place where I could vanish, 'lay low,' as Mercedes had said, somewhere that would keep me hidden and safe while I formulated something resembling a plan. Only then could I face Phoebus, and only then would I have a proper chance.

My decision made, I locked eyes with Mercedes. "They're searching for you, too. Do you intend to leave the city?"

"No, but I didn't burn anyone with magic."

I forced myself to ignore that. "Then where *are* you going?"

She sighed but leaned around the edge of the alley and pointed to the tallest and most intimidating structure looming in the distance: Cathédrale Notre Dame de Paris.

"I'm going home."

VII. THE SANCTUARY

Claude

"*H*old still, Maman."

Quasimodo's exasperated voice pulled me from my book. Lifting my gaze, I only barely stifled my chuckle at the way his face was scrunched in deep concentration. While I lounged on my bed, he sat in the chair near my fireplace, meticulously whittling away at one of his wooden figurines. He'd been carving them since he'd been able to hold a blade, and several of his finished pieces were displayed on my mantle, including one of my brother, Jehan. Quasimodo had taken extra care with this one—a likeness of me—and had been working on it for weeks now.

What, I moved? I asked when he looked up, truly unable to recall doing so.

He groaned. "Yes. You keep crossing and uncrossing your legs, and every time, it changes the expression on your face."

Ah... that certainly did sound familiar, especially given where my thoughts kept straying. *I'm sorry. I'll try harder to keep still.*

"Please do, because I'm nearly finished."

I smiled. *I can't wait to see.*

He turned his attention back to his work, and I may have done the same with my book had I actually been reading. But I hadn't turned the page for over twenty minutes. My eyes scanned the words, yet seemed unable to take in their meaning. It certainly didn't help that aside from Quasimodo's quiet scraping and the gentle crackling of the fire behind him, everything was quiet. No bells, no chorus, and no chanted prayers. No footsteps along the corridors, no faint hymn drifting from the organ, and no whispered conversations among the priests that mysteriously ceased the moment I drifted within earshot. It was well past sunset, and Notre Dame and its inhabitants had settled in for the night. No one would stir until Quasimodo and the other bellringers called us to recite the Angelus come morning.

Everything was quiet... except for my thoughts. If they could speak, they'd be deafening.

It was no wonder I couldn't sit still, because there wasn't a single second of the past week that I'd been permitted respite from Esmeralda or the night we'd spent together. I couldn't close my eyes without picturing her in that mirror, couldn't stare into the fireplace without wishing those flames were hers. I especially couldn't stand to touch or even look at her scarf, but neither could I bring myself to get rid of it. In a fit of conflicted desperation, I'd stashed it deep into my storage trunk before covering it with what I hoped was enough junk to keep me from digging it out again... or worse, running back to the faire in hopes of getting another one.

But I am *here, precisely where I need to be,* I reminded myself, sparing another glance at Quasimodo. He smiled when our gazes locked, and my heart swelled with emotion. I'd expected him to be far angrier with me than he had been, at least to my face, when I'd broken the news that we would no longer be visiting the street faire. The fact that he hadn't argued or even pushed back on it made my regret all the worse, but it was no less than I deserved.

How was your time with Henri? I asked, all but giving up on my book and hoping to steer my thoughts in a more positive direction.

Quasimodo shrugged. "Fine. He's still a little sick, so we couldn't do a whole lot. We just sat on the roof and..."

My gaze narrowed when his voice trailed off. *And did what?*

"You won't like it."

I already assumed as much.

"Henri threw a few rocks," Quasimodo confessed, but quickly added, "None of them actually hit anyone, I swear."

These teenage boys were going to be the death of me. *Sick, but not sick enough to throw rocks?*

"I told you, there was no harm done."

That may be, but if I hear about it from Father Laurent—

"He's a mage, Maman," Quasimodo cut across me. "An air mage. He manifested about a month ago, and the rocks were his way of showing me."

My spine went rigid. *And did you tell him...?*

"That I'm one, too? No, I didn't."

He turned away after that, leaving me with even more to agonize over. If life had been confusing before, I had no idea what to call it now. Quasimodo's powers weren't something we would be able to hide forever, and he shouldn't have to. As if that wasn't enough of a rift between us, I still had yet to come clean over the real reason I'd missed Mass after my night with Esmeralda; there was absolutely no way he didn't at least suspect the truth. I'd always been the repressed woman-lover, sneaking around and satisfying my lustful urges by whatever means I felt necessary: that much wasn't new. What was, however, was my fascination, borderline obsession with one woman in particular. I'd had several long-term partners, even favorites—Mercedes immediately sprang to mind—but I'd never been anything resembling loyal to any one of them. The relationships, if you could even call them that, were always left wide open. My partners were permitted to bed other people, and so was I. Such loose arrangements had always worked brilliantly. I wasn't a jealous person.

So why did the mere thought of Esmeralda lying with anyone other than me summon this uncomfortable tightness in my chest?

My world was shifting. I was shifting, and I didn't like it. We'd shared a single night; a good night, a perfect night, but how? How had it somehow been enough to turn my world on its axis, for me to no longer know my ups from my downs, my lefts from my rights? How had Esmeralda enraptured me so, at times making me forget my own name? I'd been so thoroughly convinced just one more night at the faire would be enough... but now there were only two things I knew for certain: the first was that under no circumstances could I ever see her again.

The second was that I might lose my mind if I didn't.

But it was impossible. We were impossible. Fire and... I didn't know what to call myself. Poison? Smoke? Either way, I'd be the death of her, and I simply couldn't allow that, no matter how much I wanted her. It was why I'd sent Mercedes with a message that doubled as an apology. Perhaps it was conceited to presume Esmeralda may have spared me any more than a second thought, but even if she hadn't, it felt like the right thing to do. And if there was anything I ought to start doing more of, it was that.

"...more or less done, I think," came Quasimodo's voice, once again pulling me from my thoughts. "I still need to paint it, of course. But would you like to see?"

He didn't wait for me to answer before crossing the room and holding out the figurine for me to examine. After setting my book aside, I took it with both hands, immediately struck by both the remarkable workmanship and the delicacy of it.

The detail was exquisite. Even in the dim candlelight, I could make out every line and curve that made up my broad figure.

He'd paid special attention to my vestments, even down to the stitching of the embroidery on my double orarion; such care had me swallowing hard against a sudden lump in my throat. There wasn't so much as a stray hair out of place, which was more than I could say in real life, especially when it came to early morning Masses. Though the figurine had yet to be painted, the eyes were somehow bright and full of life, especially when combined with such a genuinely warm expression.

"See?" Quasimodo said quietly. "You really do look better when you smile."

My vision suddenly became blurry, and I drew a shaky inhale, unable to form a coherent reply just yet. I ran my thumb along the figurine's smooth surface in amazement, still unable to believe that my son had managed to capture me with such... beauty. It was never a word I'd have used to describe myself, much less expect from anyone else, but to deny it would be to deny Quasimodo's artistry, and that simply wasn't an option.

The lump in my throat grew larger as tears pricked in the corners of my eyes. I didn't want to cry, especially not in front of my son, but it seemed I had no choice. All the pent-up emotions that had been building since my encounter with Esmeralda came crashing down like a wave, and a sob escaped my lips as the dam within me broke.

But before the tremors could overtake me completely, arms encircled me, pulling me into a tight embrace. I leaned into Quasimodo as I pulled him closer, using the physical contact to keep me grounded as emotions flooded through me. Sadness, grief, and fear intermingled with gratefulness I couldn't yet put into words—and perhaps never would. I may have adopted my son more than fifteen years ago when I was only a young adult myself, but I loathed the notion that I'd 'saved him.' He was no different from any other infant in that he simply needed a parent, and I was no hero for giving him what he already deserved. I hadn't saved him. Quasimodo had saved *me*, but I certainly hadn't done well thanking him as of late.

"Maman," he said against my chest, his voice barely audible over my heaving breaths. "I'm sorry. I didn't mean to make you cry."

I shook my head, pulling away to be able to sign. *Stop that. I'm the one who owes you an apology.*

For what?

Not going to the street faire tonight. I studied his reaction carefully. *I know you're disappointed, and I truly am sorry we couldn't go.*

He hesitated, and his smile vanished. *It's fine.*

It's clearly not, given that look on your face. And you're allowed to feel what you feel about it. We can talk—

I stopped mid-sentence when Quasimodo abruptly walked away, halting mere feet from the fireplace. But just as I'd caught my breath, he turned to face me before raising one of his arms, sticking it directly into the flames before I could so much as utter a squeak. Instinct screamed for me to go to him, but fear that he might do something even more drastic kept me rooted in place, as did the warning glare he was giving me.

"It's because I can do this, isn't it?" he demanded. "It's because I'm a fire mage!"

Keep your voice down, I signed desperately. *You're shouting, and someone might hear you.*

"I know you care for me, Maman. But I'm no longer a child, and I'm tired of you treating me as such."

As much as I deserved this and wanted to let Quasimodo continue, this was about the worst time he could have picked to start yelling. My gaze kept flicking to the door, where any moment now, I half-expected someone to come bursting through it. *You're right, and again, I'm more than happy to talk about this. But* please, can you be a little quieter?

He looked very much like he wanted to argue, but yanked himself from the flames instead. Though logically I knew he was unhurt, it didn't make watching it any easier, especially given that a handful of flickering embers still caressed his forearm. Guilt gnawed at my chest as I watched him—my powerful, capable son—and it was more than obvious I needed to come clean, no matter how uncomfortable the experience was likely to be for both of us. I waited until he glanced back in my direction before signing, *Do you want the truth?*

Quasimodo snorted. "What kind of question is that?"

The reason we can't go back has absolutely nothing to do with you or your magic. I paused as shame rippled through me, both for keeping it from him as well as the act itself. *It's because last week, after I took you home... I went back. And The Embermage and I did things we can never do again.*

His mouth fell open. "You slept with my potential *teacher*?"

No longer able to contain my irritation over his refusal to be quiet, my fingers flew and my movements became more exaggerated. *Yes, go ahead and shout it for all of Paris to hear.*

"First of all, I knew it, but second of all, how dare—"

It's not what you think. I stood up from the bed, needing to move around to release some of the tension building inside me. *The connection between us has been growing far longer than anyone knew you were a mage.*

"That may be true, but you still did it *after* you knew. Or was that not even the first time?"

It was the first time, and the only time. I swear.

Quasimodo crossed his arms. "Why should I believe you?"

You shouldn't. I felt like crying again. *But it's the truth.*

We stared at one another for a few long moments, with him fighting to catch his breath while I clenched and unclenched my fists in an effort to stop my fingers from shaking. It didn't work, and they still visibly quivered when I began signing again. *I am sorry—truly. And I promise that I'll find you a teacher, a better teacher—*

"Are you serious?" he cut across me, his voice deadly quiet this time. "You think you can find someone better than *The Embermage*?"

I fumbled for an answer, but before I could come up with one, Quasimodo marched over to the bed to snatch the figurine in my likeness. He went to the mantle next, selecting the one modeled after Jehan before making his way toward the door. Despite my better judgement, I chased after him, darting in his path to ask, *Why are you taking that?* It was the only physical reminder of my brother I possessed, aside from the handful of letters scrawled in his barely legible handwriting.

Quasimodo regarded me coolly. "I need a reference I can stand to look at."

With that, he sidestepped me before exiting the room, and I flinched when he slammed the door behind him. It was several moments before the weight of what had just happened struck me with force; when I sank to my knees, it was both in surrender and because they could no longer support my weight. I then turned to the only being capable of bringing me any semblance of comfort in moments like this—when not even I could stand to be in my own company.

"My Lord God," I whispered, bowing my head and closing my eyes, "I come before you with a heavy heart and an even heavier soul. I have sinned. I continue to sin, to be unworthy of your grace... yet still pray that I am worthy of your mercy. Please, if it is your will, forgive me for all I've done and all I will do in the future. But it is not only me who needs your protection and guidance." I paused as two faces flashed in my mind's eye: my son, followed by my brother. "Watch over Quasimodo. He is upset with me, and rightly so. Soothe and bless him, but also keep him safe from those who would do him harm should they discover what he is. Please also bless Jehan. I haven't heard from him in some time, but hopefully that means he is well and safe.

"And please, Lord... watch over Esmeralda, too. Give her strength when she needs it and comfort when she is feeling alone. Keep her safe from any who would seek to hurt or take advantage of her. And, as I know is your will..." My voice cracked as it trailed off, but I cleared my throat, stating the final bit with conviction. "Keep her away from me."

I wasn't sure how I felt once my prayer came to a close, because something felt... off, and it was something beyond the palpable tension still lingering in the room. The hairs on my arms stood up; not in response to the cool breeze drifting in from the open window, but as if acknowledging something I didn't yet know or see. And when I opened my eyes, a gentle rumble reached my ears. Droplets of rain began striking my windowpane, lightly at first, but soon increasing in intensity. I stood up reluctantly—I had hoped to be able to keep the window open all night—and took my time closing it, my fingers lingering on the cool frame. A gust of frigid air caressed my face, just as Esmeralda had so tenderly—

"*No!*" I slammed the window shut, crying out at the same time. Raking both hands through my hair, I began pacing back and forth in front of the dying fire, my footsteps as restless as my fluttering heart. Had God not heard me? Was Satan mocking me? Or was it both? A chill icier than the night air pierced my heart as a horrifying thought took hold. Had I stumbled down a path where not even my God could reach me? Had my night with Esmeralda been the final straw, the final indication that I was beyond saving, beyond redemption?

It was unclear if I had only just started crying or if I had been ever since Quasimodo left. Sobs racked my body, pouring from the depths of my soul, each one aching more than the last. Somehow managing to stumble to my bed, I laid in a fetal position, wrapping my arms around my knees as I curled up into myself. It wasn't just my tears that threatened to drown me, it was the overwhelming sense of despair that had seeped into my bones. Every time I thought it couldn't get any worse, it did, until eventually I found myself unable to cry any longer given the rawness of my throat and the stinging in my eyes.

I was quite certain I imagined the knock that sounded soon after. No one in their right mind would still be awake at this hour—I only was because I wasn't—but then it came again, louder this time.

Someone *was* at my door.

Forcing myself upright, my heart fluttered in anticipation. Had Quasimodo decided he wanted to talk, after all? Had he somehow found a way to forgive me of my heinous sins? Or did he simply not want to be alone tonight, just as I had no desire to be?

I yanked open my door, my fingers already signing 'come in,' but it wasn't my son who stood there.

It was Mercedes… and Esmeralda.

There wasn't time to be shocked, for Mercedes shoved Esmeralda forward before slipping in after her, closing and bolting the door in a single practiced motion. Meeting my gaze, Mercedes said, "I'm sorry. I know this is a bad idea, but she refuses to leave the city, insisted upon following…"

She kept talking, but I stopped listening, fixating instead on Esmeralda—one detail in particular. Gripping her shoulder, I stepped closer, using my free hand to lift her chin so I could better examine her face. At least half a dozen cuts marred her cheeks and forehead. They were shallow from the looks of it, and the blood had already dried and scabbed, but it didn't keep rage from flaring to life deep within my chest.

My voice was low, my tone borderline feral. "Who did this to you?"

Teeth chattering, Esmeralda took a step back, gravitating toward the fire. "I'm fine."

"Like hell you are." I was already searching for a blanket to drape over her shoulders, though it wouldn't do much immediate good. She looked as if she'd seen a ghost. What was unmistakably exhaustion had caused her usually bright eyes to go dull, and when I'd touched her, her skin had been cold. Unsurprising, given that she was soaked to the bone. It must have been raining far longer than I'd realized.

After getting Esmeralda settled into a chair near the fire and covering her in the thickest blankets I currently had at my disposal, I turned to Mercedes. I'd have offered her the same treatment, but she'd been dressed far more appropriately to traipse through the rain and mud and definitely showed it. Her skin was its normal color, she wasn't shivering, and she didn't sport any visible injuries. Having hung her cloak on the back of the door, she faced me with her arms crossed, looking very much like she expected me to reprimand her.

But I remained in a state of bewildered confusion. "What in God's name happened out there?" I asked, the question intended more for Mercedes than it was for Esmeralda; the only thing I wanted her to concentrate on was getting warm.

"Well... I gave her your message," Mercedes said slowly. "Just not in the way anyone expected or intended."

"What's that supposed to mean?"

"It means I was antagonized," she hissed, lowering her voice to an irritated whisper. "I found her in a bar sitting with some other mages. I tried to get her alone, but none of them trusted me, because why would they? And we caught the attention of the guards."

I began piecing it all together, and my heart sank to my knees. "So they attacked her?"

Mercedes hesitated, choosing her next words carefully. "She attacked them, actually. It was an accident, but she ended up burning Captain Phoebus pretty badly."

"*Phoebus*?" I bit out louder than I meant to. "And what after that?"

"A riot—"

"I can hear you, you know." Esmeralda's voice rose over our hushed whispers, her tone laced with vexation. "You may as well talk normally if you're going to converse like I'm not even here."

It felt as though she'd punched me in the gut. I badly wanted to go to her, to take her hand and apologize, but strongly suspected she wouldn't appreciate that in the slightest—not yet, at least.

Turning to Esmeralda, I said, "Our intent was never to exclude you, but you looked—"

"Like shit?" Twisting in her chair, she met my gaze, and though she wasn't facing the fire, I swore there were flames dancing in her eyes. "It's all right, you can say it. You can say it all. If your little discussion is going to end with you deciding to throw me out, just do it. I'd rather know now before I let myself get too comfortable."

At this, I did approach, kneeling in front of her before she could say anything else. "Is that what you think this is?" I asked softly, searching her face for any clues as to what she might be thinking. "Esmeralda, you're free to go at any time. But I'm not, and nor will I ever 'throw you out.'"

She shifted uncomfortably before whispering, "You should. I'm a fugitive now, a danger and a threat to you. To your son."

"Let me worry about my son." If anything, I imagine he'd be thrilled she was here, especially given our last conversation.

Silence lingered until Mercedes cleared her throat, breaking it. "So... you're all right with this, then? With her staying here?"

I nodded before she finished speaking, but when I opened my mouth, no sound came out. The mention of Quasimodo had formed an idea in my head. Though the last thing I wanted was to ask anything of Esmeralda, especially while she was in this state, if I had any hope of salvaging my relationship with my son, I needed to ask at least this much.

"She can stay... so long as she agrees to mentor Quasimodo."

Esmeralda didn't hesitate. "Of course. It's the least I can do."

"Mentor him in what?" Mercedes asked, but we both ignored her.

"And thank you. I... I have nowhere else to go," Esmeralda confessed softly. "The homes of my family and friends are among the first places they'll look, but I can't leave the city entirely. I can't. My entire life is here in Paris. I've known nothing else."

"She has a point, though," Mercedes said, her wary tone suggesting she was still choosing her words extremely carefully. "If anyone were to discover we were harboring her—"

"I'm aware of the consequences," I snapped, a little harsher than I intended.

Mercedes didn't relent. "Phoebus comes here regularly to meet with Father Laurent. This isn't exactly the safest place for her. In fact, I'd argue it's one of the most dangerous."

"How do you know you don't have it backwards? Phoebus and Father Laurent are both incredibly proud men. The last place they would assume anyone to be hiding would be in their own house."

"How do you know they won't order a search of the entire cathedral first thing in the morning?"

"We'll figure something out," I muttered to Mercedes, but then I froze... because Esmeralda was holding my hand.

Or perhaps I was holding hers. At what point that had happened, I couldn't be certain; all I knew was that her thumb lightly caressed me, and that the look in her eyes was one I'd do unspeakable things to see again. Offering me a light squeeze, she mouthed two words: thank you.

Anything for you. The words caught in my throat as my heart began to flutter, both from fear and… something else. Oh, God, what was happening? What was I doing? Hadn't I just prayed for Him to keep Esmeralda away from me, so that I might obey His will? Wasn't I supposed to be distancing myself from her, from all of this, to better protect my son? To escape eternal torment and damnation?

Or had I already started down a path from which there was no return—a path whose name was Esmeralda?

"Neither of you asked," Mercedes said quietly, shattering whatever moment Esmeralda and I had shared; we yanked our hands back to ourselves and turned to face her as one. "And I'm fully aware I'm a fucking idiot for agreeing to this. But my answer is yes. I'll do whatever I can to help keep Esmeralda's presence a secret. I'll insist that I'm the only one who cleans this room, I'll figure out a way to sneak her scraps from the kitchen, and I'll even quell any rumors that may spring up. On one condition." Glancing between us, Mercedes settled her gaze back on me. "That you *do* figure something out, an actual, tangible solution, and quickly. This cannot go on forever, and both of you know it."

With that, she spun on her heel, snatched her cloak from the door, and exited, leaving me and Esmeralda alone.

Alone.

Suddenly hyper-aware of the fact I was dressed in nothing but a chemise—my breasts weren't even bound—I rose clumsily before stumbling back a few steps and crossing my arms over my chest. "I… I'm not decent," I stammered. "I apologize."

Esmeralda raised a brow. "I'm the one who barged into your room in the middle of the night, bloodied and soaked, and you're the one who's apologizing?"

Heat crept to my cheeks, but then her words sank in. She desperately needed to get out of those wet clothes, and I couldn't stand seeing that blood on her face a single moment longer. Crossing the room, I pulled open my wardrobe, quickly locating a plain shirt and pair of breeches. After handing them to her, I turned my back, busying myself as I searched for a rag.

"I know those are too big," I said over my shoulder, "but they'll have to do for—"

"Claude," Esmeralda cut across me, but I didn't turn around until she said my name a second time. She'd stood up from the chair, holding the blankets in one hand and the clothes I'd offered her in the other. "There's no need to turn your back. You've already seen me naked. Or do you not remember?"

I bobbed my head, suddenly incapable of speech. *Of course I remember. How could I ever forget?*

"Good," she said, beginning to unbutton her shirt, but I threw up a hand and averted my gaze.

"Please don't take this the wrong way," I began, my voice low and hoarse, "but I'm not going to look. Not because I don't want to—not in the slightest—but because if I do, it might lead us down a path I don't want to walk tonight."

The faint ruffling of clothing suggested Esmeralda continued changing as we conversed. "Oh? Then what do you want to do tonight?"

"I… I want to take care of you, if you'll allow me." *And I certainly don't want to be alone—not after what happened with Quasimodo.*

Esmeralda paused mid-change. I remained facing away from her, my pulse fluttering at the thought of her half naked and only a few feet away.

"Take care of me?" she repeated softly, almost as if she didn't believe that I wanted to.

"Yes."

To prove it, I sprang into action, grateful for a distraction from my impure thoughts. I first added more wood to the fire so it would keep burning through the night. After that, I rummaged for a bucket to fill with water and a cloth rag, one I could use to wipe the blood off her face. I didn't have anything to treat her cuts, but if any looked like they needed more serious attention come the morning, we could address them then.

Once everything was prepared, I let out a deep breath and returned to where Esmeralda sat on the edge of my bed. She had donned my clothes and now held a blanket around her shoulders, informing me she must still be cold.

"May I?" I asked, dipping the rag in water.

She nodded, shifting so there was room for me to sit beside her. Firelight flickered over her skin as I settled against her, our bodies brushing as I began to clean her face. I became more and more aware of who she was with each swipe of the cloth—aware that just a week ago, I'd touched her, *tasted* her—but content with the silence, neither of us spoke.

Esmeralda didn't flinch or pull away, not even when I accidentally reopened one of the scabs. If anything, she melted into my touch, allowing me to take my time and placing her trust in me completely. When I was done, she pulled back, looking at me with the same expression from earlier, the one that immediately made me melt... and the one that was dangerous. While wearing it, Esmeralda could ask anything of me, anything at all, and I'd do it without hesitation. My heart slammed against my ribcage at the realization. *Lord, what have I gotten myself into?*

"You're good at that," she said, a smirk playing at the corners of her mouth.

"What, wiping faces? You have to be when you raise a son."

She frowned. "Don't dodge the compliment."

"I'm not dodging anything." I stood up quickly, tossing the now-bloodied rag back into the bucket; they could be dealt with later. "I just think it's time I let you rest. I'm going to—"

"If you're about to tell me we aren't sharing this bed, try again." Esmeralda shot me a pointed glare. "Where the hell would you sleep, if not here?"

"My son—"

Her jaw dropped. "You were going to sleep with Quasimodo? Absolutely not. He's what, thirteen?"

"Fifteen," I muttered.

"Even more inappropriate, far more so than us sharing. Now get over here."

I hesitated, the conflict surging within my chest threatening to tear me in half. I should stay away from her. At the very least, I should *want* to stay away from her, to keep as much distance between us as possible... but I didn't. I wanted to hold her, to trail my lips over her skin just as I had that night, to taste and touch her again. But she was right, far more so than she realized given my recent fight with Quasimodo and the fact that he'd outright said he didn't want to see me right now. I had nowhere else to sleep, just as she had nowhere else to go.

Silently praying for my God to forgive me, I climbed into bed with Esmeralda, careful to ensure we weren't touching. We lay side by side, a heavy silence enveloping us as we stared at the firelight casting long, flickering shadows across the ceiling. I wasn't sure how much time passed before Esmeralda propped herself up on one elbow, facing me.

"Why didn't you come tonight?" she asked quietly.

It would have hurt less if she had just driven a knife through my chest. Sighing, I ran a hand through my hair before forcing out, "You know why."

"I don't, actually." Esmeralda slammed back down on her back with an exasperated huff. "It's why I asked. But if you don't want to tell me, all you had to do was say so."

"It's not that, it's just... complicated, all right? As you're about to find out, that's a rather common theme around here."

"I guess that explains where you get it from, then," she muttered, and at that, I sat up.

"I have no idea how much you already know, or what Mercedes

told you about me or this cathedral," I started, meeting Esmeralda's gaze in the dying light of the fire, "but I am an Archdeacon, a member of Notre Dame's clergy. Clergymen are just that: men, or at least they were until me. Women simply don't rise to this position, but somehow, I did, and there are rules by which I must abide. And I do abide... all except one. My vow of celibacy."

She was silent for a good while. "So now every time you look at me, all you see is your failure."

"No! I mean... maybe, but like I said, it's complicated—"

"I get it," Esmeralda cut across me, rolling over until her back was facing me. "Good night."

"No, you don't get it." I placed a hand on her shoulder, daring a weak squeeze. "Do you know why Mercedes apologized so profusely for bringing you in here, why she was looking at me like that? Why she excused herself the moment she saw us holding hands?"

Esmeralda didn't move other than to shake her head slowly.

"Because even though I've lain with every woman in this cathedral who would have me, never once have I let any of them sleep in my bed." She still didn't say anything, so after releasing a heavy sigh, I kept going. "I don't look at you and see my failure. I look at you and see the woman I shared such a deep connection with that I'm terrified of it becoming more... because it quite simply can't. That's why I didn't come tonight."

More maddening silence. Finally, a shudder ran the length of Esmeralda's body; whether it was in response to my touch or something else, I couldn't be certain.

"Claude?" she whispered into the night.

"Yes?"

"Is holding me against any of your rules?"

Of course it was—she shouldn't even *be* here—but I'd admit as much over my dead body. After lying back down, I wrapped an arm around Esmeralda's waist, pulling her tightly against me and entwining my legs with hers. Closing my eyes, I inhaled deeply, letting the scent of her flood my lungs.

"No," I said softly. "It's not against my rules."

VIII. THE CONSEQUENCES

Esmeralda

ing dong. Ding dong.

Over and over, the bell tolled, though I didn't have the faintest idea which hour it was announcing given that I hadn't been keeping count. All I knew was that it was much earlier than I was accustomed to waking, and that every fiber of my being willed me to burrow back beneath the sheets. Bright morning light shone uninhibited through the window, summoning a groan as the singular bell was joined by the entire chorus, the combined might of their chimes rattling me to my core. That wasn't the worst part, though. My chest tightened when I stretched out my arm, finding nothing but empty space next to me, and the final blow sank in.

It was the second night I'd fallen asleep next to Claude, and the second morning I'd woken up alone.

I wasn't surprised. Disappointed, yes, but surprised? Not in the slightest. I wanted to believe it was because of her duties as Archdeacon, and not because I'd scared her off. It was likely a little of both, but the reason wouldn't change the truth: she'd left me.

Again.

But unlike last time, today, there was far more to be concerned about than the person who kept fleeing my bed. As imagery from last night's riot flashed in my mind's eye, so did two faces in particular: Jules and Antoine. Guilt knotted in my chest at the painful reminder that I'd left them behind. Had they made it out all right? Did they know *I* was all right? If they had, they'd probably gone straight to Papa and the council, who in turn would no doubt be searching for me... especially given what happened to Maman.

Oh, God. Icy chills shot down my spine, because I hadn't even considered that—the torment I'd unintentionally inflicted upon Papa by doing what I did, and then up and vanishing. All my efforts to not end up like Maman, and I'd become nothing but a self-fulfilling prophecy, following in her footsteps in the worst way possible. Now that the bells had finally quieted, noise began drifting from the nearby window, and despite my better judgement, I dared a peek outside. It was impossible to make out individual faces or voices from this high up in the cathedral, but the little I could see was undoubtedly unrest. A handful of guards on horseback had barricaded an entire street, while a few others were attempting to herd a small crowd of civilians to God only knew where. Whether or not they were mages was wholly unclear, but we were far past the point of that mattering.

Only when I wrapped my arms around myself did I realize I was trembling, but it wasn't with fear for myself. It was fear that everyone else may face the consequences of my actions before me, that my accidental spark had turned to a blazing inferno that no amount of fire mages could control, that far too many innocent people were going to get caught in the crossfire, including people I'd come to care for far more than I had any right—

Flames erupted along my forearms, causing me to leap to my feet. The sudden coolness of the hardwood floor against my bare skin was thankfully enough to put them out, but not enough to calm my racing thoughts; it seemed I'd need another distraction for that. Forcing myself to shut out at least the noise from outside, I glanced around, taking in my surroundings far more than I had the previous night. I lingered on every detail—the rumpled sheets where I'd fallen asleep with Claude's arms around me, my old, ruined clothes draped over the chair near the fire, and most curiously, the desk positioned next to a rather large shelf of books.

Fixating on the bookshelf, I approached it, in awe of just how many books were there. Though there was a vague order to them, it was clear they were used and read often given the obvious wear on some of the spines. Most of the titles were in Latin, suggesting they were religious texts, but a select few were in French, including *Le Paysan perverti* and *Les Liaisons dangereuses*. My jaw dropped;

Claude had her own personal library, and her collection included erotic novels? I'd have to save that juicy piece of information for later.

Placing my hand on the desk to get a better look, my fingers grazed a folded piece of parchment with a name scribbled on it—mine. I unfolded it slowly, my eyes trailing over what could only be Claude's elegant handwriting:

Esmeralda,

I hope I didn't wake you when I left. There are matters to which I must attend, but Mercedes will bring you breakfast, and I'll be back to check on you by midday. Please, stay in the room and be quiet. People are already whispering. It's not safe.

—Claude

P.S. Burn this once you read it.

P.P.S. Please don't touch anything. I'm particular about my possessions.

It was a good thing she'd told me to, because the second I finished reading it, Claude's note burst into flame. As the ashes peppered onto her desk, fire continued burning from my fingertips, its source the mild irritation her words had sparked. The logical part of me understood why I had to stay put, and I even understood why Claude had needed to leave me alone; it still didn't make the thought of waiting here for hours on end, alone and with nothing to do, any easier to bear.

Extinguishing my flames took effort, but I managed it by gritting my teeth. It did nothing for my frustration, though. That burned hotter than ever as my gaze flickered around the mess that was this room. Most of the clutter was thanks to me and all the problems I'd quite literally dumped on Claude's doorstep the previous night, but that's why I was so annoyed—if the room already looked this bad, how in hell did she expect me to make it any worse?

But I reminded myself that not only was I a guest in her house, I was lucky to be here at all. Claude could have thrown me out last night or even handed me back over to Phoebus. Instead, she was out there risking her own neck to protect me. The least I could do was show my appreciation in whatever way I could.

So for the next twenty minutes, I busied myself by tidying up the room. I folded and smoothed the bed sheets, a thrill running through me at the thought of messing them up again. I moved to the desk next, quickly making note of Claude's organizational system before returning her books to their rightful spots on her shelves. Once that was done, I pulled out some rags from within one of the dressers and thoroughly dusted every surface in sight. The windowsills were first, then the bedside tables, but as I moved toward the fireplace, I halted in my tracks as my gaze swept over the mantle.

Lined in a row were three incredibly realistic wooden figurines, each one carved and painted in the likeness of a different person. To the far left was an older man dressed in what I could only assume was some sort of elaborate religious garb; a high-ranking member of the Church, perhaps? Next was a boy no older than Quasimodo, sporting a lopsided grin and a mop of curly brunette locks.

The last one summoned an audible gasp, because it was such a spitting image of Mercedes it was almost unnerving. Though the figurine was no larger than a child's doll, the attention to detail was nothing short of masterful, especially when it came to all her freckles, perfectly placed as far as I could tell. Her hair texture was so lifelike it almost looked real, and I nearly reached out, wanting to know if that, too, was wood.

But these, I didn't dare touch. Whether Claude had carved them or not didn't matter nearly as much as the fact that they were clearly some of her most prized possessions, and it wasn't as if wood and fire mixed well, anyway. After another minute or so of admiring, I reluctantly tore myself away, turning to the garments occupying the nearby chair: my still-wet clothes as well as Claude's blanket. At first I searched for a way I might hang up the clothes to dry, but then it dawned on me that I ought to burn them. Even if they were salvageable, which I was beginning to doubt given the faint scent of mildew, I couldn't risk being seen in the same outfit I'd worn the night I maimed a captain in public.

I tossed them into the fireplace along with a few fresh logs, issuing a silent apology to Jules—I was fairly certain at least the shirt was theirs. A single snap of my fingers was all the encouragement the flames needed to roar back to life, consuming the clothes in an instant, and I stepped back as the heat seared even my skin.

Turning back to the blanket, I made short work of folding it but then stilled: where had Claude gotten it from? It didn't belong on the bed and wouldn't fit in any of the empty spaces in her wardrobe. That left an unassuming chest at the foot of her bed the only possibility.

I didn't think much of yanking open the lid, but as soon as I glimpsed inside, I gasped. Compared to the rest of her space, which was as 'particular' as she'd mentioned in her note, this chest was the opposite. It was cluttered and disorganized, containing items hastily stuffed inside with no rhyme or reason. A few loose coins here and there, moth-eaten stacks of papers hidden beneath some linen rags, some odd trinkets covered in dust. There was nothing else to call it but a mess.

But then I noticed something tucked away near the bottom: a flash of a very familiar purple. *No... it couldn't be.* Before I could remind myself that I shouldn't go digging through Claude's things, I pulled it out, my mouth agape as a mixture of shock and outrage coursed through me. She'd hidden my scarf with her *junk*?

I recalled the night I'd given it to her in pure, exquisite detail. She was so close to the stage that for the first time, I could touch her; clearly she had no idea how much I'd wanted to. The next best thing was draping my scarf around her neck, pulling our faces close in what had been an invitation to kiss me, but she hadn't—I knew why now, at least. I'd left it with her anyway, the gesture both a premonition and a promise for what was to come. It had been a gift all the same though, meaning Claude could do with it what she wished.

But if this was how she treated a scarf she no longer wanted, what in God's name did she intend to do with me?

I wasn't certain how long I sat perched on the edge of the bed, running the silk through my fingers and biting my lip to keep from bursting into flame. There could be a logical explanation—perhaps Claude simply wasn't as sentimental as I was—or perhaps I truly did mean that little to her, and her words last night had meant nothing. Or worse; what if she'd lied to me? What if she told all the women she took to her bed that they were the first one she'd permitted to sleep there, and Mercedes had stared like that because she'd known it?

Did *that* explain why there was such a gorgeously carved figurine of her on the mantle?

Bolting upright, I marched toward the door. Safety and logic be damned; I needed to get the fuck out of both here and my head and find Claude. If the streets were as bad as I'd seen from the window, surely there weren't guards sent to patrol inside the cathedral—not yet, at least, so it was likely I had time, and if not, I knew how to be sneaky. I demanded an explanation for why my scarf was where it was, for why she'd said—

Just as I was about to yank it open myself, the door swung on its hinges, revealing Mercedes. Her brows immediately shot up, and she shoved roughly against my chest, forcing me back before slamming and locking the door behind us.

"Are you crazy? Someone could have seen…" she started, but her voice trailed off as I lifted my chin to face her. I had no idea what she saw in my expression—guilt? Fear?—but it was enough to make her narrow her gaze. Her eyes darted from me to the scarf clutched in my hand, and finally, to the open trunk and its mess behind me, and she snorted as she pieced it all together. "Claude's going to kill you,"

Mercedes said simply.

"Not if I kill her first," I snapped, and I pushed past Mercedes, determined to get out of here. But she barked a laugh, and the noise was so startling I stopped in my tracks.

"You want to go out *there*? God, if you're serious, you truly do have a death wish." She shook her head, her auburn curls bouncing in my peripheral vision. "The place is absolutely crawling with guards. Phoebus hasn't been here yet, at least not as far as I know, but they're questioning anyone they know or suspect has been to the mages' faire—including Claude."

Chills shot down my spine, and I turned around to face Mercedes fully. "What? How? She always came in disguise—"

"You think that flimsy cloak was enough, or that her and Quasimodo's absence every single Friday wasn't noted? The men who run this cathedral are many things, but they certainly aren't stupid."

Fuck. Mind spinning, I sank into the fireplace chair, and Mercedes sighed.

"I warned you last night this would happen."

I shot her a glare. "If you're trying to help, you aren't."

"I'm trying to be realistic and honest, which is far more than you or Claude seem capable of at the moment. If you want to survive this, you need to be smart. You can't charge off the moment you get a little pissed off. Trust me. I know from experience that never ends well with Claude in particular." While she spoke, Mercedes produced several wrapped parcels from her pockets and handed them to me;

147

I unwrapped them to find a pair of sweet rolls and a small orange.

Nodding my thanks, I devoured one of the rolls, forcing myself to swallow before speaking. "What's the history between you and her, anyway... if you don't mind me asking?" It took effort both to keep my voice nonchalant as well as keep from glancing at her figurine. Despite how this particular interaction was going, I liked Mercedes; while I wasn't keen for that to change, I also wanted to know the full extent of what I might be dealing with, and whether or not I could fully trust her.

Mercedes sighed again, laughing darkly. "It's no secret, so I guess you ought to hear it from me before anyone else tries to tell you whatever version they've heard in rumors."

"Rumors?"

"Oh, yes." She settled on the bed, careful not to disturb my handiwork. "Honestly, I'm surprised you haven't heard them already, even being cooped up in here. Everyone loves to whisper about naughty Mercedes.

"I was a nun, you see. It's how Claude and I met—we both grew up here, spent every waking moment together... and others as well, once we began growing into our sexualities. I suppose you could say we were each other's first loves." She smiled softly. "But we were never in a relationship, not really. We were always incredibly close, and Claude often confided in me, but she was also careful to keep me at arm's length, never really letting me in the way I wished she would. And when she began working her way into and up the ranks of the clergy, that's when I truly became secondary. We drifted apart, and didn't speak for almost three years."

Mercedes's gaze clouded over. "That's when I met Elléa. The moment we discovered we both liked women, we were inseparable, but we were also reckless. I was getting over Claude, and Elléa fell too hard and too fast for me. One thing led to another, and… we were caught together by a priest." She swallowed, glancing down at the floor. "We were shamed and disgraced, of course, and banished from the nunnery. Elléa was ordered to leave Notre Dame. I would have been as well had Claude not vouched for me."

"But didn't you want to go with her?" I blurted out, but immediately regretted it. Bringing a hand to my mouth, I shook my head before adding, "I'm sorr—"

"I assume by 'her,' you mean Elléa," Mercedes cut across me. "And it's all right, truly. Again, it's not as if any of it's a secret. But no, I didn't. I cared for Elléa, yes, and we're still friends. I didn't love her, though, not in the way that…"

Her voice trailed off, but she'd said more than enough for me to infer the rest: *Not in the way that I loved Claude.* My assumption had been correct, then. There was something between Mercedes and Claude, and that something existed whether either of them wanted to acknowledge it or not.

Which begged my own question, one I could no longer keep silent. "Why help me, then? Why risk your own neck for someone you don't even know, and so willingly?"

Mercedes hesitated. "You won't like it."

"I already knew that, and wouldn't have asked if I didn't want to know anyway."

She looked up, locking eyes with me before confessing, "It's not for your sake. It's for Claude. I still owe her for what she did and continues to do for me. I... I love her, and I always will. She doesn't want me to say it, and I'm not sure she even believes it, but it's the truth. I think she loves me, too, in her way, but I'll tell you this much: she's never once looked at me the way she looked at you last night." Mercedes paused, taking a deep breath before continuing, "And even if it's not with me, even if it can't be forever, all I want is to see Claude happy."

I sat in stunned silence, letting Mercedes's words sink in. It was a lot to process—too much, if I was being honest—that middle bit especially.

She's never once looked at me the way she looked at you.

Seeming to realize I was overwhelmed, Mercedes quickly changed the subject, and we exchanged a few more pleasantries as I finished food that had lost all its flavor. I forced a smile where appropriate, doing my best to conceal the fact that, inwardly, I was spiraling, remaining fixated on two questions even after Mercedes left.

Which version of Claude was real: the one who had discarded my scarf like trash, or the one who had held me so tenderly last night?

And more importantly... which did *I* want to be real?

This was never part of the plan. None of my current situation was—I wasn't even supposed to *be* here, let alone trapped and helpless—but none of that felt nearly as dangerous as what was swirling inside me, and I didn't mean my flames. I'd intended for Claude to catch feelings, yes, but only enough to motivate her to want to help. Me, though? I was to remain at a distance, focused solely on what needed to be done, not brought nearly to tears over a damn scarf and a single conversation with her ex. And why did it mean anything? Why did that night have to mean anything? It was just sex; good sex, yes, but it wasn't as if Claude and I had professed our love for one another. Hell, we barely knew one another.

And you don't need to for this to work. You're only going to hurt yourself in the end.

But as the hours passed both fast and agonizingly slowly, the less I believed it, especially when midday came and went with still no sign of Claude and no word from Mercedes. I was left alone and in the dark, quite literally as night fell, and as I paced in front of the fireplace, snapping my fingers to ignite and then extinguish the flames within, part of me began to wonder if Claude intended to return at all.

When the door finally clicked open, the bells had just finished striking eight. I shot up, relieved, but it wasn't her standing at the threshold.

Quasimodo and I stared at one another wide-eyed for a few beats before I offered him a sheepish wave. He didn't respond, leading me to blurt out, "What are you doing here?" just as he echoed the same exact question.

This prompted even more awkward silence, so as he closed

the door, I rose from the bed and approached the desk, locating a pencil and blank sheet of parchment before scribbling out, *I'm waiting for Claude. You?*

He crossed the room to glance over my shoulder, then replied, "I'm looking for her. We were supposed to have dinner together, but that was two hours ago. She never showed."

My gut twisted into knots. I'd assumed Claude had kept herself away from me on purpose, but if Quasimodo was getting the same treatment, perhaps it wasn't that she didn't want to return; it was that she couldn't. *When did you last see her?*

"This morning." His eyes narrowed. "And you—The Embermage—have been here this entire time?"

That's not my name. Call me Esmeralda.

He repeated it slowly, and I smiled with approval when he pronounced it right. "Really, though—how long have you been here?" he pressed.

I dismissed the thought of lying nearly as soon as the notion popped into my head, because not only would doing so be patronizing, Claude could very well have already told Quasimodo the truth. *Since last night.*

At this, his eyes nearly popped out of his head. "Maman went to the faire without me *again?*"

'Again?' Oh, God—had Claude told her son we'd slept together? But I shook my head, writing out a response as quickly as I could. *She didn't go anywhere. I came to her this time.*

"Why, though?" Quasimodo asked slowly. He eyed me up

and down, and I became hyper-aware of the fact that I was dressed in what were clearly his mère's clothes. "I'm assuming it wasn't to teach me."

That certainly answered whether Claude had told him about us. Biting my lip in concentration, I wrote slower this time, not wanting him to misunderstand. *I'm here because I'm in trouble. She agreed to help, but only if I teach you. I said yes.*

"Wait…" He drew a sharp inhale. "It's *you* they're looking for, isn't it? You burned the captain?"

I gestured for him to quiet down, then nodded. *It was an accident, but yes.*

"Really? You have accidents?"

Sometimes. Fire can have a mind of its own.

Quasimodo's face fell. "Mine doesn't seem to have much of anything. I've tried, but I can barely conjure up anything. Even when I—"

He flicked his wrist, but I caught it just in time, squeezing enough to make my point. "Not in here," I said slowly, but though he nodded, he didn't look any less dejected.

An idea formed in my head as I regarded him; hopefully one that could be a compromise for us both. Releasing him, I turned back to the parchment, scribbling out the words as quickly as my reflexes would let me. *Is there somewhere safer we can practice?*

Quasimodo nodded, hope sparkling in his eyes.

Take me there, and we'll have our first lesson. But once the bells strike nine, we'll resume our search for Claude. Deal?

He blurted out his answer nearly before I'd finished the final word. "Deal."

Had I known Quasimodo was going to make me ascend even more stairs, I may well have allowed him to set Claude's room on fire.

But just as my legs felt impossible to lift even once more, we reached blessedly flat ground. Gasping for air, I clung to the nearest section of wall, trying yet failing to hide the fact that my knees were quivering as I fought to catch my breath. Quasimodo either didn't notice or didn't care, for he immediately set to work clearing a space for us, not the least bit winded by our journey. It was difficult to make out our surroundings both in my current state and given the fact that it was nearly pitch dark, so I snapped my fingers to summon a small flame for light… and that's when my jaw dropped.

He'd brought me to the belltower, but had several bells not been so clearly visible, I'm not certain I'd have recognized it as such. Dozens of art pieces occupied much of the space, causing it to resemble much more a studio or workshop than it did anything else. There was both a chaos and vague organization to it, with several of the same types of projects all grouped together to make tool sharing easily accessible, but the projects themselves were in every medium I could possibly think of. Paintings, sculptures, jewelry, and even what looked to be several inventions all sat in various stages of completion, but none caught my eye as much as the carvings.

I'd almost missed them the first time my gaze swept over the humanoid shapes, but that's when I did a double take. Nestled in the far corner was a small bench and table, and upon it rested half a dozen wooden figurines, carved in the same style as those I'd found in Claude's room. Only when I approached to get a closer look did I recognize one fashioned in the likeness of Claude herself: only half-painted, but not only was the detail exceptional, she was gorgeous.

It was all there—those faint freckles, the beauty mark, the hair I constantly wanted to run my hands through, that *smile*—and just like the ones in Claude's room, it took effort not to reach out and take it in my hands. She was dressed in what I could only assume were her Archdeacon robes, and suddenly I could see why she'd chosen this profession; even from looking at a wooden carving, it was clear this life suited her.

But then my gaze flicked to the one beside her, a man by the looks of it. This one had been completely finished, paint and all, yet still had an air of incompleteness about it; perhaps due to the fact that his clothes were baggy and dull, leading me to wonder if his maker planned to repaint him. Though slightly shorter than Claude and with blond hair instead of silvery white, the two bore an uncanny resemblance to one another, almost as if they were—

"Esmeralda?"

I nearly leapt from my skin when Quasimodo said my name. Whirling around, my flame bathed him in light even as he stood at a slight distance, impatiently rocking on his heels. "Are you coming?"

"Did you make these?" I asked, forgetting for a moment that he couldn't hear. It dawned on me the moment the words left my lips, but even as I began fishing for the parchment I'd hastily stuffed into my pocket before leaving Claude's room, Quasimodo shook his head.

"As long as you speak clearly and there's enough light, I can read your lips. And don't feel bad about it—I'm glad at least one useful thing came of the fact that people like to talk about me as if I'm not even there."

Sympathy knotted in my chest at that, but given that I suspected the last thing he wanted me to do was pity him, I didn't dwell on it. "You didn't make these, then?"

"Oh, those?" His gaze followed where I pointed. "Yes, I made them. I made everything here."

"They're stunning—all of it. But who's this, next to Claude?"

"You mean Oncle Jehan?"

Oncle? "Claude has a brother?"

Quasimodo nodded. "He just doesn't come around much. But if you don't mind… Can we begin the lesson? I'll tell you whatever you want to know about anything you want later on, but if we only have until nine—"

"Of course." Heat crept to my cheeks; why was I suddenly so interested in Claude's family, anyway? "Lead the way."

I followed him to the space he'd cleared for us, but as I eyed the wooden rafters not far above our heads, Quasimodo immediately launched into an overexcited series of questions.

"So, what comes first? Fireballs? Blasts? When will I be able to make shapes, like you do as The Embermage? How long will they take me to master? When can I…"

His voice trailed off when he noticed me standing with my arms crossed and brow raised. I gestured for him to sit, and when he did, I settled myself directly in front of him, taking both his hands in mine. "You see those?" I asked, nodding toward the rafters. "We aren't going to be blasting anything when there's a chance of burning something important. Besides, we need to start slow.

"Right now, all I want you to do is feel *my* heat. And don't worry—you won't hurt me if you accidentally summon anything—but don't try to. Just feel. Your fire, like all mages who can conjure an element from thin air, comes from within, from that well deep within your chest. Don't tap into yours just yet, but I'm going to tap into mine. I'm inviting my flames to sit just beneath the surface of my skin. Do you feel them?"

Quasimodo's lips parted in wonder. "I do!"

"Good. Now match your breaths with mine. Every inhale," I said before doing just that, "and exhale," —I breathed out— "in time with me. Fire needs oxygen, just as we do, and you cannot hope to summon it if your breaths are too erratic, whether that be from excitement, fear, or anything else."

I fell silent after that, allowing my chest to rise and fall in a visibly steady rhythm. Quasimodo watched me intently, mimicking my movements perfectly. As his breathing became more and more steady, heat began radiating from his hands, enough to overshadow mine within a minute or so. When he realized as much, he jerked them back, a look of surprise on his face.

"That's your fire beginning to surface," I said with a smile. "Now comes the tricky part: controlling it. You won't be able to do much until you learn how your emotions affect your magic. Fire can be beautiful, yes, but it's destructive if not wielded correctly. It will always respond to emotion, so you must learn to temper yours. To lose control, even for a moment, can be devastating."

Phoebus's rage-filled face flashed in my mind's eye, but I pushed it aside to focus on Quasimodo. "Let's start small," I continued. "Take a deep breath and relax your arms. Picture the flame burning in your chest. Visualize it as a tiny spark at first, then let it grow until it fills your entire being with warmth. Then imagine that warmth travelling through your veins, down your arms, and out into the air around you. Allow it to flow like a river, but not a chaotic one—you are its master, so don't let the power overwhelm you."

Quasimodo's face lit up with newfound understanding, and he nodded eagerly before closing his eyes and taking another deep breath. I watched with delight as a faint orange glow began to flicker from his palms, slowly at first but growing stronger with each inhale. Before long, a healthy flame had flared to life between his hands.

He opened his eyes, a smile of triumph on his face, but before he could say anything, I extinguished the flame with a wave of my own and gestured for him to try again. He scrunched up his forehead in confusion at first, but then nodded determinedly and began the process anew. We continued like this until he was able to summon and extinguish the flame at will without any help from me.

"Well done, that's excellent!" I praised, beaming with pride after he'd managed it three times in a row. "But remember, just because you've learned the basics of control doesn't mean you should go showing off to anyone you like. Remember, it's dangerous to— wait. I hear voices."

As I stood and turned, Quasimodo rose to his feet behind me. "Those will be the other bellringers. It's nearly nine."

"It is, isn't it?" I said once I faced him again. "That went by quickly."

He smiled. "It did."

"But now, we really need to go find Claude. Will you help me?"

"Of course. If she's not in her room, there are several other places we could look."

"Excellent. But first... I'd like to propose another deal in exchange for our next lesson."

Quasimodo's face lit up. "Yes?"

"Our next several lessons, actually. I'll keep teaching you to master your fire, but in exchange, I want you to teach me that language you and Claude speak with your fingers. Deal?"

He nodded vigorously before I'd even finished speaking, making a sign I was certain meant 'deal.'

IX. THE BATH

Claude

"For too long, the mages have been per... Claude. Are you listening?"

I snapped my head up, swallowing the lump in my throat. Of course I'd been listening; despite the familiar dull ache in my lower abdomen currently eating me alive, I'd hung on to our Bishop's every word. "Yes, Father."

Father Laurent's gaze narrowed, and he kept it on me as he continued, "As I was saying, for too long, the mages have been permitted to run wild. To display themselves as entertainment, even to stage elaborate productions, as if their magic is something to be celebrated rather than wielded with anything other than extreme care and caution. The Church has become complaisant, and the mages have become reckless, even bold. And yesterday, our own Captain Phoebus paid the price for that negligence."

As if we hadn't already noticed him lurking in the corner, Father Laurent gestured to the Captain of the Guard, who nodded at the acknowledgement. Even wounded and sporting a heavily bandaged arm, Phoebus somehow still managed to look as arrogant as ever as his eyes swept over us: the entirety of Notre Dame's clergy crammed into Father Laurent's office for what I hoped and prayed would be my final obligation of the day. From the moment I'd reluctantly left Esmeralda's side an hour before dawn until now—nearly nine in the evening—I'd been subjected to nothing but endless meetings, services, and even what could only be described as an interrogation. I had thought I'd be able to slip away to check on Esmeralda and Quasimodo around midday, but it had proven impossible. There were far too many eyes on me, and far too many whispers for me to act with anything other than unquestionable obedience.

But that wasn't the worst part. In the chaos that had ensued since Esmeralda's arrival, I'd completely forgotten that I was due to start my menses today, and I'd been caught by surprise when blood began trailing down my legs during the noon Mass. As if that wasn't humiliating enough, one of the priests tried to follow me when I excused myself to get cleaned up, and the only way I'd been able to get rid of him was by showing him the bloodied rags. The cramps had started soon after. Though I'd certainly experienced far worse, the pain was affecting my already limited ability to concentrate—an excuse I already knew Father Laurent wasn't going to tolerate when he inevitably cornered me once this gathering came to a close… *if* it ever came to a close. Father Laurent had resumed his speech, and upon realizing I'd been lost in my own head, I tuned back in.

"… why I've decided to impose stricter regulations upon the mages and their activities, effective immediately."

I stiffened. A month ago, this announcement wouldn't have given me any pause, but now I had not one but two mages to worry about. What the hell did we plan to subject them to, and how in God's name would I get Quasimodo and Esmeralda out of it?

"The guards have already begun compiling a full list of those touched with magic, both inside and outside the city walls, to be handed in by tomorrow morning. Each mage will then be required to report to the priest to whom they are assigned to declare both their element and the address of their current residence. As for performances involving magic of any kind, they are canceled until further notice."

At Father Laurent's proclamation, shocked murmurs flooded the room. Several of my brethren stood up, correctly asserting that such regulations would do nothing but antagonize further conflict among mages and civilians alike, but Father Laurent held up his hands for silence, waiting for the room to settle before continuing. "I understand your concerns," he said calmly, "but these measures are only temporary and a direct result of yesterday's altercation. Once the woman responsible for maiming Captain Phoebus is found—"

"This is all because of one woman?" I blurted out, and suddenly all eyes were on me. Blanching under the combined weight of both

Father Laurent and Phoebus's stares, I wished more than anything I could sink into the floor, but when I wasn't questioned, I pressed on. "Forgive my impertinence, Father. I only meant to say that she committed a crime, yes, but surely these regulations are too extreme of a reaction. We don't even know if she's still in the city. What about the innocents, those who have been using their magic responsibly? You would punish an entire population for something they didn't do?"

Father Laurent regarded me coolly, his expression inscrutable. "That is just it, Claude—it *wasn't* just her. A riot broke out mere moments after her attack, and many more than Captain Phoebus were injured. Or have you forgotten?"

I shook my head slowly. "No, Father."

"You understand, then. We are simply in search of any and all mages responsible for disturbing the peace, and the moment we find them, there will be no need for these temporary restrictions. What's more, Clopin Derosiers and the rest of the Mages' Council have agreed to cooperate in any way they can... on the condition that mercy is shown to the wrongdoers." Father Laurent's gaze flicked to Phoebus and back again. "A condition to which Captain Phoebus has so graciously agreed."

That hardened look on Phoebus's face looked anything but merciful, but I knew better than to press any more than I already had. "How gracious of him, indeed. Thank you for explaining, Father."

He moved on before I'd even finished, clapping expectantly. "Does anyone else have any objections?" Father Laurent asked, scanning the room a second time.

It went silent and still; either his reasoning truly had been enough to quell any doubts or no one else one was willing to dissent. Tension hung heavily in the air as everyone stood motionless, our gazes trained on Father Laurent, until finally, blessedly, he spread his hands and bowed his head.

"Let us pray."

I went through the motions, mumbling the Lord's prayer and making the sign of the cross where appropriate before all but bolting from my chair. My head was spinning, my insides throbbing, and I needed to warn Quasimodo and Esmeralda of what had transpired—possibly even Jehan. My brother wasn't a mage, but he'd no doubt be affected by these regulations too. We needed to make a plan, to prepare, to—

"A word—Claude, is it?"

I froze and bit my lip—that was Phoebus's voice—but didn't turn around. "It's Archdeacon Frollo."

"Ah. Forgive me, Archdeacon. I wasn't quite certain how to refer to someone of your…"

"My what, Monsieur?" I asked, turning around when his voice trailed off.

Phoebus cocked his head. "You are a woman, are you not?"

I bit my lip again, this time tasting blood. What the hell did it matter what I was or wasn't? Something else flared to life within me, something brutish and feral, but I forced myself to swallow it as I said, "Can it wait until the morning, Monsieur? I've had a rather long day."

"This will only take a moment."

Though every fiber of my being wanted to flee, I had no choice but to remain in place as my brethren filed out around me. Father Laurent alone lingered for a minute or so, gathering his things before heading toward the exit at a leisurely pace. "Kindly close the door once you're finished. Bonne nuit," he said cheerfully, and then Phoebus and I were alone.

The captain didn't speak right away, regarding me with an unreadable expression. On any other night, I would have proceeded with extreme caution given his reputation, but not only had every ounce of my restraint been spent hours ago, I remained on edge from his 'woman' remark. "What do you want?" I snapped, gripping a nearby chair for support as my abdomen cramped yet again. *Lord, give me strength.* "My son is waiting for me."

Something flashed on Phoebus's face, but it was gone a moment later. "The hunchbacked bellringer?"

"His name is Quasimodo." My grip tightened on the chair.

"That's it. Father Laurent was just telling me about him some hours ago and mentioned that you adopted the boy as an infant after he was abandoned as a foundling. Is that true?"

"Yes," I said slowly, not at all liking where this was going. "But why are we talking about my son?"

Phoebus ignored that. "Would you say, then, that you have a certain fondness for strays?"

"My *son* is not a st—"

"So much so, that you found yourself attracted to the mages' street faire? The one where The Embermage regularly performs?"

My heart skipped a beat, but I managed to keep my expression impassive once I reminded myself that this was information everyone already knew. I still wasn't certain who had discovered the nature of my Friday night ventures, let alone spread it all over the entire cathedral, but it hardly mattered now. Lifting my chin, my tone was icy as I said, "We visited the faire often, yes, for my son's amusement alone. He doesn't get out of the cathedral much. Just as I told your guard who questioned me this morning. I believe his name was Jacques? I'm more than certain he will tell you anything you wish to know."

Phoebus didn't relent. "And did you ever meet The Embermage? Talk to her?"

"What does that have to do with anything?"

"Answer the question."

"Am I under arrest, Captain?"

His brow furrowed. "No."

"Am I being formally detained?"

"No, but—"

"Then I absolutely will not answer the question," I snapped, taking a step toward him. I'm not sure what Phoebus saw in my face—or perhaps it was my height that did it—but it surprised him enough that he stumbled back at my advance. "The hour is late, I am exhausted, and there are matters to which I must attend. Bonne nuit, Monsieur, and safe travels home."

Heart slamming against my ribcage, I spun on my heel and headed for the door. As agitated as I still was, there was now a damn-near paralyzing fear to add to the list. Phoebus's questions had been so specific, so pointed, it was almost as if he—

"You were seen, you know."

I froze with my hand on the doorknob.

A dark chuckle. "Oh, yes. Did you really think that flimsy hood was enough to conceal you?"

They'd seen… what, exactly? I remained rooted in place as my mind raced, trying to think of a way to respond that wouldn't give anything else away. For all I knew, it could be an empty threat; after all, if Phoebus knew the whole truth, he'd have already carted me off to jail, or worse. "As I already told Jacques this morning," I reiterated, my voice low and hoarse, "the hood was because I knew how it might look should we be spotted there. In hindsight, I agree it was a poor decision."

"Perhaps I should have specified. You were seen—with *her*."

As he spoke, Phoebus stalked closer. A few more steps and he'd be upon me, but all I could think about, all I could see, was Esmeralda's face. I should go to her, should flee, should do something other than stand here helplessly, but I couldn't even bring myself to draw a breath until he came to an abrupt halt an arm's length away.

"Is that… blood?"

Glancing over my shoulder, it dawned on me that Phoebus was staring at the back of my robe, and if he was seeing blood, it meant that I'd bled through my robe. Again.

But despite the embarrassment eating me alive, and as much as I loathed my body for what it was putting me through, there was one massive benefit: I now had a more-than-convenient excuse to get the hell out of here. "If you were wondering what's between my legs, Monsieur," I hissed, yanking open the door, "there you have it."

If Phoebus replied, I couldn't hear it over the blood roaring in my ears. I ran as fast as my quivering legs would carry me down the hall and around the corner, refusing to slow even when I nearly collided with one of the maids on the night shift. Mumbling an apology, I kept going, only vaguely aware of the bells tolling nine. *Nine.* I should be laying down to sleep by now, not sprinting through the cathedral in bloodied robes fighting off a panic attack. But I couldn't go upstairs—I couldn't risk Phoebus following me only to barge into my room and discover that I was harboring Esmeralda— so I headed downstairs, taking the steps two at a time as I made for what was Notre Dame's most pleasurable secret.

The bathhouses.

Though I'd lived and worked in the cathedral most of my life, I hadn't been aware of their existence until I'd stumbled upon them by accident in my teenage years. No one save for the crypt keeper ever came down here willingly, so I'd been told, but as I quickly discovered, the lowest floor housed far more than the dead. Before Notre Dame existed in Paris, the Romans called our city home, and one of their many contributions was a series of interconnected public baths. Only a handful of such structures existed today, but the cathedral had been built on top of what were once ruins, now restored and open for use by those who were lucky enough to know of them.

I couldn't remember the last time I'd come down here, but my body knew the way. Navigating the dimly lit halls more by touch than sight, it wasn't long before I reached my destination, and I began to strip even before my eyes had adjusted. Someone else had visited earlier—that much was clear from the discarded towels and the fact that there was any light down here at all—but they were long gone by now, meaning I had the ample space completely to myself.

Steam enveloped me as I removed my robe and outer garments, leaving behind a trail of clothing as I approached the edge of the pool. Unwrapping my bindings took time and care, both because my breasts were sensitive given my menses and because I'd worn the wrappings too long, but even once they were tossed aside, I crossed my arms over my chest.

You are a woman, are you not?

Phoebus's words twisted like a knife in my gut as I stepped into the pool, hissing through my teeth when the water was warmer than I'd expected. I didn't uncross my arms until I was submerged up to my collarbone, but even that didn't lessen the discomfort I always felt when forced to acknowledge the parts of my body that had always deeply unsettled me—the parts which, according to the rules by which I lived and served, made me a woman. Tilting my head back, I tried to relax, but it wasn't only Phoebus's words echoing in my mind now; it was anyone who had ever weaponized gender against me, and the list was never ending.

Untangling what it all meant had taken me a lifetime, and I still didn't have an explanation that made any logical sense. I had known for a while now that I didn't bind my breasts, cut my hair, and intentionally deepen my voice solely to fit in with the male members of the clergy, but I also didn't fully understand why I felt compelled to go to such lengths. It wasn't shame or even resentment I felt toward womanhood; one of the aspects with which I resonated deeply was motherhood, despite Quasimodo being my son through adoption and not through birth. I held a profound respect for all the women I'd known and bedded, was attracted to their confidence and security in who they were, but proximity to them only highlighted how different I truly was. The disconnect that existed within me simply wasn't there for other women, and as much as I didn't want to admit it, it could only mean one thing.

I wasn't a woman, not fully, and not truly... but neither was I a man.

Clenching my fists as I inhaled, I relaxed them when I exhaled, repeating the process until my breathing slowed. Heat seeped into my bones as I remained fixated on my previous thought, examining it more deeply than I ever had before. God created man and woman in His image: each complements of the other, with neither intended to be inferior or superior. Several of my brethren would undoubtedly argue with me on the latter point, given that Eve came from Adam's rib, but I had my own argument: the reason Eve could be conjured from Adam at all was because they were both, quite simply, people. And in all my life, I'd never witnessed a scenario in which all of humanity could be reduced to one of two things. So by that logic, what if there was something in between man and woman, or many somethings? Infinite genders, infinite ways in which it could be expressed, and infinite ways in which man and woman could be interpreted?

Or perhaps it was wishful thinking, and this was all blasphemy. Perhaps God hadn't created anyone like me because He didn't approve of it. Perhaps—

"Claude?"

My head snapped up as the familiar voice echoed along the walls. Esmeralda, but it couldn't be; how had she of all people found me here? And what the hell was she doing out of my room, especially with Phoebus lurking about? I clenched my jaw, briefly debating whether or not I should answer, but I barked one after an awkward pause. "Are you alone?"

"I am now. Quasimodo led me here but says he's not allowed to come any farther."

"He's not." I sat up as much as I could while still keeping my body submerged. "Tell him to go back upstairs, but for God's sake, *you* get down here before anyone sees you."

Silence, but after a few moments, Esmeralda's voice came again. "I don't know where you are, exactly. Can you talk me through it?"

I bit my tongue to keep from cursing. What if someone heard us? It wasn't as though we had any other choice, but without clean clothes to change into, I couldn't go to her, and if I sent her away, I could be sending her straight into the clutches of Phoebus. "All right." Swallowing hard, I closed my eyes and did my best to map out Esmeralda's route in my head. "Listen carefully, please—I don't want you to end up in the crypt. And watch your step, because there isn't much light down here. When you reach the bottom of the stairs, turn right, keep your hand on the wall, and follow it until you see an arch."

I didn't hear anything, footsteps or otherwise, until she'd, presumably, reached the destination I specified.

"Got it," came her reply, much closer this time.

"Good." Ignoring how nice it felt to praise her, I continued, "Now keep going straight until you pass two more arches on either side. Look out for a small opening in the wall on your left. It's easy to miss."

Esmeralda's steps were light—a dancer's footsteps—but quickened as she drew ever closer. The torches had dimmed to the point where I could no longer see the entrance through which I knew she would appear, especially given the steam, but as she stepped into the room, her silhouette was illuminated by the plume of fire dancing in her palm. Her eyes widened as she took in the sight of me, and with a flick of her wrist, she extinguished her flame. She was still wearing the clothes I'd given her last night, and in her free hand she clutched something I couldn't quite make out in the darkness. We regarded one another in tense silence, with her stony expression and pursed lips more than enough to inform me she was angry... perhaps even furious. Her gaze traveled slowly around the chamber before coming to rest on me again.

"So," Esmeralda began, a hint of irritation buried in her tone, "are you going to tell me what you're doing down here, or do I have to ask?"

"Are you going to tell me what *you're* doing down here?" I fired back, my voice a low growl. "There are guards absolutely ev—"

"You told me you'd be back by midday. You lied."

I sighed, running a hand through my hair. "I didn't lie, at least not intentionally. Today was—"

"That's your tactic?" Esmeralda threw up her hands, cutting me off. "Excuses before an apology?"

"You didn't even let me finish my sentence!"

"Finish it, then." She crossed her arms and raised her chin in a clear challenge. "But if you have an explanation, it better be a damn good one."

Outrage flickered to life within me; what in God's name did she think I'd been doing all day? I looked up, meeting her gaze and wishing more than anything that I could stand, but I settled for crossing the pool and balancing both arms on its edge. "Let me get this straight," I said, fighting to keep my voice even. "I've spent nearly fifteen hours dodging questions, making excuses, and *actually* lying wherever it was necessary. Yet you're angry with me for leaving you alone a little too long?"

"I'm angry with you for making a promise you didn't keep, among other things."

"What did you think this was going to be, Esmeralda?" Though I remained angry, hints of helplessness crept in. "Did you think it would be easy? That this wouldn't be complicated or dangerous? That I'd be there to hold you every single time you got lonely or scared?"

She flinched at that, prompting my own gut to twist into knots.

"I thought you at least *wanted* to hold me."

I do, I nearly blurted out. *More than anything, I do.* But I just held her stare, forcing myself to utter the truth. "I have to think of my son."

"That's not what you said last night."

"Yes, well, I wasn't thinking clearly last night, and neither were you," I snapped, harsher than I meant but I couldn't take it back. "Mercedes was right. It isn't safe for you here. You need to get out while you still can. I can show you the—"

"Mercedes was right about a lot of things, apparently." Flames began to flicker along Esmeralda's forearms. "You do push people away."

"For good reason! Do you realize the danger you're in? Do you even care?"

"Do you realize you're still making excuses?"

"Why *are* you here?" Defeated, I hung my head, breathing hard though I hadn't moved. "Why flee here, of all places—to Notre Dame? To me?"

I hadn't meant to add the last part, but Esmeralda didn't seem the least bit surprised by it. "I think you know why," she said quietly.

Oh, no… this couldn't be happening. I'd done my best to ignore my feelings, to bury them as deeply as my lust, but Esmeralda's words made it impossible; what I felt for her went far beyond the physical. What we had wasn't allyship or even friendship, and I longed to protect her as if she was family.

But I already had a family—my son and brother—and Quasimodo and Jehan needed to come above all else. So instead of acknowledging

Esmeralda's words, I confessed, "Someone saw us. I don't know who or what they saw, exactly, but Phoebus told me himself."

Esmeralda visibly stiffened. "He's here?"

"If that surprises you, you really haven't been listening." My anger flared back to life in an instant. "But now perhaps you'll listen to me: you need to get out. I can't help you beyond these walls, but you're The Embermage. Surely you have friends, people who can—"

"I have you. And I want…" She hesitated. "Claude, I want you. Maybe that makes me an idiot. Maybe that means I have a death wish. But I think you have one too, and I think it was born the moment I gave you this."

Esmeralda held out her hand, revealing her scarf. It was more wrinkled and ragged than I'd ever seen it and was coated in a thin layer of dust thanks to being stuffed in my storage chest, but it was nothing a good wash wouldn't fix… hopefully.

"If you can look me in the eye and tell me that you *don't* want me— and you mean it—I'll leave right this second, and I'll never bother you again. But if you can't, or if you lie…" Something in her eyes flashed. "I don't know what I'll do, exactly. But it begins with setting this scarf on fire, especially given how little it clearly means to you."

This was a trap. She knew it, I knew it, and the only question now was whether I'd be able to find a way out. Because Esmeralda knew the truth: I wanted her with every fiber of my being, and that I had since the moment I first saw her. Confessing as much would be easier than breathing, but to do so would mean there could be no turning back, no second glances. This would become real, we would become real, and Lord help me… I didn't deserve it.

I didn't make a sound, but those three damning words hovered between us: *I want you.* My mind screamed it, my body willed it, and I couldn't have warred against myself any longer even if I wanted to. And I didn't. My God, I didn't. I wanted nothing more than Esmeralda, any way she'd have me, even if it killed me. It was impossible to read the emotion in her eyes, but whatever it was summoned a fresh wave of guilt. She claimed to want me, too, but had I been too harsh with her? Too mean? Too myself?

Esmeralda and Mercedes had clearly talked, and whatever Esmeralda had been told was right. I'd never been good at sorting out my feelings and had actively avoided doing so to the point where I no longer remembered how. I alone was to blame—that much was painfully obvious—but for the first time in my life, I wanted to try. Hell, I wanted to do far more than try. I wanted to heal, to be whole. For Esmeralda, yes, but also for the others who loved and needed me: Quasimodo, Jehan, Mercedes.

Most of all, though, I wanted to be whole for myself.

So with a deep, shuddering breath, I said, "In this life, there is nothing I will ever want or need more than you."

X. THE CEMETERY

Esmeralda

I didn't expect her to say it.

I certainly didn't expect her to say it like *that*.

And oh, God, this changed everything. Now that I'd forced us both to admit what was right in plain sight, this had just become messier and more complicated than I had ever intended for it to be. But then again, hadn't that been the running theme to our entire relationship? I had expected a man, for fuck's sake, a man likely to be terrible in bed at that, and what I'd gotten was… Claude. A person unlike anyone I'd ever known for more reasons than she realized. Short tempered yet introspective, intimidating yet gentle, and far more protective of me than I deserved. She still didn't know my original intent had been to use her, and now that we'd crossed this line, I needed to tell her, and soon.

But that was a problem for another day. Right now, my mind and body wanted one thing and one thing only: *her*. More specifically, the touch I'd craved so desperately since that night at the faire. So after tossing the scarf aside and in full view of Claude, I began to strip. Slowly, almost painfully so, I started to undo the laces of the shirt she'd let me borrow, never taking my eyes off her. Her lips parted as she watched me, her expression one of shock, confusion, and something else—something primal—as I let the fabric drop to the floor.

I'd never been shy about my body, and with Claude was certainly no exception. She didn't look away as she had last night, further solidifying what we had both decided: this was real. We were real. And each article of clothing that fell from me and onto the floor was a promise as much as it was a plea. The air between us was thick with anticipation as I strode closer to the edge of the pool, every button undone, every barrier removed, until finally, I stood completely exposed before her, wearing only Maman's necklace.

Claude turned to watch, never taking her eyes off me as I circled the water's edge. I had no doubt the water was hot, searing even, given the sheen of sweat glistening on Claude's exposed skin, but the temperature had little effect on me as I stepped into the pool. Tilting my head back, I closed my eyes and sighed as I felt my flames retreat deeply within me—the only thing that countered them was water—and when I opened them, I found

Claude staring at my necklace, of all things.

"That's b-beautiful," she stammered, redness creeping to her cheeks. "I meant to tell you that night, but we—"

"Wasted time talking, as you are now?" I dared a few steps toward her. "It was my mère's. I haven't taken it off since the day she died."

A shadow crossed Claude's face. "I'm so sorry."

"I'm not here for sympathy, Claude."

She swallowed. "I know. But... there's something you need to know first. Not another excuse, I swear, just an explanation that might help put things into perspective for why I am the way I am. And why we need to take this slow."

I didn't take my eyes off her as I sank to my knees, submerging myself up to my collarbone. "However fast or slow we go makes no difference to me, but I'm listening."

It was several moments before Claude spoke. "You asked what I was doing down here. I was afraid Phoebus might follow me upstairs, which is why I didn't go to you, but there's more to it than just that. He said some things, I've been feeling some things, and all of them came to a head." Lifting a hand from the water, she pointed a trembling finger toward her discarded clothing. "My menses started today. He and several others saw me bleeding."

"So what?" I spoke slowly, not intending to dismiss her, but I was genuinely puzzled as to why that had upset her so. "It's a natural thing, and it's not as if you can help it."

"I know. But the men around me aren't exactly understanding, and... it reminds me that I'm different. That I'm... confused."

I wanted badly to reach for her but didn't dare; at least not yet. "Confused about what?" I asked softly.

"About..." Claude hesitated. "About my gender. I love being Quasimodo's mother, but that's about the only thing that feels right. I don't understand why some days I feel like a woman and other days I don't. Why regardless of what I do or how I dress, something in me just feels so wrong. It's like my body is a cage and no matter what key I try, nothing fits the lock. Nothing except..." Her voice trailed off. "Nothing except you. I've felt this way for years, but you're the first person I've even thought of telling. With you, I feel safe, and I have since you asked me what my pronouns were. No one has ever done that before."

I moved without conscious thought, closing the gap between us. Reaching out, I ran my thumb over her bottom lip then cupped her face in both hands. Claude pressed into my palms, her eyes welling with tears. The moment she shifted her weight forward, silently affirming she was all right with this, I pulled her close and wrapped my arms around her. Claude's body trembled as she clung to me for dear life, and I rested my chin on her head while I gently grazed my fingers along her upper back.

"Thank you for trusting me," I whispered, though I wasn't fully certain she could hear me. "You can tell me anything, and I mean it. When I said I wanted you, I meant *you*, and that includes whatever your gender is or isn't."

She scoffed against my throat but didn't let me go. "My God. I truly don't deserve you."

The last thing I wanted to do was ruin the moment, so I didn't move but couldn't help but tense. "What's that supposed to mean?"

Claude pulled away to look me in the eye. "I'm not a good person, Esmeralda. You've seen glimpses of it, my anger, but it's far worse than you know. It haunts me, eats me alive even more than my lust—which, trust me, is bad enough on its own, but this is worse. It's a monster of my own making, a manifestation of the torment I've put myself through, and was intended as a punishment for me and me alone."

My chest tightened at that. All this talk of Claude's deepest and darkest secrets, but she had yet to know mine... so if there was anyone who deserved punishment, it was me.

"It's taken me all this time to realize I wasn't the only one I was hurting, but I won't have that with you. You deserve—"

"Fuck what I deserve," I cut across her. Lifting my chin, I gripped Claude's forearms tighter, digging my nails into her skin until she flinched. "What if I want you to hurt me?"

I was no stranger to games such as these—I'd played similar ones with other lovers before—and judging from the way Claude's lips parted, she had, too.

"You don't mean that," she said, a clear warning in her tone.

"I very much do."

"But I could—"

"What, hurt me?" I barked out a laugh. "That's the entire point. I want you to. I'm telling you that you can... if you want to, that is."

"I like being a little rough," Claude admitted, though she still eyed me warily. "But is it even possible for us? You know, with your… magic. Seems to have a mind of its own."

"Not in water, it doesn't. The flames go dormant, and I can't summon them even when I try." To demonstrate, I raised a hand and flicked my wrist, succeeding only in scattering droplets across Claude's exposed skin. "It's called a pacifier. All mages have one, depending on their element. Water does this to all fire mages. But I know that wasn't what you meant. What happened to Phoebus was the first and only time I've ever accidentally burned anyone, which is far more than most other fire mages are able to say. Water or not, I promise I'd never lose control like that with you."

Claude nodded before I finished speaking. "I know *you* wouldn't, and I trust you. I just… wondered if there was a possibility of your flames seeing me for what I am."

"And what is that?"

She swallowed. "A monster."

Sighing, I leaned in, tightening my grip on Claude's arms. I didn't speak until my lips were close enough to graze her earlobe, and only then did I whisper, "But what kind of monster has prey that's willing?"

My words turned to a yelp of surprise when Claude's hands moved from my back to my hips, spinning me around before I could even think about putting up a fight. She walked us forward then, my back pressed against her chest, and didn't stop until we reached the edge of the pool. I cried out again when she shoved my front half forward, effectively bending me over, and before I'd recovered from the sudden coolness of stone against my breasts and stomach, she secured my wrists behind my back. After transferring them to a single hand, she gathered my hair with the other, pulling my head up at a punishing angle.

Leaning over me, fully and completely rendering me immobile, Claude chuckled before murmuring, "Comfortable?"

No, but I certainly was aroused. The slight twinge of discomfort combined with her breasts pressed against my back had my hips moving of their own accord, seeking what I knew she could give me. I had no doubt Claude felt my body's betrayal, but in keeping with our game, my only response was, "You ass."

"Maybe, but yours sure feels nice." She tightened her grip on my hair, causing me to hiss as involuntary tears of pain trailed down my cheeks. "Pick a safe word."

I didn't have to ponder very long. "Ember."

"Ember," she echoed, chuckling again. "And what happens when you say it?"

"You stop."

"That's right—everything stops, right then and there. Do you have any hard limits, boundaries I can't cross under any circumstances?" While she spoke, she loosened her hold on my hair but didn't release it completely.

"None that I know of," I admitted honestly. "I've done this sort of thing before and liked everything my partner tried with me then."

"Which was?"

"Slapping, spanking, some light choking… oh, and biting. I

liked seeing the marks they left on me, and the pain was nice, too."

Claude drew an audible inhale. "Jesus, Esmeralda… it's as if you were made for me."

Maybe I was, I nearly said, but not wanting to scare her away, I bit my tongue. "Any of that is more than fine. I'll use the safe word if it gets to be too much."

"And how do you feel about this, about restraint? Me holding you down, or otherwise rendering you incapable of movement?" She began playing with my hair again, pulling and releasing over and over again as if to further test me and my boundaries.

"It's something I haven't experimented much with quite yet, but so far, I like it very much," I managed, but barely; it was getting difficult to focus on anything but the throbbing between my thighs.

"What about the things we did last time? Any limits there, or that you'd like to happen differently?"

I shuddered at the memory. "N-no. No limits, nothing different. I wouldn't mind an exact replica of that night, to be honest."

"That can be arranged," Claude murmured, a smile in her tone. "But we'll have to do it another time. I've got plenty of ideas for right now. We probably need to also decide on a nonverbal safe signal if you're for some reason incapable of speaking… but let's start here for now."

Before I could ask what she had in mind, Claude pulled my head slightly to the side and began running her lips and tongue along the nape of my exposed neck. The stinging in my scalp immediately melted away, and I gasped, my body trembling and craving more.

Her hand moved then, releasing my hair entirely and following the same path her mouth had taken until she reached my shoulders.

After skipping over my still-immobilized wrists, she continued her sensuous journey down my back and over my sides, occasionally squeezing hard enough to summon a moan that was equal parts pain and pleasure. Warmth began to spread from my core with each tantalizing touch, but she never stepped over the line into outright pleasure. Instead, Claude kept up her slow exploration until I was practically howling with need, each brush of her fingertips leaving me desperate for more.

"Quiet, Esmeralda," she warned. "We can't have anyone hearing us."

I groaned softly. "Please, it would be easier if you just—"

"Are you giving me an order?"

She didn't give me time to answer before bringing her hand down on my ass, striking hard enough to make my entire body jolt. It hurt, especially given the way she still had me bent over the edge of the pool, but immediately after the sting came a tantalizing pleasure, one that had my toes curling.

"Who's in charge here?" Claude demanded.

"You are."

"That's right. To make sure you don't forget, I'm going to hit you four more times, and not only are you going to keep quiet like I said, you're also going to count them. Do you understand?"

I nodded, gasping, "One."

"Good girl."

The second strike was just as intense, and I sucked in a sharp breath. "Two," I said through gritted teeth, barely registering the third. The fourth stung more than the first three combined, and I squirmed against Claude's grip as both pain and pleasure radiated through my body. "Four," I bit out, blinking through the tears her spanks had summoned.

The fifth and last felt almost too much to handle; my hyper-sensitive body didn't know what to make of it. I bit my tongue to keep from crying out, uttering a string of unintelligible obscenities instead, but when the agony melted away, all that remained was sheer bliss. I gasped for air as wave after wave of sensation ran through me before finally settling down into an intense pleasure so deep it left me trembling from head to toe. It wasn't an orgasm, but it certainly left me close.

"Five," I whispered at last.

Claude leaned over me, covering my body with hers once more but being careful to avoid my sore and throbbing ass. "Good girl," she praised, pulling the hair away from my face before running her hand along my back, her touch as reassuring as it was soothing. "You were perfect, beautiful. How do you feel?"

I smiled as another shudder ran through me. "Incredibly sensitive."

"The good kind of sensitive?"

"The best kind of sensitive." I wiggled my hips again, grinding against her groin. "Please, Claude. You got me close, I just need to be pushed over the edge."

My words—or perhaps my movements—summoned a moan from her this time. Wordlessly, she reached behind us while simultaneously forcing her legs between my own. She planted her feet as wide as they would go, effectively spreading me, before running her thumb through my folds. I cursed again, needing far more, and fought against her restraint, but this only made her laugh.

"Desperate, are we?"

"Of course I am," I snapped, though it came out more like a whine. "What are you waiting for?"

"*You.*"

She plunged her thumb inside me the same moment her index and middle finger found my clit. There was no buildup or tenderness; she worked me hard and fast, her fingers as punishing as they were pleasurable. Given how ready I was, how expertly Claude played the instrument that was my body, it didn't take me long at all to reach the climax I'd yearned for. I gasped her name, my body arching against the ground as an overwhelming orgasm finally crashed into me.

The force of it left me panting, my body quivering in its wake. Claude continued pursuing my pleasure, seemingly determined to drag it out for as long as possible, but pulled away once I was no longer clenching around her. At last releasing my wrists, she embraced me tightly, pulling us both back into the warmth of the pool.

It was impossible to say how long she held me. I relaxed into her completely, content to close my eyes and let the water take the edge off my pain and soreness. Claude rested her chin on my head, murmuring more praise at first but after a while began to sing what I could only assume was a hymn, judging from its simplistic melody. Her voice was low and lovely... almost too lovely. I forced my eyes open, reaching up to loop an arm around her neck as I whispered, "Don't put me to sleep—not yet. I haven't told you how well your son did at his first fire lesson tonight."

She tightened her grip on me. "Is that what you two did all day? Played with fire?"

"It's not *playing*, it's magic. And we only practiced for about an hour, right before we came to find you. All I taught him to do was breathe and summon a healthy flame, one he's able to extinguish at will."

Claude made a noise that could have been either a sigh or a huff. "Did Quasimodo enjoy himself, at least?"

"Very much."

"I'd like to watch next time, though."

I fought the urge to twist around in her arms. "Why? Because you're curious, or because you want to tell us to be careful every five seconds?"

"I just worry—"

"You worry far too much. It's not as if he could burn himself, or even me."

Claude hesitated. "I know. It's just... he's growing up so fast. When he speaks, half the time I'm shocked to hear his voice has dropped, which I know is far more my problem than his. I also know he's sick of me babying him. But he's the only family I have. My parents are dead, my brother is gone..." Her voice trailed off. "Quasimodo is all I have. And I couldn't bear to lose him, too."

"Have you told him that?" I asked.

"Not recently."

"You should."

We sat in silence for a few minutes, and though I'd have been content to lie in Claude's arms for the remainder of the night, I yearned for something else even more. "What about you?"

"What do you mean?"

"Don't tell me you're going to let me go another night without pleasuring you."

She laughed. "Just because I didn't orgasm doesn't mean I didn't have as good a time as you."

"No, but I'd like to return the favor if you'll let me." It wasn't lost on me that I still hadn't seen Claude naked. Even now, my back was to her chest. I had told her I was willing to go slow, and meant it, but it didn't quite sit right that she'd given me multiple orgasms while I'd barely touched her. "I promise I know my way around all sorts of bodies."

"I don't doubt that."

"Then what is it?" I kept my voice soft. "We can go at your pace, I swear it. I just want to make you feel as fucking amazing as I feel right now. It's only fair."

"You shouldn't use profanity in God's house." Claude reached up to pinch my nipple, making me jump in surprise. "I can think of far better ways for that mouth to serve."

"Is that so?" My heart skipped a beat; was she actually going to let me touch her?

"Yes—but not tonight. It's nothing against you, Esmeralda, I promise it isn't. I'm just not feeling like receiving for the reasons I told you earlier."

"Because of your menses?"

"Among other things."

"All right," I conceded, guiding Claude's hand as she continued exploring my breasts. "Not tonight, then. But for future reference, a little blood doesn't bother me."

She made a noise against my neck, murmuring between kisses, "I'll keep that in mind."

We stayed in the pool for another hour, and Claude made me come twice more in that time; once in her lap and the other after she bent me over the edge again. By the time we finished, I could barely keep my eyes open, and my legs were so unsteady that she needed to lift me out of the water herself. In an effort to respect her modesty, I didn't look at her again until she was fully dressed, but when I finally glanced over, I found her staring.

I raised an eyebrow as I pulled Claude's borrowed shirt back over my head. "Haven't you seen enough of me for one night?"

"I don't think I'll ever get tired of looking at you, but that's not it."

"Oh?"

"I was thinking... about pronouns," she admitted sheepishly. "She and her are still fine, but do you think you could try and mix in they and them as well? Use them both, interchangeably?"

I nodded before they finished speaking. "Absolutely I can."

"Thank you," Claude said, relief unmistakable in her tone. "It might not be forever. I just want to see how it feels."

"I understand. Just let me know when or if that changes."

They closed the distance between us, pulling me into a tight embrace. "I know I keep saying it, but I really do mean it. You're perfect."

I did my best not to stiffen. "No one is perfect."

"No. But you're perfect to me."

For the entirety of the time it took us to sneak back upstairs until the moment I fell asleep in Claude's arms, I was consumed with a single, paralyzing thought:

If she knew the truth, would she still feel the same?

Another week came and went without serious incident. Though it took a few days for the chaos to calm down, Claude and I soon settled into our own little routine—one I liked more than I cared to admit. Given their duties, she always had to leave me in the early hours of the morning, but our nights more than made up for it. We didn't return to the baths, at least not together, but Claude delivered on her promise to recreate that night at the faire… and much more. Such intense pleasure almost made up for the fact that their room remained my prison, one I was explicitly ordered not to leave under any circumstances, not even for my lessons with Quasimodo.

Almost.

As quickly as I'd settled into life at Notre Dame, I just as quickly became restless. Though my lessons with Quasimodo and visits from

Mercedes marginally helped to curb my boredom, this couldn't go on forever—a fact Mercedes reminded me of daily—and I needed a way to deal with Phoebus and his guards that wouldn't endanger me or anyone else I cared about. So for several days, I observed, tracking and recording Claude's every arrival and departure. It was soon clear that their schedule was predictable, as regular as the tolling of the bells, and the moment I memorized it, I began sneaking out.

Though Notre Dame's security remained as intense as it had since my arrival, thanks to both my own crudely sketched maps and the information both Mercedes and Quasimodo fed me, it wasn't long before I was able to navigate around the major parts of the cathedral and its grounds. I made note of the services, when and how long they occurred, and most importantly, the guards' shifts. There were a handful of close calls, but each time I was able to snap my fingers and ignite candles or torches in the opposite direction to where I was hidden, creating a crude but effective diversion which enabled my escape.

It was risky, foolish, and should Claude find out, I had no doubt they'd be absolutely furious. But I couldn't make a plan if I didn't know what I was dealing with, and I couldn't deal with anything while cooped up in the same room all day, every day. By the following weekend, however, all I had to show for my efforts were scribbled, borderline illegible notes on crumpled scraps of paper, three more people—Claude, Quasimodo, and Mercedes—I was determined to keep safe at any cost, and zero ideas resembling a solution. I didn't know what I had to do, only that I had to do *something*.

So in the early hours of Sunday morning, on Claude's longest day of work, I donned one of her cloaks, swiped a handful of coins, and fled the cathedral entirely, my sights set on a single destination. There may not be anyone I could turn to for help without endangering them further, but perhaps that was my problem: I needed to seek out someone immune to the dangers of this world, someone no longer *of* this world.

I needed to seek out someone dead.

With the number of people arriving at the cathedral to attend its services, it didn't take long to hail a carriage. All I got was a nonchalant grunt from its driver when I requested to be taken to the cemetery. Only once tucked within the safety of the covered coach did I pull out Maman's necklace from beneath my multiple layers of clothing and curl my fist around the pendant. My heart fluttered against my ribcage as we jolted forward; it had been years since I'd visited her resting place. She wouldn't have changed a bit, but in her absence, I'd grown into a completely different person: spiteful, bitter, and vindictive, much like she was before her death. What would she say if she could see me now, if she saw that I had already started down the same path that led to her own demise?

Swallowing, I released the pendant and concealed it again, forcing myself to settle in for the ride. The journey to the cemetery was long and quiet given that there were very few carriages out this early in the morning, and the sky was still mostly dark when we arrived. Only a sliver of pinkish red on the horizon indicated that sunrise wasn't too far off. My heart raced as I stepped out of the carriage, my shoes crunching against the gravel path.

I followed it through the rolling hills of headstones, some of which had been carefully maintained and others so eroded I could barely make out their inscriptions. As I walked, the sunrise illuminated the landscape with vibrant oranges and yellows, the gorgeous hues rivaled only by Notre Dame's stained-glass windows. After a few minutes, I abandoned the path, guided by muscle memory as I weaved through rows upon rows of graves. I rounded a tree and came to a halt as a plain granite slab shimmered in the early morning light: Maman's grave. Even from this distance, I made out the inscription:

> *Carmen Derosiers*
> *Beloved wife and mother*
> *Mage of the Flame*

After swallowing the lump in my throat, I strode toward it, my footsteps as heavy as my heart. I stared at her name for what felt like ages before sinking to my knees, the cloak billowing around me as I fell. Tears streamed down my cheeks as grief overwhelmed me, as did memories; the countless hours she spent teaching me how to safely and responsibly wield my magic, the innumerable nights I crawled into her bed following a nightmare, all those times we were mistaken for sisters once I reached adulthood. Anger soon followed, intermixing with the sadness that had eaten away at me ever since I'd been given the news of her passing. She was my everything, had been stolen from me far too soon, and it wasn't fucking fair.

In response to my volatile emotions, flames flickered along my palms, mirroring the way Maman's magic used to behave on a damn near daily basis. Despite myself, I barked out a laugh; we were so alike it bordered on terrifying. She'd spent her life working to undo the injustices perpetrated by the Church, but the only place it had ever gotten her was an early grave... and now here I was, about to follow in her footsteps.

My entire body quivered as I leaned over her marker, tears falling rhythmically onto the stone. She was my last and only hope. If Maman didn't have a solution, no one would, and I wasn't certain which scared me more: her silence or the loneliness. Though I'd always been independent, I'd never faced a scenario like this, one where asking for help could very well damn those I loved straight to Hell.

"What do I do, Maman?" I whispered through the tears. "How do I fix this?"

She never answered.

XI. THE SQUARE

Claude

Of all things, this morning's Masses had been about love.

Following the reading of the famous 'Love is patient, love is kind' scripture from 1 Corinthians, Father Laurent gave his homily, placing particular importance on the fact that without love, all other virtues are meaningless. "What good is it to live a life of service, of poverty and chastity," he said, "if love isn't the primary force driving you to such acts? What fulfillment do you, or anyone, get from a life which lacks love?"

I clasped my hands tightly, doing my best not to snort as I stood at my place near the altar. It was hypocritical beyond belief for Father Laurent to stand here preaching of love and acceptance when, yet again, he'd placed further restriction on the mages. Not only were they now forced to adhere to a strict curfew, the businesses and shops owned and run by them were under threat as well. Though Notre Dame itself had returned to a semblance of normality, conflict had been brewing in the streets for weeks now, and it was only a matter of time before it all came to a head.

Despite my efforts to pay attention, my mind began to wander, and I couldn't help but reflect on my own feelings on the sermon's subject. Love was something I had always resisted, never giving it a second thought or true consideration. I'd refused to open myself up to anyone who wasn't my son, and even then, there was a wall that existed between us… one of my own construction yet one I found myself unable to tear down. I had always assumed myself incapable of anything more. How could I be when being held at a distance was all I'd ever known?

Perhaps there had been a time when that wasn't true, but if there was, I couldn't remember it. My parents had died when I was eight, forcing me and Jehan to fend for ourselves on the unforgiving streets of Paris for nearly two years. Having long since exhausted all other options, we stumbled into Notre Dame on a dark and stormy night. Starving, cold, and afraid, I'd expected to be turned away just as we had been everywhere else, but once they were certain we weren't mages, we were offered warmth, food, and shelter. A different man back then, Father Laurent had been the first to greet us and would go on to become our surrogate parent for years to come, with a particular fondness for Jehan. While I was turned over to the nuns, my brother became Father Laurent's shadow, first serving as an altar boy before beginning the path toward deaconhood.

Unlike me, though, Jehan never made it into the clergy. I still don't know exactly what happened given that everyone I'd asked had a different version of the story, and Jehan himself refused to tell me anything. All I managed to confirm was that it had involved Father Laurent in some way. When I was seventeen and Jehan was fifteen, he fled Notre Dame and never returned. Though I made multiple attempts to locate him, and had even gone on several sabbaticals for the sole purpose of reconnecting with my brother, I'd only seen him a handful of times in the nearly twenty years since that day. I doubt Jehan even remembered, though; most of those times, he'd been so drunk he could barely stand, let alone form a coherent sentence, which had only worsened the guilt I felt over knowing that however indirectly, I'd failed him.

I only knew one thing for certain: Notre Dame had changed us both, irrevocably and forevermore, and love hadn't shielded either one of us. If anything, it had been to our detriment. Something had happened between Jehan and Father Laurent, a betrayal that had sliced even deeper given the bond between them, while all love had left me was confused. Confused over my gender, sexuality, even my relationship with God. If He created me this way, if He wanted me to love… why was I like this? And perhaps more importantly, why had life up until this point taught me to be like this?

My spiraling thoughts were interrupted by Father Laurent's voice, still preaching about love despite the fact I hadn't been paying attention for what felt like an eternity. His words were suddenly very relevant.

"Love is not possession. It is allowing another person the freedom to be who they truly are and allowing yourself the same."

But if there was a word to describe the hold Esmeralda had over me, it *was* possession. She had consumed my mind, body, and soul, and I was helpless to resist. I had tried, of course, attempted to convince myself that it wasn't love, that I wasn't capable of such an emotion. Yet here I was, wrestling with the overwhelming urge to keep her safe, no matter the personal cost. The mere thought of losing her flooded me with fear, dread, and a loneliness I didn't understand. I'd spent the majority of my life constructing walls around myself—walls that kept anyone from getting too close—yet in a single night, Esmeralda had cracked them, and now, they were close to crumbling. Part of me, the desperate, wounded part, wanted to let her finish what she'd started; the other wanted to rebuild the walls stronger and higher than ever. As much as they'd sheltered me, they were also my sanctuary, and I wasn't certain I was ready to leave it.

As Father Laurent concluded his sermon with a reminder that "true love will set you free," I had to bite my tongue once more.

Love may be patient, and love may be kind, but one thing love wasn't was freedom. The more time I spent with Esmeralda, the more I felt tethered to her, like she was my yoke and my savior all at once.

Once I'd completed my duties at the altar and the bells began to toll, I kept my head down and made my way toward the tower, my mind racing as anxiety dug its roots in deep. What were Esmeralda and I doing? What were we thinking? Even if what I felt for her was love—and it wasn't—it didn't matter. It couldn't. As much as I enjoyed her company and the space she occupied in my bed every night, we simply couldn't keep going on like this. We still didn't have anything resembling a plan to keep her safe, for how she might avoid Phoebus's wrath, and that needed to be our primary focus. Not one another's bodies, and certainly not feelings. But I'd barely taken a few steps when I heard someone calling to me, someone whose voice I hadn't heard in years.

It couldn't be.

Turning around slowly, my gaze came to rest on none other than Jehan. Even from where I stood, I could smell the alcohol on him, but that was far from the only indication of my brother's intoxication. His clothes were torn and disheveled, his wispy blond hair stuck out at odd angles, and he looked as though he hadn't slept in a week. In our childhood, we'd often been mistaken for twins, but in his current state, we looked nothing like the siblings we were. The innocent altar boy who believed in Father Laurent's teachings was long gone. Jehan was hardened now, rough around the edges and missing that sparkle in his eyes, the joy that was so infectious he could light up the entirety of Notre Dame. His gaze pierced through me like daggers as he stumbled closer, mumbling incoherently.

I said his name once and then twice, but my brother didn't stop. Once he reached me, he gripped my shoulders roughly, licking his lips as he repeated over and over, "Barrels of water. Round and round. Barrels of water!"

"Yes, barrels. I understand," I muttered under my breath, looping an arm beneath his elbow to keep him upright. "But quiet down, all right? People are staring."

Jehan either didn't hear me or didn't care, because he kept chanting those same nonsensical phrases like a mantra. His words were surprisingly coherent given his inebriated state, but I had bigger things to worry about, like the fact that Father Laurent had noticed us. I bit back a curse; if there was anyone I needed to keep Jehan away from, it was him. But what the hell was my brother doing here, and why? Every other time he'd cornered me in years past, it had been on a busy street, far away from the cathedral he clearly had no desire to set foot in again. Something must be wrong, seriously wrong at that, and I needed to get us both out of here so I could ask him what it was.

Deciding in that instant that Jehan was far too drunk to remember any of this—and with any luck, Esmeralda—come tomorrow morning, I began dragging him toward the tower, aiming for the stairs. We stumbled up awkwardly, with Jehan's near-constant babbling echoing off the walls. We reached the top, stopping in front of my door just long enough to catch our breath before I shoved it open, but the person who greeted us wasn't Esmeralda.

It was Phoebus.

Flanked by a guard on either side, the captain stood in the center of my room, arms crossed and brow raised as he took in the sight before him. Any other time, the current state of my room would have enraged me; my possessions were strewn across the floor, my desk had been rifled through, and even my closet had been ravaged, and I knew in an instant that Esmeralda wasn't the one responsible. But if she wasn't here, where was she? And if this was what my room looked like, what the hell had Phoebus done to *her*?

I almost didn't hear his words over the blood roaring in my ears. "Who's this, Claude? I don't think I've had the pleasure."

"Barrels of water!" Jehan declared, suddenly becoming very animated as he pointed toward the guards. "Round and—"

"What do you want, Phoebus?" I cut across him, glancing around and shaking my head. "These are my private chambers. Anything you desired, I'd have handed over more than willingly."

He laughed then, the sound sending chills down my spine. "A woman of God, lying to my face. Father Laurent would be ashamed." With a flick of his wrist, he produced Esmeralda's scarf.

I tightened my grip on Jehan and shrugged, fighting to keep my voice nonchalant. "You knew of my visits to the faire. This is just a souvenir I happened to pick up."

"The Embermage's scarf, of all things? And why do you *still* have it?"

"Round and round. Round and round."

"Shut up, Jehan," I hissed, struggling to concentrate through all my worry. "Captain, didn't you already inform me we were 'seen?' So why the interrogation?"

Phoebus cocked his head. "This isn't an interrogation. This is a trial—except you've already been sentenced."

A shiver colder than ice shot down my spine, because somehow, he knew. Perhaps not the full extent of the relationship I had with Esmeralda, but judging by that feral, unhinged gleam in his eye, Phoebus already knew more than enough to damn me—to damn *us*. So what was he waiting for, and why all the theatrics and posturing? And where in God's name was Esmeralda, where was...

"Quasimodo," I bit out. "Where is my son?"

"Seize her," Phoebus said, and before he'd finished the command, his guards were on me. Shoving Jehan aside, they grabbed me by the arms and began dragging me toward the stairs, ignoring my cries of protest.

"What is the meaning of this?" I was taller than both the guards, but they were stronger, and the one on my right threw an unforgiving blow to my gut when I struggled against his grasp. The wind was knocked from my chest, and I began to see stars, but I refused to black out. "You have... You have n-no right..."

A cry from Jehan was enough motivation for me to lift my head. I blinked just in time to see my brother attempt to throw a punch at Phoebus, except in his drunken state, all Jehan managed to do was make himself fall over. "Leave my sister alone," he slurred from the floor, trying and failing to stand back up.

Phoebus curled his lip at Jehan's crumpled form. "Pathetic runs in the family, I see. But lucky for you, I have better things to do than arrest drunken fools today."

"Like arresting innocents?" I spat, knowing full well what was coming next. Sure enough, Phoebus punched me himself this time, his fist connecting with my cheek in a way that only barely missed my nose. Pain exploded across my skull, and the only reason I didn't cry out was because I bit my own tongue.

"Get her out of here," he sneered, flicking his wrist.

I stumbled as we went, trying to keep conscious as much as I tried to keep up with their pace. Even if I could, I doubted it would have kept them from dragging me down the stairs, as they seemed intent on inflicting as much pain as possible. It wasn't long before voices surrounded me, but whether they were real or in my head I couldn't be certain... until Mercedes's cry rose over the fray.

"Claude! What's happening, where are they taking you? Please, Monsieurs, I beg you, don't hurt her!"

Her plea was enough to make me renew my struggles against Phoebus's men, and I screamed for her to find Quasimodo and keep him safe while they still had a chance. I had no idea what was happening, only that my son couldn't be anywhere near it. Though the guards didn't hit me again, my anguished cries were ignored, and my throat was raw by the time they dragged me outside. Blinking in the light of day, my jaw dropped, but not because of the roaring, bordering on violent crowd. A crude sort of stage had been constructed in the middle of the square just outside the cathedral, and on it were three human-sized barrels. Jehan's words echoed in my head then: *Barrels of water, round and round.*

Had my brother been attempting to warn me?

Before I could make sense of any of it, I was released and shoved forward, followed by one of the guards barking, "Keep moving." I knew better than to make a run for it—even if I could, I had nowhere to go— so I stumbled forward, following the directions they gave me without protest. Phoebus led the way, and though he didn't give any verbal or visible commands I could hear or see, the crowd parted for him. But if he was Moses, I was Judas; the crowd yelled and jeered as I passed.

Eventually, we stopped at a stand in the center of the square with a perfect view of the stage. Phoebus pointed to it without looking back and said, "Sit." I complied without hesitation, my heart beating out of my chest as I took in the sight before me, both of the stage and the crowd herded off to either side. I still didn't have the faintest idea what was about to happen, but if I were in any true danger, surely I would be there and not here… right?

And Esmeralda. Dear God, what had become of Esmeralda? Had Phoebus caught her in my room and taken her somewhere before I'd arrived with Jehan? Or had she somehow escaped on her own—and if she had, where was she now? Would she stay hidden, even if something were to happen to me? Would she finally take the hint and flee Paris, as she should have weeks ago?

My spiraling thoughts were interrupted as three shackled and hooded prisoners took the stage, led by Phoebus. The sight of them was enough to make my stomach churn, and I had to resist the urge to look away—because whatever was about to happen, it was clearly my punishment to bear witness. It was impossible to discern any distinguishing features given the prisoners' bindings, and their faces were no longer visible beneath the black fabric pulled over their heads. Despite my best efforts to remain composed and still, I nearly leaped from my seat; was one of them Esmeralda?

The prisoners were each made to stand in front of one of the barrels, and silence descended upon the crowd as Phoebus stepped forward. His voice echoed in the square, both commanding attention and making my skin crawl.

"People of Paris," he began, "we are gathered here today to witness justice being served upon those who have broken the laws of our great city. These three before you are mages, each of whom wielded their magic against another, causing bodily harm and even death." He paused as the crowd began to get riled up and continued only when the jeers quieted down. "They were tried and sentenced this morning. Though I campaigned for mercy, as I promised the Mages' Council I would, unfortunately, the judge did not see it that way."

Phoebus nodded to his men, who removed the hoods from each prisoner's head. I tensed, preparing to leap up should one of them be Esmeralda, but the only one I vaguely recognized was a brown-haired white woman, most likely because I'd glimpsed her at the faire. She stood to the left while her two male companions were at the center and right.

"They have all been sentenced to death: a mage's death."

It was only when the prisoners were shoved toward their respective barrels that I noticed the middle one had a fire lit beneath it. Its contents were boiling hot while, presumably, the other two contained simply water. Drowned and boiled alive—I honestly couldn't think of worse ways to die. Neither could the mages, for they began screaming and fighting, as had the crowd once more. The guards at the front struggled to keep them from pouring onto the stage, and upon noticing, Phoebus gestured for his men to hurry it along.

I should be concerned for the mages I was about to watch die. Hell, I should *do* something, anything. But as chaos unfolded around me, not only was I paralyzed with fear but my mind could only fixate on a single thought:

If Esmeralda wasn't in the cathedral and she wasn't here in the square, then where in the hell was she?

XII. THE FIGHT

Esmeralda

Maman hated flowers, but I picked her some anyway.

The only ones growing nearby were half-wilted pink roses. I pricked myself on thorns more times than I could count while gathering them but finally had a sizable bouquet to leave on her grave. "I'm sorry this is all I have," I said, tracing her name with my fingertips as I settled myself on the bed of grass next to her. "If I could risk going into town, I'd have brought you some of your favorite tarts."

A breeze drifted by, blowing a few stray hairs into my face, and a scoff escaped my lips. "Don't tell me you're surprised to hear that I'm in trouble again. I learned from the best, didn't I?"

Maman fell silent after that—or perhaps she'd never been

talking to me at all. Either way, she at least listened while I poured my heart and soul out to her. I told her of Papa and Jules, particularly how happy my sibling had been lately, mostly thanks to Antoine. I told her of my performances as The Embermage, of how well they'd been going, and how I'd been saving for Papa's future. He had served our community faithfully and still had a good many years left in him, but he wouldn't be young forever, and I wanted him to retire peacefully and without worry.

My time at Notre Dame and how I'd come to be there was next, followed by the relationships I'd been building with both Mercedes and Quasimodo. We may have gotten off to a rough start, but for the past several days, I'd been able to make Mercedes smile and laugh simply by cracking one of my own, and she was noticeably less grumpy every time she came to bring me food or the latest cathedral gossip. Quasimodo's lessons had been going better and better, and we'd moved from conjuring flame to blasting it, much to his delight. In return, he'd been teaching me to sign, and I'd been thoroughly enjoying having a new way to communicate with him.

Lastly, I told Maman of Claude, and I told her everything. From my original intent to seduce and use them, to our first night together, to how I'd fled to her side following my encounter with Phoebus and how Claude had taken care of me that night. I recounted her rules, their sternness... but also her tenderness, protectiveness, and devotion to her son and God.

"And Notre Dame itself... Maman, it's gorgeous, and unlike anything I've ever seen." I sat up straighter as imagery flooded my mind's eye. "The architecture, the stained glass, the view from Claude's window. I can see nearly all of Paris, you know, but I bet I could see even more from the belltower. Quasimodo promised to show me the bells, and he told me their names. The bells have names! Can you believe it?"

Only when tightness in my lungs forced me to take a breath did I realize how fast I'd been talking. My heart rate had accelerated, too, with excitement being the only explanation given that I remained sitting on the ground. I brought a hand to my chest and placed it where I could feel my fluttering pulse; had speaking of Notre Dame done that to me?

Not the cathedral, my inner voice chastised. *Her.*

Claude.

Heat crept to my cheeks the moment my thoughts returned to them, telling me all I needed to know, but I fought the emotions regardless. What in God's name were we doing? Or rather— what was *I* doing? I could have stopped them. I could have told her no. But I'd asked for it, time and time again: their attention, their comfort, their touch… All things which, given enough time, morphed into something else. Something neither of us could afford. Something neither of us wanted.

But… was that true? Glancing at Maman's grave, my chest tightened once again. The day she died was the day I began holding everyone at arm's length and doing everything I could to avoid true connection. It was why I'd poured so much of myself into my performances. The audience's applause was fleeting, something to be appreciated in the moment but never anything that lasted. It was why I had taken so many partners as of late, to avoid getting too close to any one of them. It was especially why I'd distanced myself from Papa even though he'd done his best to cling to me. We'd always been close, but with Maman gone, I pulled away. It wounded him, I knew, but I'd been unable to think of a better way to guard my heart against further agony. Losing one parent had been painful enough… I couldn't bear to lose him, too.

And then there was Jules. No matter how hard I tried to slip away from them, my sibling wouldn't let me, and whether that was enraging or endearing, I still hadn't decided. But if I was honest, it wasn't Jules themselves who bothered me, it was their relationship with Antoine, and what witnessing it forced me to acknowledge. When those two were together, they came alive. They understood one another deeply, often communicating without words, and rarely could be found separate from one another. It was beautiful, but most of all, it was something I envied.

The realization struck as hard as my tears, which streamed down my cheeks as I conceded that, despite my best efforts, I was falling in love with Claude. With her caresses, with how safe I felt in their arms, and most of all, *them.* The time we'd spent together had made me realize that no matter how strong and independent I wanted to be—no matter how much I pushed everyone away—I still wanted someone to catch me when I fell.

And I wanted that someone to be her.

But as much as I was tempted to laugh at the ridiculousness of it all, fear dug its roots in deep. When had this happened, and how had it happened so quickly? A flood of memories rushed through my mind—of the faire, each of our intimate nights together, our long conversations into the morning light, and laughter sharing stories. It may have only been a short time in which I'd truly known her, but in it, Claude had become far more than a means to an end.

A sob escaped my throat as the truth sank in: this wasn't just an infatuation. This was real, as real as my predicament with Phoebus, and now I needed to find a solution for them both.

I stood up then, unsure if coming here had created more problems than it solved, but either way, my time was more than up. It was early afternoon now, and Claude sometimes visited me in the break between services, so I needed to head back before it was too late. Pausing, I took one last look at Maman's grave before turning to leave. I brushed the dirt and grass off my dress, tugged my hood up around my face, and whispered, "Goodbye, Maman."

The carriage ride back into town was uneventful. To keep my thoughts at bay, I alternated between playing with Maman's necklace and the rose I'd saved for Claude, picking off the thorns from the stem so they wouldn't cut themselves, but my mind continued to wander regardless. Was it time to accept that I couldn't face Phoebus alone? That if I truly wanted to protect Claude and Quasimodo I needed to distance myself from them? Or should I confess my feelings, let Claude know that—

I jolted forward then and was nearly thrown from my seat as the carriage came to an abrupt and sudden halt. Muffled shouts sounded from outside, but though I waited and listened, no explanation came from the driver.

"Monsieur?" I said after a while, but no response came. "Monsieur, why have we—"

The carriage door wrenched open, and the white-faced driver extended me his hand. "Pardon, Madame, but you must get out now."

My flames instinctively flickered to life within me. I swallowed to hold them at bay but didn't otherwise move. "Have we reached the city?"

"No, Madame, but that's the problem. I cannot take you any farther."

"And why is that?"

"See for yourself."

Accepting his hand, I stepped from the carriage, blinking in the now-harsh daylight only to see that he was right. While the streets weren't formally blocked by anyone, guards or otherwise, they were so tightly packed with people that there wasn't any way a carriage would be able to make its way through. Even going on foot appeared as though it would be difficult.

But if I had any hope of making it back before Claude realized I was gone, I didn't have a choice, nor a moment to waste, and Notre Dame wasn't far. Nodding to the driver, I assured him he could keep his coin before tucking the rose into my cloak, checking my hood, and heading off, keeping my flames flickering just beneath the surface of my skin. Ever since the new mage restrictions, protests had been brewing in the streets, and it seemed some conflict had finally boiled over. The last thing I needed was to be caught in it, but while I was here, I may as well catch a glimpse of what we may be up against.

I kept to the outskirts and shadows where I could while weaving my way through the tangled mass of bodies, not wanting to draw any unnecessary attention. Though I did my best to eavesdrop for any clues as to what was happening, the closer I drew to Notre Dame, the more chaotic the screams and shouts became, and by the time I reached the square, the noise was deafening. All of it seemed focused on some crude sort of stage that had been erected right in front of Notre Dame, surrounded by guards, and on it stood three people bound in chains. Daring to lift my head, I stood on my tiptoes but shrank back just as quickly, because there he was: Phoebus.

His words were unintelligible given both the distance and the roaring of the crowd; whatever he'd said, they didn't like it. Protests and jeers rose up in equal measure, prompting me to swallow my fear and dare another look. Rising up once more, I fixated instead on his prisoners, two men and a woman. It was difficult to make out any distinguishing features at first, but as my gaze settled on the woman, my heart skipped a beat.

Was that *Isabelle*?

I stepped forward without thinking, abandoning any hope of cover and fully prepared to shove and fight my way to that damn stage. Those shackles must be at least partially forged from akrite— the only metal known to be a universal pacifier among mages— given that Isabelle nor her companions weren't fighting back, and the knowledge only enraged me further. I didn't have any idea what she'd done or why, but I didn't care; how dare Phoebus chain her up like an animal, suppress her magic, make her—

A hand encircled my wrist, yanking me back from the seething mob. I only barely suppressed both my yelp and my flames, though the latter lingered just beneath the surface of my skin, more than ready to defend me if it proved necessary. Whirling around, I prepared to backhand my captor… only to recognize them instead.

My jaw dropped. "Jules?"

They brought a finger to their lips, eyes darting between me and the stage. Despite their warning glance, I couldn't stop myself from speaking, my low whisper drowned out by the crowd. "What are you doing here?"

Jules offered no response. Their hand found mine, tugging me into the shadows of a nearby alleyway. Static danced along my palm, its source Jules's skin, but I forced myself to keep silent until we were well out of both sight and earshot. "Ouch," I hissed through gritted teeth, pulling myself from my sibling's grip before rubbing my twitching hand.

They shook their head, causing their own hood to fall. "I should do far more than shock you. A week. You've been missing for an entire fucking *week*, Es, with no note, no word on where you'd gone or what happened to you. Do you know how worried I've been? How worried Papa has been?"

"I'm sure you're about to tell me."

"Is that what we are? A joke to you?"

A twinge of guilt constricted my insides. "No, but—"

"We thought you were dead." Jules cleared their throat after their voice cracked, and their wounded expression summoned one of my own. "We thought Phoebus had already captured and killed you and was lying as an excuse to place those restrictions on the rest of us. Just like…"

"Just like Maman," I finished in a horrified whisper. I'd considered this the very morning after I'd fled to Notre Dame, but had never done anything to rectify it. "Fuck, Jules, I'm so sor—"

"And I'm sorry to cut you off again, but there isn't time." They took a step forward, lowering their voice even further. "We were mourning you until two days ago. Then I remembered your little friend Claude."

"They aren't exactly little."

Jules ignored that. "I also did a bit of asking around, trying to find out if anyone knew someone with white hair named Claude. Turns out they did… because she's the damn Archdeacon of Notre Dame." Pausing, they gave me a knowing glance before asking, "Did you know this whole time? Is that why you were so fixated on her, so determined to take her to bed?"

Shit, even my sibling had me figured out? Any lingering guilt quickly turned to irritation. How was it that I'd spent weeks crafting a plan only for Jules to unravel it within the span of two days? A far more pressing question clawed at my psyche—*how long before Claude finds out?*—but that was a problem for another time.

There was no use denying it, not when Jules was giving me that particular look. "Have you told anyone?"

"Jesus, that's your first concern?" They threw up their hands before resting one on their forehead. "Have I told anyone what, exactly? That you're fucking a member of the Church, or that you're even here?"

"Any of it. No one can know."

Jules snorted. "Well, Papa does, at least the latter. I told him I was

219

looking for you, and he told me to give you this." They reached into their pocket before handing me a crumpled, yet still folded letter.

I began to open it, then hesitated, suddenly nervous over what might be inside. Not only had I not seen or spoken to Papa in nearly two months, he was likely to view my actions in recent weeks one of two ways: shameful or hurtful. And I honestly wasn't sure which was worse. Turning to Jules, I asked, "Have you read this?"

"No."

With a deep breath and shaking hands, I unfolded the parchment and skimmed the hastily scrawled words. It wasn't signed, but the handwriting was unmistakably Papa's.

Ma chère,

You've kept me in the dark, but I trust it is for good reason. Now I must ask that you place that same trust in me.

There is a mage said to reside in secret at the Palais Garnier, a self-declared Phantom. Locate and inform him that he has been summoned by the council. Others have tried and failed, but if anyone can lure him out of hiding, it is you.

Je t'aime, ma chère. Be smart and safe.

I quickly relayed the information to Jules before setting the letter ablaze. The message had summoned conflicting emotions; on one hand, Papa was clearly trusting me with something he'd deemed incredibly important, but on the other, *why* was it so important? Why did a single mage matter to him so much? And just what were he and the council planning?

"He wants me to track down some phantom who may or may not exist while the people we actually know and love are treated like this?" I gestured to the square as the crowd began to roar and jeer anew. "Isabelle is still out there, we have to do some..."

My voice trailed off as Jules nodded their head in Isabelle's direction, and only then did I dare to peek from the alley. The sight that greeted me wasn't at all what I had expected. Erupting from a large cloud of black smoke, half a dozen masked and hooded figures had descended upon the stage that held the captured mages. Those who were armed took on Phoebus and his men while the rest worked to free the prisoners, guiding them to safety in what was clearly a choreographed and well-planned escape. The spectators erupted into chaos, with many attempting to escape the smoke while the rest seemed happy to follow in the mysterious saviors' footsteps. The rioters roared their approval while the remaining guards scrambled to contain them.

As incredible as all of it was, there was something eerily familiar about the way the masked figures moved; the one heading the charge toward Phoebus in particular. It was impossible to discern any identifying features beneath the disguise, but given his height and build, I could have sworn that was Papa. Had he organized this, then? And if he was fighting back, why the hell didn't he want me at his side? Was the best he could think of to send me off on some—

"Well *that* wasn't part of the plan," came Jules's voice from over my shoulder, interrupting my train of thought.

I frowned. "What do you mean? It looks like it's going well

enough to me."

"But that smoke—it isn't ours."

"Perhaps there was a smoke mage in the crowd?"

"Maybe," Jules said slowly. "But you know how rare smoke mages are."

I snorted. "At least someone is doing something."

"*We* are doing something, Es. The key word being 'we.' Though we each have our own job to do, you don't have to do this alone."

Their words stirred something in me, as did the fact that given the commotion onstage, no one was currently paying any attention to the entrance of Notre Dame. Fully acknowledging this may be my only chance, I tore off, abandoning my sibling in the darkness of the alley.

"Where in God's name are you going?" Jules hissed after me.

I muttered under my breath for my ears alone. "To find Claude."

My heart didn't stop beating out of my chest until I'd slipped inside the cathedral, and my breathing didn't even out until I was halfway up the tower that led to Claude's room. I had no idea what I would find once I reached it, and my mind raced with possibilities; the best-case scenario was that Claude would be there, angry, yes, but unhurt, and the worst...

No. I didn't want to think about the worst.

So for the remainder of the journey up those endless stairs, I worked to convince myself that Claude would be waiting for me and rehearsed my apology for sneaking out. "I'm not sorry for it," I muttered as I fished the now-crumpled cemetery rose from my cloak, "but I am sorry for worrying you."

That was the easy part. The difficult one was deciding whether I was going to tell them about Jules and Papa's request—or if I even planned on obeying it. After what I'd just witnessed—a very public spectacle in which Phoebus had been made a fool yet again at the hands of mages—I had no doubt the restrictions and danger I was in were about to increase tenfold. How in hell did it make any sense to risk my neck, crossing the city to reach the Palais Garnier in search of someone who may not even exist?

And why did it have to be me, of all people? There hadn't been time to memorize the entirety of Papa's note, but one snippet had very much rooted itself in my mind: *If anyone can lure him out of hiding, it is you.* But yet again, why? What experience did I have at convincing anyone of such things, much less finding them? And given that, what was so special about me in particular that made Papa think I'd hold any sway over this Phantom?

The endless barrage of questions my brain kept conjuring up didn't relent, and by the time I reached Claude's room, I was ready to collapse on her bed. I yanked open the door, fully prepared to plead with her to discuss everything later, once I'd had some rest and could better think straight, but though the room was occupied, she wasn't who stood there.

I frowned before taking a step back, noting the absolute mess before I did the trio of inhabitants. It was normal enough to find Mercedes and Quasimodo here, but though there was a vague air of familiarity to him, their companion was a man I didn't immediately recognize. Slumped over in the chair near the fire, his expression was as vacant as his eyes, though the latter was difficult to make out given the strands of scraggly blond hair hanging over his face. It was far from the only unkempt thing about him, though; even from where I stood, the overpowering stench of alcohol all but smacked me in the face. Was *he* who had torn this room apart, or had something else happened?

Before I could ponder it further, Mercedes whirled around, her brows shooting up when she glimpsed me. Behind her, Quasimodo offered a halfhearted wave but didn't move or get up from his seat at his mother's desk.

I opened my mouth to speak but hesitated, because the stranger could be anyone. I instead resorted to sign, recalling enough of what Quasimodo had taught me in the past week to ask, *Who is he?*

Mercedes was the one who answered and signed everything she said aloud so that Quasimodo would be able to follow along. "Claude's brother, Jehan. He's harmless… well, mostly."

I remembered then; Jehan looked familiar because I *had* seen him before, just not in person. Quasimodo's carving of him now rested on Claude's mantle, next to the one of Mercedes. "Where is Claude?"

"She's not with you?"

"I went to the cemetery. I haven't seen her since this mor—"

"He took her. Phoebus." Something flashed in Mercedes's gaze, but it was gone a moment later. "And I assumed it was because he'd already taken you. I thought your time was up and that I wasn't going to see either of you again... Not alive, at least."

Never before had three simple words affected me so much: *He took her.* Sinking to my knees, I braced my hands on either side of me, suddenly struggling to hold myself upright beneath the crushing weight of my worst fears becoming a reality. I'd known this was a possibility from the start, but I'd gotten complacent and careless, and now it had cost Claude their freedom—possibly even her life. Phoebus only had a single reason to want her or anything to do with her, and that reason was me.

Oh, God. What had I done?

"You didn't know." Mercedes stated it like the fact it was rather than pose it as a question. "Were you already gone when they came?"

"I... I must have been," I forced out, suddenly breathless, as if I had sprinted up all those stairs. "I left at first light."

"They came after the second Mass. I missed most of it. Jehan didn't, but he hasn't spoken a word since they dragged her away."

"They *dragged* her?" Flames flickered along my palms as rage overtook my shame; as much as I didn't want to believe it, I supposed it explained the mess. "It was violent, then?"

Mercedes nodded but didn't elaborate, which prompted my imagination to run wild. Even if he'd hurt Claude, I doubted Phoebus would kill her, at least right away, given that they were currently worth far more to him alive—especially if she could lure me out of hiding. But then again, if Phoebus knew I was involved with her for certain, why not simply lie in wait for me here, in an ambush of sorts? Had what went down in the square commanded too much of his attention to see to that? Or did Phoebus have yet to fully connect the dots, and we remained one step ahead?

Icy chills crept up my spine as I struggled to my feet, my mind still racing with questions. I wasn't quite sure what I was about to say when I opened my mouth, but whatever it was slipped from my thoughts the moment Quasimodo spoke for the first time.

"If you're going after Maman," he said with conviction, standing up and stepping forward, "I'm going with you."

I shook my head before he'd finished. "No. Absolutely not."

"Why not? I'm a mage just like you."

Keep your voice down, I signed desperately, but I hadn't learned enough in the past week to continue. "Claude would never forgive me if anything were to happen to you. Hell, I wouldn't be able to forgive myself."

Quasimodo didn't relent. "Isn't this why you've been teaching me? If I have these powers, why shouldn't I use them?"

Jehan finally stirred, his head snapping up. "You're a mage?" he asked Quasimodo, but we ignored him, at least for now; I for one definitely wanted to get to know Jehan better, but we needed to figure out where Claude was first.

"I've been teaching you to control your abilities, not go around hurting people with them! Even if they do have your mère."

"Isn't that what *you're* about to go do?"

"It's comple—"

"No one needs to go after anyone."

Those final words hadn't been spoken by anyone in the room; they had come from behind me, in a voice I had nearly convinced myself I would never hear again. Whirling around, a noise somewhere between a strangled gasp and a sob left my lips, and before Claude could react, I threw my arms around her, nearly knocking her over as I embraced them with all the strength I had left.

But something wasn't right. Not only had Claude gone as rigid as a board, the scent I inhaled on their clothing was strong enough to make me gag. A nauseating mixture of smoke and burning flesh flooded my nostrils, as if she had been in the middle of a fire. I pulled back to get a better look and had to force myself not to wince, because Claude was a mess. Their robes were torn and ruined, her skin was streaked with ash, and her hair was so disheveled that tufts of it stood out in every direction. That was far from the worst part; in addition to several superficial cuts and scrapes, Claude now sported a rather nasty black eye.

I whispered their name, heart rising into my throat as equal parts fear and rage coursed through me anew. "What happened?"

Ignoring me, Claude pushed me away, crossing the room to embrace Quasimodo before turning toward Jehan and doing the same. She saved Mercedes for last, lingering on the hug in a way that only worsened the lump in my throat, but I remained too frozen in shock to even think about interrupting. After exchanging a few quick signs with Quasimodo, Claude at last turned to me.

"Are you hurt?"

I shook my head before flinching at both the harshness in her glare as well as her next words.

"Then why are you still here?"

Surely I hadn't heard them correctly. "Pardon?"

"Get out." Claude turned away as she pulled Quasimodo close. "Take your things, and leave."

"I don't have any things," I shot back, doing my best to ignore the tremble in my voice. "I came here with nothing, remember?"

"All the easier for you to go, then. I need to be with my family."

I remained immobile, still struggling to process what was happening, while Mercedes turned to go. Before she took a full step, however, Claude snatched her arm, shaking their head. "Not you. You're far more family than she is."

Mercedes gasped before snapping a retort of her own, but far too fixated on Claude's words, I didn't hear it.

Far more family than she is.

I balled my hands into fists, digging my fingernails into my palms, but even that sharp pain came nowhere close to the agonizing ache that blossomed in my chest. Claude couldn't be serious... could they? We may have only known each other for a handful of weeks, and I certainly didn't expect her to place me above her family, but surely I meant more to them than being brutally kicked out like this, especially after what had just happened.

The only explanation—but not an excuse—was that this icy cold exterior was just another defense mechanism. I'd already witnessed firsthand the way Claude withdrew into themselves, retreating the moment things started to get a little too serious, and if there was any word to describe what had just happened to her, it was that. She'd been through a trauma, both physically and mentally. I desperately wanted to help and take care of them the same way they'd done for me, but not if they were going to treat me like this.

"If you're trying to hurt me," I bit out, shooting Claude a glare of my own, "it's working."

"I don't give a damn what it is you're feeling, so long as you *get out*—"

"I think it's best *we* leave," Mercedes said. "And don't look at me like that, Claude, you need to talk to her, however much you want to go on pretending you don't want to." Mercedes had already taken Quasimodo by the hand and was shooing Jehan out with the other. "Jehan, come with me. I'll get you some clean clothes."

They shuffled out quickly, clearly put off by the unsettling energy radiating between us, and in less than a minute, Claude and I were alone. I opened my mouth, fully prepared to launch into the tirade that had been building inside me the moment the door clicked shut, but they beat me to it. They didn't yell, though; they didn't even speak in a normal tone.

"Where were you?" they whispered.

"The cemetery," I admitted after a moment's hesitation. "I went to visit my Maman's grave. I brought this back for you."

Claude didn't take or even acknowledge the rose I extended to them. "How long have you been sneaking out?"

"Hang on—you don't get to change the subject. I've said what happened to me, now tell me what the hell happened to you. And if it wasn't Phoebus, give me the name of whatever bastard left that mark on your face."

"I'm fine."

"You do realize I'm the one who said that to you merely a week ago, back when you were so concerned over marks on *my* face. You can't lie to a liar, Claude."

She glowered. "I don't want to talk about it."

"Yes, I've gathered that much," I said with a snort. "But if you don't want to answer anything else, answer this: why? Why this stony façade, especially when I can see right through it?"

This prompted another long silence. After several moments, and without looking at me, they finally whispered, "You knew it would come to this. We both did."

I took a deep, full breath before uttering my reply. "Come to what—you throwing me out without so much as a goodbye?"

"Don't, Esmeralda," she snapped, and that authoritative, borderline aggressive tone was back in an instant. "Let's not make this any harder than it has to be."

"Oh, so you are acknowledging that it's hard? Because from where I stand, you're making it look awfully easy."

"I told you, don't—"

"Don't what?" I demanded, damn near shouting now. "Say the things you're too much of a coward to even acknowledge? Remind you that you do in fact have a heart? Make it so you can no longer run and hide from your feelings?"

Claude shook their head and pleaded for me to stop, but I ignored them.

"I know exactly what you're doing. You're holding me at arm's length, trying to shove me away just like you did that night we spent at the baths. It didn't work then, but keep this shit up, and it might work now. Because I'm tired of this, Claude. I'm tired of watching you be at war with yourself, and I'm even more tired of getting caught in the crossfire. So tell me..." My voice trailed off, and I swallowed before continuing, "Is this what you truly want? For me to leave? Ask again, and I will. But cross that line, and I'm never coming back."

My words were met with a deafening silence, and even more paralyzing fear crept in, this time interlaced with doubt. Had I pushed too hard? Had my words gotten through to her? Or had I just shoved our relationship even closer to the brink of destruction? All I wanted was for them to understand that she didn't have to go through this alone.

I held out my hand and waited. After a few moments of hesitation, Claude glanced up and reached for it, her grip warm and firm. As soon as our fingers touched, their face softened, her lips trembling as they spoke.

"I'm sorry," Claude said quietly, and even that was enough to quell the edges of my fear. "It's just... I'm terrified, Esmeralda. I'm terrified of losing you. An hour ago, I thought I was about to, and even worse—I would have been forced to watch."

Horrified understanding dawned on me then. "You were down in the square?"

"It doesn't matter. And neither does what either of us want…" Their voice trailed off as they took a deep inhale, exhaling with the words they spoke next. "Our time is up. This has to end."

I flinched as if I'd been stabbed, and it certainly felt like I had. There was truth to Claude's words, yes—and the longer I stayed here, the more danger I placed all of us in—but why should the truth override what we wanted, what we felt? Physically, it would be all too easy to walk out that door and never look back, but in my experience, the easy thing was rarely the right thing. Surely we were stronger together, and surely our relationship deserved a chance. Couldn't Claude see that? Wasn't she willing to fight for that?

I met their gaze for the first time since their return. I wasn't entirely certain what I'd expected to find, but it wasn't the icy cold stare I was met with, nor that distant, faraway look in her eyes. They may have come down for a moment, but Claude's walls were back, stronger and higher than ever before.

And I no longer had the energy to climb them.

With more force than I intended, I ripped myself from her grasp, dropped the rose on the floor, gathered my skirts, and marched toward the door. Claude called after me, but whatever they'd said, I didn't make out over the blood roaring in my ears. I crossed the threshold before I lost my conviction, slammed the door, and leaned against it, my chest heaving as though I'd just sprinted a great distance. My thoughts were so chaotic it was difficult to make sense of them, but before I could so much as turn, a shadowed silhouette emerged from the darkness.

I whirled around then, coming face to face with a visibly upset Quasimodo. "Where are you going?" he asked.

My chest tightened to the point it became hard to breathe. Reaching out, I took his hand in mine, giving it a gentle squeeze before pulling away to be able to sign. *I don't know. But I can't stay here any longer.*

"Because of what just happened?"

I could say yes—and it would be a perfectly logical answer—but it would be a lie. *No. Claude and I had a fight.*

"So you're just… leaving?" Quasimodo's voice cracked, and flames erupted along his forearm. "You can't."

Put those away! I hurriedly patted down his arm. *Someone could see you.*

"But this is precisely why I need you to stay. Who else is going to teach me to control this? I'm not ready to do it on my own, and you know it."

Guilt knotted in my chest once again, because Quasimodo was right. He did indeed need a teacher, but that simply couldn't be me. So with one last 'I'm sorry,' I started to walk away, but froze when he spoke again.

"I have somewhere you can hide. Somewhere they won't ever find you."

Despite my better judgment, I turned. *Where?*

He grinned. "The belltower."

XIII. THE CLOAKS

Claude

Clouds of blackened smoke had haunted my dreams ever since the first night I'd spent with Esmeralda, but that was nothing compared to the way they terrorized me now.

Everywhere I went, I smelled that acrid, putrid stench; every time I closed my eyes, endless, rolling voids of it threatened to swallow me whole. I became especially jumpy and avoidant of shadows, and despite the stupidity of it, began keeping a candle burning at night. Light only worked for so long though, and the moment I slipped into unconsciousness, the blackness was back, with no escape until I shot awake, heart pounding and covered in sweat. They were nightmares of the worst kind. An anxious person all my life, I was no stranger to them, but these felt far different. These felt… real.

I supposed it was because they were based on an experience that *was* real, or at least had been that day at the square. Phoebus hadn't released me, not willingly; I'd managed to slip away only when those masked figures created a distraction so they might free the trapped mages. The smoke had erupted from somewhere very near me—perhaps right next to me—but I hadn't bothered to figure out where, not when I became engulfed in it mere moments later. I also hadn't stopped to think about why I was the only one seemingly unaffected by the cloud of black death, and could see and breathe even while everyone else coughed and sputtered blindly around me. I hadn't thought about much of anything until I'd made it back inside Notre Dame, where I immediately fell to my knees to thank my Lord God for sparing me.

But I had far bigger things to worry about than my nightmares and trauma, and his name was Jehan. He'd stayed in the cathedral for the past three days, which was a miracle in and of itself, but hadn't said a word to me in all that time, despite looking very much like he wanted to. I'd tried everything to get him to talk: patience, time, space, and even several attempts at apologies for ever letting him flee Notre Dame in the first place, but if anything, my efforts had only pushed my brother further away. And judging by the look on his face this morning, my time was running out.

So I resorted to desperate measures, just as I knew Jehan would, and cornered him as he was raiding the wine cellars late on Wednesday evening. It took him far too long to notice my presence, but the moment he did, he whirled around, looking every bit the feral cat he'd become in all his years spent on the streets.

I held up my hands in surrender, speaking softly. "You could have asked me for help, you know. I'd have given you anything you wanted."

He curled his lip. "I don't need your help or your money."

You did, once. I only barely bit back the words as the image of my brother as a young, scared boy flashed in my mind's eye. After our parents died, he'd relied on me for everything—food, shelter, protection—and though it had been the most stressful time of my life, at least we'd been together. "So that's it? You're just running off again?"

Jehan continued rifling through the bottles and didn't respond. The easy thing would have been to walk away and leave him to it. The smart thing would be to have patience, to keep calm no matter what insults or jabs he wanted to throw at me—after all, I very much deserved it, and far worse. But not only could I not take the silence anymore, a single, burning question remained unanswered even though I'd asked him no less than a dozen times over the past few days.

"Why did you warn me?"

My words hung in the air for several moments, causing Jehan to still. But just as I became convinced he was going to ignore me again, he rasped out a response in that hoarse voice of his. "Heard the guards saying your name over and over. Mostly that blond one—Phoebus, was it? Why does he want you, anyway?"

"That didn't answer my question," I pointed out, but Jehan ignored me.

"That girl you're with—not Mercedes, the other one—she's

the mage they're looking for, isn't she? And they know you're involved with her?"

I nodded stiffly. "But please, you can't tell anyone—"

He waved his hand, cutting me off. "Save it. I just hope you know what you're doing, and that she's worth it." But then he shot me a glare, silencing me before I could tell him Esmeralda was worth all that and more. "But why did that even cross your mind? If I wanted to betray you, don't you think I would have already?"

"Honestly, you should." I was on the verge of tears, but I swallowed them back, at least for now. "You hate me, and rightfully so."

He turned at that, frowning as he fully faced me. "When did I ever say that?"

I laughed bitterly. "Did you really have to? Your avoidance for the past twenty years communicated it loud and clear."

"Has it really been that long? Feels like it happened just yesterday," he muttered.

"*What* happened, Jehan? I can't help you if I don't know."

I immediately regretted asking, for my brother's walls slammed back up in an instant. His eyes glazed over and he turned away, snatching whatever bottles were in reach as he spoke. "No one can help me, least of all you."

Mind racing, I stood there in stunned silence as Jehan packed his selection into a bag before slinging it over his shoulder. He shoved past me once he was done, but not without meeting my gaze and further twisting the knife. "Stop trying to play the hero, Claude, and stop trying to mother me. You can't save or fix me any more now than you could back then. And if you really want to know, it's this place I hate, not you, but if you don't back the fuck off, I may just change my mind." He paused as something flashed in his gaze, but it was gone a moment later. "Au revoir, Soeur."

And then Jehan was gone, and God only knew when—or if—I'd ever see him again.

Two days later, I was in my office, hunched over my desk and consumed with a singular thought.

I'd been too harsh with her.

It had been five days since Esmeralda had last shared my bed. Though I'd glimpsed her a handful of times and knew she remained somewhere in the cathedral, we hadn't spoken a word to one another ever since she'd stormed from my chambers. It didn't mean I hadn't tried; I'd lost count of how many letters I'd started but never finished, each one an attempt to communicate what I'd failed to tell her face to face… just like I had with Jehan. Even now, half a dozen sheets of parchment lay scattered before me, with each containing a few lines of hastily scrawled rubbish. They were awful, all of them, but surely I could combine bits and pieces from each into something salvageable… right?

"Wrong," I muttered to myself, burying my face in my hands after I tried and failed to do precisely that. "You're no good at this."

"I can agree with that," came a voice from my office's doorway, and I glanced up to see Mercedes leaning against it. A simple white blouse paired with a cobalt blue skirt informed me she must have been off today, as did the basket resting in the crook of her elbow. I couldn't see what was inside, but whatever it was smelled delicious.

I nodded in the basket's direction. "How was the market? Did you see Jehan?"

"Don't change the subject, but no. No sign or word of him." After closing the door, she approached my desk without prompting and snatched two of my miserable attempts at apology letters before I could rip the parchment from her grasp. Her brow furrowed deeper the longer she read, and with a scowl, she flicked her wrist and let them flutter back onto the desk. "My. These *are* terrible."

"Didn't we already establish that?"

"Yes. I just like rubbing it in."

"So you are still angry with me." At least it saved me the trouble of asking.

Mercedes shot me an incredulous glare as she settled herself on my desk—something she knew was against my rules. "And why wouldn't I be? You're being a fucking idiot, far more than usual. Do you really think these letters are the answer?"

I exhaled through my teeth as I fought the urge to scold or shove her. "I don't know what the answer is."

"I do. *Talk* to her."

"That's precisely the problem, in case you haven't noticed. She doesn't want me to."

"If you believe that, you're even more of an idiot than I already thought." Setting the basket down, Mercedes reached up and began braiding her long hair, suggesting we may be here for a while. "Esmeralda has wanted you to go and talk to her since the moment she turned her back on you. Why else do you think she's still here?"

"Because she has a death wish," I muttered again, and Mercedes laughed darkly.

"That would be you, Claude. You're the one who almost died for her."

"And what about you?" Though my door remained closed, I lowered my voice. "You shouldn't be seen with me. It's not safe." Though it wasn't constant, guards had tailed me on and off for the past several days, no doubt reporting my every move to Phoebus.

Mercedes shrugged. "Good thing no one saw me."

"How do you know for certain?"

"Because living in Notre Dame for the past thirty years, half of which I've spent fucking other women, has taught me a thing or two about sneaking around," she shot back, her exaggerated tone mimicking mine. "No matter how terrible you seem to think I am at it."

It was my turn to utter a dark laugh. "I don't 'think.' You were caught!"

"Once. I was caught once, in a moment of weakness." Something flashed in Mercedes's eyes, but it was gone a moment later. "We're getting off topic again. Do you want to hear my advice about what to do with Esmeralda, or don't you?"

I sighed. "Fine. What do you suggest?"

"Honesty, Claude. With yourself and with her. I know you'd rather die than admit it out loud—you quite literally proved as much the other day—but if you have any desire to move this relationship forward, any desire at all, you need to tell her how you feel. It's why Esmeralda is so damn frustrated with you. She's not stupid and can see it as plainly as everyone else can. Pretending any different doesn't make you strong. It makes you a coward."

A heavy silence lingered once Mercedes finished, but not because I disagreed. "Why does it sound as if you're speaking from experience?" I asked after a while, glancing up to meet her gaze.

Her bitterness returned in an instant. "Don't ask questions if you don't want to hear the answers."

The heaviness in my chest sank even deeper, because Esmeralda clearly wasn't the only one I owed an apology. Mercedes had been nothing but loyal and supportive for years on end, willingly molding herself into whatever I'd needed, whenever I'd needed it: a friend, lover, and confidant to name a few. And not only had I been ungrateful, I had been completely insensitive to her feelings all the times it mattered most.

Yet here she sat, risking her life to tell me—rightfully so—what an idiot I was. She'd taken care of Jehan earlier in the week without a word of complaint. And judging from the smell wafting from her basket, I'd be willing to bet she'd brought a few of Quasimodo's favorite sweet buns back from the market. Mercedes was irritated with me for how I'd treated Esmeralda, yes, but what had hurt the most was when I'd called Mercedes family only in the context of hurting and excluding Esmeralda.

It had been wrong, beyond wrong, because Mercedes *was* family.

So after swallowing what little remained of my pride, I rose from my seat, strode around the desk to where she sat, and spread my arms. "Come here." It was an invitation rather than a command. Mercedes was free to refuse me, but I hoped to God she wouldn't.

She visibly stiffened at first, almost like she was unsure whether I truly meant it. But then she slowly melted against me, wrapping her arms around my middle before uttering a noise somewhere between a laugh and a sob. Closing my eyes, I rested my chin on the top of her head, inhaling her comforting scent as I pulled her close. We stayed like that for some time, communicating without words; even still, there were some that needed to be said.

"I'm not entirely certain what I did to deserve someone like you in my life," I whispered, fighting back tears, "but I'm glad you're in it. And I'm deeply sorry for how poorly I've demonstrated that. Words only mean so much, I know, but I promise I'll to make it up to you through action. Whenever and however I can."

Mercedes pulled away then, and that mischievous grin I both loved and loathed was back on her face. "There are several things we could do here and now that would certainly put you back in my good graces... I'm just not certain Esmeralda would approve of them."

I raised an eyebrow. "Don't push me."

"It was a joke, Claude. But this isn't: apologize to Esmeralda like you just did to me, and I can guarantee she'll react the same way I did."

"What—make inappropriate comments?"

"Perhaps. But then it *can* lead to the real thing." Still grinning, Mercedes jumped down from the desk and began smoothing out her skirt. "So what are you waiting for?"

I did a double take. "You want me to go right now? Oh, no. I can only handle one apology like that a day." *More like a week.* "Besides, I don't even know where she's hiding."

"I do. She's—"

"Don't tell me," I cut across her, raising my hand. "I'm being followed, remember? The last thing I want to do is lead the guards straight to her."

"But if you don't know, you might lead them to her unintentionally."

"But if I do know, I'll be too tempted."

Mercedes looked very much like she wanted to argue but didn't press further. "Fine. If you don't want to see Esmeralda, at least go see your son. He's been in the belltower tinkering in his workshop all day, and I'm sure he'd enjoy the company. And take these," she added, handing me her basket. "His favorite sweet buns."

A visit with Quasimodo did sound lovely, especially given that I hadn't seen him yet today, but this gesture felt particularly generous, even for Mercedes's standards. "You're the one who went to the trouble. Don't you want to give them to him yourself?"

"Are you really going to waste precious time arguing when a guard could begin tailing you again at any moment?" Mercedes raised an eyebrow. "The reason none are in here right now is because there was another rebel mage attack on a nearby squadron. They called upon every available man to come assist in apprehending them—saw the whole thing myself when I was out and about. But they could finish at any moment, so if you're going to go, you need to go now."

Something still didn't feel quite right about this, but I could think of no further reason to argue. So after exchanging a quick goodbye with Mercedes, I closed and locked up my office before beginning the long journey through the majestic cathedral hallways. The corridors were as grand as always, and the stained-glass windows shone brightly, casting vivid hues of oranges, blues, and purples on the stone floors below in a mesmerizing display. Only when I passed Saint Mary's likeness did it dawn on me that I hadn't said my prayer for the evening, but I didn't stop, instead reminding myself that Quasimodo and I could say it together.

Keeping to the shadows, I moved silently around every corner, careful not to draw attention to myself as I made my way toward the belltower. All went well for a good chunk of time, and I'd nearly reached the stairs when I heard voices heading toward me. Though my heart began to pound, at least it gave me an opportunity to duck behind a nearby tapestry; so long as whoever was headed this way didn't look down and see my feet, they wouldn't be alerted to my presence. Their words were unintelligible for a while, but as they drew closer, I made out bits and pieces.

"…idea who's leading them?"

"Not a clue."

"Well someone has to be, and someone powerful at that. They haven't captured anyone willing to give up a name?"

"It's difficult to capture them, period. They're being as slippery as fish, from what I've heard."

"I can certainly believe it, after what happened in the square last weekend. Did you see the look…"

Though the voices trailed off not long after that, I didn't emerge from my hiding place until the corridor had once again fallen silent. Only when I was certain I was alone did I start up the staircase, moving as fast as my tired and still-aching limbs would carry me. All the while, I fought to calm the fear that had risen in my throat like bile, because although I'd managed to hold myself together in the presence of others, I'd had at least one panic attack a day since what had happened in the square. In addition to continued torment from that damn smoke, I couldn't close my eyes without seeing those mages lined up on that stage, sentenced to die horrific and painful deaths… except this time, each one of them bore Esmeralda's face.

Mercedes wanted to act as if this was simple, except it was anything but. Being honest about my feelings toward Esmeralda was one thing, our situation entirely another, and it was beginning to feel more and more like I was the only one taking this in any way seriously. How on earth did feelings matter when, at any moment, she could be found and executed, and her flame snuffed out altogether? Even if I was prepared to declare my undying love for her—and I most certainly wasn't—it felt about as useful as I'd been down in the square. My love wouldn't save her; if anything, it would damn her.

But neither could I let her go. If anything was obvious to me by now, it was that Esmeralda and I were part of each other's lives. I needed her, she needed me, and most of all, we needed to fix this.

Though Notre Dame's stairs were as endless and exhausting as always, by the time I reached the top of the belltower, both my heart rate and breathing were as steady as they were sure. The sun would set within the hour, and deep shadows as well as the final rays of daylight flooded the space before me. It had been some time since I'd been here last, and as magnificent as they were, the bells were far from the only marvel. Though Quasimodo wasn't the only bellringer, he certainly was the one who spent the most time here and hadn't hesitated to make the space his own. As I weaved my way through it, I couldn't help but admire the countless trinkets and treasures strewn about. My son had always been good with his hands, as evidenced by the expertly crafted pieces of jewelry, sculptures, and other half-finished projects that added so much life and color to the otherwise drab room.

My favorite was something resembling a chandelier, of sorts; when Quasimodo was eight, he'd collected bits of the most colorful glass he could find, sanded down their edges, and painstakingly hung each of the pieces from its own individual string. The resulting piece was as beautiful now as it had been back then, and I would never tire of the gorgeous array of colors it reflected on the wooden beams and bells alike.

This wasn't his workshop, however—simply the extension of it. But as I started in its direction, I froze in my tracks when the sound of several voices talking and laughing drifted from the partially open door. *Did he bring friends here?* If he had, the last thing I wanted to do was interrupt. Creeping nearer, I clutched the basket closer to my chest before pressing my ear to the door, listening intently. More laughter, as well as words my brain didn't fully register… and then I heard her, but not from inside the workshop.

Esmeralda's laugh rang out from somewhere behind me, causing me to whirl around so fast I nearly dropped the basket. Several different possibilities as to what I might be about to find swam through my mind as I rounded the corner, heading toward the source of the noise, but none of them included a fireball hurling straight toward my face.

I cried out, throwing up an arm to shield myself just as heat seared my skin, but impact never came. The warmth vanished in an instant, and when I lifted my head and blinked, a wide-eyed Esmeralda and Quasimodo stared back at me.

"C-Claude," Esmeralda stammered. "To what do we owe the pleasure?"

I wanted to wince at the formality in her tone—how in God's name had we gotten here?—but before I could reply, Quasimodo beat me to it.

"It's my fault, Maman. Don't be angry with Esmeralda. I asked her to stay here to teach me."

My gut twisted into knots yet again for more reasons than one.

I'm not angry with anyone, I assured him. *That just startled me, is all.* But as much as I wanted answers as to who else was up here and why, it was clear I'd interrupted their lesson, and had yet to witness just what Esmeralda had been teaching Quasimodo. So I settled myself on a nearby stool before gesturing for them to continue. *Please, don't stop on my account.*

Though Quasimodo immediately went back to being thrilled, Esmeralda looked anything but. She was trying to be discreet about it, but I certainly didn't miss that her gaze kept flicking to the basket in my lap. "Actually, we were nearly finished," she said.

"Finish up, then, but I'd still like to watch."

She gave a stiff smile before turning back to Quasimodo and signing, *Would you like to try that again?*

Quasimodo nodded vigorously before closing his eyes and lifting his hands, palms facing upward. My mouth fell open as a fireball—far larger than the first—slowly started to materialize above them, its bright orange and yellow light casting shadows on the walls of the room. Quasimodo was careful to keep the flame at a safe distance from me, but still close enough for Esmeralda to reach out and take it in her hands. She then passed it back to him, and they continued swapping it back and forth, allowing it to grow larger each time it changed hands. My grip tightened on the basket, and despite the heat in the room, my face paled; as proud as I was of how quickly Quasimodo's skills had progressed, watching this was nothing short of terrifying.

Still, I forced myself to remain still and silent as Esmeralda asked Quasimodo to hold the fireball in one hand. He struggled at first, but eventually managed to keep it steady for several moments before the strain became too much, and he was forced to let it go. The fireball dissipated instantly, and I watched as Quasimodo's shoulders slumped in exhaustion.

Esmeralda smiled, crossing the room to squeeze his shoulder. *That's enough for today. We don't want you depleting yourself over a simple lesson.*

Before I could ask either of them what depletion meant, Quasimodo skipped over to me, all but falling in my lap in his excitement. "Did you see that? Look what I can do in just a few weeks! Imagine what I'll be able to do in a few years!"

The thought terrified me far more than it excited me, but I couldn't deny that it made me incredibly happy to see Quasimodo so happy. I replied both aloud and in sign so Esmeralda might hear it, even though she'd turned away from us. "It's amazing—*you're* amazing. But what do you say to Esmeralda? You wouldn't have gotten nearly this far on your own."

He turned to her, still beaming. "Je vous remercie!"

Je t'en prie. Esmeralda gave him another smile before gesturing back to me and Mercedes's basket. *Why don't you see what your Maman has brought for you? I think she might have something for me, as well.*

I shot Esmeralda a puzzled glance, but Quasimodo descended upon me in an instant, tearing open the basket and shoving a roll into his mouth as if he hadn't eaten all day. He tried mumbling what I assumed to be thanks, but I held up a hand to silence him. *Thank*

Mercedes. She's the one who got them for you.

Quasimodo nodded. *Where is she?*

Downstairs, but I'm not sure where.

After grabbing a few more rolls, he skipped off, leaving just me and Esmeralda. I opened my mouth, but before anything came out, she tugged on my upper arm. "Come on—and bring that basket. I have something to show you."

She led me toward Quasimodo's workshop, and once she pushed open the door, I finally was able to see who I'd heard talking and laughing a little earlier. I'm not certain who I expected, but it certainly wasn't Esmeralda's sibling I'd met back at the faire—Jules, I remembered after a moment. Beside them stood someone I recognized but whose name I couldn't recall. They stood around several articles of clothing strewn across the workbench, but it gave no indication of what they could possibly be doing here.

That was far from my only question, though. What business did they have in Quasimodo's workshop, of all places? How had two mages gotten inside the cathedral with all the guards prowling around every corner, and who had helped them?

No sooner had I thought it than I answered my own question: Mercedes. Of course it had been Mercedes, because she was the one who'd set this entire arrangement up. Esmeralda's unexplained fixation on the basket more or less proved it, and a wave of irritation rose within me. *Be honest, my ass.* What in God's name had Mercedes tricked me into bringing here, and why? And how long had she known that Esmeralda was holed up here?

I shot her another look, but she didn't reply. A heavy, awkward silence descended upon the room until Jules broke it, hooking an arm beneath their companion's elbow as they spoke. "Perhaps we ought to leave you two to talk. Antoine, would you like to see the bells again?"

He muttered something that sounded suspiciously like a 'no,' but Jules dragged him out regardless.

And then it was just me and Esmeralda, alone for the first time in days.

There was so much I wanted to say I didn't even know where to start, but no sooner had I opened my mouth than she held up a hand to silence me, reaching instead for the basket.

Another wave of annoyance reared its ugly head. "Esmeralda, we need to ta—"

"We certainly do," she muttered between her rummaging, "but not now."

"Excuse me?" Surely I hadn't heard her correctly. "If not now, when? It's been days, and clearly you've been up to something in that time."

"Noticed, have you?"

My already limited patience had nearly run out. "Is this seriously how you want to do this? Weren't you the one who blew up on me over my inability to face my feelings? Here you are doing the exact same thing."

Esmeralda snapped her head up then, and I flinched both at the sudden movement as well as that borderline feral look in her eyes.

Holding up a single finger, she hissed, "One: I did not 'blow up' on you. If and when that ever happens, I assure you, you'll know. And two"—she held up another finger—"I'm not avoiding any feelings. In fact, I'm saving us time."

A chill crept down my spine as I considered the clues I had at my disposal: the pile of clothing, her obsessive fixation on the basket, and the fact that she'd brought Jules and Antoine here. "Are you... running away?"

"What? Jesus, no." Esmeralda's gaze softened, and she threw up her hands in defeat. "I'm... Fuck. I thought I'd have more time to prepare for how best to tell you this. Mercedes wasn't supposed to send you up until after my lesson with Quasimodo was over, hence nearly burning you. I can just blurt it out, but it's going to sound asinine."

My heart skipped a beat, but I nodded anyway. "Try me."

"All right." She gestured to the clothing, and I stepped closer to get a better look. It was disorganized and haphazardly thrown together, but there looked to be a pair of cloaks, a crimson-colored ballgown, and a matching men's waistcoat and breeches. On top of it all rested two pairs of matching shoes, and I hoped to God that those heels weren't intended for me.

"I'm going to the opera tonight," Esmeralda said, "and I want you to come with me."

XIV. THE OPERA

Esmeralda

"I can't believe I let you talk me into this," Claude muttered, but this time, I didn't bother glancing back.

"And I can't believe you're still complaining about it, but at least I haven't made that your problem." I dropped my skirts rather reluctantly, loathing the thought of them dragging on the ground, but Claude's outburst had shattered my concentration. We were near enough to a streetlamp so I pulled out the map Mercedes had drawn for us, squinting as I struggled to make out which direction we ought to head in next and loathing that I couldn't just summon a flame for light. "Turn back if you'd like. I won't stop you."

Claude scoffed. "If I do that, I'm dragging you back with me."

My flames flared to life beneath the surface of my skin, not at all appreciating their threat. "You can fucking try."

A groan. "Fine. But if we're really doing this, can you please watch your mouth? I can only take so much swearing in a single night."

I stopped in my tracks and whirled around at that, nearly causing the hood to fall from my face. "You're scolding me... for cussing? If that offends you, you *should* turn back. People cuss, Claude, and you're likely to witness far worse before tonight is over."

They raised an eyebrow and whispered, "Like what?"

Only then did I realize we stood chest to chest, breathing the same air as I looked up and Claude looked down, given our height difference.

Heat flamed my cheeks, and my heart began fluttering against my ribcage. This was the closest we'd been in nearly a week, and to say my body ached for her touch was an understatement. To go from near-constant access to their incredibly skilled fingers and mouth to nothing at all had been torture—but I was still furious with them, and I couldn't forget that, no matter how much I wished I could. They'd twisted their words crueler than a knife, kicked me out in the moment I most needed comfort, and hadn't made any attempt to apologize prior to now. So it was only fair that I torture them a bit and let them know precisely what they'd been missing. Forcing myself to hold her gaze, I lifted my chin and spoke with as much nonchalance as I could muster. "Like... You may see a bit of skin. Far more than you're used to."

"There's only one person's skin I'm interested in seeing," Claude said in that same breathy whisper as their gaze flicked to my chest, to the exposed skin near my décolletage. "So don't worry. I won't be looking at anyone but her."

Fuck me—they knew exactly what game we were playing. "Other people might be."

Something dark flashed in her eyes. "Not if I have anything to say about it."

"Oh?" I practically squeaked. I was losing the game, and badly, but I no longer cared. "And what will that be?"

"That they shouldn't covet what's…" Claude's voice trailed off, and they glanced away, clearing their throat. "We should keep moving."

"Now wait just a minute," I snapped, reaching out to snatch the edge of her cloak. "Were you about to say 'mine?'"

"It doesn't matter."

"It very much does, which is why I brought it up. I'm yours, now?"

The edge to their voice sounded almost pained, and they still refused to look me in the eye. "Do you want to be?"

"Five days ago, I did. More than anything. Right now, though, I'm undecided."

Claude made a noise between a snort and a scoff, finally turning back to face me. "Is that why you wanted me to come with you so badly? To stuff me in this ridiculous outfit and make me bear witness to all the men and women who are inevitably going to gawk at you tonight?"

"I didn't spend an entire month of my earnings on that waistcoat only for you to call it ridiculous." It was my turn to bristle as I eyed them up and down; though it was currently concealed by the cloaks we'd donned to sneak out of Notre Dame, I was easily able to summon a clear mental picture of how attractive Claude had looked the moment she'd put it on. "You look incredibly handsome, and I won't hear otherwise."

Their eyes widened. "H-handsome?"

"And if you think I brought you along as my *date* simply to make you jealous, you're even more of an idiot than I already thought. I brought you with me so we could talk, Claude. I want to work this out, but not if it's going to be more of the same."

She stood frozen for a moment before saying, "I'm sorry. Truly. I'm just… not good at this."

"Clearly."

They shot me a look, but then the seriousness was back. "You were right, about everything. I let my fear take over. I said some awful things for the sole purpose of hurting you, hoping to drive you away. And I stayed away hoping you might see sense and leave Notre Dame for good. If I'm being completely honest, none of that fear has gone away—if anything, this past week has only worsened it."

I swallowed, unsure where this was headed, but didn't interrupt.

"But the time apart has also made me realize what it truly is I don't want, and that's to lose you. Last week, you told me you're tired of me being distant, and my God, I'm tired of it, too. I'm tired of pushing people away the moment they get a little too close, tired of grieving relationships before they even begin. I'm tired of never knowing what I could have had."

Claude took my hand then, pressing it between both of hers. "With you, I don't want to guess. I want to know and experience you. All of you, any way you'll have me, beyond a shadow of a doubt. And yes…" They paused, a smile playing at the corner of their lips. "I want you to be mine."

If I thought my heart had been beating out of my chest before, that was nothing compared to the backflips it was doing now. Every fiber of my being was fixated on the fact that Claude was touching me, that our bodies were pressed together once more, and that they were staring… at my mouth. If not for their rule, I may have thrown my arms around their neck and kissed them.

But I couldn't do that—not without asking—and neither did she kiss me. "All yours?" I finally managed to utter, only slightly disappointed that the moment hadn't gone anywhere. "Mercedes mentioned that your relationships are never exclusive, and that you want to be free to see other people."

"Mercedes talks too much," Claude muttered, then sighed. "But yes. It's just how I am. There's no one else at the moment, but if and when that changes, I'll let you know before I pursue anything. And it works both ways—you're also free to pursue anyone you like. All I ask is that you extend me the same courtesy, and keep me informed regarding who you're seeing and when. Is that agreeable to you?"

I considered it for a moment. While I'd only ever been in a handful of serious relationships, all of them had been exclusive to that one person until the relationship ended. I'd heard whispers of those who did it Claude's way, and now that I was thinking about it, I vaguely recalled Jules being involved in a similar arrangement at one point. I'd never been a jealous person, and Claude was clearly experienced at this sort of thing, so as long as communication remained open and honesty never wavered, I could think of no downside. In fact, this might be very, very fun.

So I nodded. "It is. I must confess, though…" My voice trailed off as I stepped closer and was a sultry whisper when I spoke again. "I very much like the idea of being yours and yours alone, if only for tonight. I also like the idea of being able to flirt with anyone I choose, only for you to get jealous to the point where you feel you need to do something about it."

Claude's voice was hoarse. "Oh? And what might that be?"

"Whatever you like, but don't tell me." I held a hand up to silence her. "I want you to surprise me."

"In a room full of people? How is that supposed to work?"

"Rather easily, I'd think." I smirked before continuing, "Because I'm not wearing any panties."

I'd been waiting for the right moment to disclose that particular detail, and Claude's reaction didn't disappoint. Her mouth fell open, her eyes widened, and she sputtered a few incoherent attempts at words before I spun on my heel, pulling out Mercedes's map once again. We had to get going if we had any hope of making it to our seats before the opera began, and as much fun as teasing Claude had been, I'd have to save the rest of it for the Palais Garnier.

Looping my arm through Claude's, we set off at a brisk pace, weaving our way through the winding backstreets of Paris. The cobblestone paths beneath our feet were uneven and slick, doing nothing for my nerves and making it difficult to move swiftly despite our best efforts. Though Mercedes's directions had yet to lead us astray, I remained on high alert for any surprise patrols, more than ready to let my flames loose if it proved necessary. But as stressful as our journey was, the fleeting glimpses of the moonlit city made it all worth it, and even the cool night air on my skin alone made me feel more alive than I'd felt in weeks.

Though I said nothing, Claude had been watching me carefully. "You've been cooped up too long," they murmured after a while, a statement rather than a question.

"It's been difficult," I admitted. "I'm very accustomed to being out and about at night, permitted to come and go as I please. I've no idea how you've managed to stay as sane as you are living full-time within those walls."

"They're a comfort to me—sturdy, steadfast, and safe. But the same could be said for a prison."

If we didn't need to keep moving, I would have halted at that. "I never called Notre Dame a prison."

"No, and you wouldn't have. Which is why I said it for you." Claude squeezed my hand. "It's all right, Esmeralda. It may be my home, but I never expected it to become yours."

An unexpected wave of sadness washed over me at that, and I wasn't completely sure why. "It has, though, in a small way. Home hasn't ever been a place for me. It's where I can find the people I care about, and now, that includes you, Quasimodo, Mercedes, and Jehan. But you're not the only ones on that list, which is precisely the problem."

Claude snorted. "Didn't seem like much of a problem for you to sneak your sibling and their partner into the belltower right under my nose. Can't you just do that with the rest of your family?"

"Jules and Antoine invited their damn selves, and no—because I hardly think that hundreds of mages suddenly flocking to Notre Dame will escape anyone's attention. They're my family too, all of them." I shot Claude a glare. "Which is why so much hinges on tonight."

"Ah, right… the asinine plan to locate some Phantom mage for your père." Claude sighed deeply. "I'd nearly forgotten."

"I hope you're kidding, because I need you to be a thoroughly convincing man for this to work."

They chuckled deep in their chest. "I had you convinced for months on end, didn't I?"

"You most certainly did, and that's before you were dressed to look so handsome."

Claude yanked on my hood so suddenly I yelped, but more from surprise than pain. Tilting my head back and pulling the cover from my face, they dragged their lips and teeth along my neck, and the sensation sent jolts of pleasure straight to my groin. "Keep calling me handsome," she whispered before gently nibbling on my earlobe, "and we may not even make it to the opera before I hike up those skirts of yours and fuck you right here, right now."

I brought a hand to my mouth just in time to stifle the involuntary moan that escaped my lips. "Now who's got the filthy mouth?" I teased once my arm fell away, out of breath though she'd barely touched me.

Claude chuckled and straightened up again, flashing me what could only be described as an arrogant smirk. "I may not like swearing but I'm no stranger to hearing it, especially from men. And if I'm to be one for tonight, I plan to speak the part as much as I'm acting it."

After I'd fixed my hood, we set off once again, reaching our destination a few short minutes later. The Palais Garnier towered over us, its intricate façade illuminated by the streetlamps on either side of it. Even from a distance, we could easily make out the sculptures adorning the building's balconies and columns, every inch lovingly carved from stone into what appeared to be a work of art rather than a mere building.

But as breathtaking as the opera house was, my inner flames sensed danger almost immediately, sending prickles of unease shooting down my arms and spine. Atop the roof, a pair of guardsmen paced back and forth in opposite directions. Half a dozen more guards were posted at various points along the stairs leading up to the main doors, and I could only imagine how many more had been posted inside. We had been lucky so far that no one had noticed us dashing through the streets like the reckless fools we were, but now was the true test; now, Claude and I had to run the gauntlet.

I tightened my grip on her arm, ducking my head the moment before one of the guards glanced in my direction. Terrified didn't even begin to describe what I was feeling, but if we had even the slightest chance of making it through this, I couldn't let any of it show. "Ready?" I whispered, my voice cracking yet again. And was that my arm shaking or Claude's?

Damn it.

But they simply nodded, standing up a little straighter and holding their chin high. "Ready."

XV. THE MASQUERADE

Claude

Esmeralda had placed so much faith in me it almost hurt.

Our plan was simple enough: blend in, stay alert, and deduce whether this Phantom even existed. If he did, deliver the summons from the Mages' Council, and if he didn't, get out of there as quickly and quietly as possible. Simple indeed. But it sure as hell wasn't smart—and honestly, asinine was putting it lightly, especially when our problems started with step one.

Blending in had never been my strong suit. It was difficult enough given my tall and lanky physique; combine that with the stares I got when I didn't bind my breasts, and I was usually an eyesore in any crowd. And none of that was even touching on the fact that these guards would be looking for two people who matched the description of Esmeralda and me.

But that was precisely the loophole we could exploit: Phoebus would have told them to look for two women.

And I was anything but.

I also felt more confident than I think I'd ever been with the way I was currently dressed. I was no stranger to men's clothing, but never before had I worn anything this formal, let alone gone out in public with it on. It had felt beyond surreal the moment the fabric had touched my skin—euphoric, even—and I knew already I was going to be reluctant to take it off. The coat and breeches were a perfect fit, molding to my form as if tailored to me, and I supposed they had been, given that Esmeralda had measured the clothes I'd given her to wear to deduce my size. The waistcoat was the slightest bit too big, but the exquisite craftsmanship and skillful embroidery more than made up for it.

All in all, my ensemble was the perfect match to Esmeralda's elaborate crimson ball gown, and my jaw dropped when she'd stepped from Quasimodo's workshop with it on. Red had always been her color and never failed to enhance her already exceptional beauty. The décolletage dipped low, teasingly tracing her neckline, and the ruffles adding depth to her layered skirt swayed back and forth with each step she took. Even with her cloak still on and her hood still up, she was already attracting curious glances from the dozens of patrons beginning to line up on the stairs, but her reaction to the attention was the opposite to what I expected. In stark contrast to the confident persona she adopted while on stage as The Embermage, her quivering arm still looped within mine told me she was ready to leap out of her skin at any moment.

After taking a deep breath to steel my own nerves, I leaned in, placing my free hand on hers in what I hoped was a reassuring gesture. "It's all right, ma belle," I said, my voice low and for her ears alone. "Just stay close to me."

"Ma belle?" Esmeralda echoed.

"As much as I adore your name, uttering it here isn't the best idea."

She nodded slowly and didn't protest as I led us straight into the crowd, moving with as much confidence as I could muster while keeping my head held high. I'd never been to the Palais Garnier before—hell, I'd barely spent any time in this part of the city before—but walked as if I had, because much like what we were about to witness inside, it was all about the performance. No one would question us if we didn't give them any reason to.

We secured a place in line, which was moving quickly. Esmeralda fished out our tickets just as we reached the front, passing them to me a moment before I had to hand them over to a guard, who regarded us with a grunted and barely intelligible, "Bonne soirée."

"Bonne soirée, Monsieur," I offered in return, smiling as broadly as I could muster. "Such a lovely night for—"

"No hoods in the theater," he cut across me, pointing an accusing finger at Esmeralda. "She has to take that off."

My heart skipped a beat, but I nodded mechanically. "Of course, Monsieur."

Turning to Esmeralda, I helped her remove her hood first, then her cloak, draping the garment over my arm as it slipped from her shoulders. The lights were dim here, and she kept her gaze downcast, but I could feel her trembling, meaning she had to be thinking the same thing I was: had the guard recognized her, or was this simply a policy everyone had to follow? I suddenly wished I'd paid more attention to the couples who had gone in ahead of us.

The guard grunted again but didn't step aside. "Shy, is she?"

"Not usually, no," I replied coolly, loathing the way he spoke of Esmeralda as if she wasn't standing right in front of him. She did, too, for her head snapped up, and I didn't miss that for the briefest of moments, flames danced in her eyes. "It's just that crowds can sometimes be overwhelming."

He grunted again before finally moving aside for us to pass. *Thank God.* Draping a protective arm over Esmeralda's shoulders, I led the way into the already crowded lobby, steering us to a more secluded corner before daring to speak again. "What an—"

"Ass?" she offered, scowling in disgust. "*Shy.* What, simply because I wasn't giving him the same doe-eyed stare that seems to be the only acceptable way for a woman to communicate around here?"

I frowned, but not at her words; a sharp and sudden scent invaded my nostrils. "Ma belle—"

"I'll bet he'd piss himself if he ever had to stand in front of even the smallest crowd I've performed for!"

"Ma belle," I said again, ensnaring her wrist this time. "Look."

Esmeralda followed my gaze only to curse under her breath.

The edges of one of her sleeves had been singed off, and the smell of burning fabric had grown even stronger now. Though there weren't any visible flames, the ruined sleeve was lightly smoking; damning evidence, especially given that the surrounding skin was completely untouched.

Yanking her cloak from my arm, I draped it over hers, silently praying that no one else had glimpsed anything. "If anyone asks," I hissed, pulling her close to speak for her ears alone, "you got too close to a candle."

She nodded as I pulled away, and only then did I notice that the color had drained from her face. "I'll be more careful. I'm so sorry."

"It's all right, but let's just do what we came here to and get out." I dared a glance around, wishing we had time to be awed by the sculptures and paintings adorning the walls and ceilings, and especially by the elaborate chandeliers that glittered like stars, but we didn't. Though we'd been lucky enough to make it inside, we would be fools to push that luck any further than was absolutely necessary. "What's the plan? What sort of things are we looking for?"

Esmeralda didn't answer right away. "There… isn't one," she finally admitted. "And without knowing what type of mage the Phantom is, we could be looking for absolutely anything."

I did a double take, and it was a fight to keep my voice from rising. "Please tell me you're joking."

"I'm not. It was tricky enough to even get us here—to plan the route, secure the tickets, buy us proper attire—so beyond that, I guess I just thought we'd figure the rest out as we went along."

My thoughts were rapidly beginning to spiral, but not wanting to draw attention to ourselves, I kept a rigid smile plastered on my face. "Okay… okay. We can probably start by asking around, see if anyone has seen—"

"Are you crazy?" Esmeralda hissed, cutting me off. "If two people who look like us start going around asking about *mages* of all things, we'll be arrested within the hour."

She, unfortunately, had a point. "Do you have a better idea?"

"Perhaps, but you'll think it's asinine yet again."

I raised an eyebrow, echoing what I'd said merely an hour ago. "Try me."

"Let's just go find our seats and watch the performance. Blend in, do what everyone else is here to do. It will give me a chance to calm down and get my flames under control, and it might even give us some clues as to how everything works around here." Esmeralda paused, taking careful note of my reaction. "He's the Phantom of the *opera* house. What's the point of him being here, of all places, if he doesn't bother to attend the operas?"

I ran a hand through my hair and sighed. "Honestly? I think your first mistake is attempting to apply any sort of logic to a man who goes around calling himself a 'Phantom.'" But I could think of no further reason to argue—and at the very least, sitting still in a dark theater sounded like the perfect opportunity to come up with our next steps.

Sensing she was victorious, Esmeralda beamed before taking my hand, all but dragging me toward where people were beginning to file into the theater. "I get to watch a show rather than perform one, *and* I have the most handsome date here? It's my lucky night."

There it was again, the word that made me want to cherish and ruin her in the same breath. The word that got my heart pumping faster, that sent jolts of heat straight to my groin, and that reminded me of Esmeralda's earlier confession…

That she wasn't wearing panties.

I heard little more than the blood roaring in my ears as we were led to our seats by an usher, all the while fighting the powerful urge to pull her from the theater, pin her against a wall, and have my way with her. She'd said that I could do as much, had encouraged it, even. *Do you know?* I found myself wondering as she took my hand once again, lifting it to her mouth so she could press her lips to the back of my palm. She gave me a look that was as coy as it was alluring, and at that, I very nearly voiced my question aloud.

Do you know what it is you're doing to me?

But then the lights dimmed, and Esmeralda's face lit up with pure delight as she leaned forward to get a better look, still clutching my hand for dear life. The performance kicked off with a lively overture from the full orchestra pit below us, followed by a glorious soprano whose notes flooded the theater as much as they did every fiber of my being. Though the music was captivating in its own right, especially when the mournful aria molded seamlessly into the following chorus, it wasn't nearly enough to distract me from how badly I wanted the woman sitting next to me: the woman I could now call *mine*. We may be at an opera, at what could be the performance of a lifetime for all I knew, but all I wanted to look at was Esmeralda. At the soft curls cascading down her back, at her lips parted in wonder, at her fingers interwoven with mine.

I shifted uncomfortably in my seat as it became increasingly difficult to ignore my intense arousal. The last thing I wanted to do was break Esmeralda's immersion, especially if she was searching for clues as she'd said, but God—I couldn't take this much longer, especially once my desire began sparking mild outrage. How dare she sit there and look this good while I was forced to sit here knowing she wasn't wearing panties, and that in the present moment, I couldn't do a single thing about it? The urge to whisk her away and make good on my earlier threat became overpowering, and after gnawing on my knuckles to the point I tasted blood, I tensed my knees to get up.

Then Esmeralda made a noise beside me, somewhere between a squeak and a gasp. After covering her mouth, she glanced at me, wide-eyed, nodding with her head toward the stage. Blinking in confusion, I followed her gaze, at first unable to see whatever it was she was seeing. Half a dozen dancers skipped across the stage in colorful outfits while, in the middle, a tenor belted an impressive aria. I'd lost track of the storyline ages ago so had no idea of this scene's significance, or if that even mattered to the point Esmeralda was attempting to make. "What is it?" I dared to whisper.

"Don't you see?" she hissed, as if it were obvious. "The dancers—they're mages."

I took another look, this time focusing on the set as well as the performers. With each passing second, it became increasingly clear that Esmeralda was right, because what I'd initially assumed were mere theater tricks now appeared to be anything but. The backdrop erected behind them was of particular interest because the scenery within it was moving, and not at random. Various elements were being manipulated in time with the dancers' movements. Blades of grass swayed in the wind, flames flickered and danced along an earthen path, and even a few clouds shifted across the painted sky, all in perfect harmony with the performers' moves.

"I see it," I breathed, and Esmeralda's grip on my hand tightened.

"Oh my God. It makes so much sense—too much sense. How did I not think of it before? Mages may no longer be permitted to perform in public, but that's precisely why this works. The average citizen would never recognize what they're seeing on stage as real magic. They're hiding in plain sight." She met my gaze, lowering her voice even more. "And so is our Phantom. He *is* real."

Esmeralda seemed thrilled at the revelation, but my head was still spinning; just what exactly did she plan to do with this information? We knew nothing about this man, nor his intentions, and the reasons he kept himself so hidden could damn well be good ones. And what did we stand to gain from tracking down a man who very clearly didn't want to be found other than placing ourselves in even more mortal danger?

But before I could blurt any of that out, the theater burst into cheers and applause a moment before the lights brightened, signaling intermission, and when I turned to Esmeralda, I'd barely uttered a single word before she ripped herself from my grasp and bolted for the exit.

God damn that infuriating woman.

I had no choice but to tear after her, rushing out of the theater and down the long hallway, growing more irritated with every passing second. Esmeralda had always been reckless, yes, but tonight had been something else entirely. She may not have lied but she certainly hadn't been forthcoming about her complete and utter lack of a plan, and we both knew damn well why—I'd have never agreed to come along otherwise. Even now, what was her aim? Because all she had done was drawn bewildered glances and hushed whispers, the latter of which would reach the guards' ears in no time.

Finally catching up to her in the lobby, I grabbed hold of her arm and spun her around to face me. "What do you think you're doing?" I hissed through clenched teeth, glancing around warily. "And what the hell happened to 'blending in?'"

"Let go of me before I make you," she warned as something flashed in her eyes—something feral. I loosened my grip but didn't release her.

"Please, ma belle. I don't want to make a scene, and I want even less to argue."

"Then let *go*—"

"Not until I know you're not going to run off again. Let's find somewhere to talk, to work out a plan."

"Do you seriously think we have time for that?" Esmeralda yanked against my grip. "And what is there to plan? We know where those dancers are—backstage—and I need to speak to them immediately."

"Even if by some miracle you do manage to get back there, what will you do then? Interrogate them about the one man they've clearly all sworn to protect?" I shook my head. "Ma belle, do you hear yourself? This is—"

"Is there a problem here?"

My blood ran cold at the unfamiliar, authoritative voice. We'd been so engrossed in our argument that neither of us had noticed the guard approach, and now we were trapped. He loomed in front of us with his eyes narrowed and his arms behind his back, but given that I couldn't see his hands, this only made me more uneasy as his gaze flicked back and forth between us. And he wasn't the only one; behind him, a good number of patrons had stopped to gawk at the spectacle we'd made.

Lord, help us.

Esmeralda recovered first and smiled brightly at the guard. "No problem at all, Monsieur. I was feeling a little faint, and he was simply making sure I was all right."

If the situation weren't so tense, I might have been more concerned at the way the lies rolled so easily off her tongue, but all I could do was play along. "Yes, that's correct. It would seem we got a little carried away, and for that I apologize."

I released Esmeralda's arm to drape mine over her shoulders, more to shield her than anything else, because that look the guard was giving her felt far too predatory for my liking. Saliva pooled in my mouth as my heart began to pound; he didn't recognize her, did he?

The guard scrutinized us for a few more moments before finally breaking his gaze, and Esmeralda's body relaxed against me. "Take care of this one," he muttered, jerking his thumb toward her as he walked away. Dismissive, yes, but at least we hadn't been caught.

But before we had time to turn around, the guard spun back to face us, his eyes wide with alarm. "You!" he shouted, pointing an accusing finger at Esmeralda's singed sleeve—the damning evidence. "You're the mage they've been looking for!"

Once again, Esmeralda reacted first, ducking down before yanking me in the direction of another hallway farther behind us. She pushed over anything she could get her hands on as she went— tables, expensive artifacts on display, and even yanked down a few curtains— before setting it all ablaze with a single flick of her wrist, leaving a path of destruction in our wake yet buying us a bit of time. I tore off after her, only barely aware of the shouts and screams echoing behind us as our pursuers gave chase; as many as a half dozen now, by the sound of them.

Before I could ask her if she'd just set the whole place on fire, we fled deeper and deeper into the opera house, Esmeralda leading the way as I followed close behind her. The hallway seemed to stretch on forever, winding around and up before splitting off into several different paths, but we didn't run into any more guards as we picked one and ascended—they must all be downstairs. Still, I didn't let down my defenses for a moment, sucking in breath after breath as I kept glancing behind, expecting the mob to have caught up with us by now. Esmeralda kept up her habit of tearing down whatever she could to hinder the path of whoever might try to follow us, but at least she didn't set anything else on fire. Just as I became worried I might hyperventilate, we reached a side door, one that Esmeralda barged through without hesitation.

Stumbling out onto what could only be the roof, we doubled over, panting from exhaustion. More echoed shouts sounded from down below as our pursuers searched for us in vain, but I couldn't bring myself to worry any more than I already was; for now, at least, we were safe.

The night air was cool against our skin after such a frenzied escape, and neither of us spoke as we took deep breaths to steady ourselves. But while I remained still and stationary, Esmeralda began wandering around, muttering unintelligibly to herself.

"We can't stay here," I warned her once I'd caught my breath enough to speak. "Especially if it's about to burn to the ground. See if there's a ladder anywhere, some way we can get down without going back inside, maybe sneak down into an alley… Why in God's name are you shaking your head?"

"Because I *am* going back inside. I'm not leaving until I've delivered my père's message to the Phantom."

True fury ignited within me as she gave me that look—the one that informed me she'd made up her mind, and that no amount of reason or common sense would be able to change it. I'm not certain what possessed me to try anyway, but the words tumbled from my lips before I could hold them back. "An hour ago, you were quivering in my arms at the thought of the door guard recognizing you, and now you want to charge back in there, *willingly*, after someone has?"

"I didn't know if the Phantom even existed an hour ago."

"We still don't! We haven't seen him, Esmeralda, no one has! For all we know, he's simply a persona the mages who work here conjured up to better protect themselves."

"Which is precisely why I have to stay—*because* there are mages. And you're right. Either they made the Phantom up or he's still in there hiding, but I'm delivering my père's message to them either way."

Clenching my fists, I shook my head, already loathing myself for what I was about to do. "I can't let you do that."

Esmeralda opened her mouth, but before she could utter a word, I rushed her, succeeding in pinning her left arm behind her back almost instantly. Her right was a challenge, though, and she slipped from my grasp. Heat seared my face a moment later, and the sudden intensity of it was nearly enough to make me step back. It took a moment to deduce that a plume of fire hovered in front of my face, its source Esmeralda's palm.

"Let go of me," she whispered through the crackling of her flames, "before I make you."

We stood there in stalemate, each of us faced with the violence we were preparing to inflict upon the other: would Esmeralda actually burn me? And would it have been justified considering I'd been about to drag her off the roof by force?

I'd never know, because before either of us could react, air pummeled us in a concentrated torrent, extinguishing Esmeralda's fire in a single blast. My heart skipped a beat as, in my peripheral vision, a man stepped from the shadows, lowering his arm as he approached. There wasn't time to question why a mask covered half his face, nor why he moved with such unbothered leisure, especially when the guards' shouts were so close it was a wonder they hadn't reached us yet.

"Unless your aim is to spend tonight in a jail cell," he said calmly, his dark gaze flicking between us with interest, "I suggest you both follow me."

XVI. THE PHANTOM

Esmeralda

"Who the fuck are you?"

I hadn't meant to blurt it out, let alone snarl it as aggressively as I had. But my argument with Claude had left me so on edge that, had it not been snuffed out, I wouldn't have hesitated to hurl my flame at this masked stranger instead. I suspect he knew it, too, which was precisely why he'd done it. Claude hissed something that sounded like a scolding, but I ignored them; even if the stranger hadn't arrived, I wouldn't be speaking to them, anyway.

"Well?" I demanded when the man said nothing, wrenching myself from Claude's grip to turn and face him.

He remained silent, giving me an opportunity to study him

just as he was studying me. An air mage. That much would have been obvious even if he hadn't just blasted me with it, given the way his cloak billowed around his broad and muscular form despite the lack of a breeze. Everything about him was as dark as it was mysterious, from the midnight black of his cloak to the silver fastenings lining it, which glinted in the moonlight. He was tall, even taller than Claude, and he'd gone to great lengths to conceal his face. Half was covered by a mask molded perfectly to his pale white skin, while the other half was difficult to make out given the thick hood shrouding his features in shadow.

Though he still hadn't uttered a word, his identity struck me like a slap in the face, as did the fact that Claude truly must have done a number on me if it had taken me nearly thirty seconds to realize it.

Here he stood—the Phantom of the Palais Garnier.

An amused smirk crept over the visible half of his face as he took a few steps toward us, his movements precise and calculated. Instinct had me placing myself between him and Claude, which amused the Phantom even further, but at least he came to a halt. When he finally spoke, his voice was as low as it was velvety, almost musical, and its deep masculine timbre sent shivers down my spine. "Have you answered your own question, Mage of the Flame? Perhaps now that it's out of the way, we can greet each other properly." He bowed low, sweeping his arms in a dramatic flourish before lifting his head to meet my gaze. "May your inner fire never die."

I swallowed hard, bewildered at the formality of this

interaction. While it was once traditional to greet fellow mages in this way, it had fallen out of fashion nearly twenty years ago and was now reserved solely for greeting members of the council. I fumbled over my reply, and not wanting to take my eyes off him even for a moment, I offered only a curt nod in place of a full-on bow. "May your winds flow..."

"Freely," the Phantom finished after I clearly couldn't remember what came next, and his smirk instantly vanished. "Rusty, are you? Pity. I expected far better from the daughter of the legendary Clopin Derosiers."

Flames instantly erupted from both my palms, trailing up my arms until they reached my elbows, and given that they were feeding off irritation as well as shock, I didn't currently possess the discipline or will to extinguish them. The Phantom knew who I was, then— had he been expecting me? Had Papa warned him of my arrival? "What the fuck is that supposed to mean?"

"Forgive my interruption," Claude butted in. Their voice wavered as if fearing I might sic my fire on them; for good reason, too, considering I hadn't yet ruled out that particular possibility. "But do we really have time for this?"

"No," the Phantom said, shrugging with that same unbothered nonchalance. "But as I said, it's your choice on the jail cell."

Claude stepped out from behind me, her gaze flickering warily between me and the Phantom. "Ma belle, I think—"

"Don't call me your anything," I snapped. "Just use my damn name—he already knows who I am."

"I think we should go with him," Claude finished, ignoring my outburst. "*Now.*"

Only then did I become aware that the once-distant shouts were nearly upon us, and that there was even commotion beginning to erupt in the streets down below. It would seem news of my sighting had spread like wildfire, and it would only be a matter of time before Phoebus himself arrived—if he wasn't here already. Besides, it wasn't as if the choice was a difficult one. I'd come here to find the Phantom, and here he was.

But even as I nodded, I couldn't ignore the prickles of... *something* that shot down my spine. It wasn't unease and it certainly wasn't fear, but the Phantom's very presence had summoned an emotion I couldn't quite place. Even now, his unblinking stare felt as invasive as it did foreboding, and as much as my mind screamed for me to look away, my body simply couldn't.

"It's decided, then," the Phantom said, finally glancing away and shattering whatever connection existed between us. "Follow me."

He turned on his heel and made his way toward the opposite end of the roof from which we'd come. I trailed after him while Claude trailed after me, though they thankfully had enough sense to keep their distance as we approached a tall section of solid wall. It was much darker here and the area was bathed in shadow, so I lifted a hand to guide us, hoping the light from my flame might carry. The Phantom didn't seem to need or want it, though; he hissed in irritation when I crept a little too close, waving his hand dismissively. "Put that shit out."

I bristled, and my flames only burned brighter. "My magic is not *shit*."

"Save it for when it's actually useful, then, and I would hope that doesn't include damaging any more of my opera house." Before I could bask in the satisfaction that I'd irritated him, he halted in front of one of the darker sections, running his fingers along its surface as if searching for something. Pausing for a moment, he inhaled deeply and sharply before pressing against the wall with both hands. Expecting a blast of air to ricochet back in our direction, I threw a hand up to shield my face—but that's not at all what happened.

The wall *moved*, and not in a way that made logical sense. Stone shifted and churned like liquid, changing into various forms before settling and revealing a hidden passage. The Phantom stepped through without explanation or hesitation, motioning for us to follow. Claude and I exchanged wide-eyed glances, but if she expected answers, I had none; I'd lived among mages all my life, but in twenty-eight years, I had never witnessed anything like this. Still, it wasn't as if there was time to question it, so I gestured them through before entering after her.

We stepped into a narrow tunnel that snaked its way down into nothingness. Darkness swallowed us completely, especially after the Phantom snapped his fingers to seal the entrance behind us, but my flames were enough to light the way as we continued following the tunnel—and this time, he didn't complain. The path was steep, and more than once I stumbled into Claude's back after losing my footing. As we descended in tense silence, my heart began to flutter against my ribcage, and my earlier questions surfaced anew. If the Phantom knew my père, and by extension me, how was the opposite not true? And if he was so determined to remain hidden, why had the Phantom revealed himself to me so willingly?

I remained deep in thought when we halted in front of a door blocking our path. The tunnel leading up to it had widened considerably, and the door itself was as ornate as it was intimidating, crisscrossed with long-tarnished silver plating. Producing a key from his pocket, the Phantom inserted it into the lock before forcing it open, utilizing a combination of physical force and a powerful blast of air from each of his palms. I was immediately struck by a chill in the air the moment I crossed the threshold, and instinct had me reaching for Claude's shoulder. They covered my hand with theirs and offered what they probably hoped was a reassuring squeeze.

Except it was anything but, for things only got stranger. We descended even more winding stairs, which seemed to go on forever, until finally they led us into a massive circular chamber. The space was huge and vaulted, with towering pillars of stone reaching the ceiling high above us, and a staircase that led farther down into what looked to be an underground lake, which split off into several winding rivers. The waters themselves were illuminated by torches placed strategically along the walls, providing just enough light to make out the handful of wooden boats docked along the shoreline.

I halted then, too overwhelmed with questions to keep going without any answers. "What the hell is this place?"

Claude stopped, but the Phantom kept going, his voice carrying easily in such a large chamber. "As impatient as Clopin himself. Typical."

"Are you able to go any longer than five minutes without mentioning my père?"

"Are you able to keep quiet for three? It's just a little farther."

"But why?" I pressed. "Why reveal yourself to me, why show me all this if it's meant to be some giant secret? If *you're* meant to be secret?"

He turned then, whipping around so fast I flinched. Locking his gaze with mine, he started toward me, halting only when Claude blocked his path. Glancing over their shoulder, he sneered, "To finally prove to that damned council, and especially Clopin, that I have something worth protecting."

"As do I," Claude said, her voice a low snarl. "I may not be a mage, but touch her, and I swear to God, you'll regret it."

The Phantom's gaze immediately narrowed, and the moment he fixated on Claude rather than me, that unnerving intensity all but vanished. A shadow crossed his face, his lips parted, and his voice cracked when he finally spoke. "C-Claudette?"

I'd nearly forgotten that was Claude's full name and stiffened upon hearing it for more reasons than the gross formality of it. But Claude had an opposite reaction, visibly relaxing as she accepted the hand the Phantom extended to her. "Wait... is it really...?"

"It's me. Erik."

"*Erik?*"

He nodded vigorously, mouth still agape in wonder. "I barely recognized you with your hair this short, but it absolutely suits you. And you're still as protective as ever, I see. My God, it's been what... twenty years? More?"

"Nearly thirty, if you can believe it." Claude laughed, more easily and freely than I'd ever heard, before throwing her arms around Erik's neck and leaving me to face a single bewildering thought.

They know each other?

It struck me then how little I knew of Claude's past, particularly their early years. I'd asked her about them on multiple occasions, but every time I brought it up, she only ever talked about Notre Dame. But they hadn't been born in that damned cathedral, no matter how much she probably wished she had, so there was definitely a time before that I knew nothing about. Was that how long she and Erik had known each other? Were they close then, and were they close still? Did he also know Jehan? What about Quasimodo? Had Claude known he was here this entire time? Though I couldn't see their face, no doubt she was grinning from ear to ear as she embraced her old friend tightly. I should be happy for them, thrilled even, and I was... So why did bearing witness to such an emotional reunion do nothing but summon that familiar yet uncomfortable tightness in my chest, the one I hadn't been able to shake since Erik had first laid eyes on me?

"And Esmeralda is your...?" he questioned after finally

pulling away from Claude, glancing at me awkwardly, as if just remembering I was still there.

"So you do know my actual name. That's good—I was beginning to wonder if you thought it was quite literally 'Clopin's daughter.'" My retort was rude and probably a low blow, but I didn't care.

Claude turned at that, but when they reached for my hand, I yanked it away. Sighing, she said, "Esmeralda is my partner, and forgive her. She's angry with me right now, and for good reason."

"I'm angry with both of you!" My shout echoed along the winding chambers as I threw incredulous glances between them. "Why is it that coming here was my idea, yet I'm suddenly the one who knows the least about what the hell is going on?"

Claude frowned. "Are you insinuating that I somehow knew Erik was here and simply didn't tell you? He and I knew each other as children, but we haven't seen or heard from each other since. I had no idea he was the damn Phantom." They cast him a sidelong glance. "Or if he was even still alive."

"She's telling the truth," Erik confirmed, butting in before I could open my mouth. "Claudette didn't know where I was—she couldn't. I don't exactly make a habit of telling people who I am, if that wasn't blatantly obvious."

Right, because you made quite *the effort to hide yourself from me,* I badly wanted to snap but managed to bite at least that part back. "It's just Claude, now. Not Claudette." I knew I should have let Claude speak for themselves, but hearing their old name over and over was making my skin crawl.

Erik turned to Claude for confirmation, nodding when she did. Far more than that was exchanged between them, though, and once again that unknown emotion resurfaced as I watched them stare at each other. But if it wasn't jealousy—and it wasn't—what in the hell was it? Disdain? Resentment? Simply feeling left out?

Before I could place it, Erik snapped his gaze back to mine before gesturing toward the boats. Though narrow enough to fit down the lake's winding channels, they were quite long, and there looked to be enough room for all three of us to fit in one if we arranged ourselves properly. "You seek answers, Esmeralda, and I'm more than prepared to give them," he said, though there was the faintest hint of a warning in his voice. "Once more, I must ask that you trust me. We aren't far."

His words confirmed that it wasn't only me who sensed something off between us, and I didn't know whether that was reassuring or alarming. Still, it wasn't as if it was productive to waste any more energy arguing, and the last thing I wanted to do was make Claude uncomfortable, so I nodded. "If they trust you, so do I."

After descending the remaining stairs leading to the lake's shore, Claude and I settled ourselves into the boat Erik indicated, with me at the prow and Claude in the middle. Erik took up the rear but didn't sit as we did. Instead, he pulled a long rod nearly the length of the entire vessel from a boat docked to our right before using it to push off from shore. He remained standing, steering after that, guiding the boat into one of the more well-lit channels. Torches lined the walls, providing just enough light to see the mist rising from the waters below—but not what lay ahead.

"It's not very deep, then, is it?" I dared to ask, unable to take much more agonizing silence, especially given that I had a front-row seat to the creepiness unfolding before us. A shiver not entirely thanks to the ever-increasing cold shot down my spine, and I half-expected some demonic creature to leap out at us at any second.

Erik didn't answer right away, but he finally grunted a response. "No, it's not."

I shot Claude a look, but all they did was shrug before responding in sign language. *He's never been very talkative.*

It's not that, I shot back. *It's that he doesn't want to talk to* me.

"By all means, feel free to have your conversation aloud," Erik said with a chuckle. "If I wanted to participate, I assure you, I would."

Irritation boiled beneath the surface of my skin, as did my flames. "Didn't you just promise me some an…"

My voice trailed off as faint music began filling the air, apparently coming from somewhere ahead of us. Erik guided the boat onward, of course offering no explanation when the notes only grew louder and more distinct. The melody was as sweet as it was enchanting, and as dark and foreboding as the Phantom himself. It enveloped us as easily as the mist, the piece swirling and building, reaching its climax the moment we reached its source—and I could hardly believe my eyes.

A magnificent organ sat in the center of yet another underground chamber. Its pipes gleamed like polished ebony in the candlelight, each as intricate as it was imposing, especially given how loudly they sang. The notes came so fast now that they tumbled over one another, every new one blending with the last, yet the organ managed to treat each one with respect and care, refusing to let it die until it served its purpose. Vibrations coursed through me, relaxing and exhilarating me all at once, and I may have closed my eyes if not for its most astonishing feature.

The organ was playing itself.

I rubbed my eyes just to be sure I wasn't seeing things, but I wasn't. No one was sitting at the bench to operate the keys and pedals, yet the pipes resonated of their own accord. At first I was transfixed, unable to do any more than stare open mouthed at what appeared to be magic lacking an explanation, but then I remembered what this reminded me of—the wall Erik had seemed to melt away back when we were on the roof. So as the boat approached the shore, I shifted to face him, and only then did it become obvious what he was doing. Though he still clutched the staff tightly, I didn't miss the way his fingers flexed, nor his brow furrowed in deep concentration. Pipe organs were powered by air, and right now, that air was coming from him.

If I wasn't so unnerved, I may have actually been impressed.

The boat finally struck the shore, but while Claude leaped out almost immediately, I remained where I was, mesmerized by the sight before us. Though the organ was its crown jewel, it was far from the only thing this chamber contained, and the space was clearly someone's home. An elaborate four-poster bed sat in one corner, its blankets arranged messily over the top, while a massive closet that put even mine to shame stood against another wall. In the center of it all, an exquisite chandelier sparkled from above, each prism catching and reflecting the soft light from the dozens of candles flooding the chamber.

As if that wasn't enough to take in, the rest of the cavern-like walls were lined from floor to ceiling with shelves, each bowed forward under the weight of countless books. Statues of various creatures adorned every corner, their coal-dark eyes seeming to follow me as I finally accepted Claude's hand and stepped from the boat. Everywhere I looked there was something new, from costumes, to weapons I hoped were props, to dozens of trinkets in various states of repair. As my gaze fell upon a table containing what looked to be a half-assembled child's toy, I was struck by how much this place reminded me of Quasimodo's workshop.

"Like it?"

Erik hadn't spoken loudly, but I'd been so lost in thought that I hadn't even noticed that the organ's music had finally died away. Whirling around, I nodded mechanically, more than grateful when Claude saved me from having to conjure up an actual response.

"You've been busy, Erik," she said, glancing up from where they stood near the organ. "But it looks like you've done well for yourself."

A shadow crossed his face. "That's because you're only seeing the result—not what it took for me to get here."

"So... this is all yours? You live here?" I dared to ask, still struggling to comprehend how any of this was possible. Mage or not, this space would have taken years, if not decades to build, and that wasn't even touching on what it must have cost. Were we truly still beneath the Palais Garnier? It felt like we'd stepped into a different world entirely.

Erik chuckled. "Have I managed to impress you, Esmeralda? It's about time *something* did."

I loathed that look he was giving me, but at least the irritation it sparked was enough to shatter my doe-eyed bewilderment. "I'm more confused than anything, but I honestly don't even know where to begin. So how about this?" I stalked toward him, picking up my skirts as I weaved my way through his maze of possessions, coming to a halt directly in front of him. "I tell you what I know for certain, then you fill in the gaps."

He narrowed his gaze in what felt very much like a challenge. "Go on."

"You're an air mage, except you wield your magic differently than any air mage I've ever met. Whether that's by choice or because you've kept yourself isolated for so long remains to be seen. You cling to old customs—old everything, really—and it irritates you that I don't. And for some reason, you really, really loathe my père, and by extension, me." I paused, searching Erik's face as I did so. "How'd I do?"

"All correct, except for one thing. I'm far from isolated. I may have started out that way, but these days, I'm not the only mage to call the Palais Garnier my home. I thought you of all people would be able to empathize with how so many of us feel drawn to the performing arts… Embermage."

I fought to keep from visibly shuddering; not only from the way my stage name sounded on his lips but because of the fact we stood nearly chest to chest. How and when that happened, I had no idea. "For someone who doesn't get out much," I whispered, "you know an awful lot."

Erik's voice was a breathy snarl. "And for someone who does, you know precious little."

"Enlighten me, then." After taking a step back, I was immediately able to breathe a little easier. "You mentioned having something to protect. Did you mean this place?"

"I mean all of it—myself, the other mages, everything I've dedicated my life to building here, separate, hidden, and safe. Do you think this is the first time Clopin has sent his minions after me, seeking to drag me into some idiotic war that isn't mine to fight? And now, he has the audacity to send *you* after me? The catalyst for the latest conflict?" Erik's voice had risen nearly to a shout, and his cloak began flapping in a nonexistent breeze. "I know why you're here. And my answer, my final answer, is no. If Clopin tries to send anyone else, mage or not, I'll send their body back to him in pieces."

"*Erik*," Claude hissed from my right, crossing the room to stand beside me, but I held out an arm to stop them. If the Phantom of the fucking opera intended to frighten me, he'd have to try a lot harder than that.

"And you think that scares us—dying?" I snarled. "We already live in fear of that every single day! You're a mage just like the rest of us, and this fight is yours whether you want it to be or not."

"Do you honestly believe that?" Erik's winds died down, and his voice got deadly quiet. "Or is that just what you tell yourself to keep from losing anyone else the way you did your mère?"

I reacted on instinct rather than rational thought and hurled a plume of fire in his direction almost before he'd finished speaking. Erik dodged the blow a moment before it landed in the lake, immediately retaliating with a powerful blast of his own. After shoving Claude out of the way, I raised a wall of fire in front of me, causing Erik's magic to be swallowed by my flames.

I was about to let loose another blast when Claude's desperate cry reached my ears. "Have you lost your minds? Stop this!"

But we were too far gone. Fire and wind swirled around us like a tornado, threatening Erik's precious possessions, but knowing that just caused my flames to burn brighter and hotter. "How *dare* you bring up my mère," I screamed, growing increasingly frustrated at Erik's lightness on his feet. The man may be tall but he was proving impossible to hit.

"Touched a nerve, have I?" he fired back, followed by a cackle when one of his blasts managed to knock me off my feet. I struck the stone floor with force, hissing when I landed hard on my tailbone.

Gritting my teeth, I pushed through the pain as I struggled to stand. With a flick of my wrist, I sent another wave of fire in Erik's direction, who leaped out of the way yet again, extinguishing my wave with an even larger wave of air.

"You're strong," he conceded. "But keep pushing yourself this hard and you won't last even five more minutes."

I fucking hated that he was right; already I could feel the telltale signs of burnout, a fire mage's state of depletion. Darkness hovered in the corners of my vision, my hands were beginning to shake, and my flames were taking far too much effort to summon. I'd used up too much of my power far too fast, and if I didn't stop, and now, I risked hurting myself. Still, letting this arrogant ass of a mage claim victory simply wasn't an option. Inhaling deeply, I summoned every bit of strength I had left before raising my arm, only vaguely aware of Claude's terrified shriek.

"Esmeralda, *don't*—"

I did.

XVII. THE TRAP

Claude

I was powerless to do anything but watch as a horrifying scene played out before me. Erik and Esmeralda were going to kill each other if they weren't careful, and judging from the recklessness with which they flung around their magic, care was the furthest thing from their minds. Wind and fire clashed again and again, and Esmeralda's strikes in particular were increasing with alarming intensity. They made her performances as The Embermage look like child's play, but beyond that, a worrying thought took root in my mind: what would happen if she pushed herself beyond her limits? Was that even possible?

Erik's warning confirmed my fears, as did the fact that Esmeralda looked as though she was about to lose consciousness. Her face was paler than I'd ever seen it, she could barely keep her eyes open, and she was even struggling to remain on her feet.

Every fiber of my being was desperate to go to her, but that would be suicide given that I had no magic of my own. All I could do was scream her name until my throat was raw while silently praying to God, Saint Mary, and whoever else would listen, begging them to save her. Esmeralda either ignored me or she was too far gone, because she used what little strength she had left to conjure a final fireball—this one as big as her head—before hurling it in Erik's direction.

Then several things happened at once.

Esmeralda collapsed on the floor in a battered heap at the same moment Erik conjured up a twister the size of his body, but neither shocked me nearly as much as the massive wall of water that rose up from the lake. Surging forward, the wave engulfed both the twister and fireball completely, but not without drenching Erik and several of his bookshelves in the process. He coughed and sputtered before muttering a string of curses under his breath, but remained on his feet while the waters receded back to their normal level, settling without so much as a ripple.

Though I badly wanted to dart to Esmeralda's side, without knowing what the hell had just happened, I didn't dare move. I knew from our childhood on the streets of Paris that Erik had always been fond of tricks, but the lake certainly hadn't looked like a trick. It looked like—

"What the hell, Meg?" Erik spat as he shook his soaking wet arms, yanking me from my thoughts. "I had it under control."

I followed his gaze to where a short Black woman stood near a row of mirrors. She was very pretty, petite yet lithe, and wearing a similar costume to those we'd seen the dancers wearing on stage, but there was no time to wonder if she'd been among them, nor how she'd gotten here—not when she fixated on me before raising her arms in what I'd come to recognize as a mage's defensive stance.

"You may have, but that fire mage certainly didn't." The lake began bubbling once again, confirming Meg must have been the water mage responsible for conjuring the wave. "And this one?"

"Claude isn't a mage or a threat. Stand down, but if you want to be useful, at least go get me a damn towel." Erik unfastened his cloak, letting the drenched fabric drop to the floor before gesturing vaguely in our direction. "Meg, meet Claude. Claude, meet Meg."

Meg and I exchanged wary glances before she scurried off to do as Erik had requested. The moment she was out of sight, I darted to Esmeralda's side, kneeling on the floor and pulling her upper body into my lap. She was shaking, cold to the touch, and barely clinging to consciousness, and panic immediately constricted in my chest. "Esmeralda? Can you hear me?"

"Get her to my bed." Erik's authoritative voice managed to reach me even through the fog of worry that had drowned all other noises out. "And quickly."

I scooped her into my arms and weaved my way through the maze that was Erik's lair. Esmeralda's teeth were chattering now, rendering her feebly muttered words unintelligible, and I tightened my grip on her when she began shoving weakly against my chest. "I'm not putting you down," I warned, "so you may as well stop that."

"She's fighting you? That's good news for sure, but why am I not surprised?" Erik caught up with me easily, now wrapped in several towels, while Meg trailed behind him.

"Am I missing something?" she asked. "Didn't she attack you? Why are we helping her?"

"She was provoked," I snapped, shooting Erik a sidelong glance. "And would never have done it if he hadn't insulted her family on numerous occasions. Of course she lashed out."

"If that was simply *lashing out*, I don't even want to know what worse looks like," Meg muttered.

"This is your fault," I continued once we reached the bedroom, glaring at Erik as he yanked back his bedsheets. "And if she's been hurt in any way, my earlier threat still stands."

"Any and all damage she sustained was self-inflicted," Erik said coolly, though he helped hold Esmeralda's head steady as I laid her down. "I was merely defending myself. Meg, my tonic, if you please."

Her gaze flickered between us. "I didn't come here to be your servant. I have news."

"Which you can tell me as soon as you've fetched the tonic. Quickly, ma chérie, et merci."

Meg sighed, but obeyed, prompting me to raise an eyebrow once she was out of earshot. "'Ma chérie?' So she's your…?"

"Meg is a gifted dancer and a good friend. We also fuck occasionally, if that's what you're asking."

"I wasn't, but that certainly answers it." I rested the back of my palm on Esmeralda's forehead, which was now coated in a thin layer of sweat. "She was cold a moment ago, but now she's burning up."

Erik nodded. "She depleted her magical reserves, so now her

body is fighting to replenish itself."

"I didn't even know this could happen." I settled on the bed beside her, taking Esmeralda's hand and pulling it into my lap. With my other hand, I stroked her hair, brushing stray locks from her face. "Will she be all right?"

"She will with some rest, and she'll recover a lot faster once she's had the tonic. But she certainly shouldn't be going anywhere else tonight, especially not in this state. She wouldn't be able to defend herself should it prove necessary—and given the commotion she caused out there, I'd say it would be more than necessary. The streets are sure to be crawling with guards."

I swallowed hard, fighting back tears as I stared at my beautiful Esmeralda. This wasn't at all how tonight was supposed to go. Our first proper date, and not only had it ended in disaster, but now she was trapped. "I should never have let you come here," I murmured, lifting her hand to my lips. "I'm so sorry."

Erik watched us carefully. "You love her," he said after a time, a statement rather than a question.

I snapped my head up, horrified. "*What*? I've only known her for—"

"Found it!" came Meg's triumphant cry, and she barrelled back into the bedroom with a small glass bottle in hand. "But Jesus, Erik, you really need to organize your shelves better."

She passed the tonic to Erik, who then looked at me. "Help me get her up."

I lifted Esmeralda's front half and pulled her against my chest. She mumbled nonsensically, her skin radiating heat against my neck, but didn't protest when I tilted her head back. Erik leaned over her then, opening her mouth before gently pouring some of the tonic inside.

Esmeralda's eyes fluttered at the taste but stayed closed as she swallowed with difficulty. The tonic had a thick consistency, almost like syrup, but the earthy scent radiating from it didn't smell particularly foul. Whatever it was, it was powerful; the moment it entered her system, her quivering all but ceased.

Her breathing steadied, and her skin cooled beneath my touch. We sat in tense silence for the few minutes it took for her symptoms to fully subside, and once they did, Esmeralda began snoring softly in my arms. She looked so at peace now, so blissfully unaware of all that had happened earlier that I could no longer hold back the tears I'd been fighting. Raising my gaze to Meg and then Erik, I mouthed, *Thank you.*

"She should be fine by morning," he said quietly, gesturing for me to lay Esmeralda back down on the bed. "You can stay here tonight, both of you, and I'll—"

"Erik," Meg cut across him, a clear warning in her voice. "I'm not so sure that's the best idea given my news."

I'd completely forgotten that Meg still had a message to deliver, and apparently Erik had too, for a look of surprise crossed the visible half of his face. "And what news is that?"

"The theater is absolute chaos. We never reopened the curtain for act two, not after guards began swarming the—"

"Respectfully, ma chérie, please begin with what I don't already know."

"The Captain of the Guard was here," Meg blurted out then, "but only briefly. He left upon hearing about…"

"About what?" Erik pressed when her voice trailed off.

Meg met my gaze, hesitating, but eventually said, "He left the moment someone told him that the fire mage's companion had white hair."

Erik said something else, but given the subtext of this horrifying revelation, I didn't hear it. Phoebus had what he'd been seeking for weeks—proof of my connection to Esmeralda—so why had that scared him off? Where could he possibly have gone?

But I knew the answer almost immediately and blurted it out without thinking.

"He's gone to Notre Dame."

Erik and Meg turned to me with identical looks of confusion on their faces. "What?" Erik shook his head. "That doesn't make any sense."

"It makes perfect sense." I closed my eyes as a wave of dread washed over me, constricting my throat as I forced out, "I live there—we live there—and I have a son. Phoebus must know I left him there, which is why he isn't bothering to track us down. He doesn't need to, not when he knows I'll go to him."

Meg's mouth fell open, and Erik simply said, "Oh, shit," as I began untangling myself from Esmeralda even as my body quivered with the force of my sobs. My God, how could I have been so stupid? So recklessly and carelessly placed Quasimodo in harm's way?

"Where are you going?" Erik snatched my upper arm, stopping me in my tracks before I'd taken more than a few steps from the bed. "Don't tell me you're going to walk straight into what's clearly a trap."

"What choice do I have?" I yanked against his grip, but he held firm. "He's after my *son*. I can't just do nothing."

"How long ago did he leave?" Erik asked in Meg's direction.

She thought for a moment. "Right before I came to tell you. So about twenty minutes?"

Erik cursed, then turned back to me. "He's close, but he won't be there quite yet."

"I doubt he's even close," Meg added. "The streets are restless. Dozens of mages have broken curfew, especially after they heard Esmeralda was sighted. Guards are attempting to round them up, of course, but it's quite a mess. He won't have an easy time crossing the city right now."

"Ah, excellent point." Erik thought for a moment then gripped my other arm, turning me so I fully faced him. I didn't want to think about what a sight I looked, especially with the way I was ugly crying, but he met my gaze regardless. "Claude, listen to me. You're going to get your son, all right?"

I shook my head, unwilling to be consoled by lies. "There's no way I'll ever reach Notre Dame before Phoebus does."

"You're right—if you go above ground." Erik squeezed my shoulders. "Which is why you're going underground."

If Erik had told me 'underground' meant the catacombs before we set off down tunnels lined floor to ceiling with human remains, I wasn't entirely certain I would have agreed. Still, it wasn't as if I had a choice—not if I wanted to reach Quasimodo in time—so I did my best to keep my eyes trained to Erik's back rather than the stacks of skulls and bones that made up the walls.

He had clearly done this before, which was as comforting as it was unsettling. I could barely keep up as he guided us through the maze of narrow passages lit only by the torch he carried. Every time I stumbled or nearly impaled myself on a misplaced shard of bone, Erik simply grabbed my arm and pulled me along behind him, but he never once complained or scolded me. We walked in silence, and for that I was grateful; even the most innocent of subjects was likely to have me bursting into tears yet again.

It wasn't long before I began to vaguely recognize the architecture surrounding us, and when we turned another corner, it became obvious why: we had reached Notre Dame's crypts. For the second time tonight, I threw my arms around Erik's neck, squeezing him tightly as I murmured, "Thank you. For everything."

"Don't thank me yet," he said once I pulled away, and he wasn't smiling. "Phoebus could already be here for all we know."

I nodded, my chest tightening at the thought. But I refused to linger on anything resembling the worst-case scenario, clinging instead to hope... because it was all I had.

Though I hadn't said anything, the look on Erik's face told me he knew exactly what I'd been thinking—a talent for which he'd had an uncanny knack ever since we were children. Wordlessly, he reached into his robe producing, of all things, a dagger. The hilt was wrapped with leather, the handle made of sturdy steel, and even in the dim torchlight, I could see how well it had been crafted.

"Take this," he said softly. "I hope you don't need it, truly, but if you do, don't hesitate. Promise me."

A lump formed in my throat as I reluctantly accepted the blade, and I was immediately shocked by how heavy it felt in my hands. This was the first time I'd even touched a weapon, and the thought of using it already made me want to vomit, but I forced myself to nod as I tucked the dagger into my waistcoat. If I did have to face Phoebus, I sure as hell didn't want to do it empty handed. "I promise."

"Good." Erik gave me one last long look before turning back the way we'd come. "I'll leave a trail for you to follow back to the opera house and guard Esmeralda until you return. And Claude?"

I paused. "Yes?"

"Hurry, will you? We have a lot to catch up on."

He disappeared into the darkness without another word, leaving me to venture through the crypts alone. After taking a deep, shuddering breath, I set off, focusing on steadying my breathing rather than the blood roaring in my ears. It physically hurt to pass the baths where Esmeralda and I had once spent such an incredible night, but I pressed on, reaching the stairs leading to the sanctuary not long after. I paused then, listening intently... but there was nothing but eerie stillness and silence, like the entire world had quite literally stopped turning.

I empathized, because in a way, mine already had. Just a few hours ago I'd been faced yet again with the possibility of losing Esmeralda for good, and now, the same was true for my son, but I wouldn't lose him. I *couldn't*.

My heart was in my throat as I took the remaining stairs two at a time. Stepping into the main floor, I was struck to find my immediate surroundings empty, with no sign of Phoebus or anyone else. The atrium was as eerily silent as the crypts had been. A nagging feeling in my chest told me this should concern me, but all I felt was relief. By some miracle, I had beaten Phoebus here, and whether it was God's doing or a stroke of pure luck, I didn't intend to waste it.

At this hour, there were two places Quasimodo was most likely to be: his room or the belltower, tinkering in his workshop, and both were upstairs. But I was so close to my office that it seemed foolish not to do a quick sweep of it at the very least, so I headed there first. Instinct had me keeping to the shadows as I made my way down the hall, but it wasn't until I was a few feet away that I realized the door was open and unlocked.

I froze in my tracks, scanning the area for any signs of movement as my pulse spiked. But everything seemed perfectly still and ordinary, save for the door. Was Quasimodo already inside? Or had Mercedes invited herself in yet again?

My steps were tentative as I crept closer to the entrance, pushing the door with one hand while gripping Erik's dagger in the other. "Mercedes?" I dared to whisper. "Are you there?"

Nothing.

Only after a few more moments of dead silence did I shove the door the rest of the way open and step inside... only to find everything exactly as it should be. My desk and its contents were untouched, the shelves were undisturbed, and the furniture remained in its rightful place. Even the fireplace was precisely as I'd left it upon departing earlier today. Nothing was out of the ordinary, and no one had been here.

So after tucking Erik's dagger back into my waistcoat, I turned to go—only for a bloodcurdling scream to shatter the silence.

I reacted on instinct alone, ducking behind the door just as human-shaped shadows began to dance in the narrow space between the wood and wall. Balling my hands into fists, I fought to keep from shaking as the figures marched closer, accompanied by clear sounds of a struggle.

"Get the fuck off me!" A woman shrieked, but not just any woman. *Mercedes.*

She came into view a moment later, and it was immediately clear why she was screaming: a guard had her by the hair. Though she was on her feet now, there were unmistakable signs she'd been dragged a fair distance given her bloodied knees and torn dress. Kicking and bucking like a wild animal, she continued to put up a hell of a fight, curving her fingers like claws as she swiped them in her captor's direction.

"Shut up, you stupid bitch," he hissed, batting her arms away before slapping her across the face with his free hand.

That's when I saw red.

It happened within a matter of seconds. One moment, I was still behind the door, and the next, I leaped into view, whipped out Erik's dagger, and plunged it into the unsuspecting guard's neck—the only place he didn't have any armor. Blood sprayed from the wound like a fountain, spewing all over me and ruining the waistcoat I adored so much as he reeled back, releasing Mercedes in his shock. His sputtering and gurgling filled the air as he fell to the ground and lay there, crimson pooling around him until his movements stilled completely.

Only as I stared into the man's now-lifeless eyes did the weight of what I'd just done bring me to my knees. I hadn't meant to kill him; I'd only wanted to get him away from Mercedes. And now, with his still-warm blood staining my hands and clothes, I found myself completely unable to move. Mercedes fared only marginally better, her eyes still wide with fear as she pulled the knife from the guard's neck.

"What the hell are you doing here?" she asked between breathless pants. "You need to—"

"I... I killed him." My voice shook, and my body felt numb all over. "He's dead, and I killed him."

Mercedes shook her head as she crawled toward me to reach out and shake my arm. "Claude, listen to me," she begged. "Don't freeze up on me now. We have to get out of here."

"*Murderer.*"

"You were defending me, it wasn't your fault—"

"Actually, it very much is."

Except the words hadn't come from my mouth—they'd come from Phoebus's. At last lifting my gaze from the body, I noted that we were surrounded. In my peripheral vision, Mercedes was yanked to her feet and restrained yet again, Erik's knife wrestled from her grip before she could do anything with it. But none of them so much as touched me, which only added to the guilt currently eating me alive. Was I no longer worth even the same harsh treatment? I more than deserved it.

"Hello, Claude." Phoebus knelt to my level, completely ignoring Mercedes's muffled protests. "But isn't it Claudette?"

"What do you want?" I said, though I didn't recall ordering my lips to move.

He sighed. "Yes, I suppose we should get straight to the point—so here it is."

With a snap of his fingers, the wall of guards in front of me parted to reveal a third prisoner: my son. Quasimodo's hands had been chained in front of him and a gag had been wound around his mouth, but worse even than that was the look of pure terror in his eyes as his gaze met mine. Like Mercedes, his clothes were in tatters, and dozens of small cuts littered his arms, looking almost as if glass had been shattered over them. God, what had they done to him?

My hands shook as I raised them. *It's all right*, I attempted to sign, but Phoebus snatched my wrists before I could finish, yanking me toward him.

"We know he's a mage, and an unregistered one at that. Burned half my men almost as if she taught him how, and I'm willing to bet she did. Is that why you clung so tightly to your precious Embermage?"

I glowered, speaking through gritted teeth as I repeated, "What do you want?"

"The deal is simple, and beyond generous in my opinion. You can walk free—you, your son, and your whore of a friend—and I'll even look the other way for *this* little disaster." Phoebus gestured to the dead guard's still-bleeding body.

He paused then, and I knew what he was going to ask for before it even came out of his mouth.

"All you have to do is tell me where I can find Esmeralda Derosiers."

Never in my life had I felt more helpless, and I couldn't have conjured up an answer even if I wanted to. What kind of choice was this—I could save Mercedes and Quasimodo, but only if I gave up Esmeralda? I'd far sooner sacrifice myself for any one of them instead.

"T-take me," I stammered, my voice hoarse and pleading. "Please, take me instead, and I'll happily face the consequences of all our actions combined. Just let them go."

"Noble," Phoebus spat. "But tell me, are you truly that damn selfless, or simply that desperate to save your own immortal soul?"

His words struck me like a punch to the gut, because once again, he was right. I wanted to save them, yes, but more than that... I wanted to save myself. I didn't want the life I'd devoted to the church to be all for nothing. It *couldn't* be all for nothing. But a single moment, a single action, had changed everything, and never again was I likely to get such a perfect opportunity to wash away this blood coating my hands.

My silence damned me, and Phoebus laughed. "Just as I thought. You're no different than the rest of us. In fact, you're worse, *sodomite*— oh yes, I know all about that—and you're desperate for penance. You won't find it from me, so you may as well give up Esmeralda and preserve the minute shred of dignity you have left."

I barely registered a word he said. The world was closing in around me, suffocating me slowly, but if my time had come, I welcomed it with open arms. Blackness clouded my vision, enveloping my body and soul alike in complete darkness. It was to be Hell, then?

I'd go willingly.

"*Stop.*"

My eyes flashed open, but it wasn't the Devil who stood before me. It was Esmeralda.

XVIII. THE TRADE

Esmeralda

 'd done plenty of stupid things in the past few weeks, but following Erik's trail through a tunnel full of fucking bones was probably the stupidest of them all. Not solely because the only flame I could conjure up was barely enough with which to see, but because I had no plan or strategy other than 'rescue Quasimodo at any cost.' That, and I couldn't bear to let Claude face this alone—not with it being me Phoebus was after, and me who had placed them all in what was now mortal danger. The only right thing to do now was fix this… or die trying.

So I pressed on, conjuring up a mental image of the startled look on Meg's face rather than pay too much attention to my creepy surroundings.

She'd been less than thrilled at being tasked with guarding me, and it hadn't taken much to convince her to fill me in regarding what I'd missed. She made a feeble attempt at persuading me to at least wait for Erik to return but hadn't stopped me from barreling into the catacombs after them, muttering something along the lines of, "It's your funeral."

It was, indeed, which is why I wasn't about to let it be Claude's, Quasimodo's, or anyone else's.

The worst thing about being down here wasn't the chilling cold nor the dry, musty odor, it was that at any moment, I half-expected Erik to leap from the darkness. He wouldn't have been called the Phantom without reason and had already proven his ability to sneak around without detection. If he caught me, I didn't doubt for a second I'd be dragged back to his lair, especially when I didn't possess the strength to fight him. I hardly had the energy to put one foot in front of the other, let alone be sneaky about it.

But I wasn't stopped, not by Erik or anyone else, and made it farther than I had any right to before finally being met with opposition. I darted around a corner the moment I saw the faintest hints of light that weren't my own, but apparently not quick enough, for that irritatingly musical voice I'd come to loathe so much sounded soon after.

"Don't even bother, Esmeralda. I assumed you would follow us."

I sighed heavily before revealing myself, holding up my pathetically small plume of flame as Erik approached. His lips pursed into a thin line upon meeting my gaze, and while ordinarily his obvious annoyance may have flooded me with a twisted sense of satisfaction, we simply didn't have time for that now. "Where's Claude?"

He halted within arm's reach. "Searching the cathedral for her son. These tunnels connect to Notre Dame's crypts, and I left her there about five minutes ago."

"So this is some ultra-convenient way to get across the city undetected, and you're telling me no one else knows about it?"

"They know. But is this really the way you'd pick if you had any other option?" Erik gestured vaguely to our grim surroundings. "Besides, I have eyes and ears on all the ways in and out, and right now, the only people within these tunnels are us."

Swallowing, I took a step back. "Sounds like we're a lot safer than Claude currently is. They have no magic, and you left them *alone*?"

"If she's going to run into trouble, I highly doubt my powers alone would be enough to save—"

"More fucking excuses," I hissed, cutting Erik off. "Isn't she your friend? How the hell do you live with yourself?"

"That's precisely it. I live *because* I know how to pick my battles. Unlike you, who creates far more problems than you solve."

"What do you call this, then?" I gestured down the tunnel. "From where I'm standing, this looks an awful lot like solving."

Erik curled his lip. "From where I'm standing, it looks an awful lot like stupidity. But… I didn't confront you to try to stop you." Reaching into his pocket, he pulled out a small vial. "Like I said, I knew you'd come. And believe it or not, I truly do want to help."

"What is it?" I asked, accepting the offering gingerly.

"Power," he said simply. "Your magic remains depleted, and I'm afraid there's nothing I can do to make it come back any faster. But take this, and as soon as your fire does return, your reserves will temporarily be tripled. It only lasts until you either deplete them once again or twenty-four hours pass—whichever comes sooner— so be sure to use it, and your magic, wisely."

Unsure if I was following, I frowned. "So if I take this right now, in about eight hours, I'll be at triple my usual strength?"

Erik nodded.

"What's the catch?"

"Other than you remaining powerless until it kicks in? Nothing, really… unless you consider an increased libido to be a catch." His lips twisted into a smirk, and I stifled a gag.

"I assure you, it would take far more than whatever's in this bottle to get me into bed with you."

"Is that a challenge?" Erik stepped closer, and his voice dropped to a low purr. "I do very much enjoy a challenge."

"I'm Claude's," I snapped.

He shrugged. "You are, and I'm certainly not trying to compete in any way. It's interesting, though, that she didn't protest while we were practically eye-fucking right in front of her. Is she willing to share, then? And more importantly, are you willing to *be* shared?"

Swallowing hard, I shook my head, more to clear the alluring mental image his words had conjured than to answer his question. "You're vile."

Erik cackled as if I'd just given him the highest compliment. "That wasn't a no. But in all seriousness, I'd quit stalling if I were you. If the best-case scenario is you and Claude getting her son back, but the worst is that you find yourself attracted to me? Well… I'd say you have nothing to lose."

I rolled my eyes before yanking open the vial and pouring its contents down my throat, if only to shut him up. The taste was unexpected—citrusy, with a hint of honey and something else I couldn't quite place—but was actually rather pleasant. The moment the last drop disappeared, a shudder coursed through me. As Erik had warned, it did nothing to restore the emptiness in my chest where my magic should have been, but it certainly made me feel... *something*. An unexpected surge of confidence had me feeling like I could do anything, face anyone, and come out victorious, even against Phoebus himself.

Erik, however, frowned. "Ah, right—there is one other thing. You may get a bit overconfident prior to your magic returning, but I promise, it's simply the potion talking. Don't let it go to your head."

"Don't pretend you care about me now," I said dismissively, waving him away. "But if it's what you want to hear, I'll say it: I'll be careful."

He caught my wrist, yanking me toward him in a way that felt aggressive and intimate all at once. I was suddenly closer to him than I'd ever been, and had I taken a single step forward, our chests would have been touching. The glare Erik shot me was so full of loathing it made me want to sink into the floor, but somehow, I found myself unable to look away.

"My God, you're irritating," he spat, tightening his grip. "I can see why Claude is so attracted to you, but how the hell does she put up with you?"

It took an embarrassingly long time for me to conjure a response, which I attributed to the fright he'd given me rather than the butterflies in my chest. "She doesn't call me irritating, for starters."

"Not to your face, anyway." Erik snorted, and we were so close his breath struck my face. "Then again, love is blind."

I stilled. "What?"

"What do you mean, 'what?' Anyone with eyes can see how much she loves you. Which is why, as her friend, I'm trying to make you see sense. Go to her if you must, but for fuck's sake, be careful."

Erik released me then, but neither of us moved, still studying one another carefully. I broke the silence after a few moments. "Do *you* care whether or not I return?"

A shadow crossed his face, but it was gone a moment later. "Go, Esmeralda," he commanded, stepping aside, and for once, I didn't argue.

Following Erik's trail and making it into Notre Dame was easy—too easy. I didn't trust the silence for a second, so the moment hair-raising screams echoed along the halls with which I'd become so intimately familiar, the only surprising part was that they hadn't come sooner. I sprinted toward the sound, my pulse thundering in my ears, only to skid to an abrupt halt once I could make out what was being said.

"…tell me where I can find Esmeralda Derosiers." Phoebus, no doubt.

"… take me instead, and I'll happily face the consequences of all our actions combined. Just let them go."

My blood turned to ice.

Claude.

There they knelt, surrounded by guards as well as Phoebus himself, and was that blood splattered across their face and clothing? Was it hers, or someone else's? And the 'them' Claude had referred to, it couldn't mean…

But it did. My heart dropped to my stomach at the sight of Mercedes and Quasimodo restrained by even more guards, each of them battered and bruised, and their clothes in tatters. The still-hopeful part of me wondered if Quasimodo still had access to his magic, but one glance at his wrists shattered the idea completely, because they'd shackled him with akrite. They knew of his identity as a mage, then… meaning that unless I stepped in, here and now, he would never see daylight again, and that's if they kept him alive at all.

There was no sign of Jules, Antoine, or Jehan, but as relieved as I was that they weren't here, it also meant I stood alone. My body scarcely cared, screaming at me to move, to do *something*, but my mind kept me rooted to the shadows, as did Erik's earlier comment: *I know how to pick my battles.* As much as I was loath to admit it, he was right—to charge straight into a crowd of a dozen fully-armed guards was suicide, even with my magic at full strength, and not only was I still very much depleted, I had seven and a half hours before the full effects of Erik's potion kicked in.

I brought a hand to my mouth, barely managing to stifle my sob as the gravity of my actions nearly brought me to my knees. What had I done? The scene unfolding before me could have been plucked straight from my nightmares and was quite literally my worst fears come to life. Except it wasn't simply Claude paying the price for my actions, it was everyone and everything she'd ever held dear—her family, her title, her faith—brought down in one fell swoop. Brought down by *me*.

That wasn't even the worst part. There was only a single truth capable of twisting the knife of my betrayal even further, and it was that precise truth I could no longer outrun even if I wanted to. It had haunted me for weeks and only festered when I refused to give it life, or even a spare thought. It was hidden in every longing glance, every tender caress, every word we'd whispered to one another in the darkness. It was obvious to everyone but us: friends, enemies, and even strangers.

I was in love with Claude.

Acknowledging it was both a relief and yet another punch to the gut, because at no point had I simply *fallen*. I dove in headfirst, perhaps the very day I'd singled them out and given them my scarf, and never once looked back. She was my most addicting high and my most agonizing low, the source of both my greatest joy and my most torturous despair. Though it had been mere weeks, I was no longer able to picture my life without them in it. I simply couldn't bear to go on without hearing their laugh, without making her smile, without being near enough to drink her in… and I didn't want to.

Knowing all of that, my choice suddenly became simpler than breathing, and when I strode forward, it was without a twinge of fear.

"*Stop.*"

My voice boomed through the cathedral, continuing to echo long after I'd uttered it, and for a shockingly long amount of time, nothing happened. But when the guards finally reacted, they did so savagely, shoving me to my knees so roughly I couldn't help but cry out. Shackles encircled my wrists a moment later, and though I'd braced myself for how the akrite would feel against my skin, it wasn't nearly enough; in addition to the awful numbing sensation, a heavy fog enveloped my psyche. There were vague flares of pain, but I otherwise barely took notice as they threw me at Phoebus's feet.

He said something, but I didn't comprehend a single word until he gripped my chin, tilting my neck at a harsh angle. Only when his sinister gaze began searching my face did I emerge from the haze, at least enough to shudder beneath Phoebus's touch. I prayed he wouldn't feel it, but of course he did; the faintest hint of a smile played on his lips when he finally spoke. "Release them. I have what I came for."

As do I, I thought with relief, but even as a chorus of protests rose up from my newly-freed allies, only a single voice reached my ears—Claude's.

"Don't do this. *Please*."

They hadn't moved other than to lift their head and remained seated in a pool of blood. Tears streamed freely down her face, mixing with the blood splatters that had yet to dry, and had our circumstances been any different, I may have been horrified at the sight. Instead, I found myself drinking her in, carnage and all, because if this was the last time I was ever going to see them, I wanted to recall every detail.

I'd barely finished shaking my head before I was yanked roughly to my feet by a pair of guards, one on either side. They spun me around before I could utter a word, forcing me to whisper my confession at Phoebus's back.

"I love you… and I'm sorry."

XIX. THE JAIL

Claude

The next two hours passed in a blur.

For almost the entirety of the first, I hadn't been able to move; it had taken Mercedes and Quasimodo's combined strength to finally pry me from the bloodied floor. Though the guards had collected the body of their fallen comrade when they'd left, enough crimson stained the stone that it looked as though Notre Dame herself had been stabbed. I believed it, because nothing felt anywhere near the same. Not the stained glass, not Saint Mary's likeness, and not even the altar when we passed the sanctuary on our way to the stairs.

"I'm damned," I whispered over and over again, unable to stop even though I could tell I was scaring Quasimodo. "I'm damned straight to Hell. Take me now, Devil, if it is your will."

We spent the next hour in my room, with Mercedes signing orders to Quasimodo and occasionally yelling at me as they worked to pack as much as they could cram into various bags. But even as they bustled around me, anxious and on edge, I remained huddled in the chair near the fireplace, fixating on the burned-out embers as a single face flashed in my mind.

Esmeralda.

She was gone. She'd given herself up for me, had been arrested at long last, and I was never going to see her again; certainly not before they executed her come morning. Though Esmeralda's original crime of burning Phoebus may not have been enough to warrant a death sentence on its own, her evasion of the guards and incitement of various riots for weeks on end certainly now were, and there could be no fighting or running from it.

It was over.

So I didn't understand why we were bothering to run or even waste energy making an attempt. Where would we go, and what was the point? We had no money, no contacts beyond the city walls, and no chance of making it more than a few miles at best before guards caught up with us, because even though Phoebus claimed we were free to go, none of us believed him for a second. The moment he was done with Esmeralda, no doubt I'd be next on the chopping block, made to answer for the guard I'd killed. I deserved my punishment, and more than welcomed it.

The solution was more than clear: I needed to stay, and Mercedes and Quasimodo needed to go. None of them had committed anything resembling a crime, and the only reason they'd been dragged into this mess at all was because of their association to me. There was no fixing it, no taking any of it back, but the least any of us could do was let it die—let *me* die. Part of me already had the moment Esmeralda had been dragged away in chains, and what reason did I have for living on if it wasn't for her? The other people in my life certainly had no use for me. I'd brought Mercedes nothing but disappointment and anguish. I'd placed my son in danger on numerous occasions, and as a mage, Quasimodo needed far more than I would ever be able to give him.

And Esmeralda... oh, my Esmeralda. I'd failed her most of all, especially with how quickly I'd torn her once respectable life to complete and utter ruin. We may have been doomed from the start, but not even I could have predicted that this was how we would end; not just in fire but banished to the depths of Hell. I'd been so desperate to keep her safe that at some point I'd convinced myself such a thing was possible, but it wasn't, and never had been. Any happy ending either of us had dared to fathom was simply an illusion, one that shattered easier than glass, and we had been fools for ever attempting to hide behind it.

All that aside, I was a monster, and now a murderer. Everything she thought she knew about me, everything she may have started to love was a lie—a lie I had told not only myself but also Esmeralda. There was no way to undo it, no way to go back, but the most selfish parts of me still wished desperately that things could have been different between us. That if I'd been smarter or braver or kinder, then perhaps things actually could have been different. But it was too late now. Too late for her, and far too late for me.

I was nothing but a festering parasite, useful only for sucking the life and soul from everyone I'd ever claimed to love.

And not only did I not want to be saved… I didn't deserve to be.

I was still fixated on that depressing revelation when a hand squeezed my shoulder. Startled, I leaped from the chair before whirling around to face a wide-eyed Mercedes. She recovered quickly though, crossing her arms in a scowl. "Are you going to help us pack or not?"

"Not when I'm not going."

She frowned and glanced at Quasimodo to make sure he wasn't reading our lips before answering. "As much as I'm in no mood for jokes, for the sake of your son, I sincerely hope you're joking."

"It's precisely for his sake that I'm not," I snapped. "The two of you need to go, absolutely. But I'm staying right here."

"To do what, exactly? Jesus, don't tell me you're going after Esmeralda—"

"If I could shoot fire from my fingers, I'd burn the city to the ground if I thought it would save her, without hesitation." A lump formed in my throat and tears sprang to my eyes once again. "I guess it's good that I can't."

"I can," Quasimodo unhelpfully offered, and only then did I realize he'd been watching us this entire time, following along with our morbid conversation. "If it will help get Esmeralda back, I'll do whatever—"

"No one is burning anything," I snapped, signing it after in case I'd spoken too fast. *And please, after what just happened downstairs, I'd rather you didn't use your powers at all. No one else needs to know you're a mage.*

A wave of dizziness rushed to my forehead then, and I'd have fallen over had I not been able to grab the chair for support.

Mercedes darted to my side, placing both hands on my shoulders to steady me. "You're not the only one grieving her, Claude. What she did for you—for us—is a debt none of us will ever be able to repay. But I'm betting the last thing she would want is for her sacrifice to be for nothing. We need to calm down, make a plan, and then—"

She was abruptly silenced as the door burst open, and in walked Jules, Antoine, and… *Jehan*? As shocked as I was to see my brother in particular, a beat passed where no one spoke, and then several people did at once, talking over one another as they raised their various concerns.

"…you doing here?"

"Where is Esmeralda?"

"…look like hell!"

"Is that *blood*?"

"Quiet!" I slammed my fist on the mantle, and all eyes swiveled to me. Turning to Jules, I managed to fight through the sea of questions that had surfaced in my mind to ask the one that mattered. "How did you get in here?"

It was Antoine who answered. "What do you mean 'how?' We just walked in. The whole cathedral is empty. Everyone is either out in the streets or has already fled the city."

"I figured it was only a matter of time before you landed yourself in trouble again, Claude, so I kept close," Jehan said. "And believe it or not, I'm only a little drunk this time."

"We came as soon as we heard whispers that Esmeralda had been captured," Jules added, searching my face intently. "Is that true?"

Suddenly unable to form words, I nodded, and Jules cursed.

"Are you serious? How?"

"She gave herself up willingly," Mercedes answered once it became obvious I couldn't. "Claude tried to stop her, but she wouldn't listen."

Jules glowered, their gaze flicking to our obvious attempts at packing before fixating once again on me. "Right... which is why you're fleeing, now? Because you care *so* much about whether my sister lives or dies?"

I found my voice enough to offer a feeble protest. "It's not like that."

"Bullshit." Visible electric sparks began dancing along Jules's palms, and everyone save for me and Antoine took several steps back. "Phoebus discovered that he"—Jules pointed to Quasimodo—"was a mage, didn't he? And that you've been hiding him here all this time, unregistered and in secret? Which is why you were all-too-eager to get close to my sister, to do whatever you could to convince her to fall on the sword for him should the need ever arise."

"Are you implying that I in any way *wanted* this?" I stalked closer as rage flared to life within my chest. "That I wouldn't give anything for it to be me in those shackles instead of her?"

Jules's sparks only grew stronger. "I'm not implying. I'm accusing."

Antoine said something, but I didn't hear it, not over that familiar darkness once again creeping toward the corners of my vision. A strange tingling sensation trailed from my neck to my fingertips, flooding me with power that felt as foreign as it was intoxicating.

But before I had a chance to release it, or even properly identify its source, someone darted between us, raising both arms to forcibly keep me and Jules at a distance.

"This helps no one," Jehan hissed, "least of all Esmeralda. We ought to be working out a plan, not squabbling like children."

Jules shot him a death glare but kept their sparks to themselves, at least for now. "I presume you have some brilliant idea, then? One that's not fleeing like a coward and leaving my sister to fend for herself?"

"Quasimodo is a fire mage, is he not?" Jehan pointed out. "Who says we can't burn shit *and* run away? Burning this place would be an excellent start."

My mouth fell open. "Burn Notre Dame? Are you insane?"

"The sanest one here, I'd wager." Jehan shot me a pointed glare. "I can't believe after everything that's happened, you're still clinging to this place like it actually means something."

"And I can't believe that after all these years, you still loathe it this much." I leaned in, both berating myself for lashing out at a time like this while simultaneously not possessing the discipline to stop. "What did Notre Dame ever do to you?"

My brother's voice was deadly quiet, the same way he always got when we landed on this particular subject. "No favors, that's for damn sure."

"No one is burning anything, not unless your goal is for all of us to end up in jail," Mercedes snapped, wisely—or perhaps stupidly— inserting herself between Jehan and me.

A dark chuckle escaped my lips. "Ironically enough, that's the first helpful thing anyone's suggested—getting us in jail. At least then we'd have access to Esmeralda."

Jehan shot me a puzzled glance. "Claude, are you serious? Why didn't you say so sooner? I've been arrested enough times to know my way in and out of that place, and one of the guards owes me a favor—don't ask if you don't want to know—but I could get someone inside. Easy."

Everyone fell silent, staring wide-eyed at my brother. "What did you just say?" Jules asked.

"I can get someone in," Jehan repeated, "but only for a *brief* visit. An escape is out of the question, especially considering how heavily Esmeralda will be guarded."

"I'd like that very much," I blurted out, then blanched under the weight of everyone's stare. "I mean… it makes sense, if we can manage it. Perhaps she has a plan, and we can still help, even if we can't get her out."

Jules stepped forward without hesitation, yanking Antoine along by the wrist. "If you're serious, we're coming with you."

"You're mages, are you not?" Jehan asked, frowning upon receiving a nod from each of them. "Your powers aren't going to work anywhere within a half mile radius of the jail, let alone within the walls themselves. They're fortified with akrite, and quite a pure form of it, which is why the effects extend beyond it, as well."

"We're coming," Antoine repeated firmly. "Even if we can't free Esmeralda, surely there's information she has for us, or vice versa, that might make a difference come tomorrow."

Jehan shook his head. "Only one of us will be able to see her in person. I may be owed a favor, but it's not *that* big of a favor, and we don't have time to negotiate."

All eyes swiveled to me then, and as much as I wanted to point out that I didn't deserve this, if Esmeralda was going to want to speak to anyone, it would be me. But there was no way I trusted myself to remember everyone's messages in my current state, so I suggested an alternative. "Why don't we all write down what we'd like to tell her, and I'll make certain she gets it?"

Once I'd hunted down a roll of parchment, everyone took turns scrawling their various messages one after the other. They left ample space at the bottom for mine, but the second I was handed the quill, my mind went blank; there was so much I wanted to say to Esmeralda that I scarcely knew where to begin, so rather than waste any more time, I rolled it up without writing anything. "Mine will be better delivered in person," I muttered after several people shot me quizzical looks.

I turned to Mercedes. It didn't sit right with me not to sign for Quasimodo to follow along, but I didn't want to scare him any more than he already was. "I need you to get him out of the city by any means necessary, and stay as far away as possible until it's all over," I whispered. "Whatever happens in the next few hours, he can't be part of it."

Part of me expected her to argue, but Mercedes only nodded. Tears hovered in the corners of her eyes, and the look on her face told me there was so much she wanted to say, but her only response was, "Good luck."

But as I turned to depart, Quasimodo suddenly launched himself in my direction, darting in front of me to block my path. "Did you tell Mercedes to watch me, as if I need some kind of babysitter?" he demanded. "I can look after myself, and I want to come with you."

My gut twisted into knots as I signed, *That's not possible.*

"Not possible, or not convenient?"

Quasimodo, listen to me. I reached out to squeeze his shoulder before continuing. *I know I've kept you far too sheltered. I know you want to help. But not only am I not willing to lose you, you won't be any help at the jail given that your powers won't work, and anyone else who tags along would only slow us down.* His face fell, but I continued, *Esmeralda gave herself up so that you would be safe. Do you want her sacrifice to be for nothing?*

No, he finally conceded. *But I don't want to lose you, either.*

I very nearly signed *You won't*, but I caught myself just in time, because that would have been a lie. I instead whispered, "I love you," before pulling him into a fierce hug, locking my gaze with Mercedes as I did so.

Keep him safe, I mouthed.

She nodded, signing, *Of course.*

My son and I went back and forth for another minute or so, but I was eventually able to persuade him that leaving with Mercedes was the safest and smartest thing, at least for now, and that I'd fetch him immediately should it prove otherwise. The temptation to lie and make empty promises was strong, but I managed not to say anything he would be able to identify as a half-truth later on. He deserved at least that much, and if I had already lost Esmeralda, I couldn't bear to lose my son, too.

"All right, then," Jehan said once we'd finished. Though my brother looked less than thrilled about Jules and Antoine tagging along, Jehan glanced at the three of us in turn before settling his gaze back on me. "Follow me, and stay close."

An hour later, we'd managed to cross the city, but not without a fight. Within fifteen minutes, Jehan had apologized for originally not wanting Jules and Antoine present, for their magic proved more than useful when it came to fighting our way through the various crowds, mobs, and even several all-out riots we encountered. Antoine hadn't been exaggerating; the streets were pure chaos, and the Paris I knew and loved was barely recognizable. Mages and citizens alike were out in full force, protesting both the mages' curfew and the fact that Phoebus had burned down several structures and homes in his search for Esmeralda.

We reached the jail soon after, and the sight of it made my blood run cold. The building was massive, with tall, imposing walls as well as an intimidating gate. Even from where we remained hidden in an alley, I could feel the despair emanating from within its walls—or perhaps it was simply the akrite Jehan had mentioned, given that Jules and Antoine were both visibly affected. The color had drained from their faces, sweat pooled at their brows, and Antoine was even visibly shaking. Something seeped into my bones as well, curling around that foreign presence in my chest and constricting it, making it difficult to draw a proper breath.

Jehan alone seemed unaffected, and I wasn't yet certain if that was a good thing. After taking a long look at what we had to work with, he turned back to face us, a look of grim determination etched on his face. "Here's what we're going to do," he said, ignoring the fact that Jules looked as though they were about to vomit. "You two, stay where you can see us, at least until we're inside. Your magic should technically still work from a distance—"

"We can't get any closer," Antoine said flatly, cutting across him. "It barely works as is."

"Any cover is better than no cover, and should things go wrong, we're depending on you both," Jehan pressed, then turned to me. "Claude and I will approach the gates by pretending I'm drunk and she's the one handing me over. That will more than convince them to let us in—they know me on sight—and from there, we need to find a woman named Fleur. She's who owes me."

I frowned. "We're counting on a single person? What if she's not here?"

Jehan snorted. "If she's not there, I'll take up being an altar boy and swear off drinking forever first thing in the morning." When I still didn't look convinced, he looked me in the eye. "Translation: she'll be there, I promise. Is everyone ready?"

Jules looked the furthest thing from it, but Jehan didn't bother waiting. On his signal, I followed my brother closely—so closely I nearly slammed into his back when he came to a sudden halt in front of me.

"Here's where our act begins," he said before looping a clumsy arm around my shoulders. I gasped as he nearly threw me off balance, but all he did was sigh. "Come on, Claude. Do you want this to be convincing, or not?"

With a sigh of my own, I let Jehan lean the bulk of his weight on me in the most awkward way possible, and I was practically dragging him when we at last started forward. His head hung low and limp, bouncing against my chest with every step, and began making noises that were a shockingly good impression of the ones I'd heard him utter when he was actually drunk. He was right, there was no way we'd have any difficulty getting inside—only with what came after.

The guards posted at the gate barely gave us a second glance as we stumbled up to them. Jehan nearly fell out of my arms, and I had to bite back a curse as I propped him back up again. The guard closest to us rolled his eyes upon realizing that we had no intention of going anywhere until we were acknowledged.

"What's wrong with him?" he asked pointedly.

"He's drunk," I said, doing my best to sound annoyed rather than scared. "I found him like this and thought it best to bring him here."

The guard grunted in response before opening the gate and waving us through without another word. We made our way toward the main entrance, and once inside, it was like stepping into an entirely different world. The air was thick and oppressive, filled with the stench of unwashed bodies, urine, and vomit. A row of cells sat directly in front of us, most of them occupied, but not by mages; magic users must be kept separate from the rest of the inmates given the tall fence that ran along one side of the jail, no doubt infused with even more akrite.

I immediately started toward it, halting only when Jehan hissed at me to stop, and it soon became obvious why. Footsteps approached from behind, and when we turned, we were met by another pair of guards.

"What's this, then?" the taller one asked, their gaze flickering between me and Jehan with disdain.

"He's drunk," I repeated just as I had outside. "I thought it best to—"

"Who are you?" the guard suddenly demanded, pointing an accusing finger at my chest. "And who is he?"

Their companion saved me from answering. "Wait… I know the drunk. That's Jehan Frollo. Been in here plenty of times before."

Both turned to me then. "And you?"

A shiver ran down my spine, because what could I say? My real name was out of the question, and given how quickly we'd thrown together our plan, I hadn't thought to come up with a fake one. But if I lied, wouldn't they see right through it? Had I already hesitated too long? *Lord, help me—*

Just as they reached for me, they leaped back in disgust when Jehan suddenly vomited all over the floor. I staggered away from the mess, dragging him with me as we put ample distance between us and the guards, and though I briefly wondered whether Jehan had done it on purpose or if it had been the happiest of accidents, it seemed to have the desired effect.

The taller one waved his hand in dismissal, wrinkling his nose. "Take him to Fleur, and quickly—you'll find her office at the end of the hall. She'll know where he belongs."

I mumbled my thanks before starting off in the direction they'd indicated, still dragging Jehan's dead weight beside me. He coughed and sputtered, wiping a hand on his shirt before muttering, "Sorry you had to see that. I just could tell you were panicking."

"Of course I'm panicking. That was close, *too* close."

"Which is why we have to hurry. Come on."

The moment we were out of sight of the guards who'd stopped us, Jehan took off at a sprint, halting once he reached what was presumably Fleur's office. He met my gaze before knocking, stepping back as we waited for it to open.

I wasn't entirely certain who I'd been expecting, but the woman who emerged looked nothing like it. She was tall, her dark hair pulled back in a tight bun, and her eyes were sharp and assessing as they swept over us. Though dressed in the same uniform as the rest of the guards, her reaction was anything but typical.

"Jehan," she said without a hint of surprise, "what are you doing here? And who is this?"

He didn't hesitate to get straight to the point. "Hello, Fleur. I'm calling in my favor, and no, there isn't time to explain."

Fleur stared at me warily. "What is it?"

"We're here to see Esmeralda Derosiers," I blurted out, and Fleur uttered a squeak of shock before covering her mouth.

"You *can't* be serious—"

"Please, Fleur, we don't have time for this." Jehan took her hand then, offering it a squeeze. "We have no plans to break her out or endanger you in any way, I swear. We just want to see her—well actually, it's just Claude who wants to see her."

Fleur inhaled sharply, seemingly as she recognized both me and my name. "Claude... Frollo? She's your *sister*?"

"Not so loud!" Jehan hissed, glancing around. "Can you help us, or not?"

She hesitated, giving me a good long glare, but finally sighed. "I can get you five minutes."

"Fifteen," I said without thinking.

Fleur bristled. "Ten. But no more. And Jehan, you owe *me* after this."

I exhaled deeply and could have cried. "Thank you. And whatever you want, whatever I can give you, it's—"

"Shut up, and follow me."

We kept close as Fleur led us through the winding hallways, down a flight of stairs, and into the bowels of the prison. The farther we descended, the harder it became to draw a proper breath, but whether that was due to nerves or the simple fact that there was less air to breathe down here, I couldn't be certain. The only light came from a handful of torches, and the closer we drew, the less there were, and I lost count of how many swaths of complete and utter darkness Fleur managed to navigate us through.

At last she stopped in front of a thick metal door and gestured for us to wait as she unlocked it with a key from her belt. The moment it opened, my heart dropped into my stomach, because there she was.

Esmeralda sat huddled in the corner of her cell, her head bowed low enough that I couldn't make out her features beneath the mop of tangled hair. Still dressed in the ball gown she'd spent so much of her hard-earned money on, it was now in tatters, and unless it was a trick of the dim light, those were bruises coloring her arms. Not wanting to startle her, I approached slowly, only vaguely aware of Fleur's murmured warning. "Ten minutes. The next patrol comes by in twelve."

And then we were alone.

I knelt within arm's reach, unsure where to even begin. "Esmeralda?" I murmured softly, but there was no answer other than the raggedness of her breathing. Was she asleep? Injured? Both?

"I brought this for you." Reaching into my pocket, I pulled out the parchment containing notes from everyone. "Messages from each of us. Jules, Antoine, Jehan, Mercedes, even Quasi—"

"You shouldn't have come."

Her voice was small and soft, but more than that, it was laced with fury. She lifted her head, sending tangled curls tumbling down her back, and wrapped her arms around her knees even tighter. "You need to go. Now."

"No." I reached out to grip her hand, hoping I didn't sound as close to tears as I felt. "We have ten minutes, and I don't intend to waste a second."

"Doing what, exactly? Placing yourself in even more danger with each passing second? Wasting time you could be spending getting your family to safety?"

When she ripped her hand from mine, I winced. "Ma belle, *please*—"

"I'm not your anything. I never should have been, and I…" Esmeralda's voice cracked, and though the light was too dim to make out details on her face, I strongly suspected she was crying, too. "I never deserved to be."

"That's the most ridiculous thing I've ever heard in my life."

"No, it's not. It's the truth. I lied to you, Claude." She drew a deep, shuddering breath, and once she got going, the words tumbled out almost faster than she could utter them. "I knew who you were long before we met face to face—for weeks before we talked. I didn't know you weren't a man, but I knew of your ties to the Church. It's why I pursued you specifically, why I was so determined to get close to you, to seduce you. I thought you could help me should I ever find myself in a situation like this." A bitter laugh. "I was wrong, clearly, on all counts."

Chills that had nothing to do with the cell's bitter cold shot down my spine, and I sat back, struggling to process her confession. Several emotions had surfaced—hurt, confusion, and anger were among them—but most of all, I was simply having difficulty believing it. "So... you never truly cared for me? Only what you thought I could give you?"

Esmeralda shook her head, inching closer, and only when metal clinked together did I realize her ankles were shackled to the wall. "I have no right to ask this of you, I know, but you must believe me. Our relationship may have started as a ruse, but everything I've said to you, *felt* for you, was genuine. In fact, I think some part of me has been hopelessly in love with you ever since I gave you my scarf all those months ago."

Yet another punch to my gut, but for an entirely different reason. "You... love me?"

She nodded. "I do. More than anything, I do."

The next few moments passed in a blur. Though my mind had no idea what to say, no idea how to process all she'd revealed and confessed, that didn't stop my body from craving her touch so badly I physically ached... but not in the way either of us expected. My hands shot out of their own accord, wrapping Esmeralda's throat in a punishing grip, immediately cutting off her air supply.

"All this time," I whispered, my voice shaking. "You lied?"

She shook her head as much as she was able, but when she opened her mouth, nothing but a desperate wheeze came out. But as absolutely fucked as our current situation was, I'd suddenly be the liar if I tried to claim I didn't find it arousing—all of it. Her fingers clawing at mine, the genuine terror in her eyes, the way I'd rendered her completely and totally helpless. Once, not long ago, Esmeralda had tried to claim she was the bigger danger to me given her flames, and had even told me I wasn't a monster.

I hoped now she knew how wrong she was.

But as much as part of me wanted to suffocate her a little longer, I released her a moment later, turning away as Esmeralda collapsed on the unforgiving floor, sucking in breath after desperate breath. Only then did I realize she was crying—sobbing, even—but not even the pain in her voice had the slightest affect on me, physically or otherwise.

"I'm so sorry, Claude," she said over and over. "I never meant to hurt—"

"Hurt me?" I snapped, only barely resisting the urge to choke her all over again. "I'm the one who's supposed to hurt *you*, and only in the context of what we agreed. Not like this. Never like this."

"If that's what you need right now, do it. Please. I deserve it, and I want you to."

I swiveled my head just enough to glimpse her, and another jolt of arousal ran through me at the sight of Esmeralda quite literally begging and on her knees for me—a sight Phoebus could only dream of. A growl rumbled in my throat at the thought; I may want to do horrible things to her right now, but that didn't make her any less mine.

Mine.

Something in me shifted at that particular reminder. It wasn't forgiveness or anything close, but the reality was that this could very well be the last time I'd ever see her, the last time I'd ever hold or touch her. And as furious as I was, I also couldn't bear the thought of spending our final moments together with Esmeralda in pain. If we somehow made it through this, there would be plenty of time for that later.

I reached out, cradling her face in my hands, and a shudder of surprise rippled through her when I didn't do anything worse. Esmeralda's skin was cold and damp with tears, but the moment our eyes met, my decision was made.

Our relationship had been born of a lie. We had sinned for one another, cheated and deceived for one another, and I'd never felt more certain of anything in that moment.

If Esmeralda wasn't already destined for Hell, by God, she

would be by the time I was done with her—and I'd be there to greet her at the gates.

Which was why I didn't feel a single shred of remorse when I slammed my lips against hers.

Esmeralda hesitated, either because I'd hurt her or she couldn't believe this was happening, but a moment later, she kissed me back with equal parts violence and desperation. Her mouth was liquid fire—warm, wild, and all-encompassing, and at one point, there was even blood—and I was immediately addicted to her taste, her scent as it enveloped me in an entirely different way. We may have grown more than accustomed to one another's bodies over the past several weeks, but this particular act was entirely new, and it left me far more desperate than I wanted to admit.

"I hate you," I hissed between breathless pants. "I hate that I love you and I want... I want..."

"Tell me." A command, but given how little time we had left, I wasn't about to scold her.

"I want you to touch me."

She pulled away then, but only enough to meet my gaze in the darkness. "You're sure?"

"No," I admitted. "But if you don't touch me, I'm more afraid of what I might do to you, and if this is the last time we ever..."

I was thankful Esmeralda didn't wait for me to finish that sentence before placing a hand on my chest, directly over top of my bindings. Her touch was light and gentle, but I drew a sharp inhale regardless, because it had been years since I'd trusted anyone else with my body.

"We don't have to do this," she whispered. "I told you, you can—"

"No." I placed my hand over hers, guiding it lower. "I want this."

She nodded before placing her other hand on me in a silent, final question.

This was my last opportunity to protest.

I didn't.

But neither did she move; not right away. Esmeralda caressed my cheek, my earlobe, my neck, but pointedly avoided my lips. Her deep inhales summoned my own, and I writhed against her, which I highly suspected was her motivation behind teasing me.

"What are you waiting for?" My voice came out low and breathy.

She squeezed my upper thigh. "*You.*"

We came together not like two people making up for lost time, but as though the world would stop turning simply to wait for us. Esmeralda pressed herself to me like she belonged there, moving to straddle me as we kept kissing, gentler this time. Her lips were even softer than they'd been a few moments ago, as if she'd finally surrendered herself completely to me just as I'd done with her. She tangled her fingers in my hair, yanking hard enough to make me moan with equal parts pain and pleasure, while her free hand traveled to the space between my legs.

"I know there isn't much time," she murmured against my neck. "But I want you to come for me, Claude."

I barely registered her words, far too drunk on her taste, her touch. "Anything for you, ma—*oohhh.*"

My words turned to a moan as Esmeralda slipped her hand

down my pants, expertly and efficiently locating what she sought. A shudder ran through me as she hummed her own pleasure before chuckling softly and whispering, "So wet for me, and I've barely touched you. You've been waiting for this, haven't you?"

I'd been waiting for a lot of things, but I couldn't form the words to articulate as much, especially not when she began running her fingers through my folds. Her movements were as tantalizing as they were torturous, but she didn't linger there long, moving her thumb up to my clit once my breaths started coming in quicker gasps.

"Mon beau, look at me."

I obeyed, my eyes meeting hers in the darkness. Her gaze was heavy with desire, bright and warm even in our current surroundings. With another tug on my hair, harsher this time, she leaned forward and kissed me, her tongue teasing mine while her thumb continued its slow circles around my clit.

The sensations were unlike anything I'd ever experienced before—a dizzying combination of pleasure so intense it left my head spinning. She was gentle yet firm and patient yet swift, pushing me closer and closer to the edge until I thought I might come apart from anticipation alone. But still she kept going, her touch becoming firmer and more urgent as we raced against the little time we had left.

My hips moved of their own accord, seeking out more contact and a deeper sensation with every passing second. Esmeralda responded without hesitation, yanking me closer as my pleasure bordered on overwhelming. My hands were everywhere, as if determined to memorize the shape of her before we were so cruelly ripped apart, before we'd be forced to face demons far larger than ourselves... and before the sun rose on a Paris divided, thanks in part to us.

It was then that I came apart, every nerve in my body igniting as I threw my head back and began to cry out her name. Esmeralda covered my mouth just in time, but a bit of sound still escaped through her fingers, echoing in the cell around us. My orgasm was wild and intense, the waves of pleasure coming again and again, and I was still quivering when I collapsed in her arms, panting for breath.

"You're so handsome it hurts," Esmeralda whispered between pants of her own, cradling my head against her chest. "Especially like this, out of breath and trembling for—"

She abruptly silenced the moment a knock sounded on the door, followed by Fleur's voice calling from the other side. "Time's up."

I tensed as reality and my fears came flooding back in equal measure, drowning out any lingering desire to hurt or punish her. Even as Esmeralda tried to pull away, I wrapped my arms around her tighter, unwilling to let her go, now or ever. "What's going to happen to you?"

Curling her fingers around my chin, Esmeralda raised my gaze to hers, and her voice was so eerily calm it bordered on unnerving. "I'm going to be fine—I promise—but you have to trust me."

"How do you know?" My own voice was a plea, and I didn't move even as Fleur knocked again. "And how the hell can you be so sure?"

"There isn't time to explain. Just trust me, Claude. Please."

The door burst open then, and Jehan and Fleur charged in without hesitation. "The patrol's coming," Jehan hissed into my ear.

"Get up, *now*."

"I'll be fine," Esmeralda repeated, at last extracting herself from me. She then looked to Jehan. "Keep them safe, and make sure they don't do anything foolish, please."

Jehan cursed as he managed to yank me to my feet. "If we can get her out of here, I'll certainly do my best."

I stumbled toward the door, still in a daze given everything that happened. "I love you," I said a final time, and Esmeralda responded with a pained smile.

"I lo—"

Then Fleur slammed the door.

I'd have been angry if I had even a second to be, but given that the patrol was now so close we could hear their footsteps, I didn't have any choice but to flee along with Fleur and Jehan.

"What now?" my brother asked as we sprinted back up the stairs. "Did you learn anything useful, or did you two just pass the time fucking?"

I met his gaze as a surge of determination flooded through me. "Who do you know that could get us into the catacombs?"

XX. THE EMBERMAGE

Esmeralda

The entire city had come to watch me die, and I couldn't decide whether that was unsettling or comforting.

I had to hand it to Phoebus, though—he'd certainly gone to great lengths both for dramatic effect and to ensure he wouldn't be humiliated a second time. If the akrite shackles around my wrists, ankles, and even wound around my upper body weren't proof enough of that, the fact that he and his guards had blocked off an entire bridge certainly was. No mage's power could reach where I'd been placed, and that was if their magic even worked; many had depleted themselves in the night, which explained why the riots had been permitted to continue for as long and with as much intensity as they had. I stood overlooking the Seine, where they intended to drown me in a few short moments, once they went through the motions of reading off my supposed 'crimes.' I gritted my teeth. I shouldn't have been afraid of Phoebus, the river, or any of this, but I was, thanks to one small thing.

Erik's potion still hadn't kicked in.

Even despite the akrite suppressing my flames, I could still feel their comforting flicker rumbling deep within my chest. But they weren't at their full strength, and they certainly weren't at triple as Erik had so confidently promised. I snorted. Leave it to me to place my trust in a man, only for him to let me down at the—

The guard to my right snarled in my direction, and I wondered if he knew I could still move my legs enough to stomp on his foot if I wanted to. I might have done it—what was he going to do, kill me?—had Phoebus's voice not boomed out from behind.

"Citizens of Paris," he began, and though I couldn't see his face, the smug grin in his voice was undeniable. "At long last, Esmeralda Derosiers, the Embermage, stands before you to answer for her crimes. She is charged with assault, destruction of property, incitement of violence, and as of last night, murder."

I snorted again; at what point could I have murdered anyone given that I'd spent the night in a jail cell?

"She is to be banished to the waters," Phoebus continued, "where she and her flames will drown once and for all."

A handful of voices rose up in protest, but not nearly as

many as had spoken out against the scene in Notre Dame's square several weeks ago, and it wasn't difficult to deduce why. When I glanced at the sea of faces on either side of the bridge, I saw nothing but despair and exhaustion staring back at me. My fellow Parisians were as tired of fighting as I was, and I completely understood why most had chosen to believe Phoebus's claim: that my death would bring an end to the conflict between mages and the Church, and things could resume as 'normal.'

But that's where they were wrong. My death wouldn't be the finale—it would be the catalyst for even more hatred, conflict, and suffering, and only set a bloody precedent for the years to come. Whether the rest of the city was ready to admit it or not, there would never be any meaningful change for as long as the Church, and by extension Phoebus, were permitted to go unchecked.

They needed a fire... they just weren't ready for mine.

"...repent for her sins?"

Arms gripped my shoulders, spinning me around roughly, and then I was face to face with Phoebus. His lips were curled into an infuriating smirk as his gaze locked on mine, as if hoping I might challenge him.

My only response was to lift my chin, refusing to give him the slightest ounce of satisfaction. I may be afraid, but I wasn't about to beg for my life, and I certainly wasn't about to confess to falsified charges. My flames were suppressed, but I still had my dignity, and I had no intention of letting Phoebus or anyone else frighten it out of me.

But he wasn't deterred, and he snatched my bare shoulder before digging his nails in like talons. "Nothing to say for yourself? Come now—I expected you to at least seize an opportunity to tell me to go fuck myself."

I winced beneath his grip. "You're not worth it."

"Neither are you, apparently." Phoebus chuckled, and the sound of it sent chills down my spine. "All these people, many of them mages, and not one of them is willing to make a stand for you— especially not your *special* friend"—he curled his lips in disgust— "Claude. I hear she fled Notre Dame in the middle of the night, with the rumor being she left Paris entirely."

Even if Claude hadn't visited me, I knew them well enough to know she'd never leave—not while I still drew breath—but part of me desperately wished she had. If I truly was about to die, she didn't need to see it. "Fascinating."

I expected my cool nonchalance to irritate Phoebus; what I didn't expect was for it to fuel him. "Doesn't it bother you, knowing you've lost?"

"Doesn't it bother you that I'm still alive?"

This finally got a reaction out of him, and his eyes widened, prompting me to continue. I was in no hurry to die, necessarily, but I was tired of this senseless posturing, and if Erik's potion wasn't going to kick in, we may as well get this over with. "If you're so determined to make me a martyr," I spat with as much vehemence as I could muster, "I suggest you hurry it along."

Phoebus leaned in then, and I flinched. His breath was hot on my skin, and his words as sharp as daggers. "A martyr implies that you have an actual cause. You have anything but. You're just a silly little girl with dangerous powers you've proven time and time again you can't control. You may be remembered, but it won't be forever. Your name will just be replaced on their lips by the next mage I kill, then the next, then the next. Until there are none left, and the world is liberated of this hellish plague."

He spun on his heel before I could conjure up a response, raising his voice and addressing the crowd once more. "She has refused to repent and chosen to meet her watery grave without remorse." Nodding to his guards, they didn't hesitate to leap into action.

This crowd erupted into unintelligible shouting as arms yanked me back toward the edge of the bridge, pushing me to stand on the railing and forcing me to stare into the frigid depths below. They handled me roughly, but I barely felt it, far too overwhelmed with the horrifying truth; that I was about to drown, and there was nothing anyone could do about it.

This was it. Erik's potion had failed, but far more terrifying was that *I'd* failed.

I should fight. I should scream. I should taunt Phoebus some more, if only to get a rise out of him, and I certainly shouldn't be this cooperative with the people attempting to execute me. But resisting would only delay the inevitable, and what was the point? I'd miss Papa, Jules, and of course Claude desperately... but I'd be with Maman again at long last.

A gentle gust of wind washed over me, and with it, an eerie calm. I was ready. Death came for everyone sooner or later, and if this was mine, so be it. Drowning certainly wouldn't have been my first choice, and the minutes to come would no doubt be agonizing, but at least they were minutes rather than hours or days. At least my death wouldn't be in vain, no matter how much Phoebus wanted to pretend otherwise.

And at least I'd gotten to tell Claude the truth, and that I loved her.

I'd braced myself but still wasn't ready when they pushed me. I was even less ready for the impact, and I opened my mouth in a silent scream when my body struck the water. Icy liquid invaded my mouth and nostrils, but that concerned me far less than the rapid pace at which I sank. My chains held firm, dragging me into the depths, and refused to loosen even when I thrashed with every ounce of strength I possessed. The movement caused waves of red to pool around me—not blood, but my once beautiful ballgown—further obstructing my vision and suffocating me all at once.

But it wasn't the need for air that caught up with me first; it was the unforgiving cold. I quickly began losing feeling in my extremities, and with it, my little remaining energy. I could barely move by the time my shackled ankles struck the slimy bottom, and an ever-growing part of me didn't want to try. My lungs screamed for oxygen as my body fought to remain conscious, but my mind had already surrendered, all too happy to drift into darkness and await whatever came next.

I'm ready, Maman, I whispered into the frigid waters. *I'm ready.*

Her answer came in the most unexpected way. My helpless body jolted to the side as the water suddenly moved, shifting and rippling as if being manipulated by some outside force. A few moments later, it receded completely, and I erupted into a fit of coughs as I fought to expel the water from my lungs. My breaths came in deep, shuddering gasps, flooding my body with equal parts relief and confusion, mostly because my senses were so disoriented. My sight consisted of nothing but vague shapes and dull colors, the only sound in my ears was muffled ringing, and my nerves were so hypersensitive I doubted I'd be able to feel it even if I was stabbed. Was this what it felt like to die? And if by some miracle I hadn't, what the hell was going on?

Something encircled me then—they could have been human arms or more chains for all I knew—and lifted me from the muddy, frigid ground. I shivered uncontrollably as I was carried up the riverbed, too dazed still to make out what had happened. My hearing returned, though, at least enough to make out the eerily familiar voice.

"Hold on, ma chère fille. Just a little farther."

My eyes shot open, because there was only one person who called me chère. "*Papa?*"

A shuddering sigh escaped him, though he didn't slow his pace. "I'm going to hand you to Jules, all right?"

"What happened?" My vision began flooding back, as did the surrounding noise; shouts, violence and chaos. "Who else is—"

"Es, take my hand!"

Glancing upward, I was met with Jules's panicked face. They were balanced on the edge of the shore, offering an outstretched hand, but it wasn't enough to reach me or Papa. "Meg and Antoine can't hold back the river much longer. Can you reach?"

I briefly wondered if they meant Erik's Meg, but there was no time to question it. "Not with these." I wiggled my upper body where chains still encircled it, preventing me from stretching out my arms. "Papa either has to lift me, or—"

I fell silent as he set me back on the ground; or more accurately, dropped. A grunt escaped me as I struck the half-frozen riverbed, but I bit my tongue as Papa set straight to work. A concentrated blast of fire burst from his index finger as he pointed it at my chains, working to melt them as quickly as possible. If I were anyone but a fire mage, the heat alone would have seared my skin to a crisp, but after what I'd just endured, the warmth was more than comforting. I remained still as Papa focused on a single link, but though it was working, apparently not fast enough.

"Hurry!" Jules cried from above, and when I glanced up, I immediately realized why. In the center of the dried-up riverbank stood Antoine and Meg, facing different directions as they held back opposite ends of the river. Antoine faced the bridge, which his wave had engulfed completely, while Meg was the reason Papa and I had any chance at escape. Though there was no sign of Phoebus or his men, chaos had erupted on either side of the bridge, with various elements being slung around with more force than I'd ever seen.

But as wondrous as it was, my gaze quickly darted back to the water mages, especially when it became apparent just how little time we had left. Meg's arms quivered dangerously, and her face was contorted in pain; telltale signs that burnout was imminent. If she or Antoine were to pass out or otherwise become incapacitated, we were beyond fucked, and I'd go right back to drowning, especially with these chains still intact.

"Can't you go any faster?" I pleaded with Papa, but he shook his head.

"Akrite has an unusually high melting point, and it's dangerous to—"

"We're already in fucking danger, and it's not as if you'll harm me. Please, Papa!"

He shot me an agonized glance but obeyed, conjuring flame from his open palm rather than just a single finger. I gasped as the sudden blast of heat seared my skin, but not from pain. If anything, it was exhilarating, even more so when my sleeve caught fire, the blaze trailing up my arm until it reached my neck.

But finally, the chains began to loosen, and a few moments later, a single link finally snapped. Papa ripped them away before yanking me to my feet, shoving me toward Jules. My wrists and ankles remained shackled, but now that the chains were gone I could raise my arms enough so that when Papa lifted me, Jules's hands clasped with mine. They hoisted me up and over the wall, and I held my sibling's legs while they lifted Papa up next.

We were still helping our père get the lower half of his body back on solid ground when the river came crashing back down with a vengeance. They didn't release Papa, but the anguished cry that escaped Jules's lips turned my blood to ice even more than the residual waves that splashed us, soaking me to the bone once again. The moment Papa was safe, Jules sprinted down the bank even as I called after them, but Papa shook his head. "Let them go. We need to get these shackles off you."

"But Meg and Antoine—"

"Are water mages. Even if they did pass out, they cannot drown. They're far less vulnerable now than you are every second you're bound by those damn things," Papa pressed. "So come on."

I nodded numbly, moving as quickly as I could shuffle as he led the way toward an overturned cart. After motioning for me to duck beneath it, he got to work on my wrist shackles first, utilizing the same open-palm method to melt the stubborn akrite.

Taking advantage of the brief respite, I closed my eyes, calling upon my still-dormant flames. They were stronger now that I was nearly free of my bindings, but yet again, Erik's supposed 'power' in a bottle had yet to show the slightest signs of working. Gritting my teeth in frustration, I turned to Papa. "Have you heard of anyone making potions for mages? Ones that might enhance our power?"

He shot me a quizzical glance. "There are those who practice alchemy, yes. Why?"

"Do they work? Their potions?"

"That depends entirely on the skill of their maker." My left wrist was now freed, so Papa turned to the right. "Why do you ask?"

"Because…" I hesitated. "Because I took one."

His flames flickered for a brief second, and he did a double take. "You did what? Who brewed it?"

"Don't do this, Papa. You know exactly who."

A tense and heavy silence enveloped us for several long moments. "God damn that Phantom, experimenting on my only—"

"So you *did* know he existed," I snapped, practically ripping my wrist from his grasp once he'd freed it. My ankles remained in chains, but Papa made no move to free them. "Why the hell send me there with such a cryptic note, then? Why not go yourself? He certainly seems to know you."

"Do you think I haven't tried?" Papa reached for my right leg, and though I was tempted to kick him, I wanted access to my powers far more. "And I didn't know he was real—I swear. Believe whatever you want, but he had me convinced that the 'Phantom' was an entire group of mages rather than just one, all conspiring to make my life— and the council's—a living hell."

I sighed deeply; as much as I was loath to admit it, that certainly did sound like Erik. "Well, the Phantom is very real, he absolutely hates you, and he gave me a potion. I depleted myself last night—"

"You *what?*"

"—and he claimed that while the concoction wouldn't restore my powers any faster, it would temporarily increase my reserves three-fold when they finally did return," I finished, ignoring Papa's openmouthed glare. "The problem is… that hasn't happened yet."

He didn't answer right away, instead focusing on releasing my still-trapped ankle. When at last the akrite clattered to the stone, a jolt rippled through me, and Papa's head snapped up. "Did you feel something?"

"Just my flames eager to be free, but no more so than usual."

Only one shackle remained before I had access to my powers once again, and Papa set to work melting it. "If you're asking me how much I know about alchemy and potions, the answer is very little. If the Phantom's potion hasn't worked as intended, though, there are several possibilities: that it simply needs a little more time, that it was a dud, or that he gave you a different potion than intended, meaning the effects will be different."

I made a face. "I dislike all of those, but option one would be the most useful in this scenario."

"Why? What in God's name do you need that much power for?"

"Because," I said, lowering my voice to a snarl, "Phoebus and I have unfinished business."

Papa's flame flickered once again, this time stronger and more erratically. "Ma chère fille, violence isn't—"

"If you're going to say violence isn't the answer, don't. This ends the same way it began: in fire." The final shackle fell away, and I exhaled deeply before flicking my wrist, summoning a strong and healthy plume of some of the purest flames I'd ever produced. I may not be benefitting from Erik's potion, but maybe I didn't need to; perhaps my fire would be more than strong enough on its own.

So before Papa could scold or stop me, I crawled out from beneath the cart and stepped onto the street, already calling upon tricks I normally reserved for the stage. It would call attention to me, of course, but that was the entire point.

If Phoebus wanted to meet The Embermage, I was more than happy to oblige.

XXI. THE ELEMENTS

Claude

"Come with me."

"For the thousandth time, no."

"And why not?" I whirled around to face Erik, enjoying the rush of satisfaction that flooded through me when my cloak whipped him in the face.

He glowered. "You of all people know the answer to that question."

"Absolutely no one is going to be looking at you, because they're all looking at *her*." I pointed to the bridge where Esmeralda stood bound in chains, and where at any moment, she could be pushed off to drown. "If ever there was a day to go out in public, this would be it."

Erik remained in the shadowed alley, watching me warily. As

always, he was clad head to toe in solid black, including his signature half mask. And while I did indeed know his reasons for keeping his very existence a secret, to do so today in particular felt dramatic even for his standards. "Your statement presumes I want to," he replied coolly. "I assure you, I don't."

My chest tightened because not only was he putting up an irritating fight but we also didn't have time for this. We had a plan, yes, but that didn't mean I'd anticipated doing my part completely alone. "You're going to leave me, then? Just like you did last night, at Notre Dame?"

I didn't say the rest, but I didn't have to; Erik was fully aware that I'd murdered a man using the knife he'd given me, and that such an act may not have been necessary had he come with me. He was fully aware of my trauma surrounding the encounter, too, which was why I'd flown into such a rage when he insisted that I carry a blade again today. Though I'd vehemently fought against the idea, the knife strapped to my hip was tangible proof that I'd lost.

"Claude." A warning as much as it was encouragement—well, as encouraging as Erik ever was. "You're not alone. My mages have their orders. Meg and Antoine are in position. And in case it wasn't abundantly clear, I am here as a last resort, and a last resort only. Keep pushing me, and I may not even do that much."

As badly as I wanted to keep arguing, I knew when to admit defeat where Erik was concerned. But if I was about to head toward the bridge, alone and undefended, I at least wanted reassurance that Esmeralda would be safe. "Your potion. It's going to work, yes?"

"She needs to get those chains off first—another fire mage should be able to melt them in lieu of a key. But once she's no longer burdened by any akrite, yes, my potion will work."

I took a deep breath, steadying my frazzled nerves. He'd said 'will' and not 'should,' which was as good a promise as I was going to get, and to stall any further would do more harm than good. Erik was right: we'd planned this, everyone was in place, and he himself would be there to step in should it prove necessary, a secret weapon of sorts. All that remained was to do my part, which was to get Esmeralda to safety, and hope and pray that nothing would go wrong.

"And we rendezvous here after it's done?"

"And we rendezvous here after it's done," Erik echoed.

It was a good plan, a solid plan, and though there were many variables at play, I had no reason to be this on edge. *Here goes nothing.*

"Good luck," Erik said. Only then did I realize I'd spoken the last part aloud, but when I glanced over my shoulder to thank him, he was gone.

I supposed he wasn't called the Phantom for nothing.

Yanking my own hood over my face, I set off at a brisk pace, headed for the northern end of the bridge. It was difficult not to be reminded of all the times I'd walked to the faire dressed precisely like this, and under eerily similar yet radically different circumstances. On both accounts, the streets were bustling with activity, crammed full of bodies, and Esmeralda was the center of attention... The specific type of attention was the only real difference.

Yet another image of her bound in chains flashed in my mind's eye, but I immediately shoved it aside. Lingering on it too long only made me want to charge straight into the fray, barrel onto the bridge, and snatch her, but all that was likely to do was get me killed before I even got close. The best thing to do was watch from a safe distance, and trust that everything would go to—

A splash. I snapped my head up as my heart began to pound, and I shoved my way indiscriminately through the sea of bodies that remained between me and the river. Glancing first at the ripples marring the water and then upward to where Esmeralda no longer stood, I made the connection right as my blood ran cold.

She'd been pushed in.

No. This was never part of the plan; Meg and Antoine had sworn up and down that they'd catch Esmeralda before she went completely under, thus removing any chance of her actually drowning. So where the hell were they, and what had gone wrong? Had they been spotted by the guards? Been captured themselves? Or did they know what they were doing and I simply needed to wait?

I forced myself to do just that as I at last reached the shoreline. The Seine's waters were so murky it was impossible to make out what could be happening below, and for all I knew, Meg and Antoine had already guided Esmeralda to safety. Perhaps the delay was because they wanted to remain out of sight of Phoebus and the guards or attempt to trick them? Maybe they wanted them to believe she was really dead?

But even as I thought it, I knew immediately that if it were true, I wasn't willing to gamble with Esmeralda's life. Whipping off my cloak, I flung it behind me, tensing my knees as I prepared to leap into the water after her.

What I didn't expect was for the river to leap to *me*.

I stumbled back just as a massive surge of water rose up, completely swallowing the bridge and everyone still on it. But even as screams echoed around me, I kept my gaze trained on the newly exposed riverbed, and my heart leaped upon glimpsing her.

Esmeralda.

She may be sputtering and still chained, but at least she was alive. Not far in front of her stood Antoine, who was solely responsible for holding the massive wave that had overtaken the bridge aloft. Behind him and facing in the opposite direction was Meg, parting the Seine on the opposite side, and my God, I could have kissed them both. A small hiccup, but it appeared the plan was back on track, so long as Jules showed up, and quickly.

No sooner had I thought it than someone did scoop Esmeralda up, only it wasn't who I'd expected. The man bore an eerie resemblance to both Jules and Esmeralda, though, and I briefly wondered if this was their père before leaping into action myself. I remained on the shore but kept up with Esmeralda's savior as he carried her over to where Jules lay draped over the opposite shoreline, attempting but failing to reach Esmeralda, and I soon realized why—her chains prevented her from raising her arms, and therefore being able to reach her sibling's grip.

My blood ran cold as her père dropped her, even when he immediately set to work melting her chains. There wasn't time for this; Meg and Antoine were already struggling to hold back the river much longer, evidenced by the strain on both their faces as well as Jules's desperate cries. And I was all but useless where I stood, given that I was on the wrong side of the river and had no way of getting Esmeralda's chains off any faster.

What I could do, though, was help her up—if I found a way to cross the river. I spun around, scanning for the nearest intact bridge, fully aware that if Meg and Antoine lost control of the river, Esmeralda, her père, and possibly even Jules would be swept away with it. In desperation, I finally spotted a bridge just a few hundred yards away; much too far, but it was my only chance.

I broke into a sprint, my feet pounding against the cobblestone ground as I raced toward the bridge. My heart thundered in time with my steps as I envisioned Meg and Antoine's faces growing more strained by the second; they wouldn't last much longer, of that I was more than certain. With a final burst of energy, I lunged onto the bridge, managing to make it across just seconds before their hold on the river finally failed. The wave came crashing down like a tidal wave, swallowing the bridge whole.

There wasn't time to register just how close I'd come to being swept away; not when Esmeralda needed me. Pushing through the burning in my lungs, I took off running once again, hoping and praying that she and her family had been as lucky as I was. But when I reached the spot where the trio had been just moments before, there was no trace of them, and my heart skipped a beat; had the river claimed them, after all? My body took over without rational or conscious thought, running along the Seine's shore as I followed the flow of the current, fueled by a single thought.

You'll find them.

And just before reaching the main bridge, I did; a small group bobbed in the river, struggling against the agitated current. Jules was closest to the shore, paddling furiously as they fought to keep Meg and an unconscious Antoine afloat. There was no sign of Esmeralda or her père, which summoned an overwhelming wave of fear, but it wasn't as if I could leave these three... so wherever the other two were, they would simply have to wait.

I dove into the river, hissing at the sudden cold before swimming toward Jules as fast as I could. Once I reached them, they passed Meg off to me, which allowed Jules to focus on keeping Antoine's head from going under. We moved as a connected unit, with Jules keeping a firm grip on Meg's shoulder as I led the way back toward shore. With a weak flick of her wrist, Meg was able to raise the water level, thereby raising us, and we collapsed back onto the street in a tangled, shivering heap.

"Where is Esmeralda?" I forced through chattering teeth. "Is she...?"

"She's with Papa, but safe the last I saw. They both made it up in time."

A relieved exhale escaped me. "Thank you."

"No, thank *you*." Jules stood up first, draping Antoine's arm over their shoulders. "He's depleted. I'm taking him back to Erik."

"I'm going with you," Meg said, panting heavily. "I'm nearly there as well, so I'll be useless in a fight."

I swallowed the lump in my throat that formed at the thought of being alone once again. As much as I wanted to beg Jules at least to stay, it was obvious they would never leave their partner, and I had no right to ask them to. "Be safe. I'm going ahead to look for Esmeralda."

Once they were out of sight, I took off running in the opposite direction, at this point fueled by adrenaline alone. The streets of Paris had devolved into pure chaos, and though it was early morning, the air was so thick with smoke and dust that it nearly resembled night. All around me, mages flung their various elements around with reckless abandon, and I just barely dodged several chunks of ice that hurled through the air as I ran. Not long after that, earthen tremors started up, sending me tumbling to my knees on more than one occasion.

But still I pressed on, half-dazed as I began calling out Esmeralda's name. Was it foolish to be screaming it in the middle of a war-torn street? Probably, but I was as desperate as I was exhausted, and running on fumes. If I didn't find her, and soon—

A sudden bright light had me snapping my head up, and my mouth dropped open; not fifty feet ahead stood Esmeralda. Her arms were spread wide as she faced down Phoebus, eyes blazing with a ferocity I'd never seen before. She was completely surrounded by a sphere of fire, an orange and red halo that seemed to be emanating from the very center of her being. Phoebus's face was twisted in rage as he tried to break through Esmeralda's flames, but it was no use; every time he lunged her way, she countered it, flinging clearly solid fireballs he only barely managed to parry away with his sword.

I'd never witnessed anything like it, even in her numerous performances. Esmeralda's movements were as calculated as they were graceful, weaving between his attacks as if she were dancing—and indeed, she was. Sparks flew from her fingertips every time she launched a blast at him, each one more powerful than the last. But even more impressive than the fiery display was the look on Esmeralda's face; she was laughing as she toyed with him, enjoying every second.

It was more than clear she could handle herself and didn't need help from me or anyone. Still, I started forward, if only to get a front row seat to watch Phoebus, the man who had made both our lives a living hell, at least meet his demise.

I was so focused on her and her prowess that I didn't notice the figure barreling toward me until it was far too late.

Metal flashed in my peripheral vision, and I barely managed to duck the knife aimed straight for my face. Crouching low, I whipped out my own, on high alert as I whirled back around. I was expecting my assailant to be a random guard, or even a citizen mistaking me for one.

The last person I expected was Father Laurent.

I froze not only at the sight of him but at the unhinged gleam in his eye as he rushed me a second time. My body reacted on instinct alone, easily dodging the sloppy attack as my mind struggled to comprehend what was happening. This was the man who had taken me and Jehan under his wing, who had rescued us from a life of poverty and suffering on the streets. The man who was a mentor to me, and the closest thing I'd ever had to a père of my own.

And he wanted to *kill* me?

"I don't understand," I managed, meeting his gaze even as Esmeralda's sparks flew around us. "What did I—"

"You filthy whore," he spat through ragged breaths. "For years, I sheltered you, protected you, even promoted you! And this is how you repay me?"

"I'm afraid you'll have to—"

"Don't bother denying it. I've heard the whispers, trust me. But I turned a blind eye, especially after your fool of a brother left. I placed all my hopes on you, only for you to fornicate with *that*."

Father Laurent gestured to Esmeralda, and that's when something within me snapped. Tightening my grip on my own knife, I snarled, "Her name is Esmeralda, and you will not touch her."

He laughed then, and the sinister tone of it sent chills up my spine. "Trust me—she's not my type."

I registered the knife hurling toward me a second too late, and I closed my eyes, bracing for impact. But instead of the sharp pain of metal slicing through my skin, a sudden wave of heat washed over me before I went careening backward, striking a stone wall with force. My ears began ringing, informing me there must have been a blast of some kind, but even as I willed my body to move, it wouldn't.

Only once some of the haze cleared could I make out who stood before me. Not Esmeralda, as I had expected, but…

"Quasimodo?"

He knelt at my side, his eyes wide with fear. *I'm sorry, I'm sorry,* he signed again and again, but I shook my head, taking his hand. I was dazed and aching, yes, but not badly hurt; his blast, however out of control, had saved me.

It seemed Father Laurent had taken the brunt of the explosion, and his limp form lay draped against the opposite wall, which was now in ruins. Motioning for Quasimodo to stand back and away, I staggered to my feet before limping toward him, my knife still in hand.

Father Laurent was still alive, but barely. His breaths came in ragged gasps, blood flowed freely from an open wound on his head, and one of his legs had been crushed by a wayward piece of rubble, pinning him in place. Despite everything, the agony he must be in, he chuckled weakly as I approached, raising his gaze to mine as he twisted his lips into a smile.

"Saved by your darling hunchback, I see. I guess that boy proved to be good for something, after all."

Barely contained rage coursed through me, and I resisted the urge to run my knife through his gut and end his suffering right then and there. "Quasimodo is more of a man than you'll ever be."

Father Laurent said something else, but as blood began pooling at his lips, his words became garbled and unintelligible. It was clear he didn't have long left to live, and that even if I did nothing, the Lord would take him soon.

But was heaven really where this man was headed?

I narrowed my gaze as I took in his broken form, truly looking at him for perhaps the first time. I'd always regarded Father Laurent as me and Jehan's savior, had idolized and damn near worshipped him as a child. And he'd been good to me, to both of us once... but those days were long gone. Perhaps he'd changed around when he'd driven Jehan out of Notre Dame for good, or perhaps he had always been this bitter shell of a man who sat slumped before me, but the exact reason hardly mattered now. For someone who loved to preach about the unconditionality of love, Father Laurent's sure seemed to come with an endless list of conditions, for which the requirements could change at any moment.

And single-handedly, he'd done far more damage to my family than Phoebus ever had.

A festering combination of rage and disgust began pooling in my chest, as did the overwhelming need to sink my knife into something; ideally, the piece of filth before me. All I needed was an excuse, something to tip me over the edge of the line I'd so precariously begun to walk these past few days.

"So if I'm nothing but a whore, and Quasimodo is useless, what's your excuse for Jehan?" I whispered, though I wasn't even certain Father Laurent could hear me over the devastation still roaring around us. "What the hell did you do to my brother?"

He said something—screamed it, more like, as he realized what I intended to do—but not only did whatever it was not matter, I suddenly never wanted him to speak again.

I lost count of how many times I stabbed him, but however many it was wasn't enough. Again and again I brought the blade down with as much force as I could muster, refusing to stop even when I became coated in so much blood I could barely see. Hours could have passed, days could have passed, and I wouldn't have known; nothing existed but him and me, and me hacking his body into a million tiny pieces.

I screamed. I cried. I threw back my head and shrieked, crying out until my throat was raw and I could shriek no more. I cursed my God, I cursed the parents who died and left me with a baby brother to care for all by myself, and I cursed this wretched city. But most of all, I cursed myself.

The very moment I went still and silent, arms encircled me from behind, pinning mine to my sides. I thrashed against them, determined to break my assailant's hold by force or even my knife, but they held firm, muttering something unintelligible. It was only when I recognized the voice as Esmeralda's that it cut through my addled psyche, and her words made my blood run cold.

"Claude, that's *enough*. He's dead. It's over."

I glanced down at my hands, quivering and numb and covered in blood. Sprawled in front of me was Father Laurent's mangled body, bloodied and ravaged beyond recognition, and just as Esmeralda had said…

Dead.

Because I'd killed him.

Dropping the knife as suddenly as if it had burned me, with a strangled sob, I stumbled back as the weight of my actions struck me. Even then, I couldn't tear my gaze from the carnage, nor wipe the horrific imagery from my mind. I had killed someone—*killed* someone—and it wasn't even the first time.

"Mon beau," Esmerlda pleaded. "Stay with us. Quasimodo is watching, and you're scaring him."

I was scaring myself.

"We need to go before I burn out. I'm nearly depleted as it is, and they'll be coming for us, especially Phoebus, since he escaped… Claude. Are you listening?"

"Leave me." Ash caked in my mouth as Esmeralda's fires burned even brighter and hotter around us, and if I had the strength to get up, I may have simply walked straight into them. "Take him, and leave me."

"Don't do this, please!"

She said something else, as did Quasimodo, but I no longer heard either of them. That familiar, comforting darkness was back, the very same that had haunted me for days, and bowing my head, I welcomed it with open arms. No doubt it was the Devil finally here to claim me, but no doubt I deserved it—welcomed it, even. So why waste my final moments fighting?

But a sound pulled me back from the edge, if only briefly—coughing. Turning toward the source of the noise, I inhaled sharply when I glimpsed Esmeralda's crumpled form consumed with a violent cough. She lifted her head, revealing swollen, bloodshot eyes. Her breaths came in even shorter gasps, and she crouched, doubling over as she seemed to fight for oxygen.

"What's wrong?"

She raised a quivering finger, covering her mouth and nose with her other hand as she forced, "Claude, look."

I glanced over my shoulder, seeing nothing but black... but then I did a double take, my jaw dropping in sheer horror.

Dark. Esmeralda and I were surrounded by a void of endless, shifting darkness, powerful enough to swallow her flames entirely, and Quasimodo was nowhere to be seen. Every ounce of light had been devoured by it, and it hurled toward us next at a pace impossible to outrun.

But upon feeling a strange tingling in my palms, I glanced down, at last identifying both the entity and its source.

The blackness pouring uninhibited from my fingertips, the very last thing I saw before losing consciousness, wasn't darkness or even shadow.

It was smoke.

XXII. THE SMOKE

Esmeralda

I awoke to even more swirling blackness.

Bolting upright, my pulse immediately spiked at the same moment my flames leaped to attention, manifesting to life in my palm. The light immediately fell upon a hooded figure crouched in the far corner, who threw up his hands just as a concentrated blast of air extinguished my fire in an instant… and only then did I fully come to my senses. It wasn't smoke, but mist that enveloped me, and if a certain air mage stood in my presence, there was no way we were in any setting that resembled the public. "*Erik?*"

"Damn fire mages," he growled, pulling back his hood to reveal his usual half-masked face. "Can't help themselves even in their sleep."

I glowered. "Good to see you, too."

"What, no, I…" Erik's voice trailed off as color crept to the visible side of his face, and gingerly, he approached the bed before covering my outstretched hand with his. "I'm very glad to see you awake and well, Esmeralda. Truly. As impressive as you were out there, you had us all worried sick."

You were worried? I nearly blurted out, but then frowned. "No thanks to you. That damn potion took far too long to kick in—far longer than you said it would."

He raised an eyebrow. "And by 'far longer,' you mean what, forty-five minutes? An hour?"

"However long it was, the delay nearly cost me my life!"

"But it didn't." Erik's dark eyes burned as he stared intently into mine. "I would never gamble with your life, Esmeralda—at least no more than you yourself already do."

I glanced away, more to conceal the red-hot embarrassment that crept to my cheeks rather than to get my first decent look at my surroundings, but I looked regardless. Somehow, I was back in Erik's bed, though I didn't have the slightest recollection as to how I'd gotten there. The mist hovering in the air must be from the lake, and though I couldn't see anyone else from where I lay, idle chatter drifted from adjacent chambers, informing me we weren't alone. As for me, I'd been dressed in a simple red gown, and other than a pulsing headache, I didn't seem to be seriously injured in any way. I made an attempt to sit up, pushing through the pain in my forehead, but Erik immediately forced me back down.

"Oh, no—don't attempt any of that before you're ready."

I frowned. "How long have I been out?"

"Three days, give or take."

"Three *days*, and I still feel like this?" At least my flames were intact, hovering beneath the surface of my skin like always. Though the pain wasn't agonizing, everything ached, and the pulsing in my skull only grew more intense with each passing second.

"You burned yourself out, and under the influence of my potion, no less. All energy has a price, and every ounce of it you use must be given back. It makes perfect sense. You were at triple your strength, so naturally, your body needed three days to recover."

A glance to my left revealed that the bedside table was crammed full of various vials and bottles, several of which were already empty. "What the hell did you give me?"

"Precisely what you needed to recover without doing any further damage to your body." There was a hint of irritation to Erik's voice but he kept it mostly to himself. "I may be an alchemist, but I'm no doctor or healer. If you need one, though, we can certainly fetch—"

I shook my head and winced. "That's not necessary. But if you have anything for a headache, I wouldn't say no."

Almost before I'd finished speaking, Erik reached over, rifling through the vials before handing me one. "Just a mouthful," he warned as he helped me sit up. "That one is rather easy to overdose on."

I nodded, then swallowed the amount he'd indicated and no more. Its effect was nearly instantaneous, and a shudder rippled through me as the pain in my head began to subside. "Thank you," I breathed.

"Of course." A smile played on his lips, and he reached for my hand once more, offering a gentle squeeze. We stared at one another long enough that yet another blush began creeping to my cheeks, so I cleared my throat, breaking the silence.

"So, what happened? Why am I here?"

Erik glanced away awkwardly. "There are people far better suited than me to answer that question, and they'll be wanting to see you as well." He pulled away, but not without first leaning in to brush his lips against my forehead. A tingling sensation erupted from where he'd kissed me, but before I could identify precisely how I felt about it, Erik walked out as three more people came in.

Jules and Antoine rushed to my side, pulling me into a fierce hug without the slightest bit of hesitation, but the third halted the moment he glimpsed me. Lifting my gaze, I gasped; not because I was shocked to see Papa, but because I was shocked to see him *here*, in the lair Erik had worked so hard to keep a secret. Had he and Papa truly made amends, or had Erik made an exception solely for me and my comfort?

Questions continued tumbling through my mind, but I pushed them all aside, because we'd have plenty of time to catch up later. "Hello, Papa."

Hearing my voice shattered whatever spell kept my père rooted in place, and he crossed the room to embrace me, squeezing so hard it hurt. I barely registered the pain, though; in that moment, there was nothing but him and the overwhelming wave of pure joy that washed over me. We may have gone through hell and back these past few weeks, but in this moment, it all became worth it. Here we all were, alive, well, and most importantly, together.

"Ma chère," Papa said once he pulled away, resting a hand on my cheek. "Oh, my beautiful Esmeralda. I am so proud of you, and so happy to see you safe."

I turned to Jules, raising an eyebrow. "And you?"

They shrugged, though I could tell their nonchalance was feigned. "I wasn't worried. I knew you'd wake—"

"Oh, shut up." Antoine punched Jules in the shoulder. "They've been a wreck for days."

Jules sighed. "Please remind me why I keep him around?"

"I've wondered that myself many times before, but after his help in the river, I'll never question him again." I met Antoine's gaze, nodding earnestly. "Thank you."

But he frowned. "Never again? I'm not sure I like that. What reason do I have to be with Jules if I'm not around to piss *you* off in turn? Two for the price of one!"

I rolled my eyes as they erupted into playful bickering, but the truth was that I felt like crying all over again. All of this felt so normal, so right, that my heart felt as if it might burst from my chest at any moment. I sighed contentedly as Papa leaned against me, draping an arm over my shoulders as he pulled me close.

"I missed you," I confessed, hopefully low enough for his ears alone. "And I'm sorry for all I've put you through—you and the council."

"The council can go fuck themselves," he spat, then cleared his throat. "Sorry, ma chère. I'm just happy my daughter is safe and well. You know I'll always have your back, right?"

"Always."

"Then why didn't you tell me that Claude was a smoke mage?"

A chill shot down my spine, and I went rigid against him. I barely remembered my final moments before passing out, but the one thing I recalled in excruciating, painstaking detail was the smoke pouring uninhibited from Claude's fingertips. "Because I didn't know. I swear."

Papa sighed. "I suppose that makes sense, given how she's acted these past few days."

"Why, what happened?" I demanded, sitting back up. "Is Claude all right?" I glanced at Jules, whose smile immediately vanished.

"They're… here," they said slowly. "But just so you know, they haven't spoken a word since the battle. Not even to their son."

I swallowed the lump in my throat and nodded. "That's fine. We don't have to talk. But I still want to see them, if they want to see me."

"I need to see them, too," Papa added. "We need to talk about the sm—"

"*No*," I cut across him and reached out to grip his hand. "If I didn't know, that means she didn't know, and she might not even remember what happened, or that she was the one who did it. If that's the case, the news should come from me."

Papa hesitated but eventually conceded. "All right. I'll go fetch them."

With a final squeeze, he departed, and Jules and Antoine left soon after. Unintelligible chatter echoed through Erik's chambers, and a beat later, there was Claude.

Like Papa, they took one look at me before freezing in place, and as Jules had warned, Claude looked like hell. Dark circles were set under her once-soft eyes, her hair stuck out at odd angles, and she visibly quivered; whether it was from fear or something else, I couldn't be certain. An endless string of questions hovered on my lips—*Do you remember? Did you know? Are you all right?*—but before I could utter any one of them, they crossed the room in a handful of strides to claim my lips in a kiss.

In that singular moment, everyone and everything else melted away, and I relaxed in Claude's arms, surrendering to the calm only she could bring me. The world fell silent and still, and for the first time in days, I was truly at peace. Our kiss wasn't gentle; it was so raw it bordered on painful, yet it communicated far more than words alone ever could and left me gasping when Claude finally pulled away.

"I've never been happier to see you," they whispered against my lips, pressing their forehead against mine.

My voice shook. "Me too."

We stayed like that for quite a while—our foreheads pressed together, our hands intertwined—until our breathing steadied and our heartbeats returned to mostly normal. Eventually, though, reality came crashing down with a vengeance, forcing us apart whether we wanted to be or not. Claude shifted several feet away, but I was glad she remained on the bed.

I smiled awkwardly. "You're talking. That's wonderful."

"Yes." She cleared her throat. "It feels strange, though."

"That's all right. We don't have to talk long, and I can do most of it. I just—"

"Are you all right?" Claude cut across me, reaching for my hand. "I'm so sorry I wasn't here when you woke up. I would have been had Erik not forced me to go lay down myself."

I nodded. "Just a headache, but Erik gave me something for it."

Relief washed over their face. "Good."

"Are *you* all right?"

"Fine," Claude replied quickly, too quickly, but I didn't press her. "The city isn't, though. We've been holed up here ever since, but I'm told the riots never really stopped, and they aren't likely to—not until Phoebus is found. If Erik hadn't taken us in, we'd have been forced to flee."

"Who's we? I've seen my family, but what about…"

My voice trailed off, but Claude knew precisely who I meant. "Quasimodo is here and safe. He's absolutely enchanted with Erik's workshop, and Erik is with him. But I haven't seen or heard from Jehan or Mercedes since that night. I hope they fled the city, but… I don't know for certain."

Dread pooled in my stomach, but I forced myself to keep my tone light. "We'll find them, Claude. As soon as I'm well enough, we'll—"

"No. The safest place for you is here, and Erik has already agreed to take you on as a dancer."

I furrowed my brow in confusion. "What?"

"Well not him, precisely, but he says he has the perfect person to teach you ballet, if that's something you're interested in. You'd be safe here, living at the Palais Garnier, and you'd blend in perfectly with the other mages. And don't give me that look—it's not forever, and you're no prisoner. It's only until things calm down and we either find Phoebus's body, or..."

"Or I kill him," I finished flatly, because in my mind, there was no other option.

Claude swallowed, then nodded. "Or you kill him."

We fell silent after that, but not for long given that it was eating me alive. "What now, then?" I asked softly, and the look on Claude's face told me she knew immediately what I truly wanted to know: *Will you stay in Paris? Will you stay with* me?

They didn't answer right away and visibly stiffened. But eventually, they exhaled, squeezing my hand as they whispered, "I'm staying here... for now. Quasimodo deserves a peaceful few weeks, if I can give it to him."

"But what about what you deserve?" I brought her fingers to my lips, brushing my lips against each one in turn. "What do *you* want?"

Claude sounded as if they might burst into tears at any moment. "You," they admitted. "I just want you."

"And you have me. I'm right here."

"But it's not you I'm worried about." Her voice was laced with so much pain it made my own gut twist into knots. "I'm here, except I'm not, not really. I've barely felt anything like myself, not since..."

"Since what?" I pressed when her voice trailed off. The last thing I wanted to do was push her, but I had no idea whether she was talking about the murder, the smoke, or something else entirely.

Claude pulled their hand back. "What I did."

The murder, then. Father Laurent's mangled body flashed in my mind's eye, as did the aftermath. "That's all right, truly. You can have all the time you need to process this. In fact, I'd be far more worried if you didn't need time."

"You say that now. But it's only been a few days, and what I did will haunt me forever. What if..." She swallowed. "What if I never process it? What if it eats me alive, what if it—"

I leaned forward then, ignoring the blood that rushed to my forehead as I gripped their shoulders. Claude immediately silenced, staring at me with wide, tear-filled eyes, and the sight nearly summoned my own. "Listen to me," I began softly but firmly. "You murdered someone, yes. But not only was it self defense, not only was it protecting your son, but that man—if we should even call him that—was a monster. You saw him for what he was and gave him nothing less than he deserved."

Before I'd finished speaking, Claude burst into all-out sobs. She quivered violently, her chest heaving as she tried in vain to control her breathing. Opening my arms, I pulled her close and held her tightly, letting her tears soak my dress as I held her.

"That's it, mon beau," I whispered into her hair, resting my chin on her head. "Feel what you need to feel. I'm here."

They wrapped her arms around me, and for a long time, we sat in silence. But while Claude's breathing steadied, my own pulse spiked as conflicting emotions rose within me. On one hand, I was more than glad she'd begun to process her feelings surrounding the murder... but on the other, we still hadn't discussed the smoke. And how could I possibly bring it up now that she'd finally calmed down enough to properly breathe? The last thing I wanted to do was send her into another panic-induced frenzy, especially if she didn't know or even remember. But if I didn't, Papa would, and no doubt he'd be far harsher and more invasive with his questions. A new mage, especially one whose powers had remained dormant for so long, was nothing to be taken lightly, and whether Claude was ready to give them or not, we needed answers.

After swallowing the lump in my throat, I gently shook her shoulder. "Are you awake? I need to ask you..."

But my voice trailed off as, out of the corner of my eye, there appeared a few tendrils of smoke.

AUTHOR'S NOTE

It's becoming a rather frightening habit of mine to take an older (and usually short) story idea and turn it into an entire series, and *The Hells of Notre Dame* was no different. This novel was a rewrite of a short story of the same name I penned several years ago, and while drafting it, I discovered several things about myself—things I'm now far more comfortable to share with the world, at least when fictional characters get to say and do them. But after finishing up *A Sea of Eternal Woe* and knowing I needed a break to write something else, something entirely different and admittedly, a little self-indulgent, I immediately set to work on *Hells*.

The creation of this book was a journey in which many tears were shed, countless nights of sleep were lost, and I pushed myself to my limits both as a human being and craft-wise, but I firmly believe it's the best book I've written to date, and that's all that matters. I knew it would be niche—and at times I thought I might be the only person in the world who wanted to read a steamy polyamorous dark fantasy romance in which the main two leads were a sapphic couple—but now, you've read it, too, and all I can say is thank you. My readers, new and old, continue to surprise and delight me in ways I didn't even know were possible.

And now, let me (hopefully) delight you, too, as I tease a bit of book two, which I'm already fangirling rather hard over. Claude and Esmeralda's story continues, of course, but this time, our setting is a gothic fantasy version of the legendary Palais Garnier of Paris, and I absolutely plan to milk that for all it's worth. Anyone who knows me personally knows that I've been obsessed with *The Phantom of the Opera* for most of my life (let's just say that watching the 2004 movie version with Gerard Butler and Emmy Rossum was a formative experience for me as a child), and that I've been dying to write a retelling for eons now. But I also knew I wanted that retelling to be polyamorous, because how can you possibly ask me, a bisexual, to focus on just two people when there's an entire cast of incredible characters to pick from?

So I *didn't* pick, and neither do my characters. But it's not all alluring romance, and *The Hunchback of Notre Dame* and *Phantom* are no longer the only gothic tales I'm borrowing a bit of inspiration from as we head into the sequel. If you're a fan of Poe, you might already be able to guess which of his tales I was inspired by in book two's title alone:

THE MASQUE OF CRIMSON SHADOW

Esmeralda is fire…

And now, I'm smoke, possessing magic so volatile that I am trusted by no one, least of all myself. With obsidian poison now pouring from my fingertips at the slightest hint of emotion, the only solution is to lock myself away, to isolate myself even—and especially—from the woman I love.

But if the Palais Garnier has taught me anything, it's that the show must go on. When a deadly plague begins ravaging the mages of Paris, that becomes truer than ever, as does Erik's determination to keep the mages of the opera house safe at any cost. His scramble for a cure is as obsessive as it is unsettling… and so is his sudden interest in Esmeralda.

Unhinged as the Phantom of the Opera may be, it is for that reason I see myself in him. Erik's violent heart calls to mine, he is perhaps the only one who understands the ever growing darkness within me, and much as I am loath to admit it, our goals are one and the same.

Because I, too, will kill to protect what I love.

I already have.

PREORDER NOW!
https://books2read.com/tmocs

ABOUT THE AUTHOR

Raelynn Davennor is an author of fantasy romance and fairytale retellings. She is known for her diverse and complex characters, as well as her ability to craft heart-wrenching plots that explore heavy themes. A firm believer that light cannot be appreciated without darkness, Raelynn always ensures that her characters find their happily ever afters. When not obsessing over her latest idea, she enjoys pampering her menagerie of pets and pretending she isn't an adult. Her home base is https://rldavennor.com where you'll find more information, her newsletter, and links to social media.

Made in the USA
Middletown, DE
15 July 2024